PAWNING
PANDORA

by

Willow B. Dawes

PAWNING PANDORA

WILLOW B. DAWES

Book Cover and Formatting by Rena Violet

Map Illustration by Virginia Allyn

Developmental Edit by Kourtney Spak

Copy/Line Edit and Proofread by Bryony Leah

First Edition: 2025
ISBN: 979-8-9993017-0-3

*To those who dream of magical and mystical worlds
full of mystery and wonder.*

May you always find inspiration in the unknown.

APOLLO

Realm of Aether

HADES & POSEIDON

GUARD TOWER

HEPHAESTUS'S CAVERNS

COLONNADE

DEMETER'S PALACE

AGORA

VEGETABLE FARMLAND

FESTIVAL GROUNDS

FRUIT ORCHARD

PANDORA'S COTTAGE

NAIAD HOUSING

WHEAT FIELDS

SEA OF POSEIDON

CHAPTER 1

BITTER wind whipped my hair as I trod carefully along the icy cobblestone paths lining the summit of Mount Olympus. The white marble steps of the palace were covered in a thin layer of frost that glistened in the morning sun. My covered sandals slipped on the slick surface with every step I took toward the enormous stone doors gilded with gold from the depths of the mountain. Like all the palaces in Olympus, this one had been built to resemble its owner. The East Palace was a perfect reflection of the stony, unwavering goddess who lived within its walls.

Athena.

I'd been visiting her palace a few times a week since the day I was created, and here I learned many necessary survival skills. Or at least, that was what Athena and Zeus always told me when I asked about the importance of my lessons, since I couldn't see myself ever having a use for most of these skills.

Fighting off the chill settling into my bones, I tapped the gilded owl three times and waited.

A click of taloned feet approached from behind me.

"Apologies, I was sent out last minute," Athena's long-horned owl servant said, brushing past me and pushing open the door.

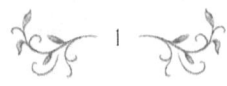

Each of the Olympians had servants who resembled their powers or their sacred animals, Athena's having distinct owl characteristics, with each differing slightly from one another in color, but maintaining their large, round eyes and hooked beaks.

"That's all right," I said through chattering teeth, smiling through my irritation as I took in the warm feathers covering his body while mine froze.

"Follow me. Athena is waiting for you," he said, waving me in with his long brown-and-tan feathered arm.

I rushed in behind him just as a gust of wind came up and followed him deep into the palace, stopping in front of a set of doors I'd come to know as well as the door to my own home.

"Come in, Pandora," Athena said from the other side of those doors.

She knew I was coming. We'd met for training at the same time on the same day for the past twenty years of my life. But her tone today seemed off. It had an icy edge to it that made my steps falter as I pushed open the doors and walked in, the warmth of the room doing nothing to chill her tone.

"Hello, Athena. How are you today?" I asked, trying to lighten her mood, which I could practically feel radiating off the palace walls. Taking a deep breath, I gathered myself and forced my lips into a smile, hoping it was as resilient as marble.

Athena's grand room was intricately carved from the same marble nearly everything in Olympus was made of. Harder for the gods to break when they lost their temper. It was difficult to forget Poseidon slamming his trident into the foyer of the West Palace, which he shared with Hades. As usual, Zeus had sparked his fury.

"I would be much better if a mortal were not twiddling her life away as if she held immortality at her fingertips. I may have all the time in Olympus, but you, dear girl, do not have that luxury." Athena's hazel eyes flashed from her seat across the room.

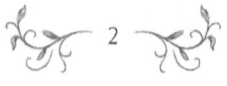

Her thick brown hair was drawn back from her temples in an intricate braid that hung down her back, as rigid as her broad shoulders and long legs. Athena was much more masculine than the other goddesses in Olympus, but I'd always assumed that was due to her role in the world. Her body was as strong and powerful as her mind, making her look every bit the warrior she was.

"Better late than never, right?" I joked, hoping it might lighten her mood.

"You spend far too much time with Hermes, girl. I can see his snark rubbing off on you."

"Ah, but by tonight, I will be wise and wondrous like the magnificent Athena." I grinned, noticing her lips twitch upward from where she was standing across the room.

"For today's lesson, we will be practicing our weaving patterns. Demeter has requested more baskets to carry her crops in."

"More? Primes, how many baskets does she need? We've made more than fifty in the past month, and now she needs more?" I sighed in frustration. I'd been so relieved to finish that last basket.

"Yes, Pandora. She needs them for Zeus's upcoming celebration. It will be held in a month's time, and as always, Demeter is required to harvest and prepare everything needed for the grand feast." Athena walked toward the corner that housed everything we needed to weave the baskets.

"A celebration?" I asked, barely able to contain my excitement. I'd never gotten to see a High Olympian celebration. Sure, the Lower Olympians had plenty of parties thanks to Dionysus, who ensured the wine was constantly flowing and the party was consistently going, but I was never invited to those. Although I may have slipped into one or two without being detected.

Athena snapped her fingers over her shoulder, her back still turned, materializing a wooden table between us and walking over to it to set down a pile of willow branches, hazel wood, and reeds.

I hated when she used her magic like this. It reminded me of how useless my *skills* were compared to the Olympians'. It also made me wonder why they insisted I make Demeter baskets when she could simply snap her fingers and create more.

"The Titan twins will be visiting from the Realm of Man."

"Titans?" My mind raced. Zeus had either banished or imprisoned the Titans when he took control of Olympus. "Why risk bringing them back?"

"They are not *all* gone," Athena said, grabbing a few reeds and motioning for me to follow as she twisted a new pattern around the willow branch. She huffed. "Do you remember *anything* from your history lessons?"

"Themis is a Titan."

Athena nodded as I plucked a bendy branch from the pile. "Themis remained neutral during the war, as did Prometheus and Epimetheus, and the few others," she prompted.

"Aside from Themis, those who remained neutral were allowed to live outside the walls of Olympus, in the wild lands of Aether, with visitation rights, but only with Zeus's approval."

A quick quirk of Athena's mouth told me I'd remembered correctly. "Good, yes."

"What about Prometheus and Epimetheus's family? Did they remain neutral?" I asked, mimicking the movement of her hands.

Athena shook her head. "Only the twins remained neutral. The other two, along with their father, did not."

"The other two? Who were they?" I asked, trying to follow her example and failing. My weave was nowhere near as tight and symmetrical as Athena's, but I was at least keeping pace.

"Move your wrist in this motion," Athena said, ignoring my question as her wrist made a scooping motion with each loop of the reed.

Scoop. Loop. Pull.

I repeated the mantra over and over in my head and successfully managed the new pattern, beaming at Athena with pride. She nodded her approval before motioning for us to continue.

We continued to weave in silence, but my mind was relentless. *Titans in Olympus . . . Why?*

"What is the Realm of Man? Why are the twins coming here now?" I blurted out.

Athena frowned, reaching across the table for another reed. "Focus on weaving, Pandora."

We spent the rest of the afternoon in silence, other than her occasional instruction when I made an error in the pattern of the basket. By the end of the day, I was exhausted and covered in a layer of sweat from the fire, which Athena kept roaring in the room for me, since the cold didn't affect the Olympians. I fell back in my chair with a groan. My back was aching, and my hands had been cramping for the past hour. I was rubbing the tender muscles in my palms when I glanced over at Athena, who took in my disheveled appearance with a smirk.

"Not all of us can glisten in Apollo's rays like the divine," I said, rolling my eyes at her amusement. "Some of us have to put in a good amount of work to achieve that goddess glow."

Why the gods had graced me with weakness and exhaustion when they created me was another mystery I had yet to figure out. The only vague answer I ever got when I asked was that "they wished to create something new."

Athena laughed lightly, taking a step toward me only to take four steps back, scrunching her nose in disgust. "Looks like all that hard work built up more than just a divine glow," she said, continuing to back away.

I lifted my arm and sniffed. My face crinkled, same as hers, and I nearly fell from my chair as I tried to escape my own smell.

"You had better go visit Poseidon's pools. We're done for today. Tomorrow, you will be meeting with Aphrodite to get fitted for your celebration gown after your history lessons with Clio in

the morning." Athena started to leave the room before turning back to me and adding, "If I were you, I wouldn't make any stops along the way. Primes forbid someone else has to suffer through that horrendous stench."

Before I had a chance to defend myself from her rude comment—about something I had no control over, and which they had cursed me with, no less—Athena disappeared.

I gathered the embroidered satchel Athena had woven for me as a child. It held my parchment, my charcoals, and a small pouch gifted from Poseidon that was spelled to stay full of water for me to drink, since the Olympians had no such need for water to stay alive.

I'd learned early on that my body differed in many ways from theirs. On the exterior, we may have shared physical similarities, but that was where it all ended. The Olympians were immortal; I was not. The Olympians had powers and abilities that gave them purpose; I did not.

The Olympians were in every way better than I was, and I had grown up my entire life knowing it.

CHAPTER 2

I WALKED through the olive groves surrounding Athena's marble palace on the east side of the summit, following the cobblestone path toward the Olympian Court and the stairway underneath it that led down to Poseidon's pools.

The court mimicked Zeus's palace, extravagant and intimidating. It was yet another space I wasn't permitted to enter without invitation. I hadn't been summoned to the court often, but I knew its layout and architecture well. Above sat the thrones of Zeus and the twelve High Olympians, who formed the Olympian Council; below, tunnels that weaved through the interior of the mountain.

A stone stairway led up to the enormous two-story rotunda housing the court, which was covered in sparkling white marble, with gold laced through it like glimmering veins. The design was open to the elements. Hephaestus had built it with no walls, instead encircling it with twelve gilded Corinthian columns, each reflecting a story of one of the twelve High Olympians, to make it feel more enclosed than it truly was. The court was said to represent honesty and equality. Its golden columns reached high into the clouds until they met the glass dome covering the second floor.

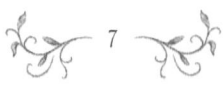

I took a moment to bask in the beauty of the court before walking through the stone archway the servants used and heading down the stairway into the tunnel system below.

The servants' tunnels were dark, damp, and cold compared to the pristine tunnels the High Olympians used. They would never be caught in the servants' tunnels. Lucky for me, that meant I could avoid them coming and going from the pools.

As I neared the entrance to the pools, I slowed, listening to the serene sound of falling water and inhaling the soothing scent of the sea: crisp, salty, and refreshing, with faint floral notes. The pools had a mysterious and beautiful tranquility about them that reflected Poseidon's home beneath the sea.

Stepping through the rocky entrance into the grotto, I smiled at the sight before me.

The large cavern was home to dozens of small waterfalls that fell from crevices and holes in the ceiling and walls. They fed cool water into the small pools lining the outer edges of the grotto. In the center was an enormous pool, small waterfalls surrounding it like the columns of the court, and in the pool's center was a statue of Poseidon and his beloved water nymphs, who cared for the pools in his absence. Surrounding his statue was a canopy of trickling water that fell from the thin crevices encircling Poseidon from above. It acted as a barrier, the thin sheet of water keeping him separate from everyone else.

I walked over to the secluded pool in the far corner—my favorite pool to bathe in. It was more private than the others thanks to the tall, bushy ferns all around it, as well as the flowing wisteria tree at the edge of the pool. They made it feel separate from the rest of the grotto, which was fitting, since that was how my life had felt since the day I was created. Me in one corner, and the Olympians in the other.

I peeked around the ferns, making sure the pool wasn't already occupied, and to my relief, there was nothing to be found but the trickling waterfall flowing down into the turquoise pool.

Quickly stripping, I dipped my toe in and nearly groaned at the warmth of the water, descending the pebbled stone steps into the pool. Sighing at the instant relaxation, I dunked my head under and folded my legs beneath me to sit on the warm stone floor, basking in the peaceful silence and the warmth before emerging for air.

Leaning back, I floated on the surface, looking up at the dangling wisteria flowers, and inhaled their sweet floral scent deeply before bringing my feet back down into the water and swimming toward the small shelf on the edge of the pool. It contained a few bottles of oils, made from herbs and flowers, that smelled divine when applied to the skin, leaving it as smooth as silk when I rinsed it off.

The gods didn't build up a "stench," as Athena liked to put it, but they never turned down something so luxurious and relaxing.

Mixing a couple of the oils in my hands to create a foam, I went to work cleaning my skin and my hair before rinsing off under the cool waterfall. The mixture of warm and cool water never ceased to shock me with its ability to take me from relaxed to invigorated. I let out a gasp at the cool downpour.

After thoroughly rinsing my hair and my body, I was moving across the water toward the steps when voices in the pool beside me stopped me in my tracks.

". . . wild ones were spotted wandering around the west side of Olympus. The Amazons reported a group of six scouting for weaknesses along the walls," a feminine voice said. I could tell it was Themis from her sharp tone and the slight rasp that separated her voice from every other goddess in Olympus.

"Coincidental timing, with the Titan twins returning from the Realm of Man. Do you think they're planning something?" a deep male voice replied. I knew without a doubt this was Eros. He spoke with a flirtatious lilt in every conversation, and if he

was in the pool with Themis, it likely wasn't just to talk about the rumors of a rebellion.

"I don't believe in coincidence," Themis replied. "If it's not them, it's someone else."

"Who would be so bold? With how swiftly Zeus ended the last rebellion, I can't see anyone having enough power to try again. Although, if they got the wild ones to align with them, their numbers would be enough to make up for the lack of power."

"As long as Zeus has his bolt and his family by his side, no one, no matter the numbers, stands a chance at overtaking Olympus. I have made sure of that," Themis snapped.

"I have no doubt about it. I am not trying to undermine you, Themis. Just stating the facts."

"You may be able to sway my lust, Eros, but do not forget who you are speaking to. I was in this realm, guiding its rulers, long before you were born. I suggest you stick to what you know and get over here," Themis snarled.

The water splashed out of their pool and rolled into mine as moaning overtook their conversation. I quickly emerged from my pool before I had the displeasure of hearing anything else.

Stepping out of the water, I leaned down to grab one of the delicate linen robes waiting beside the stone wall. I wrapped it tightly around myself before walking to the back of the cavern, where the nymphs worked, far away from Eros and Themis's love affair.

Voices carried over from the corner where the extra linens were kept.

"Good-for-nothing crete. You can't even wash a linen without ruining it. Your kind shouldn't even be allowed down here, let alone anywhere near the summit," a masculine voice said, and just as I was about to turn the corner to get a glimpse, I ran smack into him instead.

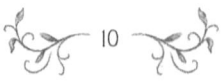

A red-haired lower god I recognized as one of Zeus's private guards stared down at me, glowering. "Get out of my way," he spat out, taking a step toward me, making me step back.

I moved to the side to let him pass before I angered him any further. I'd seen him in action before, around the creatures, and it was never good.

Most of Olympus had come to accept the creatures, but there was a time when they were just as hated as the wild ones outside the walls. Although they were accepted, most Olympians still referred to them as cretes instead of as their species, which I noticed they took offense to. I'd asked Persephone about it when I was younger, noticing she never referred to them as cretes, and she'd told me, "I choose to call them what they are, not what someone named them because they were too careless to remember otherwise."

"No one should be treated like that," I said to the nymph behind the stone table full of linens, some meticulously folded and others lying in crumpled piles. "Especially not someone who's just trying to be helpful."

Her teal scales flashed in the candlelight. She seemed slightly alarmed at the sight of me. She looked me over from head to toe, her alarm turning to anger in the blink of an eye. The nymph glared daggers at me before turning toward the opening at the back of the cave and disappearing into the darkness.

I waited for a moment, not sure what had happened or why she'd reacted in such a way. I hadn't been the one to insult her, but maybe my statement had insulted her just the same. I was about to give up on getting a thick linen peplos and head back to my cottage in the flimsy robe when another water nymph, this one with light violet scales that reminded me of wisteria flowers, returned with a fresh set of clothes.

"I apologize if Lemenia was rude. She does not take kindly to mortals."

"I'm assuming that was the one who looked me over as if I was the one who insulted her and left without saying a word?" I motioned to the opening she'd disappeared through.

"Yes, that would be her. She's new to the pools and was under the impression there were no mortals in Aether anymore, especially within the walls of Olympus—which, until recently, there were not."

Anymore? Surely, I must have misheard her, because I'd never heard of any mortal other than me residing in the Realm of Aether, let alone in Olympus.

"Why does she despise mortals so much? Surely, we can't be that bad."

"Lemenia was born in the Realm of Man and grew up surrounded by mortals," the nymph explained. "In a way, her life was very similar to yours. She was an outcast in a world to which she did not belong." Something like pity crossed her features. "When mortals were created in the Realm of Man, Olympians tried to rule them, but man did not take kindly to being ruled. Man fought the Olympians with everything they had, until the Olympians eventually decided they were not worth their time and effort and returned to Aether, leaving behind only one High Olympian who saw man's potential. Poseidon."

"Poseidon stayed?"

The nymph nodded.

"Then what happened after the Olympians left that made Lemenia dislike mortals so much?" I asked.

"I can't say. What happened next is Lemenia's story, and she has never chosen to share that part of it with me. All I know is, man did something so vile that she is now terrified of all mankind. When she arrived in Olympus, she was under the impression mortals were worlds away, that she would never need to interact with them again, but I guess everyone forgot to mention you."

"Guess so. Well, I'll do my best to avoid her for her own peace of mind. When you see her again, will you please let her

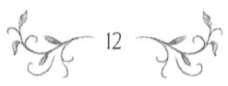

know I have nothing to do with the Realm of Man and I pose no threat to her?"

"I will make sure she knows you're not associated with them and that your home has always been in Olympus. My apologies for your treatment, Pandora. In turbulent times like these, we Olympians need to stick together." She gave a small smile and retreated back toward wherever it was the nymphs went behind that stone wall.

Turbulent times? She must be as worried about the Titans' arrival as I was. Or maybe she was talking about the wild ones outside the walls.

"Thank you . . . I never caught your name."

"Sylra. My name is Sylra," she said before disappearing through the opening.

I dressed quickly, heading back up from the pools, running my hands along the smooth marble as I ascended the tunnels. The night was cool on my balmy skin, and I inhaled the fresh mountain air, my hair floating on the night breeze while I walked down from the summit onto the small dirt path that led around Lower Olympus. There I took the bridge across the river that brought me into Demeter's land, where my cottage sat at the edge of her orchards.

The scent of flowers, grass, and soil danced in the air, and that always gave me a warm, fuzzy feeling, because I knew that smell. It smelled like home.

I followed the scent down the dirt path until I reached my small stone cottage. It rested atop a hill overlooking the river to the east, Demeter's orchards to the west, and the Sea of Poseidon to the south. My own little slice of paradise.

Persephone and Demeter had taken me in as a child and treated me like one of their own, even allowing me to live in Demeter's palace for a time. They'd taught me to plant, sustain, and harvest a garden, as well as the basics of agriculture. For my tenth birthday, they'd gifted me my small cottage, which they'd had Hephaestus build in a much humbler manner than the Olympians' palaces. Rather than being bold, extravagant, and luxurious, my little cottage was simple, with its own kind of charm, which always brought me comfort and happiness, while the palaces brought only a sense of cold, hard loneliness.

Coming home always put me at ease.

CHAPTER 3

THE town center of Lower Olympus was swarming with activity. Even the gods and goddesses had emerged into the plateia this morning, normally sending servants in their place as they found it too lowly and filled with cretes.

These servants differed from the High Olympians' servants, who were created from the High Olympians' sacred animals and thus took on their characteristics. These ones were just the average mixture of species that could normally be found walking within the walls of the Kingdom of Olympus, as well as outside its walls, in the wild lands of the Realm of Aether. Rushing behind their masters, they went about gathering fabrics, metalwork, pottery, teas, and tinctures, or any of the many other goods and services provided by the storefronts of the plateia. As usual, no one glanced my way, unless it was to glare down at me. Many Olympians had never taken to me, but there were some who treated me with respect and kindness.

After waking up to my stomach growling like a hellhound, with the rage of a fury, I'd decided to get dressed and head into the plateia early for some baked goods before meeting Clio in the Palace of Muses, and later, in the afternoon, Aphrodite.

Crossing the central square, I made my way to one of my favorite places in all of Olympus.

Hestia's Hearth.

The smell of freshly baked goods wafted through the square from the stone building, making my steps quicken as my senses were engulfed by the sweet, yeasty scent of bread and desserts. The closer I got, the better it smelled, as the baked goods mingled with the smoke from the fire burning in the hearth and pouring out of the chimney.

I took one last breath and stepped into the ever-growing line inside Hestia's Hearth.

It wasn't as bad as I expected, with only ten or so customers in front of me, and thankfully, the line seemed to be moving fast. In no time, it was my turn.

"What would you like today, Pandora?" asked a beautiful nymph I had come to know as Acacia. She had honey-blonde hair wrapped in a bun atop her head, with little flowers woven throughout, and bronze skin that glistened with her every move. Acacia was a honey nymph, a Meliae of the rarest kind, created for the protection of the honey and bees that lived within the ash tree forest, whose most striking feature was her eyes, which were a deep, smoky violet that melted into golden honey at their center.

"The usual, please," I replied, watching as she swiveled around to the rack of pastries, cakes, and breads cooling beside the roaring fire.

Acacia grabbed one of the small cakes and placed it on a tray another nymph had set beside her, along with my milk, before turning back around, tray in hand, to face me. "One lavender honey cake and a glass of milk. That will be four drachmas, dear," she said, setting the tray in front of me while I grabbed the coins from my satchel.

I passed over six drachmas.

She shook her head, trying to pass the extra two drachmas back to me, but I just smiled politely. "Those are for you, Acacia."

She put her hand over her heart. "You are too kind."

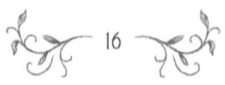

"As are you. I'll see you soon." I picked up my tray and walked it over to one of the wrought iron tables out front overlooking the fountain in center of the square.

One of my guilty pleasures in life was starting the morning like this. Enjoying a sweet treat on a sunny day while I watched the hustle and bustle of Lower Olympus, with the comfort and warmth of Hestia's Hearth enveloping me. Moments like these made my worries float away, which was why I liked coming here before a stressful day.

I carefully picked up my cake and took a bite, savoring the creamy milk, tart cheese, and sweet honey flavors. The lavender was my favorite, because the slight floral flavor complemented the cake perfectly, and as a bonus, it always seemed to soothe my nerves.

"Pandora? Is that you?" a familiar voice sang from across the square.

I squinted, light filling my vision from Apollo's rays as they reflected off the white marble fountain in the center of the plateia and its waters below. Just as I was about to get up and move to a more shaded area, a blonde-haired, blue-eyed goddess popped out from behind the fountain, sprinting in my direction.

Persephone.

"Oh, thank the Primes, it is you!" she screeched, pulling me out of my seat and into a hug, nearly knocking the small table over in the process. My milk splashed out the side of the mug, and my cake tipped over onto its side.

"Hi, Seph. What are you doing in the Plateia? I thought Demeter would have you attached to her hip with preparations for the celebration." I beamed up at her.

Persephone had been in my life for as long as I could re-member and was one of the few Olympians who treated me as an equal, not a pawn—or worse, a problem.

"As if I needed another reason to run away," Persephone laughed. "Her servants forgot to grab Hephaestus's specialty set of knives and a custom gold sickle from Forging Glory, so

I offered to come get them. His servants told me they only had the knives, though, and the sickle has not yet been delivered from Hephaestus, so I have to go up there next."

"I have to be up at Aphrodite and Hephaestus's palace this afternoon. Do you want me to get the sickle from Hephaestus while I'm there?"

"Oh, is that why you're dressed so nicely?" Persephone asked, looking me over from head to toe.

I'd settled on a soft violet gossamer dress with long, flowing sleeves and a slit running down each side of the arms, exposing my pale skin. The thin fabric had flowers and vines woven into it that would never wither or die, thanks to some magic Persephone had placed on them when she made the dress. The waist had a delicate golden lace belt, with vines looped around it that hung gracefully down the front of the dress like a golden ivy waterfall.

I rolled my eyes at her. Persephone was always dressed to impress, while I preferred comfort and simplicity. Being the only mortal in Olympus normally drew enough attention, so I didn't want to add to it by wearing clothes that made me stand out too much. But I figured my outfit wouldn't make much of a difference, as long as I wasn't meeting with any High Olympians.

"Well, I didn't wear this just to grab some breakfast," I said, laughing lightly. "So, do you want me to get the sickle while I'm there, or did you want to—?"

"No, no, no. I would love it if you could pick it up while you're there. I avoid Aphrodite like I avoid Cerberus when he's missed a meal." She cringed. Whether it was at the thought of Cerberus or Aphrodite, I had no idea.

"So, what is she teaching you today? How to walk with grace and beauty? How to seduce a man with just a few words and a look? Or maybe the elegance of table etiquette." She covered her mouth with the palm of her hand to stifle a giggle.

"All I know for sure is there's a dress-fitting for the celebration. Whatever else she has planned, I don't know, but I'm sure she's extra crazy today with the Celebration of Man coming up."

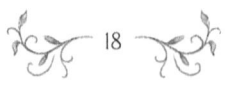

"Well, hopefully whatever she decides on isn't too torturous for you. I know she can pick the most horrendous tasks when she's in a mood."

"Every training session with Aphrodite is its own kind of torture. She says it builds character." I snorted out a laugh.

That made Persephone finally release the laugh she was holding in. "Whatever she has in store for you, I wish you lots of luck," she said, pulling me into a hug before whispering, with a little giggle, "You're going to need it."

I smiled, pushing out of the hug and holding her at arm's length before pulling her in for one more. If there was one thing I loved about Persephone, it was the way she always made me feel so loved and accepted.

"Thanks. I'll make sure to spare no details when I come over to drop off the sickle." I winked at her.

"I would have it no other way," Persephone said, smiling wide as she leaned over to the table, picked up my cake, and took a big bite before setting it back down onto the plate. "After all, what are sisters for?" she said through a mouthful of food. Then she gave me a wink and disappeared into the crowd.

Sisters . . . I smiled, thinking of how close we'd become. When I was younger, Persephone had felt more like an aunt to me, since she was born long before my creation. But in the past few years, I'd caught up with her in age, since the gods' aging slowed drastically when they reached adulthood, eventually stopping altogether, so now she truly did feel like a sister.

"Love you, Pandy," Persephone yelled over her shoulder from a few feet away.

"Love you too!" I hollered back.

I sat back down, finishing my cake and my milk while I worked on one of my recent sketches, and then I headed to the north side of Lower Olympus, near the trail that led to the summit and the Palace of Muses.

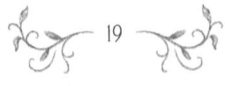

CHAPTER 4

THE Palace of Muses was my favorite palace because of its colors and the extravagant artwork throughout.

I stepped into the foyer, which opened onto nine different archways, each leading to a different muse. Without looking at the name in the center of the arch, it was easy to tell who each one belonged to thanks to their unique designs. The only two archways I'd ever entered through were Urania's—covered in deep blue, purple, and black, along with a spattering of stars and constellations that seemed to light up the night sky just as they did in reality—and Clio's. Hers was the one I started walking toward now, taking in the murals displaying the history of Olympus, from its creation by the Primal Deities, who we called the Primes, the Dark Ages under the rule of the Titans, the War of the Titans, and finally, the Age of the Olympians, who brought peace and prosperity to the realm after the Titans' downfall.

Emerging from the hallway of history, I walked into the library, finding Clio sitting behind her desk on the far side of the room.

"Lovely to see you, Pandora," she said, pushing a strand of hair behind her ear.

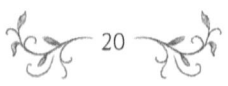

Her hair was up in a loose bun on top of her head, with small pieces falling out here and there around her pale face and her big, forest-green eyes. A beige peplos hung off her slender form, reaching to the floor, and she'd tied a golden rope around her waist. A small magnifying glass was hanging from her right hip.

I'd always admired Clio's choice of clothing. Where other gods' clothing flaunted their power, Clio's power was her mind, which contained every little fact of history she'd ever learned, so she only ever had basic clothing, with pockets lining the insides so she could carry her books, parchments, and a fine-point charcoal to take down notes.

"You too, Clio. What are you reading?" I asked, curious about the enormous leather-bound book open in front of her on the marble desk.

"Oh, nothing much. Just the history of the Titanomachy. I wanted to reference a few things before our lesson today." She closed the book with a loud thud that echoed through the vast library.

"What was the Titanomachy?" I asked, not recognizing the name.

"It's the historical term for the War of the Titans," she replied, tilting her head to the right, toward the chalkboard she kept on one side of the library for when the history became difficult to follow.

"Why not just call it that?" I asked, following her as she walked over to the chalkboard.

"Which would you prefer they call it?" She pointed to the chair for me to sit.

I sank into the soft leather chair that was worn in all the right places. "Well, War of the Titans seems more to the point than Titanomachy," I replied, resisting the urge to groan with comfort.

"Precisely. Titanomachy is the historical term because it means 'Titan battle.' However, many feel that with how brutal the fight was between the Titans and the Olympians, it should be referred to as a war, not a battle. Hence, we refer to it as the War of the Titans in our everyday language. It has always been a debate, but when a vote was cast on how to document it in history, Zeus decided it would be listed as just another battle the Titans fought and lost."

"That battle was fought for ten years. How long did it need to last for him to call it what it was—a war?"

"It is what Zeus wishes for it to be," Clio said, writing a few things on the chalkboard before turning back to me. "Today, we will be discussing the rise and fall of the Titans."

I pulled out my parchment and my fine-point charcoal, waiting for her to continue.

"The Titans were the children of Gaia and Uranus. There were twelve first-generation Titans. The six males were Cronos, Hyperion, Iapetus, Coeus, Crius, and Oceanus. The six females were Rhea, Thea, Phoebe, Themis, Mnemosyne, and Tethys." She wrote each name on the board. "Only Themis, Rhea, Oceanus, and my mother, Mnemosyne, were spared from Tartarus."

"Your mother was a Titan? What was her power?" I asked, eager to know some history on the goddess I often called "the keeper of history and mystery" because she never seemed to divulge any information from her own past.

"Yes. My mother ruled over memory and artistic inspiration. When she spent nine consecutive nights with Zeus, she became pregnant with me and my sisters."

"Where is she now?"

"No one knows. Some say her memories drove her mad, while others believe she resides in the Underworld, wandering along the edges of the River Lithe, waiting to help others erase memories that pain them as much as hers do."

"What memories would pain her?" I asked, feeling sorry for the Titaness I'd never heard mentioned before today, as if her memory itself had been wiped from existence.

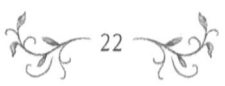

"Zeus was not entirely forthcoming during the time they spent together. Times that would eventually become memories too painful to bear." Clio's grip on the chalk tightened until it snapped in her hand.

She cleared her throat, wiping the chalk dust on her peplos as she turned to the board and quickly snatched up another piece of chalk, holding it up to write. "Continuing on," she said, clearing her throat as if a ball of emotion were fighting to get out. "The Titans also had other siblings, who emerged as different species entirely. First were the Hecatoncheires, also called the Hundred-Handed, who were known to have one hundred hands and fifty heads. The three Hecatoncheires were Briareus, Cottos, and Gyes. Next were the Cyclopes, of which there were also three. Arges, Brontes, and Steropes."

"Whose side were they on in the war?" I asked eagerly.

"They sided with the Olympians after Zeus freed the Cyclopes and the Hecatoncheires from Tartarus."

"Why were they in Tartarus?"

"Just as Cronos feared his children would usurp him, so did his father, Uranus. He feared the power of the Cyclopes and Hecatoncheires so much that he imprisoned them in Tartarus the moment their power rose to its full potential. Lucky for Zeus, they had eons of rage, strategy, and skill gathered from their time imprisoned."

"Where are they now?" I asked, sure I'd never seen any of them walking around Olympus before. I assumed either one would be impossible to miss.

"After the war, Zeus allowed them to live out the rest of their days in Aether."

"Live out the rest of their days? Are they not immortal like the Titans?" I asked, trying to wrap my head around all this.

"No. Neither the Cyclopes or Hecatoncheires are immortal, but they do have very long lifespans, as well as strength, healing abilities, and their own sort of powers to keep them going."

If they'd survived the War of the Titans, I guessed the realm outside Olympus's walls was nothing they couldn't handle.

"Back to the rise of the Titans," Clio said, pointing to Cronos. "Now, once Cronos came into power, he devised a plan with Gaia to remove Uranus from his throne. While the two were sleeping one night, Cronos snuck in and castrated him, ensuring he could never father children again. This weakened Uranus to the point they could banish him to the skies he ruled over, binding him to his duty for eternity, to never rest, leave, nor love again."

"Why did Gaia turn on Uranus? I thought she loved him."

"Gaia loved her children more than anything, and when Uranus imprisoned six of her eighteen children, she begged for him to release them, but he refused. With every refusal to release them, her love turned more and more to hate. When Cronos came to ask for her help, she happily agreed, because he swore that if she helped him, he would free the Cyclopes and Hecatoncheires."

"He never did, though, right? Zeus was the one to release them."

"No, he never did. Cronos feared their power as much as Uranus did, and he chose to keep them in Tartarus in order to secure his spot on the throne."

"So then they ruled Olympus until the Olympians were born?" I asked.

"No. The Titans ruled on Mount Othrys. During the war, they fought from their mountain, and we fought from ours."

"Where is that?" My curiosity was ever-growing.

"That is not part of today's lesson," Clio said with a proud smile. She loved it when I asked questions—encouraged it even—likely because it was the only way she could be sure I was following along with everything she was saying.

Clio tucked another stray hair behind her ear before continuing. "During the time of the Titans' rule, history was not recorded. From what we know, according to firsthand accounts, the time in which the Titans ruled was known as the Dark Ages.

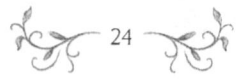

Cronos ruled with ruthless cruelty over his subjects during this time, forcing them to fall in line by whatever means necessary."

"Thank the Primes that mad Titan didn't eat Zeus along with the others," I blurted out.

"You remember this from our lessons? Would you care to tell it?" Clio asked, her eyes shining as a proud smile took over her face. It enhanced the beauty she rarely showed off.

"Cronos and Rhea gave birth to six children, called the Olympians. Hestia, Hera, Zeus, Demeter, Poseidon, and Hades," I began. "Before he bound his father to the sky, Uranus told him one day one of his children would overthrow him, just as he did to his father. Cronos was so paranoid of that coming true he began to eat his children before they could overthrow him. However, because they were gods, they never died and lived inside him. When the last child was born, Rhea wrapped a stone in cloth and fed it to Cronos in place of the child. She raised the baby in secret, and when he was old enough, she helped him to force Cronos to release his siblings from within. Once they were safe on Mount Olympus, they waged war on the Titans."

"Very good." Clio smiled. "And what can we learn from this?"

"History repeats itself?" I asked, not confident in my answer.

Clio paused to look at me, raising her brows. "Yes, history is known to do that, but what else can we gather from the Titans' story?"

I took a moment to think about my answer this time, considering the biggest downfall and the biggest strength to have been repeated with the Primes, the Titans, and the Olympians.

"Family," I finally said. "You are strongest with your family at your side and weakest when it is divided."

"Correct!" Clio exclaimed, clapping her hands.

"But how is that supposed to be avoided when your family is the problem?" I asked. If history was bound to repeat itself, then maybe the key to breaking the cycle was to fix the problem.

"Indeed, that is the question," Clio answered, tapping her chin in thought before she added, "How does one guarantee a family does not thirst for power or privilege?"

"How?" I asked, eager to hear her answer.

"They share it. That was the reason for the creation of the Olympian Court and its council. No one god or goddess holds more power or privilege than the others."

"That's not entirely true, though, right? I mean, Zeus has the largest palace, the biggest throne, and is the one who enacts the decisions made by the council," I said reluctantly, knowing Clio was very touchy when it came to her father. Some days, she defended him against all odds, while others, she seemed to almost despise him.

"Zeus was named King of the Gods by the council. They chose him to be the face of Olympus because of their respect for him, and they know without his power, it is likely Olympus would be nothing but a broken mountain surrounded by the rubble of its past civilization. Our home would look like Mount Othrys if Zeus had not been granted his bolt."

"Granted his bolt? Wasn't it gifted to him by Hephaestus?" I asked, not understanding why Clio had worded it in such a way. From what I'd been told growing up, Hephaestus had made the lightning bolt for Zeus as a way for him to harness power over lightning. Without it, he had no way to contain or control the bolts, rendering them useless in a fight.

Besides, I'd never known Zeus to be granted anything. He gained everything by either taking it or having it given to him.

Clio's entire body tensed at my question, and she stared at me for a moment before laughing it off. "Oh, yes, you're right. I worded that incorrectly. The bolt was gifted to him to help turn the tides, as Poseidon would say."

Clio pushed the conversation aside, writing a quick note on the board for our next topic, but the tension never left her body. Something about the way she'd answered didn't sit well with me. Had someone else granted Zeus the bolt as some sort of exchange or agreement, or had Hephaestus made a deal with his father when he gave him the bolt?

"After the war was won, Zeus imprisoned all those who went against him in the war to Tartarus, but some second-generation Titans were imprisoned elsewhere."

Once again, Zeus was getting all the credit for the war being won. No matter what Clio said about the council sharing their power and privileges, I knew Zeus was the mastermind behind every action they took, and he would always be the one to take the credit for their wins. If mistakes were made or battles were lost, then he had eleven High Olympians to choose from to take the blame.

"I have pulled together a collection of texts on second-generation Titans that I'd like you to read over before our next lesson. They will also give some insight on the brothers, Prometheus and Epimetheus, who will soon be arriving for the celebration. If you have any questions during your readings, write them down, and we will discuss them next time."

"Of course. I'll see you next week," I replied, picking up the books and walking over to the windows lining the far wall of the library to check the time.

I could see the sun dropping into the west, notifying me it was afternoon and time for me to head up the summit to Aphrodite's palace. I knew better than to test her patience by running late—or worse, showing up an exhausted, sweaty mess from rushing on the hike up.

I laughed to myself as I walked through the hallway toward the exit, thinking about the look on Aphrodite's face if I passed out on her floor from exhaustion, covered in dirt and sweat. She never doubted my beauty, especially since she'd helped Hephaestus in the "design phase"—as she called it—of my creation. Aphrodite was who I had to thank for my snow-white skin, my sapphire eyes, my ruby-red lips, and my ebony hair, among my other *redeeming* qualities.

It was all the things that made me mortal that she found grotesque and weak.

CHAPTER 5

"**P**ANDORA, if you drop that book from your head one more time, I will have yours on a pike. Pick it up and do it again. This time, one foot in *front* of the other, not on *top* of the other," Aphrodite said, pushing my shoulders back with more force than necessary. She fixed my posture before placing that awful book on my head once more.

I tried to make my steps more careful and deliberate this time, but I couldn't help but glance up at the book crushing me under its pages.

Ten steps. That was how far I made it before I stumbled, sending the book flying off my head onto the pristine marble floor.

Aphrodite crossed her arms, watching me expectantly.

"Don't you have a book that's maybe not so lethal?"

"Are you saying paper is too heavy for your weak little mortal neck?" she snapped.

"Paper, no. Thousands of sheets of paper contained in a book with gold casing, yes, that might be enough to break my weak little mortal neck." I glared daggers at the goddess.

Aphrodite wasn't the worst of the Olympian goddesses—no, that spot was reserved for Hera, and Hera alone—but she was definitely high up on the list, and she had a particular hatred for

mortals. In particular, me. Maybe because she had to deal with me more than any other mortal, since she spent most of her time on Mount Olympus.

She rolled her eyes, waving her hands in an exasperated manner for me to follow as she headed out of the room. "If walking is too difficult a task for you to follow, then we may as well work on getting your dress fitted. You're only expected to stand for that. Think you can manage?" she asked, flicking her light blonde hair over her shoulder and flashing me a challenging, accusatory look.

"Yes, I can manage that."

"Great. Stand up on the dais." Aphrodite led me into the tailor room she'd set up in her palace so she could be sure her clothes were as beautiful and perfect as she was at all times.

I stepped up onto the dais while Aphrodite clapped her slender hands one, two, three times, summoning her servants—three golden women—up to help me strip out of my dress. They hung the dress delicately on the handles of one of the many armoires containing fabric in all colors and textures.

"At least we have something to work with. When Hera came to me for a dress, it was like dressing a stick. Everything hung limp on her body," Aphrodite said, nodding in approval at the hourglass figure my curves created.

I didn't reply, as the golden maids were now flocking around me, with layers of fabric flowing in every direction off the dais.

I'd seen these soulless golden forms around Olympus many times before, but I normally encountered them serving their master, Hephaestus, Aphrodite's estranged husband, building or maintaining his many creations all over Olympus. Without him, the Olympians would have no weapons, no armor, nor even a palace to call home.

"No, no, no. That color is all wrong. Her skin looks like an ashy mess. Try the burgundy tulle," Aphrodite said, frustrated that the golden maids weren't working to her unreachable standards.

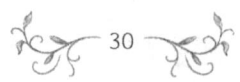

"Ouch!" I yelped as one of them poked me with a needle while trying to pin the fabric in an elaborate twirl and fold at my waist.

"Pin the dress, not the girl. Thank the Primes I had you grab the burgundy—her blood will blend right into that, rather than making her look like the target in Artemis's latest hunt," Aphrodite fumed, pushing one of the golden girls away and taking over her job of pinning the fabric into an elegant drape.

I fidgeted as Aphrodite pleated the fabric in a few more places, worried about being poked again by the minute dagger.

"Stop your moving, mortal. We can't be having our honored guests meeting you all bloody and bruised, now, can we?"

"Why would they care what I look like?" I asked, wondering once again how and why I'd been invited to this celebration in the first place. And now, why Aphrodite was worried about how the guests would perceive me, as if I were a present being gifted to them or a meal to be served on a golden platter.

"Goodness, bless the Primes you got beauty even though they forgot the brains. You will be the talk of the realm when the Titan twins visit. Surely, you will be the center of the brothers' attention."

"Yes, the Realm of Man, but I am no man. Why would they have an interest in me?"

Aphrodite threw her head back and laughed. "No man in-deed. Mortal, however, you are."

"So they're interested because I'm a mortal? Big shock there. I can't imagine they've never met a mortal before, having lived the past hundred years in a realm full of them. I would think seeing me will be no more shocking than seeing the back of their hand."

Aphrodite laughed harder and then gathered herself, only to shoot me a look full of pity and understanding. "A mortal man, yes, but not a mortal woman."

"They don't have women in this Realm of Man? All the mor-tals are men?" I tried to wrap my head around the idea. How was it possible to have a world with no women? How did they have children? Who did they marry? Questions started flying through my head, but Aphrodite's voice brought them to a screeching halt.

"It is called the Realm of Man for a reason, my dear. The Realm of Man was created by the gods, is maintained by the gods, and will forever be ruled by the gods. They have no women to love. They have no children. They know nothing of marriage or fidelity. Until you, there was no other mortal except man himself. The gods created and controlled them, but eventually, they felt the need to create another being—one who could fill their place on earth by caring for mankind in their absence. Thus, you were created to act out the wills of the gods. So, my dear, your appearance is of high importance on my list of things to accomplish for Zeus's grand celebration."

I let her words sink in. *Created to act out the wills of the gods.* I'd always thought the gods created me out of loneliness or curiosity, but it had never occurred to me I'd been created with a plan in mind. A plan for how they could use me to their benefit. I'd guessed the children of the gods were created for similar reasons, since they all had a distinct duty they were entrusted with for their eternal lives. But me . . . I'd assumed my life was too fleeting for their plans, but I guess I was wrong.

"So I am the first mortal woman?" I asked, forcing the words out of my mouth, afraid to hear the truth in Aphrodite's answer.

"The one and only," she said, shocking me when she beamed up at me with something like pride.

"Lucky me," I said, rolling my eyes.

I thought I'd felt lonely before, being the only mortal living in Olympus, but now, I felt as if I were drifting all alone through an endless abyss. The only mortal in Aether, and the only mortal woman in existence throughout all time and space.

CHAPTER 6

APHRODITE spent a few more hours playing around with the fabric for the dress and trying out dozens of jewelry choices until she finally deemed the outfit divine perfection.

"The hair and makeup will be simple. They should just accentuate the beauty already there. We want to tempt the brothers, not stop their hearts," she said, playing with my hair and admiring my features. She didn't do it in a tender, loving way, but rather in the way Hephaestus admired his lifeless creations.

"So you want me to sway them, not slay them." I smirked, making Aphrodite's face scrunch in disgust.

"Unfortunate that you must speak to them. The brothers will be enamored by your beauty until you open your mouth. Then we will just have to hope the Primes have mercy on us and the brothers don't understand a word you say," she replied, crossing her arms and turning her back to me to walk away. "Run along, little mortal. I've had enough of you for the day."

She didn't have to tell me twice. The feeling was mutual.

I slipped back into the violet dress I'd worn to come here, grabbing my satchel before heading down the hallway from Aphrodite's tailor room, toward the doorway in the foyer that descended into Hephaestus's caverns below the palace.

Rounding the corner into the foyer, I admired the way the afternoon sun made the enormous columns in the room glow with an ethereal beauty. Each pillar within the palace told a different love story for all the males Aphrodite had ever been with, as well as a few females. I'd only been down to Hephaestus's caverns once, when I was very young, and I had very little memory of it, but I had no trouble finding the entrance, considering his column was not gilded in gold or carved with soft curves that made it feel sensual. Instead, it was darker, with rough, jagged edges representing the immense struggle they'd faced throughout their time together.

Clio once told me Hephaestus had always loved Aphrodite, but she'd felt nothing except repulsion toward the blacksmith, hating him with every fiber of her being for forcing her into marriage. Before their marriage, the males of Olympus had been fighting for her hand. Many believe Aphrodite was willing to marry Ares, but Zeus feared he'd start a war to eliminate any other suitors. While Ares was planning an attack, Hephaestus trapped Hera in a throne of his making, only agreeing to free her with Zeus's blessing for her to marry him. Zeus agreed, and they were married, but Ares never gave up the war for Aphrodite's heart. He continued to see her until she became pregnant with his child, Eros. After this, Zeus forbade them from seeing each other, threatening to replace Ares's seat on the Olympian Council if he rebelled. He also reminded Ares his wars would be futile without weaponry and armor made by Hephaestus, and if he wished to remain in power, he would do well to realize allies were always better than enemies.

If only Hephaestus had known Aphrodite's beauty was only superficial, and that a life spent with her would end in hatred and heartache.

Walking around the dark column, I turned the handle on the iron doorway that led below the palace and couldn't help but

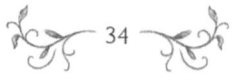

wonder if Aphrodite's bitter-cold personality was once as warm and beautiful as the columns devoted to her lovers.

The corridor was filled with shadow, the steps only visible thanks to the flaming torches lining the walls that descended deep into the belly of Mount Olympus. A metallic tang mixed with smoke filled the air, tickling my nose the further I descended, until finally, the stairs ended in front of a wrought-iron door that creaked open to the room before me.

The room was enormous, with doorways lining the walls leading to different work areas, I assumed. The ceiling reached so high up my eyes had trouble focusing. Or maybe it was the smoke filtering through the room before spilling out into the openings in the wall to my left. They looked like windowless frames built into the side of Mount Olympus.

I could feel my heart beating in time with the clang of metal echoing off the cavern walls, and I couldn't tell if it was from excitement or fear.

"Who dares enter our master's lair?" a deep feminine voice boomed from across the room as a group of Hephaestus's golden servants headed toward me.

I counted five of them approaching from every angle except my back, sending a clear message: Leave the way you came, or face the consequences.

"Pandora," I said, trying to force confidence into my tone as my throat threatened to seize up. "I came to pick up the golden sickle for Demeter."

For the most part, Hephaestus's servants avoided confrontation, but that was outside the caverns they called home. Down here, all bets were off. I was considered a trespasser until proven otherwise, simply for crossing the threshold through the stone doorway and entering into his workshop.

"Demeter sent the mortal down to the depths. How bold. Why not send the springling down instead? Maybe she fears her being underground with everything that happened with Hades.

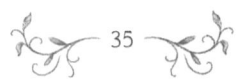

Perhaps she sent the mortal down here to finally get rid of her," they all said in unison, their lifeless golden eyes staring me down as they creeped up to me.

"Hephaestus?" I yelled loud enough for my voice to echo through the cavern, not wanting to risk the golden women coming any closer. "It's Pandora."

The clang of metal ceased, and footsteps sounded behind the wall to my right before a large, burly man hobbled out from around the corner.

"Pandora? What are you doing down here?" Hephaestus grumbled.

His servants slowly backed away, returning to whatever corners of the cavern they'd appeared from.

"Persephone asked me to pick up Demeter's sickle after my class with Aphrodite."

"Ah. Come then," he said, turning on his good leg and limping back around the corner he'd come from.

I rushed to follow him before his golden guardians returned.

I'd felt the warmth of the fires as I entered the cavern, but as I turned the corner, it became so hot beads of sweat started to drip down the back of my neck. Wiping my forehead, I looked up to see what was causing such extreme heat and stopped dead in my tracks as I took in the sight before me.

Streams of molten lava poured out of the cavern walls like a waterfall, falling into a pool of lava at their base. Flames danced across the lava's surface like a lake of fire. Over to my right, I noticed a pool of water with steam billowing up around it like the smoke from Hephaestus's blacksmith table in the center of the room, where a blazing red piece of metal was still smoking.

"Give me a moment." He pointed to where I stood. "Don't move."

I nodded, watching as he picked up the red-hot sword, which hissed and steamed as he submerged it in a nearby pool.

"Follow me."

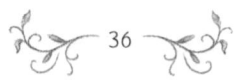

We walked back out into the main cavern and headed over to the doorway farthest from his workstation, nearly to the open windows at the cavern's edge. I couldn't help but admire the view. Walking over, I sucked in a breath at the beauty, seconds before a breeze blew in so strong I nearly lost my footing and had to reach out to the wall to steady myself. The gust of hot air blew out from behind me, and my hold on the wall faltered. I found myself teetering toward the open window in front of me.

A strong, callused grip grabbed my arm. "Hold your ground, girl. Zeus would have my head if you fell to your death from within my caverns."

"I, uh . . . Sorry. I just wanted to see the view." I stumbled over my words.

"I can assure you, the view is not worth falling from Mount Olympus."

We locked eyes for a moment before Hephaestus grunted, releasing my arm and staring down the cliffside with a knowing gaze.

"I apologize. It won't happen again," I said, taking a few steps away from the window and standing up against the wall on the other side of him. I used his body as a shield against the wind as he pulled a set of keys from his pocket and went about unlocking the cavern door.

We stepped into a dark room, and I was about to ask how he could see when, suddenly, the sound of metal striking rock sounded, and the entire room flooded with light from the flames encircling us.

The room was much larger than I anticipated, full of weapons, armor, various random metalwork such as cutlery and pans, and an enormous metal cage in its center, which seemed to glow with divine power from the fire's warm light.

"I believe Demeter's sickle was placed over here," Hephaestus said, walking to the left of the room to retrieve it, but I couldn't take my eyes off the cage.

I walked over to it to examine it closer. It was beautiful yet strange. The material was dark, more like stone or crystal than metal, and hundreds if not thousands of small runes had been carved into it and a lock made of the same black stone.

"Here it is," Hephaestus called from the corner of his room. I heard his footsteps approaching me, but I couldn't tear my gaze away.

"What is this?" I asked.

"Oh, you noticed my cage," he said, walking up beside me, holding the sickle at his side.

"It's hard to miss."

"This is my gift for Father. He's been in need of a prison of sorts for his more powerful enemies. This will provide him with the power of Tartarus at his fingertips, enabling him to imprison his enemies for as long as needed without having to open the gates of Tartarus."

"How?" I asked, trying to wrap my mind around this cage holding even a drop of Tartarus's power. After all, how could a cage mimic the power of a Prime?

"That is privileged information, child. Now, here is Demeter's sickle. You'd better be off now. The sun will be setting soon, and you have a long walk home," Hephaestus said, handing the sickle over and then grabbing my arm, pulling me away from the cage, and leading me back out into the main cavern before locking the door.

"Tell Demeter if she requires anything else to reach out. And Pandora? Stay safe out there."

Stay safe? What was he worried about? Olympus was the safest place in the realm.

CHAPTER 7

IME flew by as I went from palace to palace training with my mentors—even more so than normal, considering the list of commands Zeus had sent them to prepare me for the Titans' arrival.

It was now only two days until the ceremony, which was being referred to as the "Centennial Celebration of Man," and I couldn't contain my relief as I finished up my last lesson of the day with Clio. We'd discussed the Titans again, and she explained how they'd wronged so many and ruled with an iron fist, showing no mercy. The more I learned about these Titans, the more I found myself filled with anger at all the horrendous things they'd done. Instead of protecting all their citizens like we did in Olympus, they'd left the creatures they named cretes to wither and die, or worse, executed them by the masses.

I played the stories Clio told me over and over in my head, beginning to dread the Titans' arrival. As I headed out of the Palace of Muses, I hoped they wouldn't disturb the peace. I made my way toward Demeter's vegetable fields, west of my cottage across the river, to gather some food for dinner.

I'd always loved wandering Demeter's land, gathering whatever I needed whenever I needed it. Sure, I could always go into

the plateia and buy food from the vendors, and many times I did, but there was something about wandering the fields and orchards, gathering my own food while getting my hands dirty in Aether's soil, that brought me a sense of comfort.

While I didn't know much about the Realm of Aether outside Olympus's walls, I knew most of Olympus was formed of stone, ocean, or dense forest. Demeter's farmlands were by far the most fertile thanks to her powers, covered in a soft blanket of plentiful soil that fed the realm's celestial power into anything planted there.

"Dora? That you?" a masculine voice asked from beside me.

I jumped. The voice seemed to come from the shadows between the massive oak trees scattered throughout the courtyard. They surrounded a crescent-shaped colonnade that encased one side of the ethereal, shimmering blue lagoon, a large rotunda in its center. I prayed silently to the Primes that it wasn't Aphrodite's son, Eros, again. The flirt never passed up an opportunity to annoy me. He knew I had no interest in him, but that never seemed to stop him.

To my relief, it was not the God of Love, but Hermes.

"Hermes!" I screeched excitedly, running up to the handsome blond-haired god I'd always considered one of my closest friends. "I haven't seen you in ages! Where have you been flying off to? Come! You must tell me about all your travels." I led him over to one of the benches alongside the lagoon. Above us, a willow tree danced wistfully to every breath of cool wind that kissed its branches.

I'd always loved to hear about Hermes's travels outside the walls, especially since I'd never even had the opportunity to leave the confines of Olympus.

"It's really not all that interesting, Dora. I'm sure your stories of training with the gods and goddesses are much better than mine," Hermes said quickly, raising his thick, dark blond brow as a smile crept onto his handsome face. "I'm particularly curious

about how tightly wound Aphrodite is, considering she's the party planner, fashion designer, and responsible for everyone's attendance and for things going smoothly."

"Oh, she's definitely a little more tightly wound than normal. If I wove a basket as tight as her temper, it would snap in no time," I said, thinking about my dress-fitting.

"Don't tell me you were the target of that temper." He gave a sarcastic grin.

"On a normal day, even my mortality irritates her, but lucky for me, she was much more distracted losing her temper over all the things Hephaestus's golden women were doing wrong."

"Lucky indeed. How has everything else been on the mighty summit of Mount Olympus? Any sign of Zeus or his hellhound of a wife, Hera? Have Poseidon or Hades arrived for the Centennial Celebration of Man yet? I heard they'd be arriving early, so the High Olympians could meet before the Titan twins arrived." Hermes spoke quickly, a glimmer of curiosity and deviousness in his deep green eyes. The god had a habit of talking fast—sometimes too fast for me to keep up—but for the most part, I'd gotten used to it.

"Thankfully, I haven't seen her . . . or Zeus, really. He had the others double up my lessons so I won't embarrass anyone." I sighed, feeling the exhaustion in my body finally taking effect.

Hermes picked up a handful of rocks and skipped them across the surface of the lagoon. "Nonsense! You could never embarrass us." He paused mid-throw, looking at me consideringly. "Well, at least no more than we already do ourselves."

"So, what are you doing down here today?" I asked, laughing at him.

"Well, actually, I was looking for you." Hermes dropped the rocks, reaching into his tunic and pulling out an object wrapped in a bundle of cloth, held together with a red silk string. "I brought a present for you."

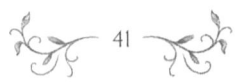

"What is it?" I asked. I started to untie the string before Hermes placed his tan hand over mine, motioning for me to stop.

"Do not open it where anyone can see it. This is our little secret, Dora. No one, and I mean no one—not Athena, Demeter, or even Persephone—can know about this. Simply having it could get me thrown off the mountain like Hephaestus when he angered father last, and I will not become a hobble like that mangled man." Cringing at the thought, he paced. "Could you imagine these winged feet carrying this beautiful body across worlds, dipping up and down, unable to keep a steady flight through the sky? If that ever happens, you have to put me down, Dora. I can't get stuck. I can't be slow. I can't be helpless. I just can't." Hermes's rambling turned to panic as he went into the dark abyss of his mind. This seemed to happen often, whenever he thought about losing his powers.

One thing I'd noticed all the gods had in common was their need to fulfill their duty. Their lives may be eternal, but that didn't mean their minds were. Without their role in the world, the gods would likely lose themselves to madness.

"Calm down, Hermes," I said, rubbing circles into his back to soothe him. I motioned to the mysterious object, not daring to try to open it again. "What is this? Why is it so important that no one sees I have it?"

Hermes leaned in close and whispered in my ear. "Protection. I found something in Father's office—something that shook me to my core. I took this from his lounge yesterday, when he summoned me to ensure the Titan brothers had received his invitation to the party."

Of course he'd been here before now. Hermes hadn't just run into me; the sneaky god had been lying in wait in the shadows so he could stop me and make this seem like a gift, not something he'd stolen from Zeus.

"Primes be with me, you *stole* this from Zeus? Why on earth would you risk something so foolish? No wonder you're worried

about ending up like Hephaestus. All he did was take Hera's side in an argument and Zeus threw him from the top of Olympus." I shook my head, glancing over at the slightly terrified look on his smug face.

"Well, we did have a little argument about the terms of the invitation he had me deliver to the Titan twins."

"What terms?"

"Just the basics. That nobody kills the messenger, and he returns with all his limbs in place." He shrugged.

I stared at him wide-eyed, my mouth agape. Sometimes, it was easy for me to forget Zeus had a habit of enacting cruelty and indifference upon his children.

"Anyway, when I got back, all limbs intact thanks to me, myself, and I,"—Hermes took a deep breath—"I paid father a little visit and may or may not have overheard him talking to Themis. I thought to myself, 'Well, if he's not worried about losing a child, then a missing object should be nothing,' and returned later that night to swipe it right out from under his nose."

"I can't believe you, Hermes. You know how your father can get—otherwise you wouldn't be so worried—yet still, you press him until he explodes." I shook my head at him, not understanding his need to antagonize Zeus at every opportunity.

"It ended up being well worth it," he said, the humor and rebellious spark leaving his face as he stared at me with a seriousness he didn't often display.

"I hope so, for both our sakes," I replied, my mind racing as fast as Hermes's with all the different possible consequences, before asking the one question I couldn't shake. "Why now? Why is everything changing so much now? Zeus has celebrations all the time. Are these Titans really so formidable that it's sending everyone into a frenzy?"

"It's not just the Titans. Everything is changing now, because it's time for his plan . . ." He paused as a door closed in the distance, alerting us to someone's presence. "We can't talk about it anymore. Look over my gift and trust no one, Dora—not even me."

Hermes leaned forward and gave me a quick kiss on the forehead before disappearing into the sky, leaping off the ground with ease. I always forgot how fast the immortal god was and struggled to ever find him after his feet left the ground. My mortal eyes simply weren't able to keep up with his immortal speed.

Tucking the gift into my bag, I headed around the back of the crescent-shaped colonnade, through the agora that was open to all the gods as a common space, and made my way across the bridge to my cottage, not bothering to visit the vegetable garden after all. I decided whatever Hermes had just given me should not be carried around in my satchel for any longer than necessary.

CHAPTER 8

I STARED at the wrapped gift for what felt like forever, debating whether or not it was worth opening. Hermes had made it seem important to open the gift immediately, but I feared what would happen if Zeus caught me with it. Maybe it was best I take it with me to my appointment with Zeus and sneak it back into his palace, so neither I nor Hermes would be caught and held responsible for stealing from him.

As smart of an idea as that was, my curiosity got the better of me, and I couldn't help but reach out and untie the silk string. I carefully unwrapped the cloth to reveal a beautiful purple stone, which hung from a golden chain, and a small piece of folded parchment.

Opening the parchment, I took a deep breath, preparing myself for whatever it was that Hermes was so eager for me to know but hesitant to say in public.

Dora,

Carry this amethyst amulet with you at all times, but be sure to keep it hidden out of sight. No one can know you have it, but you should never be without

it. A storm is brewing beyond the walls of Olympus, and many are whispering that it may already be here. Hear everyone, but trust no one.

Burn this note after reading.

Hermes

I picked up the amulet and the note quickly, carrying it over to the fire I kept burning at all times for warmth. I dropped the parchment into the flames, watching as it shriveled and burned until it was nothing but a small pile of ash.

Turning the amulet over in my hands, I noticed strange carvings within the amethyst, so small I almost missed them. I'd never seen symbols like these before. I wanted desperately to ask Clio for some of her books on runes, but I couldn't risk drawing any unwanted attention. Instead, I glanced out the window, checking the time, before running upstairs to change into something warmer and more suited to the summit's cold climate.

I settled on a deep blue peplos with golden ties at the waist and slipped the amethyst into one of the pockets I'd sewn on the inside years ago, which I used to carry extra parchments for sketching when my satchel failed to fit them all. Then I made my way up to the summit as quickly as I could, racing the sun with every step.

Finally, I passed through the summit's gateway and glanced back at the sun to find Apollo's position closer to the horizon than expected. I realized, thankfully, I had a few precious minutes left to make my way across Upper Olympus to Zeus's palace.

Up here on the summit, there was a lot more activity than down in Lower Olympus. As I walked the cobblestone paths around the court, I watched as the servants of the High Olympians hustled in every direction, although most of them were heading

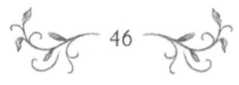

to either the tunnels beneath the court, disappearing through the dark stone doors lining its base, or gathering at the festival grounds. Today, it looked like only the west grounds were open, with a half-dozen vendors selling fruits, vegetables, and other various goods from the base of the mountain. The east grounds, between Zeus's palace and Athena's palace, were normally saved for rituals honoring the High Olympians or opened for larger celebrations.

As I got closer to Zeus's palace, I had the uneasy feeling I was being watched. Glancing around, at first I didn't notice anything, but as I scanned the shadows under the oak trees, I saw a pair of glowing eyes watching me.

I held my breath as we stared at one another, feeling an odd pull toward the mysterious figure. But I had enough sanity to realize anyone spying on me from the shadows was someone I should probably avoid at all costs.

We continued to stare, neither of us willing to break eye contact first, when suddenly a crash sounded behind me, making me nearly jump out of my skin. I quickly turned on my heel to see what had happened.

A group of servants carrying a basket four times their size had dropped it, sending the objects inside crashing to the cobblestone path. They rolled off in every direction while the servants flailed to retrieve them.

I swiveled back toward the mystery figure, only to find nothing but empty shadows under the oak trees. Staring at the spot for a moment more, I finally shook my head, wondering if exhaustion and Hermes' cryptic note were making me imagine things, and walked up the marble steps to the palace.

Zeus and Hera's palace was exactly as I remembered it, full of opulence that showcased its owners' ostentatiousness. But even with the warmth of the gold embellishments, the color scheme felt cold and lifeless.

I was lifting my hand to knock when a servant pulled open the door. He was tall and stocky, with the head of an eagle and the body of a man.

"Hi! I have a meeting with Zeus," I said, smiling kindly, which got me a cold look in return.

"Come. I will let him know you have arrived."

Not bothering to give me a name, or even to ask for mine, the servant led me into the palace. I stayed quiet, taking a second to admire the sheer size of the split staircase that twisted up the middle of the foyer from two sides. It had balusters that looked like small, slender Corinthian columns, reaching up to support a white marble railing with a decorative swirl pattern engraved into it. As we moved past the beautiful staircase, I noticed a short hallway with a door at the end of it, nestled between the two staircases, which merged into one at the top.

I must have stopped and not realized it, because the sound of someone clearing their throat in annoyance got my attention. I looked over at the eagle-man servant to find him with a feathered hand on his hip, his beak locked shut, and his light yellow eyes glaring at me. The feathers on his brow were curled down in the center.

"Sorry. I'm coming," I said, trotting over to where he stood, almost halfway down the hall.

The second I caught up to him, he began walking again, and this time, I tried not to get distracted by my surroundings. I didn't get to visit Zeus in his palace very often, so I wasn't used to its grandeur. Normally, we met at the court, or he'd show up at Athena's or Aphrodite's to speak with me.

Stopping in front of a doorway, the servant held out his feathered arm, motioning for me to walk inside.

The room looked like some sort of dayroom. On the ceiling was an extra-detailed mural of the sky, set within gold molding, and it was the most color I'd seen since entering the palace. I was looking up at it when I heard the servant finally speak.

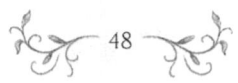

"Wait here while I inform Zeus of your arrival."

I turned around to thank him, but he was already gone.

With a shrug, figuring he wasn't much of a socializer, I stared up at the ceiling mural again, waiting for His Highness to arrive.

Zeus walked in not a minute later, his wavy, shoulder-length brown hair tucked into an oak-leaf crown and his beard longer than normal, almost fully covering his mouth. He headed over to the small table I hadn't noticed until now, which held gold-rimmed glasses and an amphora. Zeus picked the amphora up and poured two glasses of wine.

"Would you like some?" he asked, holding out the glass to me.

"No, thank you."

"Suit yourself." He downed both drinks, refilling one of the glasses before crossing the room to sit on the couch across from me. He crossed his foot up and over to rest it on his knee. "I assume you would like to know why I decided to test you today."

Over the past week, Athena had continued teaching me needlework and weaving, Apollo had made me practice playing the lyre and perfecting my pitch, Aphrodite had instructed me on beautification techniques and etiquette, and Clio had continued teaching me all the unforgivable things the Titans had done during their rule. And from Zeus I'd received a letter requesting—more like demanding—I meet with him for a series of small tests to check my aptitude in the skills I'd been taught my entire life.

"Yes," I replied.

"I need to assure the council the plans we have for you are well on track to succeed, and in order for that to happen, I must ensure your training over the years has proved beneficial." Zeus tapped his fingers on his leg like he was bored as he looked me over, taking in my appearance for the first time since he'd walked in. "My, my. Aphrodite did do well in designing your form, didn't she?" He looked at me in a way that began to make me uncomfortable. I knew Zeus's reputation for sleeping with any and every woman he could get his hands on.

Not happening. I shifted in my seat as I worked on changing the subject.

"I understand. I am eager to finally find out what it is you've been preparing me for my entire life," I offered with a smile to hide the disgust turning my stomach as Zeus continued looking me over from head to toe. Thank the Primes I'd chosen the baggiest peplos I owned, not one of the dresses I normally wore to come here. I dreaded to think how much worse that would be.

"I'm sure you are, my dear. But first, let us run through a series of tests to check you are indeed ready."

I nodded as my nerves worked their way into my system. My stomach spun. A knot formed in my throat, preventing any words from coming out.

I only hoped whatever tests Zeus had in mind for me were tests I'd be able to pass with flying colors, because if there was one thing I knew for sure, it was that Zeus did not take kindly to failure.

CHAPTER 9

ZEUS spent hours having me sing, sew, weave, and perform a dozen other "tests" that left me utterly exhausted and thoroughly confused. Why did he possibly need a mortal woman to do all these things when he had a palace full of servants and magic to help him accomplish his every desire on a whim?

"Well done. You surpassed my expectations for all these skills. I believe you are more than ready to fulfill your duty to Olympus," he said, smiling for the first time since I arrived. Although something about the way he said the last part set me on edge.

"Thank you. But if I may . . . how do these skills help me fulfill my duty to Olympus?" I hoped I didn't sound ungrateful, but these skills were common here.

Zeus grinned. "I need you to win over the heart of Prometheus."

I didn't think I'd heard him correctly. *Win over the heart of a Titan?* My mouth ran dry.

"Why me?"

"The skills you have learned are not yet common practice in the Realm of Man. Of course, the Titans know some of them to survive, but you, my dear, were taught these skills by the greatest

mentors to exist. The Olympians. Because of that, and with your experience of being raised here in Olympus, I think it best to have you show them around—Prometheus specifically. I'm sure the Titans will find your skills impressive and necessary in the Realm of Man, as well as find it interesting to view Olympus through the eyes of a mortal." Zeus gave a small grin.

"Why now?" I asked carefully.

"Man has been plagued with a poison of sorts. I am unsure of how it has spread, but I saw an opportunity to offer my help and remind them that without the Olympians, man would be no more. As such, Hecate has provided a cure for man's ailments that you, my dear, will be presenting them with at the Centennial Celebration of Man."

"Me? Wouldn't you rather present it yourself?"

"I would, yes, but that would ruin my plans." Zeus paused, grinning. "Your duty will be to present this gift on behalf of all of Olympus, and after they have accepted it, you will show them the joys of living in Olympus as a mortal, while winning the heart of Prometheus, ensuring neither he nor his brother ever think to choose man over the Olympians again."

My heart seized in my chest. "Are you sure that will work?" I asked, sucking in a breath as I saw the anger flash across Zeus's face. I quickly added, "I mean, I understand what you're saying, but why are you so sure I will be enough to sway their loyalty over to Olympus?"

"They have chosen to side with mortals for the past hundred years on the Realm of Man, ignoring every message I have ever sent them until now. You will be both the peace offering and the weapon that brings the Titan brothers to heel. Once you have won Prometheus's heart, he will have no choice but to return his loyalty to Olympus in order to protect you. After all, you could give man the one thing they do not have."

"What's that?"

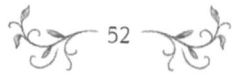

"The ability to create life. You are the only mortal female in existence. However, we have ensured that ability remains dormant until we are positive they won't try to steal you before you win his heart. Although, keep in mind, they will not know this fact. If Prometheus chose to give you to man rather than protect you, there is no guarantee of how long you would survive. Man would kill for the chance to procreate, but there is only one of you, and there are thousands of them." He smiled so wide his gray-blue eyes crinkled around the corners, and his pearly-white teeth glistened in the candlelight.

I stared at Zeus wide-eyed, panicked by the numerous outcomes playing over and over in my head. I was either doomed to live out the rest of my years with a Titan I'd been taught to hate and fear, or with man who I was beginning to think wasn't much better.

"What if I'm unable to capture Prometheus's heart? What if he doesn't bother to protect me and hands me over to man?"

Zeus's smile disappeared, and his eyes darkened like storm clouds. "If you cannot fulfill your duty to Olympus, then you have no place here."

"No place? Where would I go? Olympus is my home. It's all I've ever known."

"Failure to complete your duty will end in immediate banishment. You will no longer be allowed to live or visit within the walls of Olympus. So, if I were you, I would ensure you complete your duty or die trying, because if not, the wild ones will kill you before you even see them coming."

My breath left my body, and I fought back the tears stinging my eyes. I couldn't believe Zeus had gone from bestowing upon me such an honor to telling me my life was forfeited and the only way to keep it was to win over Prometheus. Not only that, but I had to make him fall so madly in love with me that he gave up an entire realm full of a species he'd not only created but had watched over for the past century.

"Now, off you go—you've got a celebration to prepare for," Zeus said, standing up and heading toward the door. He stopped before disappearing around the corner. "Oh, and Pandora, do not fail me. I will accept nothing less than perfection when you represent me and my family."

With that, he left me alone to process everything he'd told me.

Tears gushed out of my eyes. How could he have raised me and protected me all these years just to throw me away? I sniffled as snot started to run from my nose, and I looked around desperately for something to blow it with, finding nothing but a gold-stitched cloth napkin and a throw, which was spread across the couch behind me.

He already threatened my life—might as well leave my mark on Olympus while I still can. I grabbed the napkin and blew my nose into it before reaching for the throw to wipe my tear-stained cheeks.

After a few minutes of letting my emotions get the best of me, I was finally ready to leave. Thankfully, no servants were in the halls on the way out, so I was able to make a clean getaway before anybody saw what I mess I'd become during my meeting with Zeus.

CHAPTER 10

As I walked down the path toward Lower Olympus, I couldn't help but replay my conversation with Zeus over and over in my head. I didn't know what hurt worse: that he'd put safeguards in place in case I didn't succeed or that I meant so little to him that he'd sacrifice me to the Realm of Man, or to the wild ones outside the walls.

Tears were fighting to spill over again, but since I'd started staring at the ground instead of the view of the home that might soon be taken from me, it had become easier to pass the time without another emotional breakdown.

That is until I crashed into something in front of me. Or someone, judging by the way they screeched. I saw the metal bowls, linens, and fruit they'd dropped rolling down the cobblestone path before I had a chance to see who I'd run into.

Without thinking, I took off in a sprint down the mountainside, and thankfully, I was able to catch up to the fallen objects before they rolled right off the edge of the cliff. I gathered everything together and carried it all back up to the owner, who was crouching down gathering more fallen objects from around her.

When she heard my footsteps approaching, the water nymph turned around, yelling at me to watch where I was going. Then

we locked eyes, and her teal scales flashed as the color in her cheeks drained away.

It was Lemenia.

"I am so sorry. I didn't see you until it was too late. Here—let me help you," I said, bending down to help gather the remaining items spread around her on the path.

"I don't need your help!" she snapped, but as she leaned over to grab a bowl, she bumped the basket with her foot and nearly lost everything again.

I grabbed the basket before it could spill, and she sighed before walking back over to me, bowl in hand.

"Thank you," she forced out.

"It's no problem. I should be the one apologizing—I bumped into you and made you spill it in the first place. I promise I'm not normally so senseless. I've just had a rough day." I sighed, placing the last few linens in the basket and helping her lift it up.

"You look like you've been crying," she said, taking in my disheveled appearance.

"Yeah . . . I was trying to avoid the view so I didn't cry again, which is why I ran into you."

"The view?" Lemenia asked, looking out at the serene land and the ocean ahead of us. "What's wrong with the view?"

"Nothing. It's just . . . I might not be seeing it for much longer."

"Oh," she said, something that looked like pity crossing her features. Although I must have been imagining it, because surely, she wasn't pitying me. I was a mortal, and from what Sylra had told me, Lemenia had a traumatic history with mortals.

"I'm sorry."

"You've said that already."

"No—I'm sorry man treated your kind the way they did, and I'm sorry that when we first met, you thought I was like them. Had I known, I would have done my best to avoid you, so you wouldn't have had to relive whatever horrors they put you through in their realm."

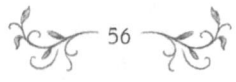

She stared at me for a moment before nodding. "You are nothing like the other mortals I've come across. I apologize for my reaction to seeing you. It was a shock more than anything, and my mind made me relive some very painful memories."

"I couldn't even begin to understand what they did to you. But nonetheless, I am sorry for whatever you had to go through in order to get here. If I were Poseidon, I would have never let the nymphs go to that realm in the first place."

She smiled. "It wasn't all bad. In the beginning, it was beautiful, and man was respectful of our waters, just as we were of their land . . . until one day, that all changed."

"You don't have to tell me if you don't want to. I don't want to make you relive any of that again."

"I relive it every day, whether I like it or not." Lemenia grabbed the basket and carried it over to one of the benches farther down the road. She sat down, motioning for me to join her.

"Man was fascinated and fearful of Poseidon. They had witnessed his beauty in the calm seas that glistened and danced, but they had also witnessed his untamed fury when the seas rose up and crashed down on everything in their path, wreaking havoc and destruction. For the most part, their fear kept them from challenging Poseidon, but there was one group of mankind they called the Clan of Adam, who sought to control Poseidon and his power by capturing his treasured water nymphs." She cringed at the memory. "They stole as many as they could on their floating vessels and slayed the others in the sea caves and grottos they found. It was a massacre."

Lemenia stared off into the distance, her green-blue eyes glistening with unshed tears at the memory.

"Man studied the water nymphs enough to understand how to catch them, but they never took into account the fact the nymphs' survival depended on being near the water. They kidnapped hundreds and took them as far inland as they could to keep them from Poseidon's reach. However, they never made it to their destination, because the farther they traveled from the sea, the more the water nymphs started dying off. One by one, each of them withered away, and with each passing, Poseidon himself felt the stab of pain and loss from his beloved nymphs."

"That is unspeakable," I said, my cheeks heating at their senseless cruelty. "So many lives stolen for what? Payback? No wonder you despise mortals—they sound like nothing but thieves and murderers. Why would Zeus and the other High Olympians fight so hard to keep their faith?"

I used to be excited to meet another mortal, thinking when I did, I would feel less alone. But from what Lemenia was telling me, and from what Zeus had said, my hatred was quickly turning into a gut-wrenching fear of my own kind.

"The Olympians created the mortals. To forsake them would be to forsake their children and their creation. When a child has a tantrum, you punish them. You don't forsake them for all eternity."

"So, were they?"

"Were they what?"

"Punished?" I asked, hoping the mortals got what they had coming to them. I knew how bad it could get for someone on the wrong side of Poseidon.

"Oh yes, they were punished indeed. Poseidon pulled all the water in the sea toward him and sent it rushing at the clan who'd committed the atrocities against his nymphs. He smashed them to pieces before pulling their remains back out to sea, nourishing his millions of creatures with the blood and bone of man in the hope of replenishing what was taken from them."

I smiled, proud of the justice Poseidon had enacted. "Good. They got what they deserved."

"Yes. However, not all were so fortunate as to have been killed that dreadful day. Some of us, like me, were forced to watch our families and friends wither away in cruel, careless deaths, seeing man's quick death as almost an act of mercy, not a punishment.

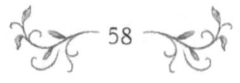

We feel man deserved to suffer more for those crimes, and we resent the mortals left to walk on the Realm of Man."

"I don't blame you. Knowing what you went through, I think your opinion of mortals is completely justified. I'd probably look at them with just as much hatred if I were in your position too."

Lemenia nodded, wiping away a few tears that had escaped. They rolled down her cheek, making her scales shimmer in the setting sun. "At least you get to live here. You don't have to worry about their cruelty in Olympus. The council would never allow them to reside within these walls," she said, smiling at me until she saw the blood draining from my face. Then her smile faltered, and her brow creased with worry. "What is it? What did I say?"

"Nothing. It's just that's what I was upset about when I ran into you. Zeus threatened to kick me out of Olympus or let Prometheus give me to mankind to do with me as they please if I can't win his heart," I said before thinking better of it. Maybe I shouldn't be telling Lemenia this. Hermes had told me to trust no one, and while Zeus hadn't explicitly told me to keep his plans a secret, knowing how mad he could get, I didn't think it wise to test him. "I shouldn't have said that."

"It's all right. Your secret's safe with me." Lemenia pulled me in for a hug.

My body froze at first, in shock that she was acting so friend-ly now she no longer thought I was evil incarnate.

"But Pandora . . . ?"

"Yeah?"

"Make sure you win his heart," she said, forcing a smile onto her lips. She picked up her basket to continue on her way, leaving me to stare out at the only home I'd ever known and pray to the Primes they'd let me stay.

CHAPTER 11

THE celebration was tomorrow, and at one time, I would have been full of excitement, but now, I felt nothing but crippling anxiety over the upcoming event. It had taken a long time for me to fall asleep after my conversation with Lemenia, my mind replaying the story she'd told me of her time in the Realm of Man.

Although, hearing her story had given me another idea that hadn't occurred to me before.

I could run.

Olympus was surrounded by walls to the north, the east, and the west, but the sea, which sat south of the kingdom, was considered an extended part of Olympus, since Poseidon ruled over it. Lucky for me, I was on much better terms with Poseidon than Zeus. I could flee to the sea, to freedom, and find an island somewhere far beyond Zeus's reach where I could live out my days. Maybe eventually I could send word to Persephone and Hermes so they could visit.

I'd already packed my bag early this morning. Sure, it would be soaked from the swim, but when I got to where I was going, I could hang all my belongings out in the sun to dry. I'd also filled my satchel with as much water-resistant food as I could

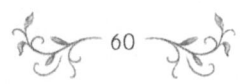

carry, including the small pouch eternally filled with water from Poseidon. Around my neck I'd wrapped the pearl necklace he'd gifted me to wear when I wanted to visit him in the depths of the ocean. It granted me the temporary ability to breathe underwater, as well as enhanced speed while swimming and gave me immunity to the effects of the pressure under the sea.

I gathered everything I needed and looked around my cottage one more time before heading out the front door, walking south toward the sea.

I cut through the orchards instead of taking the path, grabbing an apple to snack on before I crossed the wheat and barley fields and finally made my way down the hill to the sandy beach that kissed the deep blue water's edge. Turning back to the fields above me, I found my cottage in the distance. I could just barely see the smoke billowing from its chimney, and my heart ached at the sight, knowing this would likely be the last time I ever saw it.

Tears blurred my vision, and I decided it was time to go.

The only thing worse than running would be getting caught running.

I curled my toes in the sand as I touched the pearl necklace, absorbing as much warmth from the beach as possible before stepping into the cool water. Taking a deep breath in and turning to get one more look at the place I called home, I dove in, feeling my skin prickle as I paddled deeper and deeper, looking for the markers the water dwellers used to get around.

It had been years since I last visited Poseidon in Atlantis, and I looked forward to seeing his home under the sea once again. I swam back and forth along the coastline looking for the Ionic Column markers. Normally, they were easy to spot, since the stark white of the marble stood out in the dark blue waters, but now, between all the seaweed and the pull of the current, I couldn't find it.

After a few more minutes of searching further out with no luck, I turned around and swam back toward the beach.

Only, now it was nowhere to be found.

Primes, the current must have taken me down the coast . . .
I could only hope I was swimming toward land in Olympus and
not somewhere in Aether, outside the walls.

As I got closer to a rocky cliffside in the distance, I noticed
some more columns, and I grew hopeful that maybe the current
had taken me exactly where I needed to be. But the closer I got to
the columns, the more uneasy I felt, as if someone were watching
me again like they did on the summit heading to Zeus's yesterday.

Still underwater, I shook the idea off. No one even knew I
was here, so surely, they couldn't be following me.

However, as I turned the corner around the column, my
heart stopped.

Before me was one of the few places in Poseidon's waters he'd
told me to never go.

Siren's Cove.

I'd swum deeper and deeper toward the sunken column,
never even realizing I was at the entrance to the cove.

I looked around, horrified to find I was surrounded not only
by skeletons of the prey who'd fallen victim to the sirens' song,
but also by a macabre underwater palace made from the skeletons of large and small sea creatures the sirens had likely feasted
on when victims were lacking.

I surveyed the cove, thankfully finding no sirens in sight, but
I still couldn't shake the feeling of being watched.

Not wasting another minute in this underwater death zone,
I swam toward the surface as fast as I could, the sunrays making
the water lighter and brighter with every inch closer I got, until
finally, my fingertips pierced the surface.

The warm air hit my face as I greedily gulped down fresh
air. I thanked the Primes for allowing me to escape unscathed—
which, from the looks of the sirens' cove, wasn't normally the
case—and paddled toward the beach.

I was almost in the clear when I heard the water move from somewhere beside me.

A hauntingly beautiful melody filled the cove, and before I realized it, I was no longer swimming toward land but wading in place as the strange music engulfed me.

My body tensed, sensing the danger I was in.

I slowly spun, scanning the dark waters for any sign of the sirens, and noticed a faint glow that seemed to be dancing under the surface. I was about to stick my head under the water to investigate further when movement from my left caught my eye.

A siren was staring back at me from a nearby rock, eyes glowing a magnificent aquamarine—the same shade the water had been before her arrival, as if she'd absorbed the color. Her burgundy hair was braided at the crown, the rest hanging in long waves around her, reaching to her waist. Her upper body was a pale blue-green, speckled with deep teal and purple scales that became more condensed as they reached her tail, which was covered in them. The sharp cuts of her gills shadowed her rib cage and the sides of her neck. She was breathtaking, but not in the way of a flower or a view, but rather in the way a predator was breathtaking before it slaughtered its prey.

And right now, I was the siren's prey.

Glad I didn't tell anyone I was leaving. Now all they'll find are my bones. I suddenly regretted going through with my brilliant plan of running away.

The siren tilted her head, probably assessing what level of threat I posed to her and the others. I stared back, trying to look intimidating, in the hope she'd leave me alone. But I knew there was no chance of that when she smiled back, flashing a row of jagged, razor-sharp teeth that could slice my arm open as if it were nothing more than the water that surrounded me. Then she dove in.

My eyes followed her as she swam beneath the surface, and that was when I noticed the glowing lights swirling beneath me, circling me like a shiver of sharks.

Another splash sounded in front of me, and I looked up to find the siren now so close to me I could make out the shadow of scales on her face and the water droplets rolling down from her burgundy hair.

I opened my mouth to tell her I was on my way to see Poseidon and that he would come looking for me, but I never got the chance, as two clawed, slimy, webbed hands grabbed onto my ankle with an unbreakable grip.

"Help!" I screamed as the siren yanked, dragging me down to the depths of the sea. I watched helplessly as the remaining rays of sunlight faded, until I was submerged in darkness.

CHAPTER 12

I STRUGGLED to break free of the iron grip the siren had on me, losing my bag and my satchel in the process as she dug her razor-sharp claws into my ankles.

Finally, after what felt like a lifetime, we hit the sandy bottom of the cove.

I noticed the once empty area was now filled with sirens, and even more were emerging from their watery caves. I wished I could speak to tell them it had been an accident, that I hadn't meant to swim into their territory, but when I tried, my lungs started to fill with saltwater, meaning I'd been submerged for too long and the pearls were weakening. If I didn't get up to the surface soon, I'd drown before they were done eating me alive.

So far, they'd made no move against me, and I could see the burgundy-haired siren who'd smiled at me on the surface speaking to another siren. This one looked older, and all the others seemed to treat her with more respect, giving her space, not approaching her unless they were invited.

"Why have you trespassed in our cove, mortal? Do you wish for death?" she asked, her voice coming out in a soft hiss.

Having no choice, I spoke again, letting more saltwater into my lungs. "It was an accident. I was looking for the markers leading to Atlantis."

Her scaled brow lifted in question. "You know our king?"

I nodded, not wanting to consume any more water.

"Is he expecting you?" the burgundy-haired one asked, flashing her sinister smile again.

I nodded.

They looked at one another, speaking some unspoken language I couldn't decipher, but the way the burgundy-haired siren's smile grew told me this wouldn't end well for me.

"Unfortunately for you, our king has given us full sovereignty over our cove and all who enter, which makes you fair game regardless of your position with him."

"No—please! It's not just Poseidon. I have protection from Zeus too!" I panicked, scanning the area for an escape route.

"He is no king of ours. In fact, if our king hadn't made peace with Zeus, mentioning him would have been more than enough reason for us to rip you apart, limb from limb, and send your bones back as a gift," she hissed.

My heart stopped for a moment before beating so erratically I was surprised it didn't create waves. With no way out, I was about to give up when I heard a screech from the far side of the cove.

I looked over just in time to see a cloud of blood forming in the water.

Two sirens swam over to investigate but were stopped short when two fists pierced through their chests, ripping both their hearts right out. The hands dropped them in the water before moving on to a group of half a dozen sirens, who released a battle cry and swam toward their spears to take out the unwanted visitor.

I couldn't make out who it was slaughtering all the sirens, but I hoped they were here to save me, not to add me to their list of victims.

Before the sirens could make it to their weapons, the stranger—whom I could now see was a rather large male god—grabbed the two closest to him, ripping their finned arms right off their chests. He bit another one in the side of the neck, pulling hard until they all disappeared into another bloody cloud of his making.

Seeing an opening, while he had the sirens' attention, I swam as fast and as hard as I could to the surface. I emerged from the water and gulped down a huge breath of air, and the burning in my lungs ceased. I was lifting my arm to paddle to shore when my leg was suddenly yanked back down toward the ocean floor.

I kicked as hard as I could, looking down to get a better aim and locking eyes with my captive. The burgundy-haired siren smiled brightly as she dragged me down to the floor and off to the side, toward one of the caves—but not before I saw the male who'd attacked them pinned down on a table made of bone, within an enormous rib cage I could only assume had once belonged to a whale. Small shreds of meat decorated his mostly bare skeleton. The last thing I saw was him taking a piece of the bone from the table and splitting it in two, pinning it to the sides of his hips as the leader of the sirens swam toward him screaming, moments before he pierced her tail with the bone shards, dragging them through both sides of her body until they tore through her shoulders, slicing her into three pieces.

Every single one of the sirens froze as they watched their leader get torn apart. Even the burgundy-haired one stopped pulling me for a moment. Then she released an ominous hiss and pulled me so hard behind her she nearly ripped my leg off.

"Help me!" I screamed at the male, hoping he saw what cave she pulled me into before it was too late.

"He will never find you now," she hissed, pulling me through the cave system, making turn after turn, until I was so confused I knew I'd never make it out of this underwater maze on my own.

I clutched my pearl necklace in a panic as she slowed, taking one more turn before coming to a stop in a small cave with a seaweed bed in the corner and little trinkets scattered around the bones littering the room.

A room my bones would soon be adorning as well.

I wasn't even bothering to put up a fight anymore, as there was no hope of getting out. I sat awaiting the moment she'd decide to finish me off.

The siren released my leg and turned to face me.

"Hmm, what shall I do with you? Finish you off quick, so no one can take you from me, or take my time and get revenge for my dear sister your kind murdered?" The siren tapped her scaled chin with her silver talon.

"I have nothing to do with the mortals. I was raised in Olympus," I replied.

"As if that makes you any better. The Olympians treat us as their slaves. Even the mortal slaves the Titans kept were treated with more respect than you revered Olympians give us," she sneered.

"What?" I asked, hoping she'd elaborate. This was the second time someone had mentioned humans being in Aether under the Titans' rule.

She opened her mouth to speak but was cut off by a loud bang echoing through the caverns.

"Where is she?" a deep male voice roared from somewhere in the distance.

For a moment, her face froze in fear, but then her mouth twitched up into a snarl, and she launched herself at me.

I threw my arms out to stop her talons from slashing my throat. They caught on my arm as I threw them up, slicing my forearm open with four large gashes.

I screamed, forcing all my strength into pushing her away, but she was strong, and I knew I couldn't overpower her.

Remembering the lessons in battle strategy Athena had given me years ago, I used one of her favorite moves. Giving one last push, I ducked as fast as I could. The siren's claws slashed at the spot where my neck was.

Not wasting a second, I reached forward and dug my fingers into the gills at her side, making her screech and reach out to grab me. I stumbled back, out of her reach, but she was fast, not to mention mad, and coming at me with a vengeance.

She hit me in the chest, shoving me to the ground beneath her. "I'm going to enjoy this," she snarled, opening her jaws wide to reveal razor-sharp teeth that resembled a shark's. She leaned into my neck.

I felt the scrape of her teeth as they slid along the skin at my neck, one hand reaching to the top of my head to turn it to get a better angle, while the other gripped my throat.

Suddenly, her fingers wrapped around the pearls hanging from my neck, and she leaned back, still gripping them in her hands. "I saw you clutching these earlier. They must be special to you," she said, smirking at me.

More than you know.

"I like a trophy to keep from my kills, and I think these will do beautifully for my collection. They'll match your bones after I chew the meat off them." Licking her lips, the siren yanked the strand of pearls from my neck, making them go flying around her.

I clutched my throat in a panic as the saltwater rushed in, filling my lungs.

I could feel the reserved air from the pearls as it left my body, replaced by the overwhelming sensation of drowning. I'd once heard a water nymph say drowning was the best way to die, because it brought the victim a sense of peace before they passed. I was sure she'd never experienced it, or else she'd have understood that with every gulp of water, your body convulsed, fighting for oxygen it couldn't get, and your lungs burned as if a fire were raging within them as they filled with an unforgiving weight. I'd always thought it ironic that water was needed for mortals to survive, and yet it could just as easily kill us if we consumed too much.

I guess that was what the Primes meant by "all things must be balanced."

I waited for the siren to end me, craving release from this misery, but my hopes of death were shattered when the beastly roar I'd heard earlier filled the chamber.

My vision was fading fast, but I could just barely make out an enormous figure appearing in the doorway before he rushed the siren.

Vague shapes moved in front of me. I blinked, trying to clear the haze from my eyes, but it didn't work. My vision kept clouding, getting darker and darker, until I could see nothing at all.

Suddenly, the convulsions ceased as my fingertips landed on the cool sand of the ocean floor, and a sense of peace washed over me as I fell into a deep sleep.

CHAPTER 13

"**B**REATHE!" someone yelled in the distance.

I could see nothing but darkness and knew only the feeling of being lifted as a pounding in my chest began to form, picking up a rhythmic beat as the voice grew louder and louder.

"Come on, that's it, just breathe," a deep, masculine voice said.

Blue sky appeared before me, and a large figure was leaning over the top of me, shadowing me from the sun. He was saying something, but I wasn't listening as I flung my body out to the side and coughed up the seawater filling my lungs.

I sputtered out the remaining water and shivered, thinking of how close I'd been to death. One moment, I was in the darkness waiting for Thanatos to greet me, and the next, I was back in the land of the living.

I gathered my breath before pushing off the sand to sit up, coming face-to-face with the most terrifyingly beautiful god I'd ever seen.

The sun was shining down, peeking through his short, dark curls. Water dripped down the angles of his tanned face from the ringlets on his forehead. I couldn't help but stare as the droplets fell from his long, dark lashes, encircling golden amber

eyes, before running down his cheeks, past his straight nose, and dripping off his sharp jaw.

"Are you all right?" he asked, his voice deep, with a small grumble in it.

"I think so." I looked over myself, moving around, relieved to find I wasn't in too much pain.

"Why were you swimming with the sirens to begin with? Didn't your kind teach you not to swim in their territory?" he asked, frowning at me and crossing his arms. He was kneeling on the sand, leaning back on his heels.

I stared at him for a moment, shocked at his audacity to reprimand me right after my near miss with death. "I wasn't swimming with the sirens," I replied, trying to bite my tongue so I wouldn't say all the things running through my brain.

Who was this guy, and what gave him the right to speak to me in such a condescending way? Only the High Olympians ever spoke to me like that, but none of the lesser gods in Olympus ever dared to, worried they'd incur Zeus's wrath. They chose to sneer and whisper from a distance instead.

"Are you crossed? Is that why you weren't taught to stay away from them?" he asked, raising a dark brow at me.

"Crossed" was what the Olympians called those whose parents were from different species. It was frowned upon for different species to intermingle, since this was thought to weaken bloodlines and ruin the purity of the species.

"Excuse me?" I asked, glaring at him, shocked he'd asked such an insulting question so nonchalantly. I pushed myself off the ground, standing tall as I looked down at him. "How dare you ask me that? Didn't your parents ever teach you manners?" I snapped.

He stared at me for a moment before the right side of his mouth turned up and a small dimple appeared next to his half-smirk.

"Look, thank you for saving me, but I'm done with this conversation," I said, turning on my heel and heading up the beach.

"Don't you want your bags?" he asked.

I stopped in my tracks.

I'd lost my bags when I was trying to break free from the sirens. I was hoping they'd sunk to the bottom of the sea, removing any evidence of my failed runaway, but when I turned back to him, there he was, holding my bag and my satchel in his hands.

He walked toward me, stopping an arm's length away, and said, "So you're not going to tell me what you are? I can sense you're different from most, but I fear my senses are deceiving me."

"You haven't bothered to explain yourself, so why should I?" I said, crossing my arms.

"I heard a scream, ran to the water where it came from, and swam down to save you from a watery grave. What else do you want to know?" He smirked.

"Oh, I don't know. Maybe a name." I rolled my eyes at him.

"What's your name?" he asked, avoiding giving me his own.

"Pandora."

I waited for him to offer his name, but he never did, just repeating my name over again, slowly, as if he were documenting the way my name rolled off his tongue. "Pandora . . . And what gifts do you have to give?" he asked.

"What?"

His question confused me. He was the one holding my bags. Did he think I'd offer something up in return for them? If so, he was sorely mistaken.

"Your name. It means 'all-gifted' or 'a gift to all.'" The corner of his mouth turned up, and his brow rose again. "Do you not even know the meaning of your own name?"

"I do now," I snapped at him as I reached for my bags, but he took a step back, and I stumbled forward, glaring up at his face more than a foot above my own. "I have places to be. Can I have my bags back now?"

He stared at me for a moment and then stepped forward to hand the bags over to me. He was close enough now that I could see the shimmer of a silver scar across his left brow, and his lips looked swollen, like he'd been kissing.

I leaned in to grab the bags, but as my fingers wrapped around them, he paused, holding them tight in his grip.

"Don't run from your problems. They will either haunt you or hunt you. Trust me. I know better than most."

"What?" I asked, shocked at his words. It was one thing for him to find my bags, but how could he have known I was running? And *trust* him? There was no way in Tartarus I was doing that. With what he knew now, all he had to do was put together the pieces, and if he threatened to tell Zeus, then he would own me.

"Just a piece of advice. Take it or leave it," he said with a shrug, letting go of the bags so quickly I nearly toppled over.

I gathered my balance and slung the bags over my shoulder, turning to walk back to my cottage.

CHAPTER 14

AFTER my failed escape, I spent the night reflecting on everything that had happened with Zeus, the sirens, and my mysterious savior.

After a while, I realized I had run because I feared what would happen if I failed, not because I didn't think I had a chance at success. I was beginning to realize failure was not an option this time around. I would win Prometheus's heart or die trying.

But that would all start tonight, with the celebration. Today was the last day I had to myself, and I planned on enjoying it.

The orchards were covered in morning dew, which glistened on the leaves in dawn's early light. I inhaled the scent of wet soil and ran my fingers along the leaves before gathering some fruit in the wicker basket I'd brought along.

Deciding to walk along the beach for a bit, I ended up at the southern bridge that crossed over into Lower Olympus. It was made of the same stone as the bridge that passed by my house, but this one was covered in a beautiful green ivy that wrapped around the railing, blossoming with white star jasmine that smelled intoxicating as it mixed with the warm, salty breeze blowing in from the sea.

As I admired the way the waves sparkled in the morning sun, my mind flashed to the mysterious god that had rescued me from the siren's clutches. He was as infuriating as he was interesting, and I hadn't been able to wipe him from my mind since our encounter. At first, all I could think about where the rude comments he'd made about me being crossed, but then my mind had shifted to how he'd come to my aid knowing nothing about me, even going the extra length to retrieve my bags from wherever the current had carried them. I was as angry as I was grateful.

I was considering going into Lower Olympus to ask around about my mysterious savior and try to find out who he was when I noticed something—or someone—moving in the distance. I walked over, curious about who it could be. I wondered if it was my mystery god himself.

At the edge of Lower Olympus, between the servant housing and the naiad housing, was what looked like a dark cloud in the shape of a figure. I blinked a few times, trying to clear my vision, thinking I must be seeing things, but it was still there.

I wondered what—or who—it was and couldn't help but to investigate it a little more, my curiosity getting the better of me. I creeped up through the guest cottages, which were arranged like their own little village, being sure to lie low to avoid detection.

"It will not be easy to keep her away," a feminine voice whispered.

"She will have no choice. I will ensure it," the shadowy figure replied in a deep, muffled, and inherently masculine voice.

It was hard to hear them from my current spot, so I decided to risk moving closer even though every fiber of my being was screaming at me to get out of there.

"Good. Are the others ready?" the female asked as I moved toward the edge of the building I was hiding behind.

"Yes. I have him under control as well," the male replied.

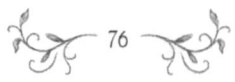

I reached my left hand out to steady myself on the stone wall and peeked around the corner.

"We have the upper hand, but we must not lose it. The rebellion depends on it," the female said. She had copper hair and was standing with her back to me, facing the shadow form head-on.

I was so focused on the female, trying to figure out her identity, that for a moment I took my eyes off the shadow form. When I looked back up, I found nothing.

I gasped, jumping back behind the wall as if it could take me back in time and save me from being seen.

"Better run. He's going to get you," the female hollered, giggling, which only made more dread sink into my bones.

What on earth was this thing, and when did it get into Olympus?

I ran as fast as my feet would carry me, feeling like eyes were all around me, knowing the shadow creature, whatever he was, could be anywhere nearby. At one point, I swore I even felt something touch me. It was as if someone had reached out and run their fingers over the skin on my arm, but when I looked, there was nothing there.

My cottage was just over the hill, and I could already see it coming into view. Slowing as I approached, I noticed a feminine figure standing at my front door.

Was this the one who'd spoken of the rebellion? Had she had figured out my identity that quickly? Was she here now to threaten me into secrecy—or worse, to kill me? My mind raced. But before my thoughts could go any further, a sweet voice sang my name.

"Pandy, open up! I brought a gift for you," Persephone's sweet voice rang out.

I breathed out a sigh of relief and sprinted the rest of the way to her, nearly making her topple over as I grabbed her in a hug.

"Primes, am I glad to see you!" I said, pulling her in even closer.

"I can tell." She giggled. "I couldn't wait until tonight. I need to see the dress Aphrodite and her golden girls made for our mortal beauty!"

"Not right now. I just had the strangest, scariest—" I started, but Persephone grabbed my hand, threw open my front door, and ran inside, pulling me upstairs alongside her.

"Oh, nonsense. You're extra cute in the mornings, and at least you're not trying to bite my head off like Hades does. That god will do anything to avoid getting up in the morning," Persephone laughed.

She and Hades had been seeing each other in secret for a few years now, and she loved to come and tell me about their time together since she had to keep him a secret from Demeter.

"He's no better than a hellhound most of the time when I wake him up. Anyway, I won't be letting any of his grumpiness or your self-loathing ruin this beautiful morning. After all, it's our first big event together!" she said, nearly skipping to the dress, clapping her hands in delight.

I watched Persephone full of glee and couldn't bring myself to ruin this moment for her. Even though I could have been killed by a shadow monster, and rebellion plots were being whispered, something inside me didn't want to take her joy away.

I decided for now, for today, I'd keep everything to myself.

"And this!" Persephone ran her hands down the burgundy tulle, which had thin gold lace woven throughout it that made the dress glimmer in the light. The bust was a mix of tulle twisted into rose patterns, and gold flakes that dripped down to my waist. "Aphrodite really outdid herself. As horrid as that goddess can be, she works wonders with fabric."

"I'm not sure if her company is worth it, but you're right. It is a pretty dress," I said, admiring the warm color, which matched my mortal blood perfectly, as the goddess pointed out. The sun seemed to light it from within. The gold shimmered as

Persephone petted the fabric a few more times, looking at it in deep thought.

"It's nearly perfect, but it's missing something. I just can't seem to put my finger on what." She stared at the dress as if it would tell her before turning to me. "Mom wanted me to come up and get you for a dawn and dine. She made your favorites."

A dawn and dine.

I smiled, remembering when we first started the tradition. About five or six years after Demeter and Persephone took me in—or more like the gods assigned me to them when they realized I needed food and water to sustain my life—they had a party to celebrate my day of creation and made me all my favorites. They would decorate a lounge area in front of Demeter's palace overlooking the orchards, and we would watch as the dawn crept across the fields, bringing with it the light of a new day, feasting for what felt like hours on roasted vegetables, figs, olives, bread, and my favorite apple tart, as we caught up on life, sipping on a warm cup of milk with steeped chamomile flowers. There was no better way to celebrate.

"Really?" I said, feeling my excitement rise and a smile break across my face.

"Really. She went a little lighter than normal and kept it inside, since the festivities have had her preoccupied and we don't want our girl to worn out before her big night, but she made a few things I think you're really going to enjoy. We need to get going, though, if we're to be back in time to do your hair and makeup."

My head snapped in her direction. "What? You're doing that? But I thought . . ."

Persephone smiled and gave me a little pat on my arm, walking past me before looking back at me over her shoulder. "You didn't think I'd let that offensive man-eater steal my chance to have some sibling bonding time, now, did you? Plus, if I let Aphrodite do your hair and makeup, it would likely end up with you looking like one of her harlot daughters, which is definitely not your style."

"And why is it important whose style I wear?"

"Because she isn't the one presenting the gift. You are. And when you present it, you will present it as Pandora, not Zeus's creation, the mortal woman, or whatever else they try to call you to showcase you as theirs. Tonight, you are Pandora," Persephone said, her eyes getting glassy as they filled with tears. She turned to walk down the stairs.

I couldn't help but wonder how Persephone knew about my role in the celebration. Did everyone except me know up until yesterday, or had Demeter somehow known and mentioned it to her?

We walked in silence to Demeter's palace, which always took my breath away, surrounded by a mix of fruit trees and green vines sprinkled with flowers and hanging fruits of all shapes, sizes, and colors. They adorned the exterior of her palace. Next to Poseidon's palace in Atlantis, Demeter's was the most beautiful palace in my opinion. Both of their palaces were covered in color and life compared to the cold, desolate, sickening opulence of the other High Olympians' palaces.

"There's my girls," Demeter said, pulling me and Persephone into a big hug.

I was smaller than the goddesses, and even now I was fully grown, I was still a good foot shorter than most of them.

"Come, come. The food is getting cold. I want to hear all about your recent training, Pandora. You haven't visited me in a while, and I've only heard what Persephone has told me—which isn't much, since she seems to be disappearing as much as you lately." Demeter looked between me and Persephone as if she could uncover our secrets with just one look. "You girls haven't been doing anything fun without me, have you?"

"Now, Mother, you know Pandora doesn't have time for fun. And as for me, well, I always have fun," Persephone said

with a wink at her mother, who just sighed and went to work eating her food.

"So, Pandora, how has your training been going? What have you learned since I last saw you?"

"Well, I learned a lot more basket patterns, since you requested we make more baskets—again," I said, looking the goddess carefully in the eye. I didn't want to argue with her about it, but I was annoyed and a little curious as to why she couldn't just create her own baskets, so that maybe then I'd have some time for fun, which Persephone had so kindly pointed out I never had.

"Mom, really, you had her make more? How many baskets do you need? You do realize they don't rot like your crops, right? You can reuse the ones you have," Persephone said as if she were talking to a child.

Demeter glared at her daughter. "Yes, I understand that. But thank you for pointing out the obvious, Persephone."

"Just wanted to make sure, since you're giving her senseless orders through Athena. Why—?" Persephone started before Demeter cut her off.

"I do not need to run my decisions or my needs by you, Persephone. You would do well to remember your place. This may be a day of celebration, but that will not stop me from locking you up and keeping you from attending tonight." Demeter's skin rippled with power as she worked to rein in her anger.

The vines around the room started to twist and turn as if they were about to strike out at us, just as their master was trying not to.

"If you must know, I needed more baskets, because this event requires copious amounts of food, which my baskets cannot handle, and more importantly, Pandora needed the practice."

"But wh—"

"Why is not your business. End of discussion," Demeter snapped, glaring daggers at her daughter. "Now, Pandora, fill me

in on the rest of the training. Maybe the stuff Athena did not teach you."

I filled Demeter in on everything I could think of, every once in a while glancing toward Persephone, only to find her sitting back in her chair with her arms tightly crossed and a stone-cold frown on her face.

After a while, the sun started to shine through the windows, signaling Apollo's descent, and Persephone finally spoke up from her withdrawn silence.

"Time to go, Pandy," she said, finally cracking that marble frown and letting her beautiful warm smile shine through . "Lovely seeing you as always, Mother." She walked out without even a glance in Demeter's direction, grabbing my arm and pulling me along with her.

"Thanks for everything, Demeter," I said over my shoulder, smiling and trying to give a little wave with my free hand.

"See you tonight, girls," Demeter replied with a sad smile and a nod.

CHAPTER 15

BACK in my bedroom, on the upper level of my cottage, Persephone was finishing the final touches to my makeup.

"All right . . . I think we are . . ."—she paused, dabbing something that looked like beet juice onto my lips and cheeks—"ready!" Taking a step back to admire her work, she smiled, clapping her hands as she jumped up and down. "Yes, that's it. You're perfect! All the gods and goddesses will envy you tonight. I know I will, you gorgeous mortal goddess." She winked at me before turning toward the burgundy dress still hanging on the armoire.

I laughed at the thought of anyone, let alone the Olympians, being envious of me.

"Doubtful, but thanks for the boost of confidence, Seph," I said, calling her by the nickname I'd given her as a child, when her name was too hard and long for me to pronounce.

"Nonsense. You won't be able to deny it when they can't keep their eyes off you." She giggled as she trotted over like one of Zeus's stallions, barely able to contain her excitement. "Okay, strip. It's time for the dress."

I quickly removed my robe, careful not to mess up any of Persephone's hard work in the process, and then she helped me step into the dress.

Persephone tied the laces at the back of the dress, tightening the fabric to my body with each knot. The dress slid over me like a dream, and when she'd finished with the last knot, I relaxed.

The dress was perfect. It hugged my curves in all the right places, accentuating my figure, and cascaded in a beautiful burgundy waterfall to the ground.

I turned to the full-body mirror in the corner of my room. It had been gifted to me by Narcissus, who was obsessed with mirrors and anything else he could see his own reflection in. He'd gifted it to me on one of my creation days.

My creation day was never a big event by any means, especially not when compared to something like tonight, but it had always felt important to me, and it was a way for me to tell which gods and goddesses cared for me more than their own selfish needs. Unsurprisingly, it wasn't many.

"Not yet!" Persephone panicked, grabbing my arms to turn my body back toward her. "I think I figured out what's missing."

She smiled and raised her slender hands in a twirling motion toward me. Slowly, my body turned as if I were on a spinning pedestal, stopping almost as soon as it started. The air had a sweet floral scent to it, which I recognized as Persephone using her power.

"Now you're perfect," she said, stepping to the side and helping me turn toward the mirror this time.

My breath caught in my throat as I stared at the mesmerizing beauty in front of me.

I was . . . *beautiful.*

Persephone had pulled my long onyx hair up at the top, twisting it into an elaborate design on the back of my head, while the rest spilled down my back and over my shoulders, the dark curls a stark contrast to my alabaster skin. She'd done my makeup in a way that accentuated my natural features, making me feel more ethereal than I'd ever felt in my life. My lips looked fuller and redder, my eyes looked wider and brighter, and my skin had

a healthy glow to it. It was so simple, yet somehow, it made me look and feel like a completely different person.

The dress, though . . . The dress was what took my breath away.

In the burgundy tulle, the golden strips glittered in the light and seemed to move even when everything else was frozen in time. Now, dozens of red roses cascaded down from the bust into a waterfall that flowed over the skirt. I could never have imagined a more beautiful dress.

"It's . . ." I started to say, but I was at a loss for words, emotion clogging my throat as my eyes watered.

Persephone's hand came up to my cheek to wipe the tears away before they fell. "You are perfection, Pandora. One more tiny thing. Every goddess needs a crown." She smiled as she placed something onto my head.

"I'm not a goddess." I cringed, feeling the weight of the situation pulling me down again. It threatened to crush me with the pressure to succeed and make my family proud.

Who was I kidding? I was just hoping tonight would make them see me as something more than a failed, pointless creation.

"You are. You're the Goddess of Mortal Women," Persephone said, and she removed her hands, revealing a rose crown held together by a golden chain of thorns. "Don't let them forget that."

I looked at the beautiful girl standing before me and thought of all the things she was created to do. She looked every bit the goddess Persephone had described, except for the fear and denial shimmering deep within her eyes.

But I could hide that. I would hide that.

I always do.

"Goddess of Mortal Women," I repeated to myself, hoping speaking the words aloud would help me to believe they were true.

CHAPTER 16

THE carriage Demeter had summoned to take me to the celebration dropped me off at the base of the cobblestone steps leading to the south entrance of the court. Persephone had wanted to come with me, but she'd run off, saying she had other obligations and she'd meet me there.

Glancing up at the first level of the court, where the celebration was being held, I saw warm light flooding out from between the columns. Sounds of laughter and music were being carried across the summit by the gentle breeze.

I always dreaded the walk up these huge stone steps. The gods were all much larger than me and most of the cretes who resided within the walls, but they certainly hadn't taken us into consideration when they'd designed Olympus. Especially on the summit. The higher you climbed, the larger everything became, as if it had been built for giants. The court itself was so enormous that even the gods seemed dwarfed under the huge glass dome.

My legs were burning by the time I reached the top, and I leaned forward, bracing my hands on my thighs as I struggled to catch my breath. Looking around, I prayed to the Primes no one had witnessed me nearly dying after one flight of steps, no matter how oversized they were.

Finding no one had noticed me yet, I took a moment to fix the few strands of hair falling into my face instead of around it and wiped the small beads of sweat from my brow. Then I headed into what was sure to be the most important night of my life.

Servants dressed in shimmering silver robes carried trays of food and drinks around. Some glasses were filled with the familiar burgundy liquid from Dionysus, but the other glasses were filled with a light-colored drink, little bubbles floating up to the surface and forming a light foam.

"Would you like one?" a servant asked from beside me.

"What is that one?" I asked, pointing to the bubbly liquid.

"This is a drink made special in honor of the Titans' visit. Dionysus created it using white grapes, as a symbol of the continued peace between the remaining Titans and the Olympians. He added honey, as well as a secret ingredient he got from Hestia, to create what he calls 'the fizz,'" the tall servant said. It was easy to tell he was a satyr from the horns and ears poking through his curled blond hair, along with the lower half of his body being that of a goat.

"Sounds lovely," I replied, grabbing one of the glasses from the back of the tray and a bite-size fruit tart from the front. "Thank you."

He nodded and turned away, toward a group of partygoers, as I popped the fruit tart into my mouth, savoring the tart berries, tangy custard, and buttery crust.

I didn't recognize anyone around me, so I decided to set off in search of someone to talk to until Zeus came and found me to give the speech. I figured I'd try to avoid him for as long as possible tonight.

Finally, I spotted Hermes across the room, flirting with one of the handsome satyr servants. I started to head toward him, but as I passed a large group, their conversation caught my attention, and my curiosity made it impossible to keep moving.

"Mankind have come far in the past century. They have begun gathering in different areas across the continent and have built shelters spanning large and small stretches of land that protect them from Gaia, whom they've started calling Mother Earth in some parts and Mother Nature in others. Some regions even worship her as their god, because they have witnessed her wrath, as well as her mercy," an extremely tall god said from beside me.

I stayed out of his sight, a few feet behind him, keeping people in between us so as to not seem obvious, and continued to listen.

"Worshipping a Prime instead of the High Olympians? Zeus will be *thrilled* to hear that," one of them snickered.

"As I was saying, mankind have shown great progress adapting to their chosen environments by building shelters for large groups in what they call 'villages' and establishing a way of life and government among themselves. In the past few decades, they have also begun to design weapons, shields, and methods of transportation, farming, and agriculture using the animals created by Epimetheus that roam their land." The male looked around for someone and didn't seem to find them before continuing. "They have learned to use the available resources to their advantage and are resilient in their will to survive and thrive in their realm."

Epimetheus? Then this must be his brother, Prometheus. The man I'd been created to win the heart of.

I took a step forward, dying to see what he looked like. From this point of view, all I could make out was his tall, lean build, wavy, shoulder-length chestnut hair, and a chiton made from a fabric I couldn't pinpoint from here, though I could tell it was off by the way it hung stiff on his body. From the way he spoke, I could tell he was kind and compassionate, with a levelheadedness not often seen in Olympus.

"I am pleased to hear of my children's success," a deep voice, full of command and power, boomed from behind me, making me freeze as my heart dropped into my stomach.

I would know that thunderous voice anywhere.

Zeus.

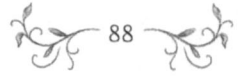

Spotting a large centaur to my right, I slowly creeped over until I was standing along the back side of his body, facing the group of gods and Prometheus. I peeked over the centaur's back just in time to see Zeus walking up to their group, his golden tunic flowing with ethereal grace as he approached.

He was the same as he looked when I last saw him, full of pride and power. His rich brown hair matched his flowing beard and fell in waves to his shoulders. It was pulled back from his face, secured by a crown of oak leaves that rested on a high forehead, above his curiously kind gray-blue eyes, which I knew could change at a moment's notice and fill with storm clouds lit from within by a silver power that pulsed and streaked across his irises like lightning in the skies.

"Although I am displeased to hear of their misled worship." Zeus's kind smile dropped for a second as his eyes flashed silver. It happened so fast I would have thought I'd imagined it had I not felt the electricity pulsing through the air at the same moment, making the hair on my arms stand.

I glanced around to see if anyone else had felt the pull of power and quickly found it was just me.

"Surely, you remember you're there to represent me in my absence and to guide them in the direction of Olympus's rule," Zeus said, looking between Prometheus and another figure I could only see a small portion of, whose back was to me.

That must be Epimetheus. I wished I had a better view of them.

"We have guided mankind in prosperity and innovation to reflect your power as not only the father of man, but the creator of mortals," Prometheus told Zeus.

"Hmm," Zeus said, giving Prometheus a look from head to toe, his lip curling back for a flash before it transformed into a show-stopping smile. "Well, we can talk about that after the celebration. Let's not let the silly beliefs of mortal men get in the way of the party." He was acting as if they were old friends. "I have a surprise for you that should be arriving soon. Please do enjoy the party until then, and welcome home. I'm sure you both have a lot of catching up to do." Zeus gave them a pat on the shoulder before walking off into the crowd, swallowing the brothers from view as he came directly toward me.

Time to go. I ducked down behind the centaur, hiding from sight until Zeus had passed and then moving as quickly as mortally possible toward the opposite side of the celebration.

Once again, my curiosity had nearly gotten me caught. Just another curse the gods had given me during my creation, this particular one having been *gifted* to me by the queen of the heavens herself, Hera. She'd granted me curiosity when Hephaestus was working on my creation. I confronted her about it once and asked why she'd given me such a dreadful gift that always seemed to get me into trouble. She'd sneered at me and said, "Stupid mortal. That 'horrendous gift,' as you call it, will one day be the only thing to set you free. Without curiosity, you are nothing but a puppet for a man to use. With it, you can determine your own destiny. Curiosity can be used to your advantage or your downfall. It's up to you whether to let it save you or imprison you."

After that, I never asked another Olympian why they'd given me the gifts they chose. Instead, I did what Hera said and tried to use my gifts to my advantage, in a way the Olympians would hopefully never catch on to.

Much as I disliked Hera, her advice that day had made me see everything in a different light and heightened my curiosity about the role I was meant to play among the gods. I'd always hoped my curiosity would grant me the opportunity to be the conductor of my own destiny rather than fall blindly into whatever plan they had for me, but as of tonight, the destiny they had planned was going to consume me whole.

CHAPTER 17

WALKING to the edge of the court, I glanced up at the glass ceiling above me that separated the celebration room from the throne room.

I'd always loved to admire the High Olympians' thrones. Each represented its owner, with sacred plants, trees, or the elements. The largest throne was Zeus's, which was carved from the trunk of an ancient oak tree said to be as resilient, well-rounded, and majestic as Zeus himself.

"Pandora, Zeus is requesting you behind the stage," Athena said. She was wearing a beautiful violet peplos, a golden tie encircling her waist, and her thick brown hair was twisted back from her temples and wrapped into her olive-branch crown, which had small flower buds sprinkled throughout.

"Already?" I asked as dread washed over me.

"Do not fear your duty, Pandora. Tonight marks the beginning of your destiny," Athena said, staring at me for a moment.

I opened my mouth to ask if something was wrong, or if maybe she knew something I didn't, but I didn't get the chance.

Athena cleared her throat. "Come on. Best not keep him waiting."

I followed her through the crowd toward the stage, each step feeling heavier than the last, until there were no steps left to take.

"Ah, there she is," Zeus said from ahead of us, clapping his hands as he walked over to meet us halfway. "I've been looking for you all night, Pandora. Where have you been hiding?"

"I wasn't hiding," I said a little too quickly. "I was just wandering around trying to find anyone I might know, and there are so many guests at your celebration I had trouble finding anyone in the crowd."

I was lying through my teeth, hoping and praying he hadn't caught a glimpse of me earlier, when I was eavesdropping on his conversation. I painted the most innocent smile I could muster onto my face to really sell it.

Zeus stared at me for a moment before smiling back. "You're right. This celebration has turned out perfectly thus far. Let's just hope the speech I wrote for you will make it even better. Here is the amphora holding the cure, which you will be presenting to the Titan brothers." He handed me a large amphora covered in runes, scriptures, and illustrations depicting the steps to recreate the potion contained within. "Remember what we discussed, Pandora. Do not fail me," Zeus said before straightening out his golden tunic and turning toward the stairway leading to the stage.

Each of the High Olympians made their way up the stairs, with Zeus following behind them, motioning at the last moment for me to follow.

Thankfully, these steps were more average than the ones leading up to the court, and as I made it onto the stage, I noticed Athena subtly motioning for me to stand beside her, on the opposite side of Zeus.

Hundreds of eyes focused on the stage, making my palms go slick with sweat. I hated attention like this, and more than that, I hated the pressure of this situation. I began to tap my fingers on the amphora as I fought the urge to run offstage, until a hand gently squeezed my shoulder.

Turning around, I found Persephone smiling softly at me. She nodded for me to turn back around.

I released a sigh, feeling a little better knowing she had my back and was here if anything happened.

Zeus clapped his hands, and a lightning bolt struck the tip of the throne behind him, lighting up his silhouette in a way that made him look every bit the almighty god he claimed to be.

"Welcome, friends and family, to the Centennial Celebration of Man. We are gathered here tonight to celebrate one hundred years of mankind living in the realm created by the great Prime Gaia, who slumbers deep within the realm's core. Under Olympian guidance, and with the help of the Titan twins Prometheus, the creator of man, and Epimetheus, the creator of animals . . ."—Zeus paused, motioning to where the two brothers stood in the center of the crowd—"mankind has not only survived, according to Prometheus, but thrived. However, much as the mortal men want to rule their own world, they do not have the power nor the capability to survive without us. I heard just tonight that Epimetheus himself even sacrificed some of his creations so mankind could survive without being poisoned by Gaia's *gifts*, simply because they are not wise enough to understand them as we are," Zeus announced to the room. "As their protectors, we have called the Titan twins here so we can grant this gift to them, in order to help save the mortal race of man from their own ignorance—which we cannot fault them for, since their kind is still young and naïve to the dangers of their world." Zeus finished by motioning for me to come up and stand beside him.

I walked forward the few steps that separated us, and for a moment, I forgot to speak. Zeus knew my nerves had hit the same moment I did, and he nudged me in the arm.

I cleared my throat and took a breath, rolling my shoulders back and straightening my spine, until I was standing straighter than I had done all evening. "I present to you Methydrium, a potion created by Demeter and Hecate from herbs found in the Realm of Man, and also grown here in Olympus. The scripture on the amphora describes the exact mixture of herbs that can be used to recreate it, and when taken orally by mankind, it will heal all ailments caused by the sickness overtaking them. All of Olym—"

Zeus grabbed my arm and squeezed, cutting me off. "On behalf of Olympus, Pandora, the first of her kind, extends this gift to you in order to cure mankind's ailments . . ." Zeus paused, looking down at me with something akin to pride or admiration, before turning a seemingly kind smile to the audience and the two tall men standing near the center of the room. "She also offers her guidance around our exquisite home, providing an intriguing point of view, as an added bonus for all your hard work on . . ." He tapped his chin in thought. "What did you say they liked to call it?" he asked a lesser god standing off to the side of the dais.

"Earth, your grace," the lesser god replied.

"Ah, yes. Earth," Zeus said, smiling back at the man I now recognized as Prometheus from his height and his wavy chestnut hair.

"You said she was the first of her kind . . ." Prometheus started.

"What is she?" the male standing beside Prometheus, whom I assumed was his brother, asked. I couldn't make out too much of his face from my vantage point, but the voice sounded oddly familiar.

"*She* is mortal," Zeus said, pulling me into his side as he looped his thick, heavy arm around me, looking down at me with unsettling admiration. "With the grace and beauty of the Olympian gods who raised her."

I looked away from Zeus just in time to see the one I assumed was Epimetheus grabbing his brother by the arm and pulling him to the back of the room. They disappeared into the crowd before Prometheus could answer. I could see the fury blooming on Zeus's face as he watched them, but then it washed away as a tiny flash of pride streaked over his features, covering the anger with a sly smile.

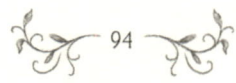

CHAPTER 18

AFTER the speech was over, Zeus and the other High Olympians exited the stage, some hanging back to speak in private, while others headed out into the celebration.

"Well done, Pandora. You presented yourself beautifully, and I noticed *both* brothers could not take their eyes off you," Zeus said from beside me. He pulled me into a hug the way I imagined a proud father would.

It caught me off-guard, and I froze, as still as the marble Corinthian columns surrounding us.

"Now that we have Prometheus's attention, I want you to personally deliver the amphora to him," Zeus said, turning to leave before stopping to add, "Don't waste this moment. You may not have another chance to catch the Titan off-guard again, and if you want to fulfill your duty to Olympus, this conversation will be vital."

I glanced down at the amphora in my hands and nodded. "I understand."

"Good. Make me proud, Pandora," he said finally, walking away into the crowd and leaving me to a moment of peace before I had to go confront the man who held my future in the palm of his hand.

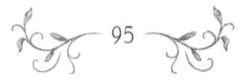

Taking more time than I should have, I finally emerged back into the crowd, beginning my search for the tall, chestnut-haired Titan. It shouldn't be too hard to find him—he stood at least a foot over most of the guests here.

"Pandy!"

Persephone's voice sounded from behind me, making me twirl around. I locked eyes with her right before she pulled me into her arms, squeezing me tight.

"You were fantastic!"

"Thanks. I didn't really get a chance to come speak. Zeus has me hunting down Prometheus to give him this amphora," I said, still scanning the crowd for any sign of him.

"Yeah. I asked around, and everyone seems to say he's very wise and has a soft soul compared to most Titans. Really, it's his brother you need to watch out for."

"Why?" I asked.

"I heard he's just as wild and unpredictable as his creations. Just try to stay away from him. He's bad news," Persephone warned, her eyes holding mine.

"That might be a little easier said than done." I smiled softly at her before adding, "Don't worry. I'll be careful and try to avoid him as much as possible."

Persephone nodded and pulled me in for another hug. "I just worry about you."

"I know, and I appreciate it, but I'll be okay," I said, hugging her back tight before releasing her. "Right now, I need to go find Prometheus and give him the amphora before he leaves, if he hasn't left already."

"Oh, I saw him heading over there." She pointed to the far side of the room.

I followed her gaze, finding a group with none other than Zeus at its center. Of all the places Prometheus could be, he had to be standing with Zeus.

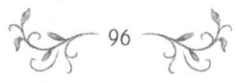

"I have to go," I said, rushed, to Persephone. "I'll come see you tomorrow to fill you in on everything."

Persephone's brow furrowed, and for a moment, I worried she might not let me leave. But as I turned to go, she only said, "Be careful, Pandora."

"I will."

I rushed through the crowd, trying to get to Prometheus, but the room had become so congested with bodies I could barely get through. Seeing an opening between two servants, I dove as quickly as I could, but they closed the small gap just before I got through, making me bounce right off them and onto the floor, taking one of the trays full of glasses down with me.

Glass was shattered all around me, and my palms were covered in small cuts from where my hands had hit the floor. I winced as I pushed them into the ground in an area without as much glass, trying to get up off the cold, hard marble. Reaching over and grabbing the amphora—which, miraculously, had not shattered—I slowly stood up.

"Is getting injured a habit for you?" a deep, sultry, all-too-familiar male voice said from above.

Warm, golden amber eyes framed with thick, dark lashes met mine, and I felt myself freezing like a statue again.

This was the same god who'd saved me from Siren's Cove. Although, now I was close enough to fully see him, I recognized him for who he truly was.

This was Prometheus's brother—the same one Persephone had just warned me to stay away from.

Epimetheus.

CHAPTER 19

"**P**RIMES got your tongue?" he asked, looking down at me as I scrambled to my feet, no longer caring about the glass.

"You're Epimetheus."

"I came for my antidote," he said, flicking his finger toward the amphora, which I'd smeared with blood when I picked it up. Carrying it tenderly in my arms now, I was careful to avoid contact with my torn palms.

"Oh—" I started to hand it to him but stopped short, remembering what Zeus had just said. "Actually, I should probably give this to your brother." I held onto the clay pot as if it were a lifeline—which, as Zeus had made clear, it basically was, since I could use it to talk to Prometheus.

"Funny. My brother just sent me over here to get it from you." The corners of his mouth lifted as he tried to hold back a smile.

"Well, uh . . . Zeus just told me to take it to him, so I'd better go do that." I started to walk away, brushing past Epimetheus's muscular body, which was like brushing up against a boulder that had been kissed by Apollo's rays.

He grabbed my arm, stopping me. "Zeus is distracted with Prometheus right now. I don't think either one of them will

mind. Me, however . . . well, you might hurt my feelings if you leave now without finishing our conversation and handing over that very important little present you're holding."

I tried to wiggle free of his grip with no success, which brought a smug smile to his lips. He was close enough that when I stared menacingly up into his glowing amber eyes, the glimmer of a silver scar running through his left brow caught my eye, and before I could gather my thoughts again, Epimetheus spoke.

"So, you are a mortal," he said, still holding my arm. "No wonder you didn't want to share that. How is it that a mortal survives, here in Olympus?"

"What do you mean? Olympus is the safest place a mortal could be," I replied, matter-of-fact.

His grip loosened, and I took my opportunity, pulling away from him and putting some space between us.

"Far from it," he said, holding my gaze.

"And what—you're going to tell me Earth is safer?" I asked, trying to maintain control over my emotions. Something about this Titan ignited the anger within me. I'd met gods who annoyed me and even made me mad at times, but never had one gotten under my skin with such infuriating ease as him.

"Well, yes." He paused before asking, "Do you not wish to be with your own kind?"

I looked him over for a moment, finally taking in his outfit, which looked like it was made of the same leather used to bind books and cover furniture throughout Olympus. The peachy glow from the orb of light circling the center of the rotunda, like an orbiting chandelier, reflected off the deep brown leather, making it feel warmer and softer than any leather I'd ever seen.

"My kind," I scoffed. "I may be mortal, but I am no *man*, and as far as I'm concerned, I am every bit the *Olympian* I was raised to be."

"They may have raised you, but from what I've seen so far, you're nothing like them," he said, looking into my eyes as if he were looking through them, past them, into my soul.

"How dare you?" I seethed at him. "You know nothing about me or how the Olympians raised me. They have treated me with nothing but love and respect throughout my life. My family are not a threat to me. You and your men on Earth are." I felt the lie as it left my lips. The truth was, I didn't know if there was anywhere or anyone that could keep me safe from the destiny the fates had laid out for me.

He stared at me as if he saw right through me, but instead of calling me out for lying to him, he just said, "I apologize. I didn't mean it as an insult. In fact, that's probably the nicest thing I've said to anyone in the past century."

I scoffed. "You might want to work on that."

"Indeed. I see now that we have very different views of your world and mine."

"You no longer consider Aether your world?"

"Not for the past century." He smiled sadly, which made me feel bad for the slightest moment, but then he added, "I should not have assumed that because you are mortal, you are like mankind."

"I am nothing like mankind, nor do I want to be."

"And why is that?"

"I've heard stories, and I've come to the conclusion mortal men are nothing more than a bunch of ruthless, cold-blooded, power-hungry monsters. Your choice of clothing proves those stories were not all wrong," I said, looking him up and down.

"And what is so cold-blooded about my tunic?"

"It is leather, is it not?"

"Yes . . . and . . . ?" He lifted a brow, daring me to continue.

"You don't find it cruel to kill your creations in order to steal their hide? What could possibly be worse than creating a species only to slaughter them and wear their skin around for fun? I'm

not sure what life was like with the Titans in control, but I can assure you, Olympians would never do something so unthinkable." The words spilled out of my mouth like a flood, unable to be stopped.

He stared at me in silence for a moment, then he released an almost pained sigh as he said, "We do not slaughter my animals out of boredom or fun. That's more of an Ares or Artemis thing. My animals are only killed on Earth when necessary for survival, which cannot be said of Aether." He paused, his mouth turning down into a frown, before continuing. "Man consumes the meat and the organs of the animal and saves the bones and the hide in order to make clothing and tools to help him survive." He tilted his head at me curiously. "As a mortal, you must be familiar with hunger and know food is necessary for survival."

"Yes," I said, crossing my arms over my chest, not liking being compared to the *men* who roamed his realm.

"Have you ever eaten something not meant to be consumed by mortals?" he asked.

I thought back to the time when I was little, wandering the berry bushes. I'd been nibbling on a handful of sweet purple-black berries when, at some point, I passed out, and Persephone found me purple-skinned and foaming at the mouth. I'd fallen into what they called a coma. I was lucky Demeter knew all the cures and healed me in no time. Later, she told me what I'd consumed were Atropa berries, but some called them deadly nightshade. When I asked why she'd grow such a terrible plant, she said it wasn't grown for her but for Hecate, and for Atropos, who was one of the three Moirai who controlled the threads of fate.

While the sisters of Atropos spun and gifted the threads of fate, Atropos severed them, killing whoever she had her sights set on, often using deadly nightshade as her chosen weapon.

"Yes."

"Well, same thing happened to man, and it's not because *they do not have the power nor the capability to survive without*

us." He paused, glaring into the distance, where I could see Zeus still standing with Prometheus. "Humans fall victim to toxins, because it is how the gods created them. I can guarantee Demeter has never poisoned herself. That knowledge is ingrained into her, down to her very essence. Mortal men were not granted the same luxury. When they were starved and had to choose between risking their lives or sure starvation, they ate any and all vegetation they came across, not knowing if it was safe or not. I stepped in and offered them another way. I gave up some of mine to save most of theirs. It worked until the last year, when, suddenly, a new poison began to spread like wildfire, killing mankind faster than we can risk if they are to survive. And so here we are, in the home we were thrown out of, getting help from the same gods who cursed mankind to this fate to begin with," he said, clenching his jaw.

"That's . . ." I couldn't find the words. If this Titan was telling the truth, he'd done something more selfless and honorable than I'd ever even heard of from any of the Olympians. "You said the same could not be said for Aether. What did you mean?"

"Many in Aether, not just within the walls of Olympus, stalk and kill the animals I was forced to leave behind, but most do so for sport or decoration. The Olympians find the animals' natural hides to be too primitive, and they prefer to have them dyed or bleached to conceal their true nature, which is why this leather, in its raw form, looks so different from what you've seen on furniture or on books." Epimetheus cringed. "Figured it was fitting to wear it to Zeus's 'Celebration of Man.' Remind him that without my animals, there would be no man for him to control." The corner of his mouth turned up into a smirk, but his eyes . . . his eyes looked different than they did when we started talking. They'd gotten deeper, darker.

"Why are you telling me all this?"

"You asked," he said simply, shocking me to my core. I was so used to my questions being brushed aside or given cryptic answers that I couldn't help but feel uneasy at his openness.

Epimetheus looked around us before his frown formed into a spectacular grin. "Looks like we have some admirers," he said, not breaking eye contact with me as he tipped his head to our left.

Looking over to the group, I froze, finding more than a dozen pairs of eyes watching us. I sighed as I locked eyes across the room with the one god I truly dreaded.

Zeus.

At the moment, he looked like he wanted to strike me down.

"Does Olympus still feel like the safest place for mortals?" Epimetheus whispered, low enough for only me to hear.

I didn't have to turn around to know his handsome, smug face was probably grinning, likely even bigger than before.

"Stop talking to me," I said as I walked away, trying to put some distance between us. The tempting Titan was about to get me kicked out of Olympus, and Zeus might actually be mad enough to just bolt me and be done with it. End of mortal woman.

"He's already seen us. Can't hide it now. Might as well—"

A scream rang out from the far corner of the room, stopping Epimetheus short.

"Who dares enter this celebration without my invitation!" Zeus's voice boomed so loud throughout the room that it shook the columns holding up the rotunda's gold-and-glass dome, which was now vibrating above us.

Another scream sounded, and I saw a flash of dark hair as a goddess ran from someone—or something—toward the dais. I squinted as hard as I could against the bright light to see who could be so scared they would run away.

"Artemis," Epimetheus said, almost to himself. "Who could have the Goddess of the Hunt running? I've never—"

Whatever words he was about to say fell flat when a beautiful man with silver-white hair stepped up onto the dais, stalking toward her as she scrambled backward, tripping over her feet. Something I would never believe could happen to Artemis if I weren't witnessing it with my own eyes.

"It can't be . . ." Epimetheus said, shaking his head in disbelief.

"What? Who is that? Another Titan?" I asked, tugging on Epimetheus's leather sleeve.

"He was exiled," he said to himself, completely ignoring me.

I pulled on his sleeve harder, until he looked at me. "Who is it? Who is after Artemis?"

"Otus. One of the Aloadae twins."

"One of them?"

"If Otus is here, then Ephialtes can't be far behind." Epimetheus scanned the crowd frantically before his eyes froze on the corner of the room where Zeus sat for the banquet, beside Hera. "So predictable," he said, his eyes flashing to mine in worry for a second before darkening.

I followed his gaze to where the other Aloadae twin, Ephialtes, was cornering Hera in a similar way to his brother cornering Artemis on the dais.

"Hera? They're targeting Hera and Artemis? Are they crazy?" I asked, outraged at their bravery and their stupidity. No way would these two see Apollo's next dawn.

"Well, on the bright side, I don't think you need to worry about Zeus anymore," Epimetheus joked. "He's going to have his hands full for a little bit."

"Who are these—?"

"If I were you, I'd stay as far away from those two as physically possible." Epimetheus nodded in the direction of the Aloadae twins, leaning toward me. Before I could process what he was doing, he grabbed the amphora from my arms and disappeared into the crowd, leaving me standing there like a stunned idiot.

CHAPTER 20

EPIMETHEUS was right. Everyone forgot all about us, including Zeus, who was now hovering in the air above the two brothers, threatening to rain lightning bolts down on them.

"How dare you enter my domain!" Zeus yelled as thunderclouds started to form in the peaks of the rotunda, creating an entire storm system in the ceiling.

"Touch me, and you lose that hand," Artemis seethed from between the enormous thrones, where Otus was approaching her slowly, reaching out as if his touch alone could calm her from her panic.

Zeus never turned toward the cornered goddess; his eyes were on Hera and Ephialtes, who was sitting beside her. At first, I thought she was accepting his invitation, but then I saw the fear in her large blue eyes, and her mouth seemed to twist as if she were in pain.

"Step away from my wife," Zeus said, turning the full force of his lightning in Ephialtes' direction.

"Surely, you don't want me to do that," Ephialtes said to Zeus with a sly smile, not taking his intense gaze off Hera.

"Remove your vile talons from her mind immediately, and maybe I will let you and your insufferable brother survive the night."

Ephialtes curled his fingers under Hera's chin, turning her face toward his in a way that might seem gentle, if not for the pain and internal struggle shining in her eyes. I hadn't realized I was moving closer to the action until I felt the electricity sizzle in the air at my proximity to Zeus.

Survival instincts started to kick in at the tingle, and I walked back to the corner of the room I'd been talking to Epimetheus in. If I were really smart, I would've walked right out of there, but curiosity got the better of me, and I stayed peeking out from behind one of the marble fountains containing wine at the edge of the room, watching as the scene unfolded.

"Release my wife," Zeus boomed again, the electricity in the air intensifying. Gasps traveled throughout the room as the guests felt his power wash over them. "Now!"

Hera stood up from her chair and moved closer to Ephialtes, fighting every movement as if she weren't in control of her own body.

"Calm down, sparkles," Ephialtes said, smiling at Zeus hovering above him, electricity glittering at his fingertips, ready to strike lightning down on his enemy the moment Hera was clear. "Hera doesn't seem to mind—do you, Hera?"

Hera smiled, not of her own will, and turned on Ephialtes' lap to face him. "Not at all," she said in a voice that wasn't her own.

"I will give you one more warning. Let my wife go, and tell your brother to do the same with Artemis, or I will incinerate you where you sit." Zeus's eyes flashed to Hera, probably trying to figure out a way to keep her safe from his bolts.

"Now, now, sparkles. That is no way to talk to your nephew after centuries apart." Ephialtes twirled Hera's dark bronze hair in his fingers, reminding Zeus that if he killed him, Hera would

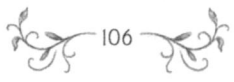

be incinerated as well. "After all, you have not even asked why we're here."

"Why are you here?" Zeus asked hesitantly, as if he were weighing up his odds of killing the Aloadae twins and being done with this.

"Well, Otus and I missed our family. Our home. After centuries of exile, we decided a family reunion was in order. Although we hoped you would have all been a bit more excited to see us after so long."

"You and your brother have not been talked about or thought of since the day you were exiled, and I can guarantee you, no one will miss you when you leave again. In fact, I promise to make sure of that by removing your names from all our texts. It will be as if you never existed, not even a blip in our immortal lives." Lightning flashed in Zeus's eyes the same moment the sinister smile took over his face at this idea.

"Now, that's not very nice, Uncle. After all this time, you're still mad that Hera found me so irresistible she sought the warmth of my bed instead of yours."

Hera flinched and tried her hardest to pull away, but Ephialtes caught her and pulled her even closer, burying his nose in her neck as he looked over her shoulder at Zeus.

"After all, I only returned to take what's mine."

"I will kill you before you can even try."

"You could, yes. However, I have a feeling you'll reconsider, seeing who is currently keeping my lap warm."

I couldn't believe how flippantly Ephialtes was challenging Zeus. Surely, he stood no chance against him.

"Plus," he added, "you haven't even seen the best part."

Artemis screamed again, and this time, Zeus couldn't resist turning toward his daughter, taking his sparkling silver-blue eyes off Hera.

"Take your hands off me!" Artemis yelled at Otus, who had her wrists twisted behind her back, trapped tightly in one of his enormous hands, which I swore were bigger than most gods'.

"You were meant for me, Artemis. After centuries alone, hiding in the night or getting lost in the hunt, I have returned for you, this time with something Zeus will never be able to ignore." Otus was almost pleading for Artemis to accept him; to return the look of longing and sorrow that flashed across his gaze.

"I don't care what you're offering, you fool! I have never and will never love you the way you love me. You bring me nothing but dread and doom. I'm disgusted by your very presence," Artemis spat, glaring so coldly that if Otus were mortal, he would have surely died on the spot from that look alone.

Something she'd said made his face flare with fury before he whispered something in Artemis's ear that made her go completely still.

"I would suggest you both take the hint these powerful goddesses are giving you, for it is not only my wrath you should fear." Zeus's lightning calmed, as did its master.

Maybe Zeus knew the brothers wouldn't hurt them, but Hera and Artemis looked anything but calm. Hera's chin quivered. Whether she was fighting against Ephialtes' control over her or just upset, I wasn't sure. Artemis stood stock-still in Otus's grasp, nostrils flaring.

"Finally, something we agree on," Otus said from behind Artemis, speaking directly to Zeus for the first time since his arrival.

"Something we agree on indeed," Ephialtes chuckled. "If you had more intelligence, maybe you would have stopped before the sparkle show and asked why we were here *now*."

"Why *now*?" Zeus grumbled out.

"Well, Uncle, it seems over the centuries, you have isolated and insulted many of your people, and you see they are not happy to watch as the Olympians living on this mighty mountaintop

ignore them while you create more than you could ever need, and they suffer." Ephialtes' gaze turned icy. "We have come back for what is ours, yes. However, we have also come for more."

Zeus opened his mouth to speak, but Otus interjected. "We came for what is yours too." He smiled, pulling Artemis closer.

"You fools have no power here. If you want to try to take what's mine, go ahead." Zeus opened his arms wide in challenge, releasing strings of lightning that flooded behind him, lighting his frame in pure power that almost seemed to resemble wings. "The second you drop them, you will be no more than dust."

Otus and Ephialtes laughed loudly before Ephialtes spoke.

"Still so naïve, sparkles. You think we came here alone? Waited centuries to make our move, only to walk in and have you incinerate us? You still seem to be missing the point. We are not the only enemies you have made in this realm, and if you have any hope of saving Olympus, I suggest you take the time to find out before it is you who gets incinerated."

Zeus was silent. Eerily so. The only noise coming from the enormous room was the gasps from onlookers, and the buzzing energy that had once felt fuzzy now felt like little electrical shocks, signaling Zeus's anger and his struggle for control.

Luckily, he had his bolt at his hip, so he could take aim and not burst into a massive explosion of electricity, taking everyone out. But the feeling of electricity moving throughout such a large area was extremely unsettling, especially for someone like me, who could be killed by Zeus's untamed power.

Ephialtes stood up, pulling Hera with him, before sliding her down his torso to set her back on the throne at the banquet table beside Zeus.

Zeus's throne stood out among the others thanks to the golden lightning bolts adorning the back of it. Electricity charged as Ephialtes walked away from Hera, around the front of the table, which was the only thing protecting him from Zeus sending a bolt right through him.

Just as he rounded the table, Zeus took his chance and rained lightning down on Ephialtes from the clouds hovering ominously above him. I pulled myself into a hug as if that would stop me catching a shock from the air and getting electrocuted myself.

Lightning bounced off an invisible shield around Ephialtes, and Zeus roared in fury as every strike he threw missed him.

"Pretty light show, but it seems our welcome has worn out." Ephialtes smiled innocently at Zeus, making a mockery out of him and his almighty power, which hadn't singed a single hair on his head.

"You were never welcome to begin with!" Artemis yelled at Ephialtes and then his brother, who still held her hands in his unbreakable grip. Otus was probably smart enough to realize Artemis would waste no time fulfilling the threat she'd made earlier, and he would quickly be missing a limb.

Ephialtes glared at Artemis in warning, which earned him a glare of his own from Otus. He shook his head and laughed again. "Well, as much fun as this has been, Otus and I have more important places to be."

A horrifying shriek rang throughout the rotunda, and shadows passed overhead.

I barely had time to register what was happening before Ephialtes said to Zeus, "I hope you don't mind some friends stopping by." Turning to Hera and picking up her slender hand, he pulled it up to his full lips and placed a kiss on her knuckles. "See you soon, my love."

Dark figures filled the sky, swarming around the rotunda, as the Aloadae twins disappeared into the chaos.

CHAPTER 21

ORRIFYING winged creatures flew in and out of the rotunda, swooping down to attack. Picking up gods and goddesses with their razor-sharp onyx talons, they flew them high into the rotunda before dropping them onto the marble floor. The fall wouldn't kill the gods and goddesses, but it would leave their bodies and their egos a little sore. The cretes, however, could die from the impact, same as me.

I scanned the room from my hiding place behind a large fountain at the edge of the rotunda. Wine poured down its white marble edge onto the floor, splashing at my feet. One of the winged creatures had flown into the fountain minutes before and tipped it into the column I'd been hiding behind, making the perfect little hiding spot. It wasn't safe, necessarily, but it was better than standing in the middle of the celebration room, which had become a war zone.

"Hera!" Zeus yelled, turning around in a full circle as he searched for his wife in the mess below him.

"Zeus!" Hera called back, fighting off one of the creatures that had its talons all twisted in her hair, trapped as if it were in one of Arachne's webs. The creature was pulling so hard it kept lifting her off the ground, until it finally untangled itself.

"Alert the Amazons and call the sphinx down here," Zeus said hurriedly to his wife as a dozen winged monsters flew toward him, each getting struck down by a bolt of lightning before they came within ten feet of the god. "NOW!" Zeus's voice boomed, and Hera took off down the path leading to the palace.

Bodies were piling, both Olympian and creatures, and my view had become blocked by a creature Zeus bolted down right on top of the fountain.

Being unable to see what was going on was worse than witnessing the bloody battle. I couldn't stand it.

Gathering my courage, I moved from my *safe* spot—now a blind spot—anchoring one foot on the edge of the fountain as I reached up to get ahold of the toppled column, since the floor and the fountain were both slick with wine.

I had never seen so much blood. Or death.

I'd heard stories of the epic battles that had taken place when the High Olympians gained control over Mount Olympus, but I'd never witnessed such a thing in my life.

"Pandora! What are you doing? Get out of here!" Athena yelled from across the ballroom, swinging two mighty swords through the air. She sliced through the torso of one of the creatures, while simultaneously slicing the membranous wings off another.

I stared at her, frozen in fear, watching as her gold-and-silver swords cut through the air, taking out creature after creature that flew across her path as if they were nothing but an annoyance. Although, when she looked at me, I could have sworn fear shone in her eyes.

Not for herself, but for me.

I watched for longer than I should have, mesmerized by the fluidity of her movements as she danced across the mayhem to a song only she could hear, never missing a beat.

A scream sounded. Guttural, terrible. A creature tore into the faun standing nearby. It ripped at her skin, tearing large pieces away from the bone.

Bile rose in my mouth.

The faun locked eyes with me, full of agony, pleading for me to end it. But what could I do? I had no weapons—I was just as mortal as her.

The creature let out a bloodcurdling screech, and the faun let out one final scream before her throat was torn away.

I screamed. The creature released the faun. Her blood poured from the gaping wound, pulsing in even beats. She reached for me, her movements slow, until she stopped moving altogether, her wide eyes as empty and soulless as the monster on top of her.

The creature shrieked again, turning its attention to me. I turned, hoping I had the strength to outrun it.

One step, two steps. My foot slipped in the wine, sending me sliding, until my chin collided with the marble floor.

Panicked, I stared at the creature's feral eyes, shrieking as it tried to release its talons from the unmoving body below it. I fumbled around on the wine-slick marble, grappling for something to use as a weapon.

Finding a cylindrical piece of marble that had cracked off the side of the column, I held it firm in my hands, readying myself for the winged beast to attack. I looked up just in time to see the creature fling its body toward me.

Swinging the piece of marble as hard as I could, I made contact with the beast's side, launching to my left, where it hit a column before sliding down to the ground, leaving a thin black streak of blood on the once pristine marble.

I breathed a sigh of relief, but I breathed it too soon, because the creature was lifting its battered body off the ground, looking even more ferocious than before.

I pushed my legs out, slipping through the wine as I tried to gain some sort of cover from the creature crawling toward me,

dragging its broken wing behind it. My back hit the broken fountain, leaving me with nowhere to go. In my haste to find cover, I'd done nothing but back myself into a corner.

I held the marble "weapon" in my hand, realizing I couldn't swing it from this angle, and as I struggled to figure out my best course of action, the monstrous bat creature flung its body at me.

Bringing the marble up in front of me, I pointed it at the creature's chest, screaming as its body collided with mine. The point of the marble shard went directly through its chest and pierced its heart.

The creature fell limp on my body.

Pushing its dead body off me, I tried my hardest to pull the marble piece out, even bracing a foot on the side of the fallen fountain to get a stronger hold, with no luck. I couldn't get the piece of marble to even budge from its spot, buried deep as it was within the creature's chest.

Hearing more commotion a few feet away from me, I decided it best to leave the creature and the weapon behind before another monster attacked.

I crawled over to the back of a column that was still standing and peered around the side, looking for anyone who might have a weapon or something that could help me. Athena was closer to me than she had been before, now fighting alongside Artemis. I yelled, screamed for her through the chaos, but she couldn't hear me.

Get closer, I told myself, getting to my feet. *Get closer.*

I was considering my chances of making it to her when an ear-splitting screech sounded over my head, pulling my attention from Athena. Looking up just in time, I noticed the creature diving from the peak of the rotunda before making a sharp turn in my direction.

For a moment, time seemed to slow as I watched it dip and dodge others of its kind, setting its sights on me.

I scrambled around the back of the column, heading toward the path that led away from the rotunda, hoping I could lose my assailant in the boulders lining it.

I didn't.

The ear-piercing shriek of the creature followed, but once out of the chaos, the sound worked to my advantage, warning me of its approach.

I wished I had a sword, but as I looked around, I noticed large pieces of rock littering the ground. Slowing for a second, I picked up a handful, hurling them over my shoulder at the creature. I missed every time, only slowing it down slightly as it maneuvered to miss them.

I ran as fast as I could, dropping to my stomach every time I noticed it tuck in its wings to descend. In the time it took to circle around, I tried to gather more rocks to hurl at it before it came back.

When I hurled a few more, one of them finally hit. Releasing a ferocious shriek, the creature dove, tucking its wings tight into its sides to gain speed.

I dropped to the stone-cold ground, wincing as my banged-up knees made contact, skidding to a halt on my stomach as I waited for it to pass before getting up to run again. Only, this time, I was a little too slow, and the creature was far closer than I could have imagined.

The razor-sharp talons shredded my dress, slicing through skin, all the way down to the bone. Flesh ripped from my back as the creature tried and failed to lift me into the air.

I screamed in agony as I dropped to the ground, sobbing.

"We need to go—now!" a male voice shouted as I was pulled to my feet as if I were as light as a feather.

Crying out in pain from the movement, I finally caught sight of my rescuer.

Epimetheus.

Time slowed as I stared into his molten amber eyes, which had turned deep and dark as he stared back into mine with worry.

Peeking behind him, I saw the beheaded body of the creature lying on the cobblestone outside the court. I recognized it from the hundreds of identical ones thanks to the burgundy scraps of my dress wrapped around its bloody talons. Black, tar-like blood dripped from its wounds.

I was frozen in fear until Epimetheus grabbed me by the arms and gave me a good shake, bringing me back to reality and the deadly situation I was in. Even though this attack was on the Olympian gods and goddesses, they were the only beings here tonight who couldn't be murdered by these winged monsters.

"Pandora! We. Need. To. Go."

I nodded at Epimetheus before nearly falling back to the ground in pain after one step.

"I can't . . . I don't think I can walk," I blubbered out through the tears as snot streamed down my face from the sobs overtaking my body.

"Okay. I'm going to get us out of here, but it's going to hurt," he said, looking around for any other option to escape the chaos.

I nodded.

Epimetheus bent down, swooping his strong arms under my knees, and picked me up gently, careful not to touch the wounds on my back that were beginning to throb with a pain so deep it coursed through my entire body. He cradled me in his arms against his warm chest, which was as hard as stone.

"Ready?" he asked.

I nodded into his shoulder, suddenly feeling like I was going to pass out.

My eyes fluttered closed as a gust of powerful wind rushed around us. It felt as if my body were being propelled into the heavens. All I could focus on was the warm, steely grip pinning my body against his before everything went dark.

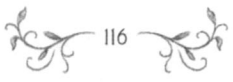

CHAPTER 22

"WHY does it look like that?" someone whispered from what sounded like miles away.

"The Keres have poison talons. Normally, they don't do much damage to immortals, but I've never seen their effect on a mortal," another voice answered in the distance.

"You said you could heal her. *That* does not look healed to me."

"I've healed as much as my powers will allow, but I can only paralyze the poison that has latched onto her, not remove it. It's up to her now to stay strong until Hecate is able to come up here herself and withdraw the poison from her system."

Silence filled the room, and my eyes fluttered open just in time to see Apollo's blond hair and warm glow leaving. I turned my head to see who he'd been talking to. I expected to be in pain, but instead, my body was completely numb. Even turning my head took every bit of strength and willpower I had left.

Epimetheus was sitting on a marble chair in the corner of a room I'd never seen before. The room was filled with pristine white marble, and the ceiling was nonexistent, leaving the room open to the cloud-filled sky above us.

I could have sworn I was dreaming as I watched birds fly overhead, dipping in and out of the clouds over and over again.

One even flew close enough that I could make out some details: brown feathered wings, with bronze tips that looked like daggers, stretching more than twice the length of their body, and the face of a beautiful woman.

The harpies, which could only mean one thing...

We were no longer on Mount Olympus. We were in the clouds above it, in the Palace of Dawn and Day. Apollo's palace, high in the heavens, which until now had never been accessed by those who dwelled below the clouds in Olympus.

"Is this heaven?" I asked, struggling to get the words out.

"Some might call it that." Epimetheus scoffed. "We're in Apollo's home. He helped heal you."

"Heal me? What hap—?"

Memories flooded in. Screaming. Crying. The dead faun. My shredded back.

"How?" I asked.

"Athena caught my attention when she yelled at you to run. I made it just in time to see a Keres diving toward you, chasing you out of the rotunda. My brother and I figured it was in our best interest not to let the only mortal woman in all existence be shredded to pieces," Epimetheus said, his voice a monotone.

"I remember that much." I rolled my eyes. "How did I get here?"

"I flew you up." Epimetheus shrugged.

"You *what*?" I stared at the beautiful Titan, trying to figure out how that was possible. I thought only Zeus, Artemis, Hera, Apollo, and Hermes could make it this high into the heavens. "How?"

Epimetheus leaned back in his chair, crossing one of his massive legs and resting his ankle on his knee. He tapped his leg with a long finger, looking me over like he was deciding how much to tell me. "I created animals. My powers allow me to take on their forms as I see fit. So, you see, I flew us up here."

I attempted to wrap my head around what he was telling me. I'd never heard of a god or a goddess being able to change forms. At least, not any I'd met in Olympus—or none that I knew of. I was beginning to wonder how much outside the walls of Olympus I'd never been told about before now.

I tried to move again, fighting the fatigue and the numbness in my body, but no matter how hard I tried, I couldn't so much as lift my arm.

"Why can't I move?"

"The Keres got ahold of you before I was able to get there. It ripped your back up pretty good. That was why I brought you to Apollo. You were losing a lot of blood, and I've seen what small injuries and ailments can do to end a mortal's life. Rather than chancing it, I flew you straight up here to him, and he healed all your injuries, but the poison the Keres's talons are coated in has not been easy to heal."

Epimetheus didn't break eye contact as he spoke, those amber depths seeming to look straight into my soul. The Olympians were intense, but he was . . . different. While the Olympians always had cold, calculating looks, Epimetheus seemed to have an untamed wildness in him that I'd never seen. It was as beautiful as it was terrifying.

"The Keres? I heard you and Apollo talking about them before I woke up, but what are they?"

"Nyx had a thousand daughters known as the Keres. They're the spirits of violent and cruel death. Normally, they're found on battlefields to help the dead travel to the Underworld, but when the Keres taste blood, they go into a frenzy that makes them nearly impossible to control. I haven't seen them in eons. Last I heard, Zeus had most of Nyx's creations either slaughtered or imprisoned in Tartarus."

"If they can't be controlled, then how did the Aloadae twins get them to attack the celebration?"

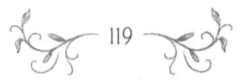

"That is the question indeed. The Keres could not have completed an attack as effective as the other night with only the Aloadae twins in charge. Someone must be helping them. Someone who has the power to access Tartarus."

"The other night? I thought the attack happened hours ago."

"It happened four nights ago. You've been recovering since then. It took Apollo a while to figure out how to stop the poison from spreading any further throughout your body, hence the paralysis." Epimetheus gestured to my unmoving body, sprawled out on the four-poster bed.

"I thought you said I couldn't move because of the poison," I pointed out.

"Semantics. The poison nearly killed you and had already started to immobilize your body before Apollo stepped in. This"— Epimetheus flung his hand at my statuesque body again—"is the reason you're not dead. So in a way, it was the poison."

I stared at him. Maybe it was whatever magic Apollo had used on me, but that didn't make one bit of sense. Looking down, my gaze caught on the tunic covering my body. A tunic that was clearly not mine and seemed to be tied at my neck, leaving my back open and covering my front like a blanket.

"What am I wearing?" I asked, my fingers itching to touch the fabric but unable to move an inch from the paralysis.

"A tunic," Epimetheus said, raising his brows at me.

"I know that, but how did I get into the tunic?"

"Apollo's servants changed you into it so it would be easier to inspect your wounds. The tunic was put on backward so they could adjust the ties as needed around the injury site. Not to mention, your celebration gown wasn't covering much of anything and was dirty enough that Apollo feared your wounds would become septic, killing you even before the Keres poison could." He shrugged, refusing to meet my eye, as if he were hiding something and feared his expression might give it away.

"Oh, okay," I said, suddenly feeling awkward as I imagined how exposed I'd been when he carried me up here.

"Now that you're awake, I need to return to Mount Olympus and check in on things with my brother. Hecate should be up soon, and I'm sure she'll figure something out to get you back onto your feet." He stood up from his seat, rolling his shoulders before turning to walk out the door.

"Epimetheus—"

He stopped and looked at me over his shoulder.

"Thank you."

Without a word, he nodded and walked out the door, leaving me in a lonely silence to stare out at the rolling clouds filled with a mix of blues, purples, and pinks—the colors of dusk. Soon, Artemis would be illuminating the night sky with her silvery glow.

CHAPTER 23

HECATE appeared from the shadows. "Hello, Pandora."

Her approach had been silent. Yellow eyes glimmered in the darkness. If my body weren't paralyzed, I would have jumped out of my skin.

Tossing her long black hair over her shoulder, she slowly leaned over, placing a slender hand on my forehead. "Keres are horrid things, aren't they?"

I shivered. Never had she touched me before. Her magic thrummed against my skin. It was easy to forget how much power she wielded.

"Hecate," I choked out.

In the weak moonlight, her lips tugged into the smallest smirk. "Death hovers around you like Aphrodite's lovers."

Was she joking about how close I was to death? Sure, I'd heard stories of her raising the dead and romping around with ghosts for fun, but I'd never stopped to consider how odd it would be to find yourself in the presence of someone so unfazed by death. Especially as someone who seemed to dance with it every day as a mortal. Death was not as finite for her.

Hecate sniffed the air. Could she smell the poison? The death?

"It's a good thing Apollo froze the poison when he did. Bringing you back from the dead would have been troublesome."

"Troublesome?" I wished she'd stop touching me. I swallowed. My mouth was the only part of my body I could still use.

"It doesn't always turn out the way most assume. Your soul would be broken, your mind would be lost, and your body just a husk." She grinned, the corners of her mouth lifting into a lethal smile, revealing a set of brilliant white teeth that would make her even more beautiful if I didn't know what sinister secrets she held. "Rather unpleasant."

My face must have said everything I was thinking, because she laughed and patted my shoulder—as if I could feel anything in my current state. She pulled out a glass bottle and a small dagger, which looked like it was made of stone rather than metal, and set them on the table beside my bed.

"No worries, little mortal. Although it will be excruciating, I should be able to draw the poison from your body and trap it in this vial." She smiled to herself before adding, "Might even come in useful as a weapon one day."

"Wh-wh-what do you mean, ex-excruciating?" I stuttered—out of fear of the goddess or what she'd said, I couldn't be sure.

"Well, in order to pull the poison, I first must stop the paralysis. At the moment, the poison is stuck in your body. If I leave you in paralysis, the poison will shred you from the inside, just as the talons did on the outside. However, if I remove the paralysis as I pull the poison, it should flow through your body, similar to a stream of water."

"Is there no other way?" I asked as panic settled into my bones.

"Sure, there is," she said, smiling in that sinister way of hers. Her yellow eyes flashed in delight. "Death."

My heart hammered in my chest so hard I swore I could feel it pulsing throughout my body even in paralysis. I took a deep breath before answering, trying to gather a morsel of strength for what I was about to agree to. "Okay. Pull the poison."

She grinned at me. "As you wish, little mortal."

I was already lying on my stomach, so the wounds on my back were only covered from her sight by a sheet, which she pulled back, revealing the mangled skin left behind by the Keres. She chanted words in a language I'd never heard, and everything went white as the paralysis was removed and pain descended in its place.

The pain was worse than I imagined, like molten lava being pulled from all around my body. Hecate's lips moved, but I could hear nothing beyond my own screams.

The burning sensation paused. I took a breath, savoring the icy breeze in the room and the relief it brought, before it started all over again.

I screamed, gripping onto the sheets with all my might. It felt as if Hecate were pulling every vein in my body out through the wounds in my back. Surely, this would kill me. How much pain could a mortal take?

Her lips kept moving, but I heard nothing as my vision began to blur and fade away, taking my pain along with it.

Death. This must be it.

Hours—or maybe days—passed before the warm light of dawn flooded my vision. The excruciating pain was gone, but my entire body ached as if I'd been trampled by a herd of centaurs.

I glanced around the room, finding no sign of Hecate. The only thing left in her absence was a note, a glass of water, and a vial of a deep burgundy—almost black—liquid that swirled within the glass like smoke.

Picking up the water first, I chugged it down, relishing the coolness, which put out the inferno raging in my throat. Reaching

across the nightstand for the paper, I unfolded it and winced as I shifted back on the bed to read it.

Pandora,

The poison from the Keres has been successfully removed.

In the process of extracting the poison, your body coped with the pain coursing through your veins by temporarily relieving you of consciousness. I thought at first you were dead, but alas, you were not.

I have left a portion of the poison within this vial, should you ever need it in the future for protection. I caution you to not let the poison contact any part of your skin, though, as I cannot predict the ramifications of such an act. It is a miracle your mortal form survived with the amount of Keres poison coursing through your veins.

Apollo will handle the remainder of your healing, as it is in his power now.

See you soon, Pandora.

Setting the paper back on the nightstand by the enormous white four-poster bed, I picked up the small glass vial and twisted it carefully in my palm, entranced by the ominous swirls held within. I couldn't help but be reminded of the shadow figure I'd seen ahead of the celebration.

Could the shadow figure have been the one who orchestrated the attack with the Aloadae twins?

I swore, as soon as I was able, I'd head to the library to find as much information as I could on shadow creatures.

Setting the vial back down before I did something stupid like drop it, I wiggled to the edge of the bed, relishing in the movement my body was once again able to make. I would never take movement for granted again.

As I stood, my feet wobbled slightly, getting used to my weight on them again. I walked over to the far wall, taking in the view of Olympus from above. It all seemed so small from up here.

Was this what it was like for the giants—feeling larger than life, as if one wrong move could crush a kingdom? I considered this as I watched the citizens of Olympus moving about their daily routines.

Glancing down to see more of the summit, which was partially covered from view by clouds, I suddenly noticed the lavender dress stretching all the way to my toes. Someone had changed me out of the oversize cotton tunic and put me in a lavender silk nightgown, with a floral lace trim that flowed down to my ankles, and a slit up the right side that reached almost halfway up my thigh, leaving it exposed to the cool morning breeze coming through the large arched windows.

It was more revealing than I would have chosen for myself, and my face flushed beet-red as I tried not to imagine what Epimetheus would think. I silently cursed myself for thinking about him when it should be Prometheus I was imagining.

CHAPTER 24

"**Y**ou're awake," a feminine voice said from behind me.

As if summoned by the rampant thoughts that had been running through my head, Artemis walked into my room. If you could call it walking. The goddess was so quiet in her approach she might as well have appeared from thin air, just as Hecate had.

"How are you feeling this morning?" she asked, carrying a tray of bread, juice, an apple, and a bowl of ambrosia. I'd never been allowed to eat ambrosia. The elixir of life amplified powers or granted immortality.

"I can't eat that," I said, pointing to the ambrosia before even thinking about the outraged tone I'd used toward the intimidating goddess. She was looking at me as if I'd just called her stupid.

"If you couldn't eat it, I wouldn't have brought it," she said, rolling her eyes as she set the tray on the table beside the window. "Zeus and Demeter consulted each other regarding your health and agreed, given your recent injury, consuming ambrosia would be in everyone's best interests."

"Won't it make me immortal if I consume it?" I asked.

"No. Not this small amount. It will, however, make your mortality less *fragile,* and it will also help to expedite your healing."

"Hecate said Apollo would be handling that."

Artemis scoffed. "For as much as that death goddess knows, she always seems to forget some of us are required to be places and can't just arrive whenever we feel like it. You see the sun shining up in the sky, don't you?" Artemis pointed to the sun, which was rising to the east of my enormous guest room.

Clio had once told me that after the war with the Titans, Zeus imprisoned the old gods Helios, Selene, and Eos with Uranus in the skies covering the mortal realm. Ever since then, it had been up to Apollo and Artemis to take over their duties, transforming themselves into the sun and the moon over the Realm of Aether. I'd never understood exactly how they accomplished that, but Clio had said they simply became the embodiment of their powers over light, filling the sky with sun—or, in Artemis's case, lighting the way through the darkness Nyx released into the realm every night.

I rolled my eyes at her. "I had my back torn open, not my eyes, Artemis."

She looked me over before her stony face cracked into a smile. "Zeus has been impatient since the attack and has requested you be brought back to Olympus for the announcement he plans to make today. Hermes will be up shortly to escort you down." She turned on her heel and headed for the door, taking the conversation with her.

Before she could even make it halfway across the room, I asked, "Artemis, are you all right?"

"I am. Why would I not be?" She stopped in her tracks to turn around and look at me.

I shied away from her steely gaze, picking up the loaf of bread for something to do with my hands. "The other night . . . I have never seen you so frightened before."

"I was. Otus brings with him a sense of doom that I loathe." She rubbed her arms as if she were cold, but the breeze was warm, and Olympians were not affected by the weather. "What

was most concerning was the power I felt coming from him and Ephialtes, as if they were children of Nyx."

"I thought they had giants' blood." Giants weren't known for having powers beyond being strong and durable.

"They do, but their powers far exceed those of a giant," Artemis said. She clarified, "When the giant started to emerge within them, they did something we'd never heard of any giant doing. They controlled their size."

"Like the gods?" I asked, remembering the time Demeter had grown in order to reach the tops of the trees in her orchard.

"Yes. It wasn't long before their exile that powers started to emerge. Some sought to control the Aloadae twins by influencing them to do their bidding, while others tried to accept them for who they were, until the day their powers became greater than we could control." Artemis stared off into the distance as if she were reliving the moment their powers had emerged.

"Is that why no one except Zeus intervened at the celebration?" I asked, pulling her attention out of the memory and back to me.

"Not everyone agreed on the twins' exile. Many argued their powers could protect Olympus. Others feared they would eventually try to take Olympus for themselves. As time passed, their powers grew, and everyone except Poseidon agreed to exile them. For a time, there was peace with their exile, but then man attacked Poseidon's nymphs, and Poseidon tried to argue man was as much of a threat to the Olympians as the Aloadae."

"He couldn't possibly think that, could he?" I balked at the idea. Sure, man had numbers, but they held no actual power—not like the gods, and especially gods with the blood of giants.

"He did. He still does."

"But how could he compare the two when they're totally different?"

"Imagine it from Poseidon's point of view. Zeus's children, mankind, murdered millions of his nymphs and were gifted

their own realm, where they were allowed to stay as they saw fit, while the Aloadae were punished with exile simply for growing powerful enough to threaten Zeus's rule."

"So is that why no one stepped in—they didn't want to anger Zeus, knowing how he felt about them? And why target you and Hera? Just to anger Zeus even further?"

"No one stepped in because they fear them. The Aloadae have been gone for millennia, and no one could possibly know how powerful they are now," Artemis said, releasing a sigh before continuing. "They targeted me and Hera because, before their exile, we were both in love with the Aloadae."

"What?" I asked, unable to believe her words. "No offense, but I assumed you were like Athena—celibate and bound only to your duty."

Artemis laughed, smiling as she said, "I was, but I'd never met anyone like Otus. He was kind, caring, and had more passion than any Olympian I'd ever met. We met in secret for a while before his brother, Ephialtes, shared his connection with Hera. Then the four of us would meet at her palace in the Lower Heavens, or in the Aloadaes' home in the Eastern Sea, outside Olympus's walls and in their father's territory rather than Zeus's." Artemis glanced out the window to the eastern sea.

I followed her eyes, admiring the view and noticing I could see the long strip of land beyond it I knew to be Themyscira, home of the Amazons, which I had seen countless times on maps of Olympus and the Sea of Poseidon in my lessons with Clio.

"Are you saying Hera used the Aloadaes' love for her to inspire a rebellion?" I asked, hating her even more.

"Yes. That is when everything changed. Otus's kindness turned to hate, and the loving energy he once exuded turned, leaving only doom in its wake. Hera said a similar thing happened to Ephialtes. She claimed he went from being the god of her dreams to the monster of her nightmares. Hera has a tendency to overreact, so I didn't think much of it after they were exiled, but

when they returned, all I sensed from those two was anger and power." A shiver traveled through Artemis's body as she spoke.

"Do you miss him? The old Otus, I mean."

"Every day. But the monster he became will always over-shadow the love I once had for him." Artemis stared down at her empty hands before adding, "Enough of the Aloadae. You need rest, and I must be going." She turned and walked to the door.

As her hand reached for the door handle, I said, "I meant to ask. I was wearing a tunic before. Who put me in . . . this?" I pulled the sides of my silk nightgown out and looked down at the beautiful fabric as if it offended me.

"Hecate. She figured Epimetheus would have preferred to leave you in his clothes, but she knew this was more suitable for a mortal beauty such as yourself." With that, she turned the door handle and stepped through, closing the door behind her.

CHAPTER 25

HERMES flew me down to my cottage, carrying me as if I were as light as a feather. He wasn't as muscular as most Olympians, with a lithe build that hid his strength beneath a thin layer of sinewy muscle.

He made a point of telling me my weak body could never complete such a task, and that I was lucky to have such a masculine friend to fly me around. I assumed he was referring to himself before he snorted and said, "Not me, Dora. Your Titan. Now, that god has muscles to make most Olympians look puny. If he gave me half the time of day he gives you, I'd climb him like a mountain goat."

I laughed as I thought of the mountain goats I passed on the trails running along the cliffs of Mount Olympus. Then I felt the blush creeping onto my cheeks as I imagined climbing Epimetheus in the way Hermes suggested, and I quickly changed the subject.

"So, what have I missed? Have the Aloadae been found?"

"No, not yet. Zeus has announced that until they've been caught, Olympus is on lockdown. No one comes in or goes out." He paused for a moment before adding, "Except for your Titan,

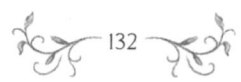

Epimetheus. He traveled back to Earth the night before last to deliver the cure to mankind."

"He's not *my* Titan," I said, rolling my eyes at Hermes, which only made him grin wider.

"Worry not, dear Dora. Your Titan will be back in a few days' time. He wouldn't leave Prometheus here with Zeus for a moment longer than necessary—not after what Zeus did to his other brothers."

"What happened to his other brothers?"

"They got on Zeus's bad side." Hermes shrugged as he walked over to the front door of my cottage. "Speaking of, I'm supposed to be up at the summit for a court meeting. Primes forbid I get put on Zeus's list of enemies for being late."

I ran over to Hermes, throwing my arms around him and pulling him in for a hug. "We can't have that. After all, you're my favorite big brother." I winked at him as I mimicked what he'd said in our last conversation.

He laughed and hugged me back. "You know it."

From the front lawn of my cottage, I squinted up into the cloudless blue sky as Hermes took off. I was always at peace watching the gods and goddesses fly. They'd soar through the sky as if the moment their feet left the ground, all their weight and the worries of the world fell away, replaced by wondrous freedom.

After Hermes was gone, I couldn't seem to relax. Energy coursed through my body almost as quickly as questions raced through my mind.

Suddenly, I remembered something. With everything going on, I'd forgotten about the book on the Titan brothers Clio had given me to read.

Running over to the far wall of my cottage, I scanned the row of books on the shelf until my eye caught the one I was searching for. I pulled out a dark leather-bound book, titled "Tales of the Titans," and carried it over to the couch, where I settled in and found the section on Prometheus and his brothers.

According to the text, Atlas had been born first, followed by Prometheus, and soon after, his twin Epimetheus, and finally, the youngest brother, Menoetius.

While Prometheus and Epimetheus had sided with Olympus during the War of the Titans, Atlas and Menoetius had sided with the Titans.

I flipped the page, sucking in a breath as I took in the illustration covering the entire left page. It depicted three Titan males leading a group of cretes and other Titans into battle. They roared into the sky, signaling the attack. The artist had captured the fury in the three males' faces so well it made me uneasy the longer I looked at it. I glanced down at the description, which read, "*Iapetus and his sons Atlas and Menoetius leading the right wing into battle.*" Out of the three Titans, the one labeled "Menoetius" seemed far more menacing than the others.

I scanned the text on the next page to find out more about him, tapping my finger on a line separated from the rest that seemed to be a poem written for the mighty Titan.

"*Doomed by might and fated to fight,*" I read.

Scanning the text a little further, I came across a passage that described his downfall.

"*Fighting with fury and force, Menoetius made his way across the battlefield until he was in front of Zeus himself. Zeus smiled, sensing the Titan's fury. Falling right into his trap, Menoetius descended into a rash storm of rage, attacking Zeus before noticing the bolt he was holding in his palm. Zeus struck the Titan down with a single bolt.*"

The section continued to describe the other Titans who fell, but it never mentioned Atlas or Menoetius again.

I flipped forward a few more pages until I found the section on Titan imprisonment. There was a list of all the Titans charged with eternal imprisonment in Tartarus. I scanned it, finding Iapetus and Menoetius, but there was no mention of Atlas.

Finally, at the end of the list, amid descriptions of various other imprisonments, I found Atlas's name.

"Zeus discovered that the Titan who gave Cronos the idea to overthrow Olympus was Atlas. As a result, Atlas was imprisoned separately from his family in Tartarus, cursed to live out eternity alone, holding the weight of the world on his shoulders."

Literally.

If these texts were correct, then Zeus, knowing Gaia's feelings toward Uranus, had cursed Atlas to forever keep them separate, holding the heavens high above the Earth, which was now filled with Zeus's creations. Only Atlas prevented Uranus from crashing down on them.

I kept reading for what felt like hours, absorbing as much information about Epimetheus and Prometheus's family as I could, until eventually, I drifted off into a deep sleep.

CHAPTER 26

KNOCKING at my front door jolted me awake.

I had no idea how much time I'd spent unconscious, but I figured the divine snack Artemis had given me was to thank for my deep sleep. Ambrosia, I'd found out, was drizzled in nectar, a thick syrup that came from the bees Demeter kept in hives in the center of the ambrosia fields.

A loud noise came from the kitchen, where Persephone was standing with a basket full of fruit. "Hey, Pandy! I come bearing gifts," she sang, dancing her way over to the small, two-seater dining table.

The kitchen in my cottage was attached to the dining area and consisted of a large marble slab that made a sort of island in the center of the space, a few cabinets, and a small basin I could rinse fruit and clothes in, since it had been fitted with pipes and running water by Hephaestus and Poseidon.

Poseidon had once found me trying to drink water from the sea because I was too lazy to travel up to the freshwater springs farther up Mount Olympus. He'd explained drinking seawater would do nothing but intensify my thirst to the point of dehydration, and eventually, death. That was the last time I'd let my laziness get the better of me. I began taking the trail up to the

springs at least four times a week to gather enough water to keep at my cottage. That is, until he and Hephaestus put their brilliant minds together and gave me access to fresh water in my own home, and Poseidon himself gifted me the pouch of never-ending water so I would never be caught thirsty again.

I yawned, stretching my arms as high as they could reach above my head, and headed toward Persephone, rubbing the sleep from my eyes. I heard her snicker before I saw the grin on her face.

Persephone eyed my dress, her gaze lingering on the high slit that nearly exposed my hipbone. "Where did you get that?"

"Hecate put me in it after she pulled the Keres poison from my body in the Palace of Dawn and Day."

"Hecate?" Persephone nearly choked on the name as her eyes widened in shock. "I thought Apollo was healing you. I've never heard of her visiting Apollo's palace."

"Well, she did. I guess it was out of Apollo's scope of healing, and he summoned her." I shrugged.

Persephone laughed, shaking her head. "Zeus won't be too happy about that."

"What do you mean? Why would he care if she was in Apollo's palace? Artemis suggested both Zeus and Demeter should know I was up there, but I guess I never considered Hecate."

"Zeus held a meeting at the court with all the High Olympians to discuss what preemptive actions we should be taking to prepare for the Aloadae twins' next attack. I guess Prometheus had a vision, but it was pretty vague, and Zeus got a temper, demanding Hecate be summoned to wield her magic and figure out the vision—which, of course Hades didn't like. It ended in a glaring match between the two of them before Zeus had Hades hauled off to the dungeons, where he was to be kept until Hecate decided to show." She laughed a little more before adding, "The almighty Zeus didn't even take the time to consider Hecate was right above his nose, healing you, the whole time."

"She didn't seem very worried when she was helping me. Not that I saw her when she left, since I was about as conscious as a rock."

"She probably wouldn't have shown it even if you did see her leave. As Hades made very clear, no one, not even the King of the Gods himself, can order Hecate around. She answers to no one but herself."

"Why take Hades as prisoner then?" I asked, trying to put the pieces together.

Persephone shook her head as if she didn't want to reveal what she was about to tell me. "Hades and Hecate have a very close relationship."

"I thought you and Hades had a close relationship." I winked at her as the corners of my mouth turned up in a teasing grin, which earned me a glare.

"Not that way, Pandy. He looks at Hecate like a little sister and feels a sort of protective affection over her. In fact, I'd go as far as to say she is one of the best friends that temperamental man has ever had. Why do you think he allows her to live in the Underworld and help him rule part of it?"

"She *what*?" I asked louder than I meant to.

"Do not tell anyone what I'm telling you now. Hades likes to keep to himself, and what he shares with me about his domain is not to be shared with anyone else. But considering the Goddess of Magic saw fit to come save your life, I feel you have a right to know the basics in case Zeus hears about your time with her in the Palace of Dawn and Day." She looked at me, waiting for me to agree to secrecy.

"I won't tell a soul. Not that I'd talk to anyone other than you regarding Hades. I've kept quiet about your late-night rendezvous, haven't I?" I smirked at her, which earned me another glare—only, this time, it was more playful.

"Hades gave her dominion over the in-between."

"The in-between?" I tilted my head to the side.

"It's the liminal space that lies between the living and the dead. She controls the doorways and the crossroads the dead must travel in order to cross over into the Underworld. Basically, no one gets in or out of the Underworld without Hecate knowing."

"That is a pretty massive job. How does Zeus not already know this? And won't Hecate realize Hades hasn't returned?"

"As I said, Hades likes his privacy, so at first, she probably won't find it uncharacteristic of him. Zeus is too self-absorbed sitting on his perfect mountaintop to pay much attention to anyone or anything below him—which, in his eyes, is basically everyone. If you ask me, his hunger for power is what got him into this fight with the Aloadae twins."

"I thought they were exiled for trying to attack Olympus," I said, remembering the way the Aloadae had acted as if Hera and Artemis were owed to them, using their powers over the goddesses to instill bloodcurdling fear.

"Attacked his ego, maybe, but no, they never made a physical attack on Zeus. They simply wanted to be accepted by a family that didn't want them, and when their power started to grow, Zeus grew jealous—some might even say fearful—of what they might one day become. So *before* they got the chance to attack, he ordered their execution."

I nodded, remembering as much from my conversation with Artemis, but the execution part made me pause.

Persephone looked at my wide eyes and raised brows, taking in my shock, before continuing. "It didn't help that Ephialtes was so enamored with Hera it bordered on obsession. But before Zeus got the chance to execute them, Poseidon came to Zeus from his palace under the sea and begged for their lives to be spared." She grabbed an orange from the basket and squeezed it into a glass with ease, making the juice magically pour from the fruit's center. "Poseidon and Zeus came to some sort of agreement and decided on the immediate exile of the Aloadae twins, making it clear that anyone who sought to help them during their exile would be executed for treason against the orders of the court. After that, the Aloadae twins were never seen or spoken about again . . . until the celebration."

Persephone slid the glass of freshly squeezed orange juice over to me and sat down.

"Who was their mother? I know Poseidon was their father, but you never mentioned the mother." I played the conversation back over in my head, feeling like I might have missed that important piece of information.

"Their mother was Iphimedia, a sea nymph married to Aloeus," she started, but I was already interrupting her.

"Poseidon's son, Aloeus?"

"Yes, but Iphimedia never truly loved him, because he was always overshadowed by her obsession with Poseidon. She made it her life's mission to have Poseidon's children and to win his love, but he refused, swearing loyalty to his wife, Amphitrite. However, Iphimedia didn't take no for an answer.

"What do you mean? What could she have done to sway Poseidon?" I asked.

"She went out into the sea and cast a spell—"

"I thought Hecate was the only one who could use magic," I blurted out.

"Hecate is the mother of magic, but she does not have complete control. Magic is a force of nature and cannot be contained. That is something Iphimedia unfortunately learned the hard way."

"Why? What happened?"

"The spell worked, and after hours of sitting on the beach letting Poseidon's waves wash over her, she became pregnant. What she failed to understand is that magic does not come free, and in using such a strong spell to trick Poseidon, she brought a curse upon her unborn children."

"What was the cost?"

"The one thing she was working so very hard to get. Poseidon's love and power."

"I can see Poseidon hating her, but why the children? They were innocent in all this," I said, starting to feel bad for everything the Aloadae twins had been forced to go through since their creation. I couldn't help but see the good in them, which had been twisted and turned into something evil by those they thought cared for them the most.

"At first, Poseidon loved Ephialtes and Otus, and he raised them on his own at the edge of the sea, outside the walls of Olympus."

"What about Iphimedia? What happened to her?"

"Iphimedia was punished—first by Poseidon, and later by Hecate, who found out she'd stolen her spell book to cast the magic on Poseidon in the first place."

"Where is she now?" I asked.

"Some say she was locked in Tartarus after the Aloadae attacked the summit, and others say she's imprisoned as Hecate's servant in the Underworld."

"Wait," I said, processing her words. "This wasn't the first time they've attacked Olympus? I mean, the first time they've succeeded at attacking Olympus?"

"They tried but barely made it past the gates. Poseidon took them in for their first few years of life but soon realized they were not like the other Olympians. Whatever spell Iphimedia cast had imbued them not only with the blood of the giants, but also with an unknown dark power."

"How?"

"No one knows. And honestly, if you're asking me, I think the Fates have a sick sense of humor and thought it would be amusing if Zeus's greatest weapon became his greatest downfall."

It took me a moment to understand what she meant, but then the pieces fell together. The giants had helped Zeus rise to power, and they would also be what made him fall from power.

"But the Fates sided with Zeus. Why would they turn on him?"

"The Fates side with no one."

"Not even their mother?" I asked. If anybody could sway them, maybe it was Nyx herself. I remembered Artemis saying their powers resembled those of the Primes.

Persephone's face paled. "Their *mother* is not someone we should ever want to or try to understand. To do so could mean a worse fate than Tartarus itself," she warned, staring off into the distance, toward the front door, as if Nyx would walk through it at any second.

Changing the subject, I asked one final question. "Why do you think the Aloadae have returned now?"

"If I had to guess, I'd say they've come back to finish what they started. To either rule or ruin Olympus."

A shiver ran through my body at the thought of my home, the only place I'd ever known, being destroyed.

CHAPTER 27

THE letter from Zeus came early the next morning, summoning me to the court. By the time I'd made it there, the High Olympians were just exiting the lower level.

Walking up the steps, I passed by Dionysus, who smiled kindly at me, and Aphrodite, who looked me up and down, huffing as she leaned into Dionysus and whispered something that made him laugh. They cast one final look in my direction and descended the stairs.

Taking a deep breath, I gathered the bottom of my deep purple peplos and climbed the remaining steps.

"Ah, Pandora," Athena said, coming over to meet me at the entrance to the court, which had already been repaired and now looked as though the attack had never even happened. "Zeus is waiting for you on the court level. Follow me."

I followed her to the center of the room, where she twirled her wrist. The floor shook as the area we stood on broke away in a clean circle, lifting us all the way to the glass ceiling that acted as a second floor. Athena closed her fist before opening it wide, and the glass above our heads shimmered as we passed through it like it was nothing at all.

She stepped off the platform, turning to face me on the glass floor, which was solid beneath her feet. "Step off."

Knowing the High Olympians did this nearly every day, and that she was standing on solid glass currently, I had no reason not to trust her. I stepped off the platform and onto the glass beside her, feeling it vibrate slightly as the platform descended. My legs went weak at the extreme height, and an uneasy feeling overcame me.

"About time," Zeus said from behind me.

"Yes. I apologize. I got ready and came up here as fast as I could at your notice," I said, turning to find him glaring at me with one eyebrow raised. He was sitting tall on his oak throne.

"My notice was plenty," he said, never breaking eye contact.

"You're right. My apologies." I didn't want to argue with Zeus when he was already on edge.

"I summoned you here because things have begun to escalate in recent days. Now more than ever, it is imperative that you win Prometheus's heart and ensure he stays loyal. I'm sure I don't need to remind you of the consequences you'll face if you fail," he said, watching me closely.

"I understand. I will not fail you, Zeu—" I started.

"You say you will not fail me, but have you even spoken to him yet?" Zeus asked, raising his eyebrow again.

"Well, I haven't spoken to him yet, but—"

"There is no 'but,' Pandora. You had a chance to speak with him before the attack at the celebration, but instead, you spoke to his brother, and he came and spoke to me instead of you," Zeus said, standing up off his throne and walking over to me, stopping only when he was looming over me.

"It's not what you th—"

"It is exactly what I think. I'm tired of excuses. You will win Prometheus over, or else you are gone. I will not have such a waste of space within the walls of Olympus."

Tears welled in my eyes at his words. I couldn't meet his stare, and I had no words to reply—but, thankfully, I didn't need any, because Athena spoke up from behind me.

"Father, do not let your anger about the unease of the realm fall onto Pandora. She has only just had the opportunity to begin fulfilling her duty, and although she has not yet spoken to Prometheus, she has the eye of Epimetheus, and you know how those brothers can be when one has something the other wants."

Her words settled me enough to finally look up at Zeus. To my relief, he seemed to be settled by them as well, because his anger was fading, and a smug smile split his face.

"My wise daughter," he said, walking over to her and cupping her cheek. "You are once again right. How happy I am to always have you by my side."

"Always, Father," Athena replied, smiling up at him.

Zeus walked back over to stand in front of me, his proximity commanding my attention. "Athena is correct, but I don't want to hear of you spending any more time with Epimetheus that could have been spent with the real goal. Do you understand me?" Zeus asked, his voice booming with authority.

"I won't fail," I replied, holding my chin high, wanting to prove to him I could do it, much as I feared I couldn't.

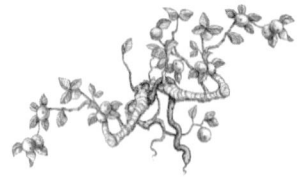

I PULLED ON A sage-green satin tunic with small chamomile flowers embroidered into it and quickly tied it at my waist with a gold-threaded rope, pushing the sleeves down slightly to expose my shoulders, before twisting my hair into a knot at the back of my head, which I fastened with two gold pins.

I looked in the mirror at the familiar stranger staring back at me. It wasn't that I looked any different physically, but the fear of failure was painted all over my face.

A couple of loose curls fell around my face, and I tucked one behind my ear as I smiled to myself, silently repeating, *You are the goddess of mortal women. You can do this.*

Taking a deep breath, I looked myself over one more time before heading out the door.

The guest cabin the Titan brothers were staying in was the farthest from Lower Olympus, just at the edge of a beautiful grass meadow. It was one of the closest to the sea and the place where I'd first met Epimetheus—Siren's Cove.

Knocking on the wood door of the cabin, I focused on keeping my breathing even and wiped my clammy palms on the fabric at my hip, hoping I could camouflage the panic rising to the surface.

The door swung open, revealing a very tall, very handsome Titan.

Prometheus looked a lot like his twin, except where Epimetheus embodied wild, untamed power, Prometheus exuded a refined intelligence, similar to Athena.

I only hoped he'd be more entertaining company than her.

"Pandora," he said as if he'd expected to find me when he opened the door. He wasn't shocked by my presence in the slightest.

"Hello," I said, wishing I could say more, but I was suddenly at a loss for words.

"Can I help you?" he asked, raising his perfectly full chestnut eyebrows.

Primes, I hope so.

"I wanted to invite you to the festival this afternoon," I said, twisting the end of the gold rope at my waist between my fingertips before adding, "If you're not busy. I know it's late notice."

"A festival?" he asked, seeming curious.

"Yes. I'm not sure if they had them when you were here last, but every week, the cretes in Lower Olympus hold a festival along the river, to the west of the town center." I hated using the derogatory term, but I knew it was the Titans who'd given them the name.

"Will the High Olympians be there?"

"Not normally," I replied, wondering why he'd care even if they were.

"All right. Are drachmas still the currency in this realm?" He headed further into the cabin, toward a dresser on the back wall.

"Yes, but some vendors will make trades as well."

He nodded and picked up a leather pouch that jingled with the sound of coins. Then he returned, stepping out onto the dirt path before closing their front door and saying, "Lead the way."

We walked in silence to the festival grounds, only speaking when he asked about the buildings that separated the guest cabins from Lower Olympus.

"That is housing for the cretes who reside in Olympus. They're separated into species, and each housing unit is close to that species' home." I pointed to the housing unit closest to the river. "See that one? That's the naiads' housing, and it's built right into the widest and deepest part of the river, which they have complete access to whenever they need."

I expected him to ask more questions, but he just gave a grunt and continued walking in silence until we made it to the festival grounds, where he stopped in his tracks, staring at everything around him.

"It's beautiful, isn't it?" I said, smiling as I watched dozens of vendors laughing and bartering. Young satyrs and centaurs ran around the center of the grounds, kicking what they called a ball, made from fabric scraps tied together and soaked in a sap that hardened, so it was strong and waterproof.

"Yes," he said, following me as I led the way to one of the first stalls.

"Did they have these when you were here last?" I asked, curious.

"No. Nothing like this."

Two Meliae nymphs, one older and one barely out of her teen years, were selling jars of honey they'd collected from the bees that lived around—and even sometimes within—the ash trees, and some bark from the tree itself.

"Hello. May I interest you in some honey or ash bark? Both provide wonderful benefits to health, vitality, and even beauty. Though you seem to have more than enough beauty already," the older Meliae nymph said. Her deep violet eyes didn't have the same golden center as Acacia or the younger nymph working with her, which told me she didn't deal with the honey, only the trees.

Clio had once told me the Meliae were related to the sacred mountain nymphs, oreads, who lived within the sacred ash forests deep in the mountains. They were the guardians of the trees' healing powers, while the Meliae had the power to tame the bees that swarmed the trees' leaking sap. They could even pull the sap from the trees without harming them. The sap, called honey, was similar to the nectar the gods used, but it didn't have the immortal healing powers and simply boosted the body's natural abilities.

"I'll take one of each, please," I said, pulling out my pouch of drachmas as she passed the jar of honey and a small bunch of ash bark, tied with a ribbon, over to me.

I reached my hand out to pay her, but a large tan hand stopped me.

"How much?" Prometheus asked.

"That will be twenty drachmas," the nymph said, suddenly uneasy as she took in the Titan standing before her.

Prometheus pulled out a small handful of drachmas and dropped them into the Meliae's hand. She gasped the same as I

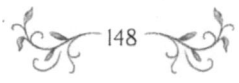

did. The handful of drachmas was well over her price, but when she started to hand some back to him, Prometheus stopped her.

"Keep it," he said, collecting my honey and my bark before turning and walking into the next booth, leaving me standing there in shock.

The nymph and I looked at each other for a few more seconds before I gave her a quick thanks and ran over to join Prometheus, who was already pulling his pouch of drachmas out again.

"Whoa, you might want to slow down. We still have a good amount of the festival left to get through," I said, grabbing his arm and pulling him away from the booth selling dried leaves to make teas and spices. "Why don't we go sit for a moment?" I offered, leading him over to one of the marble park benches along the river's edge.

"I love this spot," I said almost to myself as I watched the children playing while taking in the sound of running water flowing across the river rocks behind me.

"It is nice, as far as Olympus goes," Prometheus said, looking around at everything and everyone except for me, as if he were purposely avoiding eye contact.

I shifted toward him. "Wasn't this your home once too?"

"No. It was not," he said bluntly.

"What's so bad about it? When I look around, all I see are Olympians making a life for themselves. Happy and safe," I said, a defensive edge to my voice.

"*They* are," he said as if he meant it as an insult.

I picked at the fraying edge of my gold belt, biting my lip, until I finally quelled my anger enough to meet his eye. "And you think that is a bad thing?"

"Only for those who aren't considered Olympians," he said, staring off into the distance at something that had captured his attention.

I followed his gaze, but I couldn't see anything from this distance except the fuzzy outlines of bodies walking around.

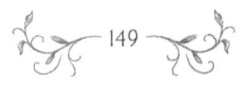

"Here—buy whatever catches your eye. I'll be back in a moment," he said, dropping the pouch of drachmas on the bench between us before standing up and walking over to the area he'd just been staring at.

He disappeared from my sight into the ever-growing crowd of people.

I walked around the vendor booths for almost an hour, buying things I needed for my cottage here and there, even grabbing a slice of bread with goat's cheese and apricot to snack on while I waited, but Prometheus never returned.

Finally, having had enough of waiting around, I decided to grab my things and head back to my cottage, figuring the Titan had no plans to return anytime soon, if at all.

CHAPTER 28

A KNOCK on my cottage door startled me as I worked over the running tap water, rinsing the residue of my meal off the cast-iron pan. I expected to find Persephone or even Hermes waiting at my door, but when I opened it, Prometheus was standing on the other side.

"Hello, Pandora."

"Prometheus," I said, crossing my arms and looking up at the tall Titan in front of me. "I didn't think I'd be seeing you again after you disappeared at the festival."

"Yes. I'm here to apologize for that."

"All right. I'm listening."

"I'm sorry for leaving you at the festival. It was very inconsiderate of me to do so, and I will refrain from doing it again," he said, only serving to irritate me as he avoided telling me why he'd done it.

"What was so important that you needed to run off and couldn't at least return to tell me you had to leave?" I asked, raising my brows at him, daring him to tell me the truth.

"Nothing important, but nothing I could avoid," he answered, shifting on his feet as if he were uncomfortable. Anyone would think he was on trial with the way he was acting.

I sighed, closing my eyes so he wouldn't see them roll. "I accept your apology."

Prometheus nodded, staying silent, leaving me to once again keep the conversation alive.

"Listen, I know things between us didn't get off to the best start . . ." I paused. "But maybe we can start over. Are you busy today? Should we maybe try again?" I asked, looking up at him through my thick lashes sweetly, just as Aphrodite had taught me in our "Basics of Seduction" training.

"No," he replied, staring down at me.

"No, you're not busy, or no, you don't want to try again?" I asked.

"No, I'm not busy today. Tonight, I do have a prior engagement I must be in attendance for though." He didn't bother to elaborate on what that might be, which made my curiosity soar.

Maybe this Titan is interesting after all . . .

"Great! How about a walk around Olympus? It's a beautiful day out, and I'd love to hear how things have changed since you were last here." I smiled up at him, praying to the Primes he'd say yes.

"I would enjoy that." Prometheus finally cracked a smile, stepping outside to wait for me as I ran to grab a wrap in case it got cooler, since I was wearing a lighter tunic than normal.

"Lead the way," he said when I returned, extending his arm out for me to walk ahead of him.

We walked the coastline, past Siren's Cove, following the eastern wall of Olympus north.

"Well, is everything as you remembered it?" I asked, breaking the silence that was starting to become deafening. I often found peace in silence, but that wasn't the case yet with Prometheus. Instead, I felt a little uneasy. Probably my nerves over the situation overwhelming me.

"Close enough. Though I don't remember the walls being so fortified," he said, taking an interest in the eastern guard tower.

"Athena says it's better to be overprepared than under-prepared."

"Are all the towers like this?" he asked, examining the tower with intense interest.

"What do you mean?"

"Are they all this protected?"

"Well, yes. I assume that's the reason for calling it a guard tower, because it's guarded," I joked, smiling at him.

He didn't laugh.

"I am aware," he said, still staring up at it.

Way to go, Pandora. He's more interested in the tower than you. I seethed at myself, wishing there was some way I could loosen him up.

"Is there anything like this in the Realm of Man?" I asked.

"Somewhat. The materials used are different, and it is not as clean-cut, but they have figured out how to build defenses against all sorts of things."

"Like what? What would mankind have to defend themselves against?" I asked, genuinely curious.

"Animals, the elements, and on occasion, each other," Prometheus said, looking over at me.

"Man attacking man I can understand, but animals and the elements? What threat could they pose, with Epimetheus ruling over animals and the elements being evidence of the Primes or gods around them? Wouldn't those things make them feel closer to the gods? Why wouldn't they want to feel that?" I asked, confused at how this Realm of Man worked and eager to know more about it.

"Epimetheus does not allow animals without the ability to take flight or fight to be slaughtered. Many of the predatory species can kill dozens of humans alone or in pairs, so humans have adapted. As for the weather, the gods and the Primes on Earth do not care about the human lives they take. To them, they are expendable, as easy to kill as they are to create."

"So they fear the gods and the Primes?" I asked, not able to envision a world where the gods were feared or even hated instead of being worshipped.

"Yes. My brother and I gave them comfort by providing them with the ability to fight, flourish, and fend for themselves, granting them the opportunity to be the rulers of their own destiny." Prometheus's lips curled into a proud smirk that made him look even more handsome than normal.

I couldn't help but envy the opportunity the Titan twins had given to man, since I couldn't imagine having control of my destiny—not when I was created with a purpose in mind and seen as useless unless it was fulfilled.

"I have an idea," I said, grabbing his arm excitedly and squeezing the lean bicep hidden under the sleeve of his tunic. "How about we cut across the meadow over to Dionysus's vineyards on the way to Lower Olympus? I'm not sure about you, but I could use a snack." At this, my stomach growled.

He glanced at me and then looked further north. I followed his eyes to the next guard tower. What was it with him and these towers?

I opened my mouth to ask why he was so interested in them, but he surprised me by saying, "That sounds wonderful."

I grinned up at him, and he smiled back, but it never quite reached his eyes.

When we arrived at the vineyard, I pulled a couple bunches of grapes before leading him to the north side, where Dionysus had built a sitting area in an open colonnade that had grapevines crawling up each column, encircling the top and growing together to make a canopy over the marble tables. I pulled Prometheus over to one of the tables, motioning for him to sit before setting the grapes down beside him.

"I'll be right back."

There were a few fountains on Dionysus's land that were normally filled with wine, and the Primes must have been on my

side today, because I found two chalices and a fountain filled to the brim with red wine.

Filling the chalices, I walked as quickly as I could without spilling any, back to Prometheus, who was staring out at the land with a dazed look on his face.

"This is one thing I'm sure you missed during your time on Earth," I said, smiling as I placed the chalice in front of him.

"You would be correct." He smiled too as he held the chalice, twirling the burgundy liquid until it just touched the rim before bringing it up to his nose to inhale. He eventually took a long pull from the glass and sighed.

I pulled a couple of grapes off the stem and popped them into my mouth, savoring the sweetness as they burst.

"Do you mind?" Prometheus asked, motioning to the grapes.

"Not at all," I said, pushing them closer to him.

I watched as he popped the deep purple morsel of fruit into his mouth, and his smile grew even more.

"I can see why your face lit up like the sun. These are better than I expected." He grabbed another grape off the stem to pop into his mouth.

It took me a moment to realize I was staring, and I cleared my throat. "These are sweeter than most. I often grab some to take home so I can have them with fresh goat's cheese from the weekly festival."

"You come here often then?" he asked, leaning back in his seat as he sipped more wine.

"Not as much as I would like."

"Why not?"

"Normally, I'm too busy with my . . ." I stopped, thinking back to my lessons. Probably best not to mention those.

"Too busy with what?" he asked, suddenly giving me his full attention, as if he could sense I was hiding something.

"Oh, you know, life," I said, shrugging my shoulders and fumbling for a grape. I tried my hardest to seem relaxed even though every fiber of my being was panicking.

"Life?" he asked. "And what is life like for a mortal in Olympus?"

"Wonderful."

"Hmm." He rubbed his chin. "Have you ever been outside Olympus?"

"No," I said, confused by his question. "Why would I ever want to leave Olympus?"

"Why not?"

"Because, as I told your brother, I'm safer in Olympus than anywhere else."

"And why is that?" Prometheus asked, not showing any sign of surprise that I'd had a similar discussion with his brother.

"Considering I'm the only one of my kind, I'd rather be in a place where I know I'm loved and protected than trapped in the unknown." I didn't want to elaborate any further.

"Do you know how mankind doesn't just survive but thrives on Earth?" Prometheus asked, not breaking eye contact.

I shook my head. "No."

"Mankind have made it their life's mission to know the unknown. They take risks every day in their lives, but through trial and error, they learn how to overcome the threats facing them. Without facing the unknown, they would have died off decades ago."

I considered what he was saying for a moment and had to bite my tongue to keep from asking what I really wanted to ask: *How many deaths did it take to know the unknown? Hundreds? Thousands?*

"Lucky for man, they have you to guide them," I said, smiling over at the Titan.

Prometheus stared at me, clearing his throat before he spoke. "Indeed. The sun is beginning to set—shall we head through Lower Olympus and get you home?"

"If you're ready," I replied, secretly hoping he'd say no. I was shocked at how much I'd come to enjoy my time with him.

"I am," he said, making my hopes fall as he extended his hand to me.

I grabbed it, letting him help me off the seat.

We walked mostly in silence again, but as we crossed the bridge, I stopped.

"I hope I didn't bore you too much today."

"Not at all. In fact, I found your company surprisingly enjoyable," Prometheus said.

"You must not have ever had great company if you can call that enjoyable," I joked, smiling up into his deep brown eyes.

"You have met my brother, yes?" He smiled back, sarcasm shining through his eyes. He seemed much more relaxed than he had been earlier in the day.

"My deepest apologies. Well, now you know where I live if you ever need someone to hold a decent, somewhat enjoyable conversation with."

"I do indeed." He stared down into my eyes. "Would you like to do this again, maybe tomorrow?"

"Sure . . . I mean, yes. Absolutely," I replied, smiling even wider than before and surprising myself at how much excitement I had for what tomorrow would bring.

CHAPTER 29

PROMETHEUS showed up on my doorstep the next morning just as he'd said he would, and I couldn't help but smile from ear to ear.

"Good morning, Pandora."

"Good morning, Prometheus. It's nice to see you, but I didn't think you'd be here so early." I stifled the yawn that tried to escape.

"I apologize. I was eager to see you again and thought we could go on a morning stroll through Lower Olympus." Prometheus rubbed the back of his neck.

"That sounds lovely. Let me just go get ready really quick. You can come in and wait on the couch if you'd like." I opened the door wider, stepping to the side and motioning toward it.

"Thank you." Stepping inside, he smiled at me. "Take your time."

I dressed quickly, wearing a forest-green peplos with golden vines embroidered into the thick fabric, and left my hair down, pulling one side back with a small clip.

"I'm ready," I announced, meeting Prometheus at the bottom of the stairs, where he grabbed my hand, and we headed out the door to Lower Olympus.

The plateia was quiet this early in the morning, and Hestia's Hearth was just opening their doors for the day.

"Do you mind if we stop for something to eat? I'm pretty hungry first thing in the morning," I said sheepishly, the smell of warm baked goods carrying over to me on the cool breeze, making my mouth water.

Prometheus laughed. "Of course."

We both ordered a lavender honey cake and a glass of milk, which Prometheus was pleasantly surprised with. His eyes grew wide and he groaned as he savored each bite, seeming to enjoy each one more than the last, until he was done.

I couldn't help but smile at how nice the morning had been and felt it growing as I watched the plateia start to get busy, when a flash of copper caught my attention.

I did a double-take, squinting to see the figure better, not sure if I was imagining things—but then she turned around. It was the same woman I'd seen whispering with the shadow figure.

"It's her," I accidentally said out loud, not able to peel my eyes off her.

"Who?" Prometheus asked from beside me.

"That girl with the copper hair. I saw her with . . ." I started, but then I stopped, thinking better of it, not wanting to risk him thinking I was crazy or dramatic. I glanced over at him quickly before pointing to the area I'd noticed her. "She was up to some-thing . . . something bad." But when I turned back, she was gone.

"I don't see any females with copper hair." He furrowed his brow as he scanned the plateia before turning back to me, confused.

"Never mind. I must have just been mistaken," I said, shak-ing my head, pinching at the space between my eyebrows and laughing it off.

I opened my mouth to speak, but he beat me to it.

"Yes, surely, that must have been it," Prometheus agreed, looking back to the spot where the girl had been and giving it a

good once-over before turning back to me. "I understand Zeus has asked you to show me and my brother around Olympus," he said, at which I nodded, swallowing a gulp of milk. "Well, there is one place I've missed dearly, and I was hoping you could take me to see it during my stay."

"Of course. Where would you like to go?" I asked, smiling, my excitement rising at the thought of him initiating the plan for the day.

"The Library of Olympus."

"Oh . . . well, actually . . . normally, guests are forbidden, but I guess you are different than most guests. As long as Clio is there, I don't see why I can't take you." I thought it over, not seeing a reason why he couldn't see the library. I realized no one had mentioned *anywhere* off-limits for our tour. "Shall we head up to the summit then?"

"We need to stop and grab my brother first. He'd be furious if I went without him."

"Oh . . . all right." My excitement plummeted at the idea of Epimetheus getting in the way of my time with Prometheus, while at the same time, my heart raced at the thought of seeing him again.

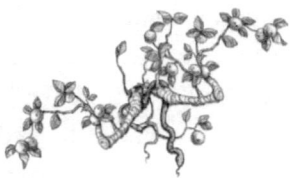

THE THREE OF us walked to the summit, Epimetheus mumbling about how he could have flown up and met us, not suffered through the hike too. We descended into the tunnels underneath the court, where I led them through the twists and turns one needed to know in order to find the library, before we arrived at the two gilded doors.

Thankfully, the entrance was unlocked, which meant Clio was working today.

Clio watched over the library and ran it during certain hours of the day for lower-level gods and goddesses, as well as cretes. The High Olympians had access to it whenever they needed.

"Pandora? What a surprise," Clio said, taking in the two Titans standing beside me. "And you brought guests."

"Yes. I hope that's all right. I was showing Prometheus around Olympus, and he mentioned he wished to see the library before he left." I gestured to Prometheus, who was already scanning the shelves nearby.

"Is that so . . .?" She looked over at the brothers suspiciously, her gaze landing on Epimetheus, who was standing uncomfortably close. Clio quirked her brow up at him.

"Oh, Prometheus didn't want to leave him at home," I said, motioning to Epimetheus. "He insisted we bring him with us."

Epimetheus turned toward me, his brows shooting up, hidden beneath his dark curls.

Clio laughed. "Come find me at my desk if there's anything I can help you with." Walking away, she disappeared within the shelves.

I looked up at Epimetheus and shrugged, not saying anything as I walked away from him and over to Prometheus. He had his arms full of books and was still pulling more off the shelves.

"Wow . . ." I said, taking in the number and size of them. "Looks like you found some books of interest. Is there anything you were looking for in particular?" I asked, trying to glance at some of the covers in his arms.

He caught me looking and turned away before I could see. "Nothing in particular. Just a little bit of everything. You can go take a look around yourself, if you'd like, while I finish up here," he said kindly, but I read between the lines. He wanted to be alone, and I was interrupting him.

"Oh . . . I guess I can go look around," I said, scanning the rows of shelving like I wasn't sure where to go or what to do, since he'd invited me here but now wanted me out of his space.

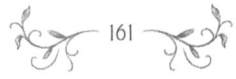

Thankfully, I'd been wanting to visit the library anyway to find some books on shadow powers.

I walked around, not having any luck finding the section they must have been hiding in on my own, and went to find Clio instead. She was much easier to find.

"Ah, Pandora. Did you need help finding something?" she asked, looking up from her book.

"Actually, yes. I was looking for books on shadows or shadow beings."

She tilted her head. "Why would you be interested in books like that, my dear?"

"No reason. Just something I heard that got me curious. You know how incessant my curiosity can be." I laughed, hoping she wouldn't dig any further into why I wanted them.

Normally, I would have told someone by now, but with the Aloadaes' attack, it didn't feel right to talk about what I'd seen, for fear someone would try to connect me to the Aloadae or the rebellion.

Thankfully, Clio asked no more questions, walking me over to a set of shelves in the far back corner of the library, where she pointed out a couple different books that might include what I was looking for and left me alone. I read through half a dozen of them before I found anything close to what I was looking for.

About three quarters of the way through a book titled "Ancient Aether," I found a section about shadows—specifically, how they came from the Primes Nyx and Erebus. I skimmed through the section describing how, as a result of creating children, Nyx and Erebus's shadows had spread throughout the universe, embodying the dark unruliness of their masters— meaning any offspring they had could have the ability to wield power over the shadows and possibly even more of their dark powers. It was thought the more corrupted their soul, the more power the shadows gave them.

Giving up on my search after finding nothing else other than that small passage of text, I headed back to Prometheus, who was leaning over the table, his attention lost in the pages beneath his nose.

"Are you about ready?" I asked, sitting down at the table across from him and taking the opportunity, in his distraction, to look at the titles of the books he'd been reading. "Olympian Customs," "Runes & Ruins," "Olympian Court Proceedings," and "Amplifiers, Dampeners, Containments & Power Transfers." It seemed like an odd group of books. Although, considering what I knew about Prometheus, he did seem abnormally curious and had a fair amount of knowledge on . . . well, just about everything, which I guess we had in common.

Reluctantly pulling his eyes away from the book, he looked over at me. "Yes. Let me put these away," he said, gathering up the pile.

"Where did Epimetheus go?" I asked, wondering if I should track him down before we left.

"He left already." Prometheus shrugged, carrying the books off in Clio's direction.

We walked back to my cottage, laughing and talking about our mutual love of books and history.

"Would you like to come in?" I asked, holding my front door open for him.

"Oh, I can't stay. I have a meeting soon. But I wondered if you'd like to meet me later this afternoon for some lunch on the beach. I was hoping to try the goat's cheese combination you mentioned yesterday. I'll bring the grapes." He looked at me expectantly.

"Of course. That sounds lovely. Do I need to bring anything else?" I asked.

"No. Just the goat's cheese," he said, smiling before looking over to where Apollo was peeking over the horizon. "I apologize, but I must be leaving now in order to make it across Lower Olympus."

"That's all right. I'll see you this afternoon," I replied, smiling, surprised at how much I was looking forward to spending time with him.

"I'm looking forward to it," Prometheus said, grinning at me before turning to leave.

Maybe I had a chance at winning his heart after all, and who knew—maybe he could win mine too.

CHAPTER 30

I SAT on the beach from midday until the sun dipped below the treetops of the wildlands outside the wall. With the goat's cheese nearly gone and the one remaining apricot I'd brought for Prometheus staring me in the face, I picked up the orange-skinned fruit and threw it as hard as possible into the Sea of Poseidon, watching as it tumbled through the surf and disappeared into the ocean's abyss. Gathering the wooden cutting board, the blunt-edged knife, the cotton blanket, and some cotton cloths I'd brought with me, I wiped the sand from my tunic and headed toward the apple orchard, needing some reprieve from Prometheus standing me up.

After the wonderful time we'd had earlier, I was surprised at how hurt I felt by his failure to show up again, but I couldn't help it. I was so invested in getting him to fall for me that I'd forgotten his emotions weren't the only ones being influenced. Every time I was with him, I learned more and more about the Titan Zeus had made me for, excited to see what we could—and would—grow into.

Spreading my blanket out under one of the apple trees, I grabbed a couple of apples to snack on while I sketched.

I chewed on an oversized chunk of apple, its edges pressing into the side of my cheek, as I rubbed my finger into the charcoal to shade and smudge dark clouds into the sketch I'd been working on for the past week. It depicted the forest outside the walls on a rare day when one of the unspoken gods had wandered too close, bringing with him a ferocious storm that nearly swallowed Olympus whole, with winds strong enough to rip entire orchards from the ground.

I'd swallowed the apple piece and was ripping off another chunk, picking up my charcoal to add a few more details, when, suddenly, the hairs on the back of my neck rose in alarm at the feeling I was being watched.

Looking around through the rows of apple trees, I tried to find whoever—or whatever—it was that was spying on me. I wondered if maybe Prometheus had seen me leaving the beach and followed me here, but that hope quickly dissipated as a tiny hiss sounded from my left, pulling my gaze to a tree a few feet away.

I squinted into the branches, but I was too far away to make out anything except the foliage moving every couple of seconds. As I took a few steps forward, my eyes caught on a large shape moving through the branches. It made me jump back so fast I stumbled over a root and fell to the ground, just as an enormous python slithered through the tree, making the branches creak and the leaves tremble with its weight.

I scrambled backward on the ground, trying to get to my feet, while my heart did somersaults as the massive snake seemed to grow in size even as I put distance between us, until it slithered out along an exposed branch, curling its tail around it and letting its body hang to the ground.

I watched the creature in front of me, trying to fight the urge to run. Just as I was about to bolt, the snake's reptilian body shifted, morphing into none other than Epimetheus. He swung from the branch with knees bent, wearing clothing on his bottom

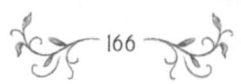

half made from a fabric that looked an awful lot like snakeskin mixed with leather. It reached from his waist down to his knees, leaving his chest completely bare.

Epimetheus reached his muscular arms up to the branch, gripping it in his hands, and tucked his legs. Then he flipped over, landing on the ground with deadly accuracy. He pulled down a perfectly ripe red apple and bit into it, his eyes not leaving my face as the juices ran down the side of his mouth. His eyes taunted me to look away first, as if he were trying to make me uncomfortable with his presence and was curious to see what my reaction would be.

"What are you drawing?" he asked nonchalantly, taking another bite out of his apple. Plucking two more apples from the tree, he walked over and dropped down onto the blanket covering the ground beside me.

"I think the better question is, what are you doing?" I said, pulling the paper to my chest, not wanting him to see. "Did you come to apologize on behalf of your brother?" I folded the paper and shoved it back into my pouch with the charcoal. The sketches were for my eyes, and my eyes only.

"And why would I be doing that?" Epimetheus asked, stoking my fury as he took another bite from his apple.

"Because he once again left me waiting for him like a fool. Is that how you Titans work? You make plans and then don't even have the decency to cancel or say you must leave? You get a girl's hopes up only to let them crash and burn when you never show up," I said, staring him down.

Epimetheus stared back, brows pulled together as if he were at a loss for words, but he finally cleared his throat and spoke. "I cannot speak for the actions of my brother, but I assure you, it was not with malicious intent. Prometheus would never hurt anyone or anything without due cause."

Epimetheus was trying to assure me, but the confused look on his face only made me worry more.

"He may not have intended to, but I can assure you, his intent does not need to be malicious in order for him to still cause harm." Anger seeped into my words. As cautious as I was around Prometheus, I couldn't seem to keep up the act of the perfect, levelheaded woman around his brother.

"Prometheus may be the one with the power of forethought, but he does have a tendency to get absorbed in his duties more than most."

I scoffed. "So is that why you're here instead of him—because his duties are more important than yours?" I asked, crossing my arms defiantly and refusing to break eye contact as I waited for an answer that didn't sound like an excuse.

"As surprising as it may be, I am not my brother's servant. He has his duties, and I have mine. Which are equally important," Epimetheus said, finishing the apple off and leaning back to get comfortable beside me on the blanket as if he either didn't care I was angry or was choosing to ignore it.

I turned in my spot on the ground to face him. "Do you plan on staying?" I asked, motioning to his body sprawled out , dwarfing mine.

He shrugged. "As long as you do."

"What's that supposed to mean?"

"Well, considering my brother was supposed to keep you company and failed, I figure I might as well step in. Primes forbid he sullies our family name."

"Your what?" I asked, suddenly curious enough to stay beside him.

"Our family name." He rolled his head in my direction. "It's something mankind started. There are so many now that some have grouped up, calling themselves family, and to show which groups are families, they've given themselves family names."

"That's very progressive of them," I said, shocked. "Did they come up with that themselves?"

"Actually, no. It's something that was first done here in Aether," Epimetheus replied, watching me closely.

"If that's true, then why have I never met a single family in Olympus with a family name?" I asked, raising my brows in challenge.

"Not Olympus. Aether. Many families outside these walls have family names separate from their species or their homeland."

"Why not in Olympus?"

If a time ever came when I could no longer depend on Prometheus being there, I would need all the information I could get in order to survive the wilds of Aether—or worse, possibly Earth—on my own.

"I always figured it would challenge the only true family that matters within these walls. The High Olympians," he said, still holding my gaze.

"If you hate the Olympians so much, why not side with your father and brothers?"

"You know of them?" Epimetheus asked, shocked.

"Only what I've read in books."

"And were those books written by Titans or Olympians?"

"I think you know the answer to that."

"Uh-huh. Well, let me tell you what the Olympian stories miss out." He sat up and leaned against the tree trunk, his legs crossed.

I settled in, waiting for him to elaborate.

"My home on Mount Othrys was not much different than yours. Ruled by the powerful but kept alive by the servants and the cretes who secretly ran everything . . ."

I hung onto his every word, comparing this to what I already knew.

"The High Court was looking to expand its terrain, and my brother, Atlas, provided them with options that could not only increase the Titans' power over Aether, but also, if done correctly, liberate those who lacked the power to liberate themselves."

"The Titans had a court?" I asked, remembering Clio telling me the High Olympians had created the Olympian Court to avoid a fight to rule like the one with the Titans.

"Yes. As did the Primes before them," Epimetheus replied. "Atlas had heard of the mistreatment of the cretes living in Olympus and sought a way to help them."

"If that's true, then why did you and your brothers not side with your family during the war?" I asked.

"I almost did, but Prometheus had other ideas." Epimetheus paused for a moment, "Regardless, Prometheus sided with the Olympians to save his precious mankind and swore to me the only way to save my animals would be if I joined him. So I put my duty before my family and went with him to Olympus."

"What!" I coughed from inhaling the half-chewed chunk of apple, struggling to control myself as the apple fought its way down my throat, nearly choking me.

Epimetheus smacked me on my back, dislodging the apple chunk, which flew abruptly across the blanket. "Are you all right?" he asked, alarmed, his palm still spread across my back as I coughed.

"Did you say 'mankind'?" I coughed out.

"Yes." His brows pulled together in confusion.

"As in, mankind was here in Aether?" I asked. "*Before* they inhabited Earth?"

"Yes. Although not exactly the same, mankind once lived in Aether. Both Othrys and Olympus."

I stared at him. I would have normally said he was lying and just left, but this wasn't the first time there'd been mention of mankind in the Realm of Aether, although it was the first time anyone had bothered to go into detail. Before now, I wasn't sure if those who'd mentioned mankind hadn't just misspoken or, if they were telling the truth, when mankind would have been here. I never suspected it was even before their creation on Earth.

"I figured you would have known that, considering you're mortal," Epimetheus said softly, as if he too were surprised by my revelation.

"I suspected but never knew for sure. What happened to them?"

He opened his mouth to reply, but the crack of a branch in the distance made us both go silent.

"I think I should walk you back home now," Epimetheus insisted, scanning the surrounding orchard, suddenly on high alert.

"You do realize I grew up in these orchards, right? Maybe I should walk you home." I put my hands on my hips and looked up at him.

He turned back toward me, the corner of his mouth lifting. "I do, but I doubt monsters were roaming Olympus back when you were growing up." His grin grew as he moved closer to me.

"The only monster I see out here is you." I suddenly remembered why I shouldn't be anywhere, let alone in the middle of an orchard with him.

Epimetheus leaned in closer and whispered in my ear, "The worst monsters are the ones you never see coming."

The warmth of his breath tickled the hairs on the back of my neck, making me shiver as a cool breeze surrounded me. I couldn't help but inhale his intoxicating scent of sandalwood, leather, and musk, forgetting for a moment there might be someone lurking nearby and I might be in danger.

Then two large, rugged hands grabbed my shoulders, forcing me out of my daze.

Taking a step back and putting some much-needed space between us, I looked up at Epimetheus, trying my very best not to focus on the inky curls dangling over his eyes and the fullness of his lips.

"We should go," he said, his voice a few octaves deeper than it was before.

I nodded, suddenly not wanting to argue about how I could take care of myself. I was more worried about whether I could indeed.

Epimetheus walked me back to my cottage, never letting his guard down. He kept about a foot of distance in between us the whole walk, and by the time we were at my doorstep, he seemed to have finally started to relax a little.

"Thank you for seeing me home safely," I said, turning toward him, with my back to the door.

"I was heading into Lower Olympus anyway." He shrugged.

"Oh, I hope I didn't keep you from anything too important." I avoided his intense gaze.

"You didn't."

"Well, thanks again for the walk home." I moved to leave, but he grabbed my arm, stopping me.

"Wha—?" I started to say before he cut me off.

"Do not mistake Olympus for being today what it was in the past. It is not safe for anyone right now, but especially you." He gave my arm a quick squeeze and then walked away.

CHAPTER 31

I SPENT a couple of days endlessly searching Olympus for Prometheus, having no luck in finding him or his brother.

Plopping onto my couch in utter exhaustion, I couldn't help but think about the Titan brothers and what Epimetheus's ominous warning could've meant. Prometheus hadn't shown up or apologized like he did last time, but I was secretly grateful for that, because as much as I knew I should be daydreaming about falling in love with him, his face wasn't the one I saw.

In every way, Prometheus was the safer, better choice for me—well, if I had a choice in the matter—and safety had always been my number-one priority as the most vulnerable being in this realm. Yet Epimetheus, with his wild, untamed nature, somehow seemed to always be the one ensuring I was safe. I knew I should fear him and what being near him could mean for me, but I couldn't bring myself to feel anything but intrigued by the forbidden Titan.

It was late in the evening when the Zeus's letter arrived. I ran my finger over the lightning-bolt wax seal before ripping it open.

Pandora,

I have received unfortunate news today from my eyes and ears around Olympus. It seems you have been entrapping the wrong Titan once again. I was immensely clear about your duty to Olympus and what would happen if you failed, but worry not: I have decided to grant you mercy and help. Tomorrow morning, at the break of dawn, Hermes will deliver the celebratory news of yours and Prometheus's engagement to all of Olympus. Additionally, to honor your upcoming nuptials, we have planned a feast to commence the month-long events of the Gamelion leading up to the proaulia and, of course, your wedding day.

This is your last chance to succeed in your task, and I will not be so kind as to extend a helping hand again.

— Zeus

Sleep was elusive to me after reading that letter, and for a while, I tossed and turned in my bed, until finally, I gave up, deciding to make a cup of tea and watch the sunrise.

The warmth of the tea calmed my nerves, and I could have passed out in the plush grass of my flower garden, there on the hillside overlooking the sea, if it weren't for the cold breeze and my racing mind. I couldn't decide if I was more upset about being forced into a marriage or that Zeus had such little faith in me that, after just two witness reports, he'd rip away my opportunity to set my destiny in motion.

Time flew by as fast as the birds over the sea, and before I knew it, dawn had arrived, and with it, so had Hermes. I wanted to talk to him, hoping he could cheer me up, but by the time I heard the knock on my door, he was already flying off to the next Olympian to deliver the big announcement.

I jogged over to retrieve the letter and picked it up swiftly, but it felt heavy in my hands, and I couldn't bring myself to open it. Luckily, I didn't have to, because the next second, Persephone was there, standing behind me.

"You're engaged?" she yelled, her normally kind face scrunching up in rage.

"I guess so," I said under my breath, walking into my cottage and holding the door open for her to follow me.

"You don't seem excited about it." She took in my disheveled appearance, and the anger slipped off her face, replaced with worry.

"I didn't know until last night," I said, avoiding her prying eyes as I poured another cup of tea.

"What? Did Prometheus stay the night?" she asked, which nearly made me laugh. She was so far off the mark.

"Hardly. We've never even kissed, let alone spent the night together." I shook my head.

"Well, something had to have happened. He asked you to marry him!" She sounded surprisingly excited.

"He didn't ask me," I sighed. "Zeus informed me we were to be married in a letter."

"Unfortunately, that does sound like something my father would do. I'm sorry he ruined such a special time in your life." She paused, walking over to me and pulling me into a warm hug, which I was desperately in need of. "And to think I came over here furious at you for making me find out in a public announcement."

"I can't blame you. The arranged marriage isn't even the worst of it." I put my head in my hands, wishing I could curl in on myself and disappear

"What do you mean? What else is going on?" Persephone asked, leading me over to the couch to sit down.

"Zeus threatened me with exile if I fail to win Prometheus's heart. I guess this is his way of ensuring I do."

"Primes . . . That man has no boundaries when it comes to what he'll do to stay on top." Persephone shook her head. "As horrible as it is to say, maybe he proposed the marriage to protect you, in his own distorted way."

"Zeus didn't propose the marriage. He commanded it, and he isn't protecting me. When he gave me the ultimatum, he didn't fail to mention that if I couldn't win Prometheus's heart and protection, then there'd be nothing to stop him from stealing me away to Earth to use as he pleased." I cringed at the thought.

"I would never let that happen, Pandy."

"Primes, this is a mess. There's no way Prometheus will grow feelings for me now Zeus has forced his hand."

"That's not true. He just needs to get to know you more, and then he won't be able to resist you." Persephone rubbed circles into my back as I struggled not to have a full breakdown in front of her.

"Doubtful. Much as Zeus claimed to be helping, he knew what he was doing. He's forced Prometheus into this engagement as much as he did me."

"Prometheus doesn't seem so bad though. Maybe you'll grow to love each other over time," Persephone said softly.

"Maybe," I said, hopeful she was right and that this wouldn't sour Prometheus's feelings toward me—if he even had any. Sure, I thought I'd been making progress, even if it were small, but now, I couldn't help but feel like every step forward had taken us ten steps back.

A knock sounded at the door, making me and Persephone jump.

"Are you expecting someone?" Persephone asked, getting up from the table and peeking out through the curtains as another knock sounded.

"Who is it?" I asked, getting up to stand by her and peek out too.

"Speaking of . . . there he is!" Persephone said optimistically, at the same moment as Prometheus's dark eyes met mine.

Walking over to the door, I smoothed down my wild hair, tucking it behind my ears, before opening it.

"Hello," Prometheus said.

"Prometheus."

"I'm sure you know why I've come," he said, making me work to suppress my anger.

"Was it because you invited me for lunch at the beach and never bothered to show, or because Zeus forced us into an engagement?" I asked, harsher than intended.

"Both, I suppose," he said under his breath before speaking up to ask, "May I come in?"

I opened my door, stepping aside so he could walk in. He had to bend slightly to get through the doorframe.

"I want to start off by—"

"I'm going to go now," Persephone said, cutting Prometheus off. "Pandy, you know where to find me if you need me." She walked over and pulled me in for another hug.

"I apologize. I didn't know Pandora had company," Prometheus said to Persephone, but she wasn't having it. Striding right up to him, she poked one of her slender fingers into his chest.

"I'm not the one you need to be apologizing to," she said before brushing past him and walking out. She locked eyes with me right before she closed the door, leaving just us standing in my cottage, both of us staring at each other in awkward silence.

"She's right. I should be apologizing to you," Prometheus said, shifting his weight between his feet as he added, "I've mistreated you not once but twice, and worse, I broke my promise to you by leaving you the second time."

"Then why do it? Or better yet, why even invite me in the first place?" I asked.

"I cannot say, but be assured it was not you who prevented me from coming." Prometheus was clearly hiding something, as he continued to avoid looking me in the eye.

"I am not assured, Prometheus. I can somewhat understand you disappearing after our first time together. I thought maybe you didn't enjoy our time as much as you seemed to or got nervous, maybe even overwhelmed, but not this time," I said, pacing around the room before finally planting myself on the couch. "This time, I was excited. I went into the plateia and bought a cheese knife and some fresh goat's cheese from one of my favorite sellers, went into the orchards to collect a few apricots, and went back to the beach to make a sitting area with the linens, where I waited for you. When a couple of hours had passed and I realized you weren't coming, I was confused and upset with you for putting me through this."

"I know there is no excuse I can give to make up for my actions, but I hope that through our marriage, I can atone," Prometheus said, watching me closely.

"Our marriage? You mean you're okay with Zeus forcing us into this engagement?" I asked, astounded. Maybe he cared for me more than I realized.

"He may have forced my hand, but he is not forcing me to marry you. I've chosen to do that on my own."

"Why?" I asked before I could think better of it.

Prometheus looked at me, his brow furrowed. "I'm not sure I understand what you mean."

"Why do you want to marry me?"

He sat there in silence for a moment, rubbing the back of his neck with his hand. "I have always had an affinity for mortals, and although I have lived among man for the past century, spending time with you has reminded me of what is missing on Earth." He spoke softly, sitting down beside me.

"And what is that?"

"A woman. I have spoken to those closest to you, and each one has assured me you are everything a woman should be— kind, obedient, nurturing, trustworthy, and a beauty to rival the gods. I couldn't imagine a being I'd rather be married to."

Prometheus reached out and grabbed my hand in his. His were lengthier than Epimetheus's and surprisingly cold to the touch. They also had a softness to them, which Epimetheus's did not, as if he'd never done a rough day of work in his life. Something I couldn't relate to.

"Well?" he said, waiting for me to answer.

I felt relief at his heartfelt statement, but all I could think of where his hands and the fact most of what he'd described was not truly me but the mold the High Olympians had shaped me into.

"That is very kind of you," I said, looking away bashfully as I tried to hide the realization I'd come to. Everything Prometheus felt for me was based on a lie. A lie I would never be able to escape.

"It is only the truth," he said, holding my hands in one of his as he reached up with the other to grip my chin. "I will be honored to have you."

I smiled at up at him and said, "Does this also mean you won't leave me again without giving me a reason?"

"Never again," he said, grinning down at me hard enough that I could see the crinkles in the corners of his eyes. For a moment,

I imagined those eyes being amber and felt myself inadvertently leaning in even closer to him.

I tried my hardest to wash Epimetheus's face from my mind and focus on the Titan in front of me, but just as I was about to pull away, the hand that was pinching my chin a moment ago slid to the back of my neck, pulling me in, until his lips met mine.

I'd never kissed anyone before, as no Olympian had ever been bold enough to tempt Zeus's rage, but I'd always imagined it being full of passion and energy. Kissing Prometheus was tender and slow, but something about the way he paused and his hand tightened on my neck made me think he was holding back.

Before I knew it, the kiss was over, and I was trying to catch my breath.

"That was . . ." Prometheus began through panting breaths before laughing to himself. "I don't remember it being like that. That was . . ." He shook his head, smiling down at me, and I smiled back up at him as if the kiss had been as grand as he seemed to think it was.

"Wonderful?" I offered.

"Yes," he agreed, pulling away and rubbing the back of his neck, which I was beginning to think meant he was uncomfortable.

"It was wonderful for me as well," I lied, wanting to see that smile grace his face again. To my luck, it did. "So, what should we do now that we're officially engaged?"

"Get married and start our lives together on Earth," Prometheus said, smiling from ear to ear.

I smiled back, but I couldn't help but wonder if maybe I'd live a happier life if I gave up and just let Zeus exile me into the wilds of Aether. At least then I wouldn't be committing myself to a life of lies in a world away from everyone I knew and loved . . .

Now I had the eye of Prometheus, I doubted he'd ever let me stay.

CHAPTER 32

THE remaining days before the feast were a blur. Prometheus came to see me every day. Sometimes, we explored Olympus, while other times, we just stayed in my cottage talking and taking the time to get to know each other.

He asked me what it was like growing up, and I told him a version of the truth. When I asked him about his childhood, I was met with only one-word answers or long descriptions that would divert from my question. In fact, Prometheus left almost all the questions I asked unanswered.

Although he played his cards close to his chest when it came to his past, and although I hadn't been given much of a choice regarding this marriage, I was finding more and more that I enjoyed the time I spent with him. We grew closer with every moment we spent together.

By the day of the feast, I was beginning to accept my fate as the wife of Prometheus and found myself thankful my attempt to run away hadn't succeeded.

Persephone stayed the night before my engagement feast, and although she never directly said it, I could tell she was missing Hades.

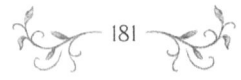

"Are you worried about him? I mean, with Zeus keeping him prisoner and whatnot," I asked as she walked around my room gathering things to help me get ready for the night. I watched for her reaction, knowing even if she didn't want to tell me something, her face always gave away what her mouth would not.

To my surprise, she cracked a smile and shrugged. "I am going to miss him, sure, but, honestly, I'm more worried about Zeus than Hades. I don't think Zeus realizes the enemy he's making. The only reason Hades hasn't attacked Zeus is because he has more control than his megalomaniac of a brother. But you can only push someone so far before they crack, and Zeus is on thin ice threatening Hecate. The only one I think Hades would blow up over is me, which is why we keep our little rendezvous private. You can't be someone's weakness if no one else knows that weakness exists."

Laughing at her, I picked up the wooden comb and started to work on taming my tangled hair, which had formed into a hideous mess overnight, much worse than the bird's nest I normally woke up with.

Sighing as my comb got stuck in my hair again, I tried to maneuver it past the knot, which wouldn't budge more than an inch. I set the comb down and reached for the bottle of oil I used to moisturize my skin, thinking maybe it could help to loosen the knotted nest, which had begun to give me a headache as I'd spent so much time trying to detangle it.

Persephone watched me in amusement before finally offering to help. She carried the bottle of oil as she led me to the bathing room at the back of the cottage. Filling the copper tub with warm water, she poured in a mixture of sweet, floral-smelling oils and helped me to step over the edge of the bath.

"Primes, this is nice . . ." I breathed out as my body settled into the silky warmth of the water.

"For you and me both. You were beginning to smell like a one of Hades' hellhounds." She laughed, scrunching up her nose

in mock disgust. "You didn't think I was helping you bathe out of the kindness of my heart, did you?"

I snorted out a laugh. "Of course not. Especially not with your weak stomach. Remember when we had to pick up the rotted fruits for Demeter's compost pile, and you dry-heaved every step of the way?"

She scoffed at me, pulling my hair lightly as she replied, "If I recall, you were dry-heaving pretty hard as well."

"Touché." I laughed.

Persephone helped me through the rest of my bath, and finally, after what seemed like hours, she'd pulled through the last tangled strand of hair and was helping me out of the tub to dry off and get dressed for the night.

She held out a beautiful pale teal dress, which would drape across my body like the waves moving through the ocean, but I shook my head.

"Actually, I had a special dress made for tonight," I said, pulling out the dress, which was still wrapped in the button-up fabric sleeve it had been delivered in, and hanging it on the armoire to admire it.

The dress was made from white gossamer fabric that hung loose, with flowing white sleeves and a square neckline. Strips of leather hung down from the waist to the floor, attached to a leather bust. I'd bought the dress off the premade rack in the Weaving Web and modified it to match the idea in my head, having the leather strips and golden lace sewn in as a final touch. The gold reflected beautifully off the dress.

"Oh, Pandy." Persephone ran her hands down the leather bodice. "It's beautiful."

"I wanted to wear something that reminded Prometheus of Earth, since he's so fond of it. I remembered the brothers arrived in leather tunics, and I thought this would be a nice way to show him I accept him and his world."

"He's luckier than he'll ever know," Persephone said, pulling me in for a hug before ushering me back to sit in front of the mirror so she could finish getting me ready.

We decided on leaving my hair down, except for two small braids on each side of my face, which Persephone tied at the back with a leather-and-lace ribbon I'd made from the fabric scraps of my dress. She left my face bare, aside from a bit of kohl lining the tops of my eyes and swooping out at the edges into a small wing. She also added a touch of gold dust to my eyelids and their inner corners, which accentuated my eyes like someone had lit a fire within them.

"Wow! You look amazing." Persephone beamed up at me as she helped me twirl, admiring her work.

"Not too wild for an Olympian gathering?" I asked, suddenly unsure if adding leather into my dress had been the right move.

"I don't think 'wild' is the word to use." She tapped her chin, a smile lighting up her face as she said, "You look powerful."

I laughed. "Looks can be deceiving."

"They can, but not tonight—not for you. You are the Goddess of Mortal Women, remember." She glanced out the window. "We'd better get going. We can't have the guest of honor be late for her own party."

I grumbled, walking over to my nightstand to grab the amulet Hermes had given me and tucking it into the small pocket I'd asked to be sewn in so the amulet could be hidden within the square neckline. "You're right. We'd better start now if we want to make it in time. I can't move so fast in the shoes you picked out for me." I huffed out a laugh as I wiggled my feet in the golden sandals Persephone had laid out and went to work looping the gold ribbons up my calves, securing them in a bow at the back.

She scoffed. "As if I'd let you get that beautiful dress covered in sweat and dirt stains. We're going to ride in style." She winked at me before opening my front door to reveal two beautiful black stallions pulling a bronze chariot behind them.

My jaw slackened as I stared at the opulence of the carriage, so shell-shocked I barely noticed Persephone giggling as she pulled me gently by the arm toward it. I'd ridden in carriages before, but nothing as extraordinary as this one, and never one pulled by the High Olympians' personal stallions.

"How much did this cost you?" I asked, astounded that she'd go so far as to rent a High Olympian chariot to transport me. I'd never seen one of these up close, and although Persephone got to ride in them with her mother and father frequently, I didn't think she'd be granted access as a lower god. She wasn't one of the twelve ruling High Olympians like Zeus and Demeter.

"No, no, no. No money talk. It doesn't matter what it cost. Seeing the look on everyone's faces will be worth every penny. Plus, as I mentioned, I will not be having you ruin everything I worked to create." She gathered the reins in her hand and gave them a light tap to get the stallions moving.

I watched the horses' powerful muscles as they started to trot and found myself mesmerized by the control and power they exuded. They weren't like Pegasus, who had wings; they were massive creatures whose backs reached at least twice my height. I tried to imagine myself riding one and laughed at the thought. I'd have no idea how to even get on top of a stallion, let alone stay on top of one, but I still found myself dreaming of the freedom and power one would feel to ride these majestic creatures.

As we crossed through the gate to the summit, I could already see the line of Olympians waiting to get inside Zeus's palace. I was relieved to see Zeus had invited the cretes rather than forcing them to work as the cost of their attendance. It was a shock to see how many had decided to come.

People started to turn our way as we approached, their jaws dropping with realization when they saw us, the two females riding in on the chariot.

"At least try to look less mortified, Pandy. It's not often you and I get to make everyone in Olympus jealous at once." Persephone

laughed, stepping down from the carriage before helping me. She held her chin high, beaming her ethereal smile upon every Olympian we passed on our way up to the front of the line.

One of Zeus's servants held a scroll, but as Persephone approached, he put the scroll down and held out a winged arm for us to pass.

"What do you think was on that scroll?" I asked. "It looked too short for a guest list, and so far, it seems everyone received an invite."

"Probably a list of enemies." Persephone shrugged, walking through the door and grabbing my hand to pull me along when she saw me hesitate at the top. "I'm honestly surprised it's not longer."

I couldn't help but laugh at her even as every nerve in my body screamed in anticipation of what the night would bring.

CHAPTER 33

"I'LL meet you in there," Persephone said, squeezing my hand in reassurance as the servant at the doorway to the ballroom prepared to announce her.

All the High Olympians and a few lower-level Olympian gods and goddesses were required to be introduced. Persephone was considered higher-ranking among the lower Olympians.

"Are you sure we can't just go in together?" I asked, close to pleading with her not to leave me on my own just yet.

"Don't worry, Pandy. Everything will be fine. Just remember, everyone in there is here to celebrate you tonight, and if anyone messes it up, Zeus will strike them down."

She was trying to make me feel better, but the pit in my stomach only grew until it threatened to consume me whole.

"Persephone, Goddess of Spring," the yellow-eyed servant announced, opening the door with his winged arm and pulling it shut behind her before I could make out anything except a warm glow and the flow of voices.

He looked at me expectantly, and I copied what I'd seen Persephone do when I'd snuck into parties with her in the past.

"Pandora" I said, raising my chin high as I readied myself for him to open the door.

But it stayed shut.

"What do you rule over?" he asked, raising an eyebrow at me.

"I don't rule over anything. This is my engagement celebration." I waited for him to just open the door and let me in.

"What are you the goddess of?" he asked and then sighed. "I need to know so I can announce you. Only gods and goddesses are announced."

I turned that over in my head for a moment, and before I could think better of it, I said, "I'm the Goddess of Mortal Women."

He nodded, turning the golden knobs of the enormous oak door and pushing it open. "Pandora, Goddess of Mortal Women," he announced to the room, turning toward me and motioning for me to enter.

I walked forward, picking up the skirt of my dress as I held my head high and descended the steps into the ballroom.

The normally empty white ballroom in Zeus's palace was full of color and warmth. Demeter and Persephone had definitely lent a helping hand in decorating the room, because every wall was covered in oak branches that climbed like vines, and tiny little purple, blue, and white flowers grew among the green oak leaves. Glowing orbs danced across the ceiling, casting a warm glow on the mural of the open sky, and four enormous oak trees reached their limbs up to the ceiling from the corners of the room, their branches fanning out, making the sky look even more realistic.

I was so caught up in the decorations it took me a moment to notice the gasps quickly spreading throughout the room.

There had to have been hundreds of Olympians in attendance, some holding their partners on the dance floor, while others were already seated at the long oak tables stretching along each side of the room. But the one thing they all had in common in this very moment was that they were all turned in one direction, staring at me.

I stepped off the stairway onto the floor, desperately searching for a familiar face among all the guests. My gaze trailed the

two long oak tables all the way to a riser with stairs leading up to another table, this one with only six chairs. It sat above all the rest in its own little acropolis, and there was Zeus, sitting in one of the center seats like an eagle perched in his nest.

He smiled but made no motion to invite me over, so instead, I headed to the only place I could think of at a time like this. The wine fountain.

As I poured wine into my glass, the Olympians poured their whispers into the room. My ears felt like they were burning; I ached to hear what they were saying. But before I could focus on any of it, suddenly, everyone silenced.

I turned, expecting to see Zeus, but I found Epimetheus instead. Olympians parted for him the same as they did for Persephone, but instead of admiration in their eyes, they looked at him with fear.

I smiled at him—more than I should have—as he approached, but the closer he got to me, the more I noticed he didn't look happy at all.

"What's wrong?" I asked, worried something had already happened to ruin the night.

"My brother is waiting for you over there," Epimetheus said, motioning to the far left side of the room, under one of the oak trees. "He sent me to bring you over to him."

"Oh, okay," I said, confused. I let him lead me toward his brother. "Why are you upset?"

"I'm not," he snapped, making me flinch at the anger that seeped from those two simple words.

"I can tell something is—"

"Ah," Prometheus interrupted, "there is my wife-to-be. Pandora, I'd like you to meet Ryxan and his partner Drusilla." Prometheus gestured to a male and a female standing beside him. I assumed they were lower gods, since they had no defining creature features I could see. "These are friends of mine from Othrys."

"It's lovely to meet you both," I said, smiling at them.

"You as well. I can't believe our dear friend Prometheus is going to wed an Olympian, but I can see now why he agreed," Drusilla said. Her hair was as dark as mine, but somehow, her eyes seemed even darker, with pale skin that looked silvery, even surrounded by all the warm, glowing light of the room.

Drusilla's partner, Ryxan, had dark hair like hers, with bright, icy-blue eyes that seemed to glow against his deep skin like stars in the night. I couldn't help but think they made a beautiful couple, even if something about the way they were looking at me made me uncomfortable.

"Thank you," I said, looking between them and Prometheus. "So, how did you all meet? I'd love to hear more about Prometheus before the Realm of Man. I'm sad to say I don't know much from that time of his life." I hoped someone would share the stories of his past he seemed to be trying hard to keep hidden.

"I wouldn't say we became friends until after the war, although we did frequently pass by one another in Othrys," Ryxan said, smiling over at Prometheus as if he were expecting to be stopped from sharing anything else.

Then Prometheus spoke up. "They had the important task of guarding the Stones of Baetyl, which were not technically in Othrys but close enough that they called Othrys home for a time. I got to know Ryxan and Drusilla better after I was assigned my duty on Earth." He looked nervous to be revealing this information to me.

"I've never heard of the Stones of Baetyl. What are they?" I asked, curious at Prometheus's sudden change in demeanor at their mention.

"The stones act as a portal, made from the remnants of a Prime who has long been forgotten. They give certain gods the power to travel through them freely. That is how your friends in Olympus and your Titan here travel between realms."

I stared at him, unsure of how to answer as curiosity burned through my brain. Just as I was about to launch into questions, Prometheus spoke again.

"Epimetheus, would you mind taking my betrothed to dance? I'm sure she would love it, and I have some private matters I must discuss with Ryxan and Drusilla." He spoke over my shoulder to Epimetheus, who was hovering behind me.

I could already tell from the looks Prometheus had given me that speaking my mind was not an option. He needed me removed in order to finish his conversation.

Great start.

"Pandora, would you like to dance?" Epimetheus asked.

I nodded in reply, and for the first time tonight, I saw the anger fade and Epimetheus's eyes visually lighten as I grabbed his hand and followed him to the dance floor.

CHAPTER 34

EPIMETHEUS spun me on the dance floor, making me giggle as I glided across the marble.

"I didn't know you could dance," I said, smiling up at him.

"There's a lot you don't know about me." He led me in the dance everyone else in the center of the room seemed to know.

Orbs of light danced in the air above us as if in tune with our very movements, and one enormous chandelier with candles aflame floated midair in the center of the dance floor. A few other chandeliers floated above the dining tables, the diamonds dangling from their golden arms glittering like Asteria's stars in the night sky.

Epimetheus moved effortlessly and with a grace I would never have expected from him. I was beginning to realize he was right. There was a lot I didn't know about him, but I wanted nothing more than to learn.

I looked up to find him staring down at me in a way that made my cheeks flush.

"Stop looking at me like that," I said, shaking my head clear of the cloud of lust that overwhelmed my senses.

"Like what?" he asked, feigning innocence.

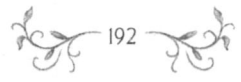

"Like I'm marrying you, not your brother," I said, harsher than I meant, but I was all too aware of the eyes on us, watching our every move.

"And what if I said I wish you were?" he asked, staring at me as if he could see through my soul to the hidden part of me that wished that were true.

With all the ups and downs with Prometheus over the past few days, much as I tried, I couldn't seem to feel anything more than a strong friendship toward him.

"You shouldn't," I answered, starting to pull away, but Epimetheus pulled me even closer and leaned in.

"I wish you were," he whispered, lifting my chin with his hand and forcing me to look up at him. "You look beautiful tonight. I especially like your dress."

He was the beautiful one. It wasn't like I was unfamiliar with beauty; I was surrounded by it. But something about the way Epimetheus carried himself, with untamed power rather than perfection, drew me to him like a moth to a flame.

"You can't say things like that. If anyone were to hear you say that, Zeus would . . ." I paused, remembering I couldn't say anything about Zeus's threat to exile me without explaining why.

"He'd what?" Epimetheus asked.

"Nothing. I just can't have you saying things like that, especially at my engagement party. I'm marrying your brother. Think of what people would say." I prayed he'd listen to my reason and not ruin this for me, tonight of all nights.

"I never thought you'd be one to worry about what others think."

He couldn't be farther from the truth. I'd tried time and time again not to get upset about what others said about me, because I knew their opinions were never good. But every hushed insult and hate-filled rumor the Olympians threw at me seemed to always hit home.

"I don't," I replied, which made the corner of Epimetheus's mouth twitch. He could see right through my lie.

"No one would believe we were together even if I kissed you right here, right now, in front of everyone," he said, clenching his jaw as he looked around. He glared in the direction of the Olympians still watching us.

"I highly doubt that," I said. "Why would you think that?"

"My brother is respected among his peers and always does the right thing. If he kissed someone else's betrothed, everyone would be shocked to their core. Me, however . . . They would fully expect me to do something like that. I am, after all, the fearsome fool, never as wise as my brother, but stronger and meaner than he could ever be. I'm the rebel they would expect to ruin your perfect image, not to uphold it like my brother." Epimetheus paused as if thinking to himself. "Maybe you are better off with him."

I watched him grappling with something deep in his mind and then glanced around at the onlookers, realizing for the first time they were watching him, not me, as if waiting for Epimetheus to commit some unspeakable act instead of flirting with me like I was the most precious being in the realm.

"Maybe you're right," I replied, making his head shoot up.

Epimetheus looked at me like he couldn't tell whether I was joking or not. He opened his mouth to speak but was interrupted when an announcement echoed throughout the room.

"My fellow Olympians, thank you for honoring me today with your presence in this dire time, and for coming to my home to celebrate my dear Pandora and her betrothed, Prometheus."

The enormous crowd answered in a chorus of claps, which brought a prideful smile to Zeus's lips.

"As many of you know, the Aloadae twins have returned to Olympus, ignoring their exile, and launched an attack on the Olympians who were present at the Centennial Celebration of Man. We have reason to believe that attack was just the beginning

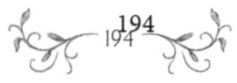

and that they have something much more sinister planned. Fear not, my fellow Olympians. We will fight these atrocious beasts until they take their last breath, and we will not allow them to tear apart the beautiful kingdom we've built on this sacred land."

More cheers rang out as the Olympians hung on his every word.

"In times like these, we are stronger together than apart, and as one united force, the Aloadae brothers will stand no chance."

The crowd roared in agreement.

"As a united force, I suggest we hold our heads high and celebrate this wondrous night with a performance from a few of our beautiful muses, Terpsichore, Euterpe, and Melpomene." He raised a hand, motioning for the three muses to join him on the dais before adding, "Ladies, if you would be so kind as to provide some much-needed entertainment."

"We would be honored, Father," the muses said simultaneously as they sashayed their way up the steps, starting their performance well before they'd even set foot on what would become their stage.

I was mesmerized by the way the muses performed together. Melpomene sang melodies that harmonized perfectly with Euterpe's double flute, while Terpsichore glided across the stage as if she were floating on air, dancing with such grace and ease along to their music. It was impossible to take my eyes off her. The three of them together captured the crowd, leaving all of us lost to the ethereal wonder of their performance.

"I always forget how beautiful they are when they're performing together," I said, unable to ignore the magnetic pull. It was as if they'd cast a spell on their audience, making it impossible to ignore them.

"They don't hold a candle to you," Epimetheus whispered from behind me.

I couldn't help but smile, even though I knew I shouldn't.

I was turning around to remind Epimetheus that while flirting may not be dangerous for him, it most definitely was for me, when an ear-splitting scream rang out.

"Primes, what's wrong with her?" someone shouted from the back of the crowd, where a tight-knit group seemed to be forming around the source of the screaming.

"Make her stop!" another yelled.

More and more people began to scream and run in fear from what I could now see was one of the muses screaming in terror, running in circles, with her hands over her face.

"What's happening?" I asked, walking over to the crowd forming close to the exit.

"Stay behind me," Epimetheus said, moving his body in front of mine as if he were my shield.

I pushed my way around him, attempting to see where the screaming was coming from.

As we got closer to the crowd, I saw the back of a woman's head. Her dress was a deep navy, with silver stars falling from the waist, denser the closer they got to the floor. It was Urania, and she wasn't simply covering her face with her hands; she was clawing at it like a rabid animal. Strips of skin had been peeled off with each scratch of her perfectly manicured nails, and blood was streaming down her pale skin, saturating her blue dress so much the bodice had started to turn a deep purple.

"What's wrong with her?" I asked, unable to look away from the horrifying sight, until I realized no one was stepping in to help her. Everyone was just standing around her in shock, watching as she continued to rip herself apart. "Why is no one helping her!"

"Self-centered Olympians," Epimetheus said under his breath, searching the room for someone. His eyes lit up as he found who he was looking for. "Prometheus!" he yelled to his brother, who was making his way through the frantic crowd.

"My premonition. It's happening," Prometheus said, panicked, as he jogged over to us.

More Olympians began running hysterical in all directions, but no longer from the fear of Urania attacking herself. It was as if they were fighting off their own unseen evils.

I searched around for what was causing everyone to panic and found nothing at first—until my eyes settled on a shadowy figure in the corner, near Urania. I was about to ask if they could see it too, but Epimetheus walked up to Prometheus—who seemed to be zoning out, stuck in his own mind amid the chaos—grabbed him by the shoulders, and shook him out of it.

"Prometheus, I need to help her before she does something irreparable. Stay with Pandora," he ordered.

Prometheus looked at me in a daze and nodded. "Maniae. It's here," he said to himself.

Epimetheus stared at him, fear settling into his features, but it didn't stop him from backing up in the direction of Urania. "I have to help her! She's one swipe away from scratching her eyes out," he spat at Prometheus before looking at me. "Stay with my brother. He'll protect you, but if he starts to go mad like the others, run."

I looked at him wide-eyed. "He looks like he's going to pass out," I said, pointing to where Prometheus now stood zoning out, his arms wrapped across his chest as if he were hugging himself. I didn't know what madness they were talking about, but it looked to me as if whatever was happening had already begun to affect him.

Epimetheus ran back to his brother and slapped him across the face, waking him from whatever wallowing trance he'd put himself into. "If he looks like he's lost, do that. Brings him back to reality and out of his visions. But if he starts to see things that aren't there, run."

I stared between the two brothers, trying to wrap my head around what was going on and who Maniae was, and nodded to Epimetheus. He wasted no time in running over to Urania's side, grabbing her hands and pulling them from her face. He turned

her around to pin her arms behind her back, between his body and hers.

Urania screamed as she fought him with every ounce of power she had left.

"Calm down!" Epimetheus yelled, holding her hands as she raged.

She most definitely did not calm down. Instead, she bucked like an angry bull, kicking her legs out and hitting him in the shins multiple times. He cursed as she kicked him particularly hard.

"Get them off! Get them off! Get them off!" she screamed over and over, thrashing her head back and hitting Epimetheus in the jaw. The blow split his lip open, and blood streamed down his chin.

"What? Get what off you? I don't see anything," he said, searching her body for whatever it was she thought was on her, patting her down and finding nothing.

"The bugs! Get them off!" she screamed and screamed, growing more crazed by the minute.

"There's nothing on you! You have to calm down, Urania. There are no bugs on you. It's only in your mind." He tried to console her to no avail.

"What's happening to her, Prometheus? Who is Maniae?" I asked, turning away from Epimetheus and toward his brother, who was looking around the room frantically.

"We must go. Maniae are the spirits of madness, and this is how they attack," he said, grabbing my hand and pulling me past Epimetheus just in time for me to see him punch Urania square in the face.

I gasped, covering my mouth with my hands as her bloodied, mangled face hit the ground, completely and utterly unconscious. I tried to see if she was all right, watching as Epimetheus flung her limp body over his shoulder, but a group of cretes who'd gone mad ran at him as if he were a threat they must eliminate. Fighting against Prometheus's hold, I grappled to get back to him, but it was no use. Before I knew it, Epimetheus had disappeared from sight.

"We have to help him!" I yelled, pulling against Prometheus with all my might.

"We can't. I slipped an amethyst into his tunic in case this happened. Right now, we need to focus on getting you out of here," he said, urging me to follow him to the side door in the back corner of the room.

I thought of the amethyst Hermes had given me, telling me to wear it at all times, but how could he have known something like this was going to happen, and why did the amethyst help against this madness?

I was about to ask, but I never got the chance. A centaur came charging out of nowhere, hitting Prometheus right in the side and ripping his hand from mine. I stared hopelessly after it as it carried him off into the chaos, leaving me all alone.

CHAPTER 35

I KEPT searching for any sign of the Titan brothers as I moved along the wall, but they were nowhere to be seen. I was heading for the side door Prometheus had been trying to get to but was stopped in my tracks as a shadowy figure emerged, blocking my exit. This looked like the Maniae who'd sent Urania into madness, distorted but obviously there.

I approached it cautiously, watching its arms move like a puppet master pulling strings as it stared out into the crowd at where a group of cretes were attacking one another. It reminded me of the shadowy figure I'd seen talking to the woman about the rebellion, except where that one had seemed to have a cloud of shadow distorting its true form, this Maniae was made of pure shadow, with small tendrils trailing after its movements.

I took another step forward, and the shadowy figure—which I could now make out as a female from the curvature of her form—dropped her hands, turning her full attention straight onto me. A screeching filled my ears. I wanted to scratch the sound from my head. Suddenly remembering the amethyst in my side, I pulled it out, wrapping the chain tightly around my hand and clutching it.

Soothing silence filled my mind, and in that same moment, the Maniae screamed, launching herself at me.

I expected it to be a figment of my imagination and figured it would pass right through me like smoke on a breeze, but instead, the Maniae hit me with the full force of a solid body. Clawed hands gripped me around my neck, and I scratched at her as she pinned me down, screaming for someone to help, though I knew my screams would likely be drowned out by all the other screams.

My vision started to blur, and I gasped for air as her sharp nails threatened to pierce my neck, the pressure increasing, until something—or someone—threw her off me.

I looked up, expecting to find Epimetheus saving me again, but it was Dionysus. He stood there, blood dripping down from his warm brown hair, which was wrapped up in a grapevine crown, with little purple gems shimmering all throughout. I sucked in a breath.

Amethyst.

Of course! Dionysus was never without his amethyst crown to ward off the effects of his constant consumption of wine. At the sight of the gems on his crown, a memory flashed through my mind of Clio's short lesson on the stones and their history. *That must have been what Prometheus meant. Amethyst clears the mind, and these are mental attacks.* I gripped the amethyst in my palm even tighter.

"Come on!" Dionysus pulled me to my feet. "More are likely coming. We need to make haste."

"How many are there?" I asked.

"I don't know, exactly. Maniae poison the mind with madness. The more it spreads, the more powerful they become, and with everyone in Olympus stuffed into this room, their power is growing to an unstoppable point. We need to get those doors open. The Maniae are guarding them, making sure no one leaves until their madness has consumed everyone in their reach."

I followed his eyes to the shadow figures littering the room, either blocking the exits or standing in the groups that seemed to be the most affected.

"Why is no one fighting them, only each other?"

"Only those wearing amethyst can see the Maniae," Dionysus explained.

"And you don't know how many there are?" I asked, hoping the Maniae weren't like the Keres and that we would suddenly have hundreds upon us.

"No one knows for sure. Some say it is one being, and some say they are infinite." Dionysus ducked as a winged owl servant I knew to be Athena's flew right over our heads, crashing into the wall behind us and sliding to the floor, its beak bloodied and its body crumpled.

I moved to help, but Dionysus grabbed my arm.

"No. We can't help. We just need to get the exits open and run. Madness may not cloud our minds, but it can still hurt us." He paused, looking at me sadly before adding, "It could even kill some of us."

"So how do we get around them to open the doors?" I asked, unable to see how he thought this would work with only me and him against what I counted as six Maniae.

Dionysus looked around, a smile spreading across his features as he said, "I have a plan. Follow me."

I followed him up to the edge of the dais, where we crouched behind the stairs, hiding from view.

"The Maniae want chaos? Then let's give them some chaos." He smiled down at me and gave me a wink before jumping over the edge of the steps, running up to the table, and climbing on top of it. He lifted his arms, and I watched as wine levitated out of the fountains in an endless stream, flowing across the ceiling before gathering in an enormous wall of burgundy liquid, which crested over at the top like a wave preparing to crash on the beach.

Dionysus's arms began to shake with the enormous amount of power he was using not only to draw the wine to him, but to hold so much of it behind him at once. The Olympians turned toward him, the madness clearing for a moment, and as I looked around at the Maniae, I noticed they too had set their sights on Dionysus.

Letting out an enormous roar, Dionysus brought his arms down, sending the wall of wine crashing down onto the Olympians. It burst through all the doorways and washed countless Olympians and Maniae out with it.

"It worked." Dionysus gave an exhausted laugh that came out as more of a huff.

"You didn't know it would?" I asked, realizing he was shocked by his feat of power.

Dionysus may have been one of the twelve High Olympians, but he was the youngest god within Olympus, leading many to forget what power it took to sit on the council.

"One could hope," he said sheepishly. "We need to get out of here before the Maniae recover."

Shadow figures began to appear throughout the celebration room.

"I think we might be too late for that."

"When I say run, I want to you run out the door behind me as fast as you can, okay?" Dionysus said, his eyes not leaving the group of Maniae stalking toward us from all around the room.

I could see a couple of shadow figures around the door he wanted me to escape through, and I took a deep breath, grabbing my skirts and tucking them into the leather rope at my waist. Dionysus clenched his fists, and the wine at my feet began to rise, little red droplets floating through the room until they shot toward Dionysus's side, hardening and forming into what looked like shards of ice.

"Run!" Dionysus yelled through clenched teeth.

My feet landed on the marble floor at the same moment as the shards of wine flew forward.

I never saw if they hit their targets—my eyes were on the Maniae standing in front of the doorway. I screamed, releasing a battle cry full of fury and fear as I charged it, slamming its body into the door as hard as I could. It crashed through, sending us tumbling out into the oak grove at the side of Zeus's palace.

We grabbed onto one another as we tumbled, trying to get the upper hand, until we hit the trunk of a tree and broke apart.

I groaned, my back aching from the impact, and pushed off the dirt, forcing myself to my feet. I looked over just in time to see the shadow figure doing the same thing.

Grabbing one of the broken branches, I readied myself, holding it in both hands, with the end above my shoulder. It had been a while since my fights with Athena, and right now, I wished Zeus had never ended them. I wondered what he'd have to say for himself now if he could see me.

The shadow figure screeched, launching herself at me, and I swung the branch as hard as I could, hitting her in the side.

The figure doubled over and launched herself at me again. I lifted my branch too late, and she collided with me, sending us rolling even further into the grove, down the hill, toward the cliff edge at the back of the palace.

Flinging my arms out, I tried to grab anything I could to stop us from rolling. I caught onto a tree trunk and gripped it with all my strength, coming to a sliding stop right as the cliff edge came into view.

I looked around frantically, trying to find where the Maniae had landed, but I could see no sign of her. Standing up, I grabbed another branch in case she appeared again and followed the dust trail leading to the cliff.

Maybe she fell off.

I slowed as I got closer to the edge, wondering if there'd even be a body to find or if the Maniae might have fallen all the way to the base of Mount Olympus.

Figuring she'd fallen, I turned around just in time.

The Maniae jumped on top of me, forcing me to the ground, so close to the edge my arm holding the branch dangled off the side into thin air. With the other, I gripped the Maniae's arm.

If I go, you're coming with me.

My heart raced as I tightened my grip, ready to accept my fate—but then she went for my throat, strangling the life from me once again.

I fought, but it was strong. So strong.

Tears filled my eyes as I gasped for air. It was becoming clear there was nothing I could do to get it off me.

But then I remembered something. How it had reacted when I'd hit it in the side, as if the shadowy form could feel every bit of the impact, same as me.

If it could be hurt so easily, then maybe it could be killed.

Tightening my hand on her arm and the hand holding the branch, I used every bit of strength I had left to heave the branch up and into the center of her chest, where it was easiest to pierce the heart, if her anatomy were anything like my own.

I felt the Maniae go slack above me as the branch pierced through, and then the full weight of the shadow figure fell on top of me. I tried to shove it off, but I was too weak. Just as I was about to scream for help, the body disappeared, shadows floating away on the breeze as if the Maniae were never even there.

Getting up off the ground, I forced myself to push through the pain pulsating through my body and climbed back up through the oak grove toward Zeus's palace. Dionysus may have stopped the madness inside, but now, there was an even bigger problem.

The Maniae had taken over all of Olympus.

CHAPTER 36

I WATCHED as Olympians ran from or toward the mania being waged on their minds. I hadn't seen any High Olympians other than Dionysus and figured they'd either run off to safety or were just as affected by the madness as anyone without amethyst in their possession.

I was scanning the crowd, searching for a way through the rampage, when I noticed a group of shadowy figures cornering someone. One of the shadow figures was launched backward hard enough that her body slid through the dirt, knocking over a couple of cretes running for their lives from an unseen assailant.

It gave me just enough of an opening to see who they were cornering.

Epimetheus.

Without thinking, I held my branch tight and ran at them, piercing one of the shadow figures through the back before they even saw me coming. Epimetheus met my eye, staring at me in bewilderment.

"Pandora?" He blinked as if he were seeing me for the first time.

Hands ripped me off the back of the Maniae seconds before its body disappeared. The hands dragged me back, and shadows floated past my face as they picked up speed.

Remembering another of the moves Athena had taught me years ago, I flipped onto my stomach, causing the Maniae to lose her grip on me, and pushed my legs out hard enough to stop myself from skidding further. The Maniae turned back to attack, but I was ready, rolling out of the way and jumping to my feet as I threw myself onto her back. I didn't have my branch anymore, but there was the leather rope at my waist, and the one in my hair.

I couldn't reach the rope at my waist, since it was pinned between the Maniae's body and mine, so I pulled the one from my hair and wrapped it around its throat, pulling as hard as I could until it fell to its knees, ripping at its throat in desperation, the same way Urania had ripped at her face. I couldn't tell if it was my rope or the Maniae's claws that were suffocating her. I didn't know if these things needed to breathe, but right now, it didn't matter.

The next thing I knew, smoke was billowing out from the wounds she'd made at her neck, and she disappeared.

Epimetheus had taken care of the last few Maniae around him and was running over to me by the time I stood up. "What are you still doing here? Where's Prometheus?" he asked frantically, pulling me into his strong embrace.

I pushed out of it, looking up into wild eyes. "We don't have time for that. We need to get off this mountain. Now," I said, just as a group of Olympians started to head our way.

He followed my eyes and growled, moving me behind him and pointing to the hidden path down to Lower Olympus that seemed open for the moment. We headed straight toward it.

"When I tell you to, run as fast as you can to your cottage and lock the door behind you. Do not open it for anyone except me or Prometheus," Epimetheus said, never taking his eyes off the manic group of Olympians stalking toward us, crouching as if they were about to attack.

I nodded seconds before they sprang into action, flying through the air, right at Epimetheus. He stared them down with such intensity I nearly missed the scream coming from his mouth.

"RUN!"

I took off in a sprint along the open path, fighting the urge to look back, even though I knew the Titan could hold his own in a fight. My legs burned as I hurled my body down the side of the mountain, ignoring the twists and turns of the road and going off on the path the mountain goats often took, heading straight down to my cottage. My feet slipped a few times, sending me skidding through the rocks and nearly falling to my death. If I were less concerned about my life, I might have laughed at the image that popped into my head as I descended the steep slope, thinking I probably looked like a human avalanche barreling through the gravel and the dirt.

I could see my cottage in the distance now and nearly slowed in relief, fighting to catch my breath as fire burned in my lungs and I tasted the metallic tang of blood in my mouth. But I knew better than that, so instead, I buried the uncomfortable feeling and powered through, forcing my feet to move even faster as the ground leveled out.

I nearly face-planted the door in my rush, but luckily, I slowed enough to grab the handle. Yanking the door open and slamming it shut behind me, I rested my forehead against the wood to catch my breath. Then, reaching up, I pushed the steel locking pin into the doorframe before reaching down to put the one in the floor as well. I'd never understood why Hephaestus insisted on putting locks on the doors and the windows, but I couldn't be more thankful for them now.

I sank down to the ground, holding my head in my hands as I pulled my knees up into a hug. *I made it. I'm alive. I'm home.* I

kept repeating the words in my head until my heart rate slowed and my breathing returned to normal.

Pulling my body up from the dirty wood floor, I quickly went around to all the windows in my cottage, making sure they were locked tight and that no one would be able to sneak in. I was worried the Maniae or one of their victims would show up. I even went as far as putting some of my clay pots on the ground below each of the windows in the hope that if anyone did sneak in, they'd hit my trap and alert me to their presence.

Luckily, there was only one door in my cottage—the front door—so I went to work tightening the rope I always left hanging from a beam, which I used as a reinforcement to make it a little harder to get through if anyone managed to split the doorframe or the floorboards holding the locking pins. Grabbing the rope, I pulled it over to the left side of the door, looped it around the handle, and pulled it taught so the pressure would make it more difficult for someone to pull the door open.

Not fully trusting the rope and the locks, especially since I wasn't sure if Maniae even used doors and windows versus just appearing, I decided it was probably best to get a weapon—or the closest thing I had to one, since I'd dropped the daggers Athena had gifted me off at Forged Glory to be sharpened. Looking around, I grabbed the closest object to me: the cast-iron frying pan Hephaestus had gifted me when he heard of my cottage being finished. He'd called it a housewarming gift and insisted every new homeowner should get one.

Holding the cast-iron pan in both hands, I gave it a couple of swings, trying it out, and decided it would work pretty well if I could hit the intruder over the head with it. If I were lucky, they might even be knocked unconscious, but if not, the frying pan might be big enough to use as a shield when they came at me.

I'd been hesitant to accept the pan as a gift at first, figuring I wouldn't have a need for it, since the Olympians had never bothered to teach me how to cook. Even Demeter hadn't thought

to teach me until later in life, figuring the produce from her farmlands was enough. But now, it was proving more useful than I'd ever imagined. Not only could I cook all sorts of food in it, but it might also be a formidable weapon. Not to mention, it was a weapon nearly every being in Olympus would never see coming. After all, an Olympian with a sword or a bow and arrow was predictable, but a mortal woman with a metal pan? They'd be too confused at the sight to realize I was about to hit them over the head with it.

I sat in front of the door, frying pan at the ready, listening to the distant screams of the Olympians and hoping everyone I cared about was safe from whatever nightmares were spreading.

I thought about everything that had happened tonight. No one knew for sure if the Aloadae twins were behind the Maniae attack, but I couldn't shake the feeling something didn't add up. They could attack anywhere and at any time. Sure, it was convenient, with so many Olympians of every power level gathered in one place, but the similarity I couldn't shake was that both attacks had happened when the Titans were the guests of honor.

CHAPTER 37

Y backside ached from sitting in my chair near the door, cast-iron pan in hand. The screams went on for hours, until finally, the sun set, and Aether grew quiet.

The chaos of the day and the sweet silence of the night must have swept me off into a deep sleep, because before I knew it, I was being startled awake by fists pounding on my door.

"Pandora, it's me!"

Epimetheus.

I pulled aside the canvas curtain covering my window and peered outside, just to be sure my mind wasn't playing tricks on me. I still had the amethyst held tightly in my palm. I sighed in relief as my eyes proved my ears right.

Epimetheus was leaning with one hand against the top of the doorframe, his head dipped in exhaustion. He started to lift his other hand to knock again, but I was already undoing the rope and opening the front door.

His golden amber eyes met mine, and the corner of his lips turned up in a smirk, blood trickling out of his mouth. He was covered in dirt and blood, most of which didn't seem to be his, since there were no immediate injuries in sight.

I couldn't resist—I leaped out through the front door and pulled him into a hug, glad to see him still in one piece and sane.

"Miss me?" he said, his voice cracking as he winced in pain.

I let him go quickly, worried my hug might have hurt him. I held the door open for him, pointing toward the dining room.

Epimetheus moved past me, limping as he favored his left leg and dragged the right one, which looked to be crooked at the ankle.

"Here—let me help you," I said, moving to his side and trying to lift his arm, but he winced and pulled away, shaking his head.

Resting his left hand on the table, Epimetheus carefully lowered himself into the dining chair I'd pulled out, which creaked beneath his weight as he settled into it, letting out a relieved sigh.

"What happened out there?" I asked, worry filling my voice as I looked him over for any sign of injury.

"Maniae kept appearing and causing more and more Olympians to go mad. They repeatedly launched attacks at me until I had no other choice than to jump."

"Jump?" I asked.

"Well, the road down was flooded with the crazed, so I did the only other thing I could think of. I jumped off the summit."

"You mean you flew?" I asked, remembering how he'd flown me up to Apollo's palace.

"No, I mean I jumped," he said, attempting to laugh, but it came out as more of a hiss as he clutched his side. "I had a group of Olympians rushing at me and a Maniae following me. One of them jumped on my back, pinning my wings down, and so I jumped with him still attached. I must have been knocked unconscious, because by the time I woke up, everything had calmed down. There are still crazed Olympians running around, but most of them have locked themselves in their homes to wait it out. The larger wards surrounding Olympus are back up now, so they're safe to wait it out there."

"The wards?" I asked, not remembering ever hearing anything about wards inside Olympus.

Epimetheus started to loosen the clasps holding his chiton over his broad, blood-covered shoulders. I watched, unable to pull my eyes away, as the fabric dropped into a puddle at his waist, deep bronze abs glistening in the sunlight, rippling like the small mountain range that surrounded Mount Olympus.

"See something you like?" he joked, bringing me back to reality.

I snapped my mouth shut and shook my head, trying to remember what it was I was supposed to be doing.

Grabbing a wet towel and a bowl full of clean water, I came back over to him, setting the things down on the table and pulling over a chair of my own. I placed it directly in front of him, so we were now sitting knee-to-knee. More like calf-to-knee, considering the massive height difference.

"We need to set the ankle first before it starts to heal," I said, bending down to pick up his foot and resting it in my lap.

Epimetheus watched every move I made. "I know that. What are you doing?" He lifted both brows in question.

"I just told you. I'm setting your ankle before it heals like this." I stared at him, wondering if he was being stubborn or if he was still suffering from head trauma after falling off the summit.

Hopefully, his head heals faster than his ankle.

He stared at me but never said a word.

Guess that's a yes. I kept his foot cradled between my legs.

Grabbing the ankle as gently as possible, I removed his leather sandal, tossing it to the side as I assessed the damage. It looked twisted, with a small fracture, not a full break. *Thank the Primes.* I cringed at the memory of the sickening crunch from the last time I'd had to set a broken bone, when I'd repositioned it into a splint.

I turned Epimetheus's ankle slightly, adjusting it back to a normal position and being careful of the fracture on the upper section. When I felt satisfied with the position, I tightened my legs as much as possible without causing pain.

Epimetheus sucked in a breath, and my gaze shot up to meet his.

"I'm sorry!"

"I'm fine," he grunted.

I glared at him. "Okay. I just wasn't sure when you gasped like a—"

"I said I'm fine."

"Fine," I grunted back, continuing my work by wrapping the now set ankle and tying it off a quarter of the way up his calf.

I looked up at him, holding my hands out to show my fantastic work.

He only gave me a grunt before lifting his foot off my lap and leaning back in the chair, staring at me again as if he couldn't make sense of what he was seeing.

Trying to ignore the ripples of lean muscle staring me in the face, I went to work washing the blood from his body, noticing the purple-and-blue bruises blooming across his skin.

"What are the wards you were talking about? Why weren't they active when the Maniae attacked?" I asked, wiping away another streak of blood, this time his own, from a nasty cut he'd gotten. It reached from the base of his rib cage at his back and wrapped around to his front, ending near his belly button. If I had to guess, someone had probably tried to gut him but was unable to finish the job before Epimetheus took them out.

"Someone deactivated them. All of Olympus has been warded against mental attacks since the War of the Titans, the walls and every building within them. That's why no one believed my brother when he had a premonition of this attack." Epimetheus winced as I ran the towel over the angry red opening, which was already starting to stitch itself back together.

"Who would have the power to do that? And how, with Olympus being so heavily guarded since the Keres' attack?" I

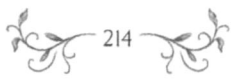

asked, racking my brain and not liking the answers I was coming up with. Even more so when Epimetheus proved my suspicions correct.

"Hecate made the mental wards and could have removed them, but really, anyone who had the spell and the runes she used to create them could have done it," he said, sitting up straighter in his chair as he realized something. "What's odd is, whoever is behind the Maniae attack is keeping the Aloadae twins out of it. But why would the Aloadae hide it if they were behind the attack? Why not flaunt another strike against Olympus?" Epimetheus seemed so wrapped up in his thoughts I couldn't tell if he was speaking to himself or me anymore.

"Do you think that's why Hecate is so reluctant to help with anything involving the Aloadae twins—because she's worried someone's trying to frame her?" I asked, trying to put together everything I'd gathered from various conversations over the past few days.

Epimetheus scoffed. "Zeus is an idiot to threaten a Titan who rivals him not only in age and wisdom, but power."

"Hecate is a . . ." I paused as my mind grappled with the revelation.

"A Titan," Epimetheus repeated, leaving me stunned.

CHAPTER 38

EPIMETHEUS looked me over, taking in the shock on my face before asking, "How much do you know about the Titans?"

"Not much. Just that a few sided with Zeus, like Themis, and a few decided to stay neutral in the war, like you and Prometheus. Other than that, I assumed the rest were imprisoned, whether in Tartarus or somewhere else, after losing the war." I tried to recall what I'd read about the fate of Epimetheus's brother Atlas.

"Hecate is one of the few beings in Olympus whose origins are shrouded in mystery. It was thought in the beginning that she was the daughter of the Titan Perses and the nymph Asteria. However, as Hecate's powers started to grow to levels that surpassed both Perses and Asteria, it was thought her heritage was wrong, and that Perses may have had an affair with none other than Nyx, the Prime Goddess of Night."

If Hecate was the daughter of Nyx, then it was no wonder Zeus, along with the other High Olympians, held no power over her. From what little I knew about Nyx, I'd gathered pretty quickly she was feared by everyone in Olympus, even Zeus.

"Once that theory came to light, Hecate was free to roam as she wished, and lucky for Zeus, she chose to live in the

Underworld with Hades. Until the Aloadae twins' arrival, I don't think Zeus has attempted to summon her for anything."

"So, if Hecate is a Titan, why did she choose to stay neutral in the war—or did she side with Zeus?"

"Hecate hadn't yet been created during the War of the Titans, but it is thought she was conceived during it. As Perses was on the Titans' side fighting alongside Asteria, and the Titans had reached out to Nyx for help, no one could ever be too sure exactly how her creation came about." Epimetheus laughed lightly before adding, "The Goddess of Magic is about as mysterious as they come."

Now it was my turn to laugh. "She didn't seem that mysterious to me. In fact, she seemed pretty normal, all things considered." I laughed even harder as a memory popped into my head of my torturous time with the goddess. "Well, until she almost killed me and acted as if it were nothing more than a scratch."

Epimetheus made a grunting noise, his golden eyes darkening.

"She didn't mean to . . ." I started. "Well, I mean, I don't think she meant to . . ." I was having trouble speaking as I watched the dark storm brewing in his gaze. "I mean, she had to get the poison out, or I would have died anyway, but the extraction was a little worse than she let on, and I guess I passed out from the pain."

Epimetheus launched into the air, his wooden chair scraping against the floor as it was pushed out of his way. He looked as mad as the Olympians rampaging outside.

"I'm going to . . ." he began, making his way to the door and nearly tripping over the shoulder ties of the chiton, which were dangling dangerously down to the ground in front of him.

I stepped forward to block his exit before he did something stupid like attack Hecate for saving my life, no matter how unorthodox her treatments may have been.

"You're not going anywhere," I said, pushing against his chest and not moving him an inch. "Have you gone mad!" I seethed, finally getting his attention as he looked down at me. "She did what she had to do to save me. Did it hurt? Yes. Did I die? No. That is all you need to know. I hold nothing against her, so neither should you."

Primes, this Titan was built like marble. I'd have about as much luck moving him as I would a boulder.

"Now, sit back down before you get blood all over my floor." I pointed to the seat he'd knocked over, now lying on its back against the wood floor.

He growled as he turned around, grabbing the wood chair and sitting it back up before plopping down onto it, making the wood creak from the force. "I can't think of the last time I let a mortal order me around," he said with a huff that almost sounded like a laugh.

"Well, maybe you need more of it if you're going to go around attacking anyone you disagree with."

"It's worked out well for me so far." He shrugged.

I scoffed. "Worked out for you, huh?" I shook my head as I wrapped a loose gauze fabric around his torso, tying it tight to stop the flow of blood.

Even though I knew the blood would stop soon enough anyway, with his immortal healing abilities, this was more to prevent me from having to clean up even more later. It was always a pain to get blood out of wood after it dried. Immortal or not, bloodstains were equally as troublesome. Already, I could make out a large puddle under his chair, and dribbles that had followed him to his seat from the doorway.

He looked at the wrap in confusion before meeting my eye. "Why?" Epimetheus asked quietly, all the anger that had been blazing in his eyes now gone.

"Why what?" I asked, not having a clue what his problem was.

"Why did you do . . ."—he paused, trying to figure out what to call the makeshift wrap—"this?"

"Are you trying to ask why I helped you, or why I bandaged an immortal?"

He looked even more perplexed as the words left my mouth. "Both."

"Should I not have done either?" I asked, earning a shrug from him. "I helped because not only have you gotten me out of some dicey situations, but you've also saved my life on more than one occasion." I pointed to the wrap. "As for that, well, I guess that's more for me than for you. I wasn't kidding about not having you bleed on my floor. Blood's a pain to clean up. It soaks into the wood like a sponge."

He stared at me in disbelief, shaking his head. "I've never met a mortal like you."

"Obviously. First mortal woman and all that," I said, rolling my eyes.

"That's not what I mean," Epimetheus said as I stepped into the kitchen to rinse the red-tinged bowls and wring out the towels.

"What did you mean then?" I asked, setting the damp towels down on the counter and giving him my full attention.

"I mean . . ." He paused, scratching his head and giving an awkward smile. "I've never had a mortal go out of their way to help me, especially when there was nothing in it for them."

I opened my mouth to reply, but he cut me off, saying, "I couldn't even imagine them wrapping me in this." He pinched the gauzy fabric between his fingers and pulled slightly.

"I find that hard to believe, if mankind is as wonderful as you and Prometheus make them out to be. Besides, what makes you think there's nothing in it for me?" I asked.

Epimetheus quirked one corner of his mouth up in a seductive grin. "What's in it for you, Pandora?"

Something about the way he said my name, along with the heat in his gaze, sent a shiver through my body. It took me a minute to realize I hadn't answered, and worse than that, I was staring at the rugged beauty of the Titan in front of me.

"Guess you'll have to wait and see." I shrugged, ripping my gaze from him as I walked out the door with the damp towels, needing to put some distance between us so I could clear my mind.

I swung the front door shut behind me, kicking it lightly with my foot as I carried the towels to the line tied between two massive oak trees. I used it to dry my clothes, towels, and any other linens under Apollo's rays. It was night now, but there was a breeze, and between that and the morning sun, I hoped the towels would be dry by the afternoon.

I went to work hanging the linens on the line, but a voice made me jump.

"I never thought I'd see such normalcy and mortality within the walls of Olympus," Epimetheus said from behind me. *Close* behind me.

I felt the urge to spin around but resisted, continuing my work and trying to ignore his presence.

"Who taught you all this?" he asked, so close now I could feel his breath tickling the hairs on the back of my neck.

Unable to ignore my curiosity any longer, I tossed the remaining linens in a pile on the drying line, promising myself I'd get back to hanging them as soon as I was done telling Epimetheus off for distracting me.

Joke was on me though.

I spun around, and he was so close that my nose nearly brushed his bare chest. I jumped back again, looking up into his eyes, which were turning molten like lava. Primes . . . he was even more intoxicating than I remembered. Even Dionysus's wine didn't have a flicker of the effect Epimetheus had on me.

"Pandora," he said, his full lips turning up in a sinful grin.

"Huh?" I replied, shocked I was even able to spit that out in my current state.

"You're staring again," he said, not breaking eye contact.

The way he was looking at me, it was as if he could see through my eyes all the way into my soul. As if he could find every answer he was looking for without me even having to open my mouth.

"I, uh . . ." I tried to gather my thoughts, but it was useless as he continued to stare. "I'm sorry. I don't know what keeps overtaking me."

His grin grew into a full-blown smile that showcased his perfect, gleaming white teeth, now free of blood, along with the dimples I'd never noticed before. He leaned in, grazing my neck with his lips as he whispered in my ear, "I do." His lips brushed my earlobe and moved across the edge of my jaw, sending shivers down my spine as he lifted my chin to look at him. He was now standing in front of me.

I was breathless, unable to even form a sentence, as I tried my hardest not to fall victim to the temptation pouring off him in waves, begging me to give in.

"Let me know when you figure it out," he said with a smirk.

I wouldn't have had a chance to answer even if I could form words, because the next thing I knew, he'd turned on his heel and was strolling off like the powerful, prideful, perfectly infuriating Titan he was.

CHAPTER 39

PROMETHEUS showed up at my door three days after the attack to check on me and tell me what Epimetheus already had—that Zeus would be sending out notice of the wards in Olympus being reactivated. He didn't stay long after that, saying he had important matters to attend to.

Honestly, I was thankful he didn't stay. I was slightly annoyed it had taken so long for him to make sure I'd survived the attack, but also, I couldn't get what Epimetheus had said out of my mind.

Needing some relief from my cottage, which had begun to feel like a cage since I wasn't able to leave it, I headed out for the path to the summit, intent on visiting Athena. I was tired of being weak and depending on others to protect me. During the Maniae attack, I'd been full of fear and self-doubt, knowing my chances of survival in a situation like that were low. If the attack had proved anything, it was that I needed to focus on learning how to save myself. If Athena hadn't taught me battle strategy all those years ago, I would have been as good as dead. Surely, Zeus could no longer argue that training with her in defense and battle was unnecessary.

As I walked up Mount Olympus toward Athena's courtyard, I couldn't tell if my body was buzzing with excitement at having

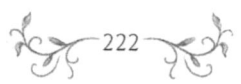

something to do other than be attacked, or if it was buzzing with fear because of the abnormally quiet roadways that led through Lower Olympus.

Scanning the desolate agora leading up to the lagoon, I noticed a good amount of damage throughout the area. Numerous Corinthian columns had crumbled to the ground, bringing pieces of the roof they'd been supporting down with them. Dozens of oak trees and bushes also seemed to have been ripped from the ground and thrown around haphazardly.

The silence began to feel like it would swallow me whole. Even the birds that normally relaxed by the lagoon were nowhere to be seen. I picked up my pace, clearing the path to Athena's palace in half the time. My lungs burned—my legs did too—but I didn't mind. I loved the feeling; it was powerful.

After a few minutes of wheezing, I walked up the stairs and knocked on the front door.

No one answered.

Odd. Maybe she's out the back. I recalled the times I'd seen Athena training in her courtyard.

I walked around the side of her palace, down a long stone stairway leading to a courtyard right on the cliff edge, overlooking Olympus and the wildlands of Aether beyond the wall. Since I'd never gotten to go beyond those walls, every time I got a chance to see the views from this high up, I couldn't help but wonder what was out there. The Realm of Aether was enormous, home to so much more than its prized kingdom Olympus, but Zeus kept Olympus so isolated from everything else that it might as well have been its own realm.

Athena was standing in the middle of the courtyard, her back to me, looking out at the view. She had two swords strapped to her back, and a vest—which I knew contained daggers—was wrapped around her. I couldn't understand how she was so prepared for combat training when I hadn't even asked her for it, but Primes, was I happy.

"I never knew you could read minds too," I said as I stepped down into the stone clearing.

The courtyard was surrounded by Ionic columns, but it had no roof, leaving the cloud-covered sky in clear view. The center was sunken into the mountain by a couple feet and had four steps lining the stone floor.

"Would you consider asking Zeus to clear me for combat training? I'm hoping he might change his mind with everything going on."

"Combat and battle strategy," Athena corrected, turning around with a rare grin on her face. "We will start your training immediately."

She normally presented herself as calm and collected, but I knew better than to think those were the only emotions held within this formidable goddess. Athena loved blood and battle almost as much as Ares, the God of War—she just resisted the urge to fight as much as her bloodthirsty nephew. Where Athena fought with focus and strategy, Ares fought with rage and brutality.

I pulled each of my ankles up to my butt, stretching my sore leg muscles, before crossing my arms over my chest and stretching those as well, knowing the pain I'd be in at the end of the day if I skipped these stretches. When Athena trained, she was relentless, and sometimes, she seemed to forget I didn't have the same energy and power level as her. It was both a blessing and a curse to be treated as more than mortal.

"Well, I'm glad Zeus reconsidered," I said, transitioning into another stretch. "Thought it might be a long shot."

"No." Athena's hard expression didn't change. "He did not reconsider."

I straightened, my heart rate kicking up. *Is she going against Zeus?*

"Zeus may be the King of the Gods, but that does not mean his decisions are always the wisest, especially when it comes to you."

I smirked. *She* is *going against Zeus.* "That's becoming increasingly clear."

Athena unstrapped the two swords from her back. They were covered in gold and silver, with olive branches engraved on the handles and scripture on the blades in the ancient language of the Primes. It translated to "Warrior of Wisdom."

"That doesn't matter now. What you need to focus on is learning to protect yourself from both seen and unseen threats. We'll start with the threats that can be seen." Athena spun the sword and caught the blade in her hand, not even drawing a drop of blood. Then she held the hilt out to me.

I grabbed the sword, relishing the weight of the pommel and the perfect balance of the blade, and tried to resist the pride that overcame me knowing I'd get to train in combat. In Zeus's mind, women had no need to fight, and when I'd asked him why I couldn't fight when goddesses and other beings such as the Furies were allowed to, he'd replied, "They were born to fight. You were not. You were born to be the beauty others battle for, not the beauty they battle against." I'd told Athena about it, and she'd only said I should choose my battles wisely, especially when it came to Zeus, and that if I could win with my wits, anyone who went against me would be as unprepared for the fight as I was.

"Brains over brawn," I accidentally said out loud as I rolled my eyes, earning a small smile full of pride from Athena. She was crouched with her arms open, taunting me to make a move.

"Glad my lessons weren't forgotten," she said before launching herself at me, apparently tired of waiting for my attack.

I spun on my heel, dropping low to the ground, as she swung her arms out to grab hold of me, narrowly missing. I kicked my right leg out, attempting to trip her, but missed completely, spinning right onto my butt as she jumped flawlessly into the air. Athena pulled a dagger from its sheath before dropping to a crouch on top of me, the dagger pointed straight at my heart.

I widened my eyes, shocked by the swift agility she rarely showed outside of battle.

Sheathing her dagger, Athena extended the same hand that had just held my life in it, offering to help me up. I grabbed it and flew to my feet as she pulled my body up as if it were nothing but air.

"Again. This time, focus on the areas I'm not able to move. Avoid the arms and the legs unless they're in a position of weakness. Instead, aim for the torso or the neck when in close range, and if the limbs are the only thing in reach, sever the tendons."

I nodded and crouched into position, preparing for the next attack. Athena darted to my right instead of coming straight at me like before. Instead of running to the left or spinning to meet her like I knew she expected, I spun to the right with her, following on her heels as I launched onto her back and wrapped my arms around her to pin my sword at her throat. I'd almost succeeded when, suddenly, my body was being launched from her back, over her head, and onto the ground in front of her. I felt her dagger pinned against my throat in a similar move to the one I'd just tried to pull on her.

"Better," Athena said, helping me to my feet again and falling back into her battle stance.

CHAPTER 40

WE went through a few more rounds of me landing on my butt in front of Athena, with her weapons pointed at my most vulnerable spots. I had a dagger to my heart, my throat, my spleen, and every artery in my body that could make me bleed out in minutes—or even seconds—if it were cut in the right way.

I panted in exhaustion and embarrassment at having been beaten in battle for more than an hour. Sweat, blood, and bruises were already starting to bloom across my body, while Athena barely even had a hair out of place, her braid still sitting atop her head like a crown.

"What's the point in showing me my vulnerabilities if I can't use them on the immortals I'll be fighting?" I asked through rushed breaths.

"What will kill you may not kill an immortal, but it will slow them down more than the other attacks you could use against them. It will also remind you of your vulnerabilities so you can adequately shield them, which will hopefully prevent an untimely death on your part."

She had a point there.

I nodded, and when she began to crouch, I hurled my petite form at her. She saw it coming, but a second slower than normal, and that was the second I needed.

Pulling my sword into my body as she swung her arms out to stop the attack, I dropped to the ground just as I had earlier—but this time, I used my speed to propel myself forward. I slid past her on the stone, which would surely leave my legs shredded, but I ignored the fire burning in them as I skidded across and pulled a dagger out of one of the sheaths dangling from Athena's waist. In one fluid motion, I sliced the backs of her knees and launched my sword up through the right side of her rib cage, puncturing a lung, as she swung to grab me.

Got her. I smiled with pride as the goddess dropped to the ground beside me in a pool of her own blood, smiling at me broadly.

"That's more like it," she said with an approving nod as she yanked her sword from her side and placed it back in its sheath on her back. Blood poured out of her wounds, but it had zero effect on her.

I laughed, a little dizzy, as my own blood loss started to kick in and the world spun around me. Athena, missing nothing, noticed this, and her brow creased with something akin to worry, though I knew better. She may have been kind to me, but I wasn't foolish enough to think she felt bad about the blows she'd landed on me throughout the day.

"I guess I'd better start heading home before the sun sets," I said, pushing myself to my feet.

"No. You will stay with me tonight. I won't have you stumbling down the mountain with night approaching. You may have beaten me in one battle, but without the adrenaline that propelled you a few minutes ago, it's unlikely you'd win any fight you might face on your way home."

I opened my mouth to protest, but then I swayed on my feet and grabbed my head as if that would keep my exhausted body upright.

"At this rate, a pebble could take you out."

"I . . ." Struggling to find the words, I stared at her in shock. Athena had never opened her palace to anyone—except maybe Artemis, whom she showed more fondness than any other god or goddess in Olympus. She most definitely hadn't opened it to a mortal like me. Especially in my current blood-covered, sweat-slicked state.

She waved me off before I could finish my sentence. "There is no debating on this matter. You'll stay here tonight, and the first thing you will do is bathe. I can already see I'll have to get someone to come clean the blood trail you'll leave on the way to your room."

"I don't know what to say. Thank you, Athena," I said quietly, avoiding eye contact, because the shock of her offer likely had my eyes looking as big as her shields, which were hanging on the wall behind her.

"Nonsense. I'm doing us both a favor. I'll have one of my servants come show you to your room, and I expect to see you at dinner tonight. We have much to discuss." With that said, Athena clapped her hands, and one of her servants appeared. "Tyto, lead our guest to her room."

Like all of Athena's servants, the young woman had the features of an owl and a body similar to mine in size and stature. Her skin was covered by a layer of gray-and-white feathers, and in place of her nose and her mouth was a dark gray, almost black beak. Although what struck me the most was her large golden eyes, which seemed to follow my every move with precision, the same way an owl would look at its prey before swooping in for the kill.

As if sensing my curiosity, Tyto swiveled toward the steps, swinging her winged arm toward me in a way that said, "Follow."

She led me up the stairs alongside the olive grove and through a doorway that opened into an enormous sitting room overlooking the valley. I'd thought the view from the courtyard was beautiful, but this vantage point was better than I could have imagined. From this height, we had an unobstructed, almost bird's-eye view. I didn't realize I'd stopped, stunned by the beauty before me, until I heard a clipped voice say, "Come, mortal. You are bleeding all over the marble floor."

I glanced down at the spot Tyto was looking at, and sure enough, there was a tiny puddle of blood forming at my feet.

"Sorry. I've just never seen—"

"I do not care." She walked toward the hall, ready to leave me lost and bleeding in the middle of the room, like an idiot. "Follow," she said, disappearing behind a large white marble wall and forcing me to run in a half-limp, half-sprint to catch up.

More blood dripped from my wounds as I turned the corner to find her waiting for me.

"Keep up," she said, turning her back to me again, her pace much slower now.

I smiled as I realized she wasn't leaving me behind and slowed to a leisurely walk, favoring the leg that didn't feel like it would twist and fall off with the wrong move. I was no longer bothered about keeping up with her. Instead, she'd have to slow down for me.

Tyto huffed as if she realized what I was doing and stopped to wait for me again.

We did this dance down a few more hallways and up a flight of stairs before she stopped in front of a door, pushing it open and extending her winged arm out to the room before her. As I entered, I sucked in a breath as if I were worried the beauty of the room would pull every ounce of air from my lungs.

Inside, the room was floor-to-ceiling marble, just like the rest of Athena's palace, but instead of being plain, boring white, the marble was covered in intricately carved friezes. They seemed to

decorate every inch of wall space, depicting scenes of battle and glory with none other than Athena herself.

As I took in the glory of Athena braced in battle, Tyto spoke from the doorway.

"You will have time to fawn over those later. For now, I suggest you bathe and dress your wounds. There are bandages and salves from Apollo on the shelf over there." She pointed her winged arm toward a doorway I assumed led into the bathroom. "Athena expects you in the dining hall at dusk. I'll return before then to escort you." She started to pull the door closed but added, "Hopefully, you'll smell better by then."

I laughed a little to myself as I thought of what Tyto must look like trying to scrunch her beak in a similar way to the other Olympians when they found the unfortunate features of my mortality disgusting.

Walking through the lavish room, I ignored the friezes on the walls, instead focusing on the ceiling, which was covered in glass, allowing me to see the sky above it. Olive branches twisted between the panes of glass as if they were supporting their weight, which I knew was impossible. It was more likely that during the building of Athena's palace, Hephaestus had fortified the branches like I'd seen him do in the past, hollowing them out and filling them with liquified metal.

Stepping into the bathroom, I expected to see a claw-foot tub or something similar to the copper tub in my cottage, but I could not have been more off the mark. Instead, an enormous glass pool had been sunken into the floor. It spilled over the edge of the room, out into the exposed air, between two Corinthian columns.

I was expecting a room similar to the bedroom, but this bathroom was designed in a way that you could bathe outside, on a large balcony of sorts, overlooking the olive grove below. It had a glass roof, the same as the bedroom, to protect from the elements when Zeus lost his temper, but it also allowed a cool breeze to dance through the space and tickle the hairs on the back of my neck. I quickly stripped down and stepped into the pool, pleased to find the water warm to the touch. It smelled of citrus and peony and a medicinal scent I couldn't put my finger on.

The pool was intoxicating, and it lulled the aches and pains in my body, along with the chaos I hadn't realized was consuming my mind. I'd expected it to sting my wounds as I entered but found it to be soothing instead, washing away the blood, giving the once clear water a red tinge.

Primes, I could stay in this pool forever . . . I rested my chin atop my arms, which were folded on the edge of the pool, and watched as Athena's sacred animals, owls and snakes, swooped and slithered through the grove.

Once I felt my eyes start to drift shut, begging for sleep, I gathered all my willpower and forced myself from the pool, wrapping myself in some of the coziest linen I'd ever experienced. Patting myself dry, careful of the cuts, I walked over to find the salve Tyto had mentioned. I grabbed the glass jar and some cotton wraps to use as bandages and went to work applying globs of the soothing salve onto my wounds before wrapping them carefully.

When I walked back into the bedroom, I was pleased to find a fresh peplos laid out neatly on the bed. I loved a peplos because of the fabric, which was pinned at each shoulder and secured with a rope at the waist. Considering how frigid the night had become, I was grateful for the extra warmth. Looking to the horizon, I watched as the sun descended toward the Sea of Poseidon, drying my hair in its final rays before braiding it down my back and getting dressed for my dinner with Athena.

CHAPTER 41

By the time Tyto had led me into the dining chamber, Athena was already seated at the table, swirling a deep red liquid in her chalice.

"Come," Athena said, motioning to the chair made entirely from olive wood, then across the white marble table, which had olive tree trunks for legs. They twisted and climbed around the edges of the table.

Tyto walked ahead of me, pulling the chair out and grabbing me a chalice of my own, which she promptly filled with wine.

I gulped the wine down eagerly, craving the relief it brought. It dulled my aches and pains, as well as the mental warfare I'd been going through lately with the Titan brothers. It was as if my heart and my mind were pulling me in opposite directions, threatening to rip me apart if I didn't make a choice.

"I see I'm not the only one craving relief from the world tonight," Athena said, flicking a relaxed finger at my chalice as I took another gulp.

I cleared my throat and set my chalice down as I racked my brain for a way to reply.

"Don't stop on my account," Athena said with a carefree shrug.

What was up with her today? She'd always been so strict with me, and she never, ever went against Zeus's commands, but today, it was like she was throwing all that to the side to let me have a taste of not only freedom but something else I'd never known.

Equality.

"Is this some sort of test?" I finally asked, eyeing her with caution. I didn't want my words to come out as an insult; I was simply trying to figure out what her motives were.

"No test. I just thought you deserved a little reward for your success today. I cannot tell you the last time someone drew so much blood from me." Her lips pulled up into a small grin. "Not even the Keres were able to."

I smiled back, my heart swelling with pride at her appraisal. "They didn't train with you," I said, bringing the glass to my nose and inhaling the fruity, floral, earthy scent. Something about this wine felt different from the wine I normally drank, but I couldn't put my finger on it.

"True," she said, taking a sip from her glass. "Are you enjoying the wine?"

"Yes," I said, sipping it slower this time to savor the taste.

"This blend is more of an acquired taste than the wine Dionysus serves in Lower Olympus."

"Why? What makes it different?" I asked as Tito came by and refilled my chalice.

"This blend was made specifically for the High Olympians. There's a small dose of nectar in it, so I suggest you drink it fully if you don't want that porcelain skin of yours to be black-and-blue tomorrow." She took another sip before adding, "Plus, I'd hate for Tyto to have to spend all her time tomorrow scrubbing your blood from the bed linens."

I stared at her for a moment, unsure of her intentions, and then decided I agreed. I didn't want to be bruised and battered when I woke up either. I took another deep gulp, coughing as

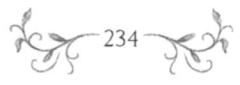

the liquid went down wrong, making me feel like I'd swallowed a rock. It finally settled, flowing into my stomach.

"Good," Athena said, setting her chalice down and waving Tyto over to fill it. "Now then, shall we get back to the reason for this dinner?"

I nodded, sitting further back in my seat as the effects of the wine started to spread through my body, making it feel tingly and numb.

"Zeus may be the elected ruler of Olympus, but he is not the wisest when it comes to looking past his own ambitions and focusing on the bigger picture, especially where you're concerned."

I listened eagerly, thankful someone might finally be able to shed some light on what Zeus was thinking. I'd just never expected that someone to be Athena.

"When I was first assigned to teach you the ways of womanhood, I was honored. That soon changed when I realized what Zeus intended for you was not at all what you would need to survive this world and the next. He wanted a woman who would make mankind fall to their knees worshipping her beauty and kindness until it blinded them from the true threat to their existence. Zeus."

This world and the next? Was she talking about Earth?

"But Zeus didn't just send Prometheus to create man. He became their father, their protector, their savior. Why would he be a threat to them?" I asked, wanting badly to bring up why man had been roaming Aether before Prometheus created them for Earth but not wanting to push her.

"Zeus did not have man created. He stole them," Athena said, confirming my suspicions.

"From who? Prometheus? Is that why he sided with Olympus—to get man back?" I asked.

"No." Athena stared at me, her head tilted to the side as if she were wondering how much of the truth I could handle.

"Then who? I thought Prometheus created man and joined Olympus in the war to protect them." I paused, adding, "Were they alive during the Dark Ages of the Titans' rule?"

"Yes. Mankind lived long before they arrived in Gaia's realm, and they were much different than the man we know today. Prometheus did create today's version of man, but he did not create the first. That was another Titan." She was being as evasive as ever.

"If it wasn't Prometheus, then which Titan created the first man?" I asked again, this time more forcefully than I meant.

Athena raised her brow at my tone. "Epimetheus."

CHAPTER 42

"**E**PIMETHEUS created mankind?" I asked, feeling like I might have misheard Athena. "How could he have created mankind, and not Prometheus? Epimetheus created animals," I clarified, confused at what she was telling me, which was the opposite of everything I knew.

Athena smiled. "Right you are, but as I said, the first of mankind were not the same as those who roam Earth, as they call it, today."

I lifted my chalice to my lips, listening to every word, no longer settled in my seat but on the edge of it. The numbness in my limbs faded as energy coursed through my body at the revelation. "What do you mean by that?"

"When Epimetheus created animals—thousands, if not millions, of species—one of them was mammals. These mammals were different from other species, because they were more similar to our forms than the cretes who roamed Aether. They were born alive and fed on milk produced by the mother. They also had fur and were warm-blooded to help weather the cold other species could not withstand. But most importantly, their minds became more complex than other animals."

"So were all mammals considered the first humans then?"

"No. As Epimetheus created more and more mammals, he created a type that began to evolve on its own, without his help— whether through the Primes' intervention or because they'd simply been able to understand enough to mimic the gods they encountered, we're not sure. But one day, they changed."

"Changed, how? What were they?"

"They came from a group of mammals known as primates. Among the vast number of primates, there was one small group that seemed to be more separated than the rest. This group was named the Hominidae and consisted of four families, but only one of the four families evolved without Epimetheus's guidance. The Homo sapiens," Athena said slowly, watching me carefully as she spoke.

"So if these *Homo sapiens* evolved into mankind, why does Prometheus get the credit, not Epimetheus?" I asked, trying to understand how the history books had gotten it so wrong.

"Although they evolved, they were never seen as anything more than another of Epimetheus's animals. That is, until the day Cronos decided he could use the Homo sapiens as slaves and realized they weren't as wise and powerful as the cretes who'd served him before. He bargained that after living in the wild for so long, fighting everything around them to survive, all they needed was food and shelter to feel indebted. It worked for a while, until talks of the war began to spread."

"I don't understand. Didn't Prometheus join Zeus to save mankind? If he was living among them in Othrys, then why would he go to Olympus?"

"Prometheus envied the attention Epimetheus's creations were getting and secretly went to Zeus, offering his help, saying he could recreate the species his brother had made, but that this time, they'd be created in the Olympians' image. He promised Zeus he could have a world full of them if he allowed Prometheus to take control of their creation. Zeus agreed, under one condition. Prometheus needed to watch over mankind and personally

ensure they understood they wouldn't survive—would not even be alive—without the help of the Olympians."

"Why would Epimetheus go along with that? Surely, he must have known when he followed Prometheus to Olympus."

Athena looked at me sadly. "If I had to guess, I'd say he felt a responsibility toward mankind, and to his twin brother. With his creation being used by the Titans, maybe he wished to see them live a better life than one of slavery, so he put his own ego aside and let Prometheus take credit for their recreation on Earth."

I shook my head. This was all too much. I'd been desperate to find out more about mankind in Aether, hoping it would clear everything up, but instead, I was left only with more questions.

"So that's why Zeus is using me to get close to Prometheus. To tighten his power over mankind," I said, remembering the vague version of the story Zeus had told me when he tested my training before the Centennial Celebration of Man.

"Part of it. Zeus had no reason to control Prometheus until a century ago."

"When were mankind put on Earth? Wait—were they created on Earth, or in Olympus?"

"At first, both, but then Prometheus lashed out, wanting to give mankind the opportunity to control their own destiny."

"How did he do that?"

"He stole all the men within Olympus's walls and sent them to Earth, then he returned to Olympus to steal the one thing he'd seen in his visions mankind would need to survive, at least for a time, without the gods. Fire."

"Fire?" I asked before it dawned on me. "Wait . . . he stole Hestia?"

"The eldest of the Olympians, and the most peaceful. He stole her away to Earth, forcing her to gift mankind with fire. When Zeus found out, he was furious, and he sentenced Prometheus to an eternity of torment."

"How did he get out of that? Zeus isn't exactly the forgiving type."

"Epimetheus petitioned on his brother's behalf, explaining to Zeus that the rate of mankind's creation and the animals filling Gaia's realm were too much for him to handle alone. He swore to stay by Prometheus's side and make sure he never attempted anything against Olympus again if they would spare him. Zeus agreed and sent Prometheus back, letting them rule in peace for nearly eighty years before the idea for a new creation came to him. One that would ensure the Titan Prometheus never chose mankind over the Olympians again."

"Me," I said, remembering what Zeus had told me about being able to create life. But something still wasn't adding up. "Wait. If Homo sapiens were animals, then they would have had females in the time of the first man, right?" I asked, adding, "Epimetheus granted his creations the ability to procreate, so they must have had women among them, even children." I smiled at the thought. Maybe they'd led me to believe I was the only woman in existence to control me. Maybe that had all been a lie. Maybe I wasn't alone.

Smiling sadly, Athena said, "At first, but when Cronos realized the power the Homo sapiens held to procreate, he ordered all the female Homo sapiens to be executed on the spot. This meant the population would be controlled and gave the gods yet another thing to hold over mankind to ensure they stayed in Othrys as loyal slaves."

"He murdered them . . . all?" I asked, feeling sick at the thought of so many innocent lives being lost for something so trivial.

"Every single one in existence. That was one of Zeus and Prometheus's earlier agreements—that the gods would not bestow upon mankind the power to procreate. Which they both upheld, until Zeus decided to create you. A mortal woman raised by the Olympians, loyal to the Olympians, would be the one thing Prometheus could never resist."

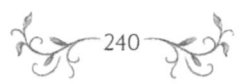

"But am I even able to procreate? Was that included in my creation? I mean, not that I've ever tried, but I'm pretty sure it's something I would know, or at least something someone would have told me about by now, so it didn't accidentally happen." My mind felt as turbulent as the sea. Maybe it was the information, or maybe it was the amount of wine I'd consumed, but the room seemed to be spinning.

"Not yet," Athena replied before everything went dark.

CHAPTER 43

WOKE up with my head flat on the marble table and someone shaking me.

"Pandora, are you all right?" Athena asked in a worried tone I'd never heard her use before.

"What happened?" I asked, squinting at the pool of wine rolling across the marble toward my face.

"You had too much wine and passed out." She helped me to sit up in the chair. "Tyto, I think our guest may need some assistance getting back to her room for the night." She whipped her head toward the plate I noticed sitting to my right. "Take her food up when you're done. She'll need it when she wakes up."

I stumbled out of the room alongside Tyto, who'd wrapped a winged arm across my back and was gripping my side to help support me.

Somehow, I made it back to my room in one piece and didn't waste a moment, flopping onto my bed to stare at the star-filled sky above me, thinking of how I wished I could be anywhere else other than Olympus, and anyone else other than Pandora, the only mortal woman.

Primes, this was going to be a rough night, if the spinning sky was any hint at what was to come.

I lay there for a while letting my mind wander, going over the massive amount of information Athena had dropped on me tonight. I'd never seen her so vocal and open. Normally, Clio was the one I went to with my questions, but even Clio hadn't told me the version of events Athena just had.

The spinning sky began to fade, and I was thankful for the reprieve from my mind as my eyes drifted shut into a deep sleep, where there was nothing but the peace and silence of the void.

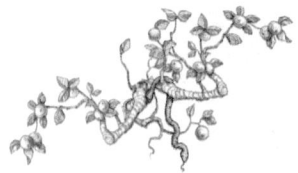

I WOKE UP early and headed downstairs in the hope of running into Athena before I returned to my cottage. To my surprise, she was waiting in the sitting room, holding a small glass with tendrils of steam rising past its rim.

"Pandora, glad to see you doing better today," she said from her seat, motioning for me to sit in the one across from her overlooking the view. "Would you like some tea?"

"Yes, please," I said, watching as another owl creature, who must be Tyto's replacement, went about fixing me a cup before setting it on the table at my side.

I grabbed the cup, inhaling the floral scent and taking a sip, and nearly moaned as the tea coated my parched throat, warming me from the inside out.

"Did you sleep well?"

I laughed. "Like the dead."

"Well, I must say, when I saw your eyes roll back into your head and your entire body slump forward, I feared for a moment you might have been. I've never drunk wine with a mortal, let alone in such large volumes."

"I can't say it was just the wine that affected me." I paused, setting my cup down. "You were pretty open with information last night. Between that and the alcohol, I'd say my body was more overwhelmed than it could cope with."

"I agree. I apologize for laying so many truths at your feet in one sitting, but in light of recent events, I felt it prudent to give you all the information I had. It isn't fair to keep you in the dark any longer."

"Was it ever fair to begin with?"

"For a long time, I believed so. I may not seem it, but I do have a heart, Pandora, and after training with you for so long, I've become quite fond of you. I wanted you to be prepared for what was to come, but I also didn't find it necessary to burden you in your youth, choosing instead to let you enjoy your life here."

"Until it was ripped away from me. I was never going to be allowed to stay in Olympus, was I?" I asked, even though I was pretty sure I already knew the answer.

"No. You were always meant to go to the Realm of Man. You were to act as a bridge, binding the Olympians to mankind right under Prometheus's nose."

"So what am I supposed to do now—just go back to normal, pretending to be naïve to the political ploys around me?" I shook my head. "I don't think I can do that."

"You must," she snapped. "If Zeus knew of our conversation, it would mean more danger than you know."

"How so?" I asked, crossing my arms.

"You care for your sister, Persephone, do you not?"

"Of course, but what does she have to do with this?"

"Not her directly, but her mother, Demeter." Athena looked at the confusion plastered on my face before adding, "Demeter is the ruler of fertility, but Persephone also has the power to create life. If you were to let on about what I shared with you, Zeus might try to double down and use them as pawns in the process." She shifted in her seat. "He has Hades imprisoned—it isn't unreasonable to think that by imprisoning them as well, he'd have a tighter grip on you. But he would also control their ability

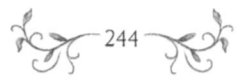

to grant you fertility, which Zeus ensured they blocked at your birth so Prometheus couldn't simply steal you away from under his nose."

"They *what*?" I asked, my chest tightening. Had they been in on it this whole time? Was their love for me all a ruse? A means to an end?

"Those who have kept themselves closest to you are the ones you must be the most careful around. No one is who they seem, especially in Olympus."

"Why are you helping me then? You're one of those closest to me, so wouldn't that go for you as well?"

"As I said, I no longer see the wisdom in Zeus's plan. Now, I think the wisest move is to do what everyone else is too afraid to do. Tell the truth."

I watched her closely, waiting for any warning sign that might appear to tell me whether she could be trusted or not.

"If you really aren't a threat to me, will you help me?"

"I have. I've just told you everything you need to know," Athena said, frowning at me.

"And I appreciate that, but that isn't the help I was referring to. Train with me. Teach me how to defend myself. I know we used to train frequently, but over the years, my skills have faded," I said. "Will you keep training with me as we did yesterday, so I may yet have a chance to survive this dreadful destiny the fates have laid out for me?"

Athena smiled. "It would be my pleasure."

CHAPTER 44

IT had been a few days since I returned to my cottage from Athena's palace, suddenly fearing my home and everyone within it now I was viewing them in a new light. I'd once admired Olympus's beauty, but now, all I could think of when I looked out my window were the evils that beauty might be hiding.

A knock sounded at my door, and I rushed to open it, hoping it was Athena finally stopping by for our lesson.

"It's about ti—" I began, but the words got stuck in my throat as I looked up to find Epimetheus standing in front of me, smiling, with his scarred brow pulled high into the curls on his forehead.

"Not who you were expecting?" He looked me over as a frown formed on my face.

"No, you were not," I said, moving to close the door—but he put his hand out, stopping me from moving it more than an inch.

"Listen, I'm sorry about the other night. I shouldn't have said those things. I was wrong to have put you in such a position." Epimetheus's eyes pleaded with me as he pulled his hand through his hair, mussing it up and somehow looking even more handsome for it.

"You're right. You shouldn't have," I said, taking my frustration out on him even though I knew full well I'd played a part in the flirtation, much as I didn't want to admit it.

"Are you all right, Pandora?" he asked, looking me over again before his eyes drifted past me and took in the mess of my cottage—evidence of locking myself in for the past few days as my mind spiraled with possibilities.

"I'm fine," I said, moving to push the door shut again, but he put his foot in front of it.

"No, you're not." Wedging his body between me and the doorway, he forced his way in and immediately set about picking things up throughout the kitchen and sitting area.

"What in Primes do you think you're doing!"

"Exactly what it looks like. Helping," he replied, not bothering to look at me as he gathered soiled linens that had been thrown around the room, where they were doomed to stay until I had the motivation to clean them and hang them out.

"I don't need your help, Epimetheus." Putting my hands on my hips, I glared at him.

"Don't need it or don't want it?" he asked, still not stopping.

"What I need and what I want is for you to leave," I said, my voice rising with my temper.

"Fine. I'll leave right after I finish picking this stuff up." He threw a few sheets over his shoulders, then he rolled the soiled linen into a ball and tucked it under his arm.

Helpless! That's what I was as I put my hands in my hair, wanting to scream. If I couldn't even keep my house under my control, then how was I supposed to ever have a chance at controlling my destiny?

I dropped onto the couch, holding my head in my hands, tears welling in my eyes as my nostrils began to burn. Everything came crashing down on me so fast I didn't even have it in me to worry about Epimetheus bearing witness to my mental breakdown.

"Pandora?" he said softly, resting his powerful hand on my shoulder. "Please, just let me help you."

"I can't," I sputtered out, tears dripping off my cheeks as my nose began to run.

"Whatever is going on, I can help. You don't need to tell me anything you don't want to. Just let me help you."

"Why?" I snapped, glaring up at him through tear-filled eyes. "What's in it for you? Are you going to go back and tell your brother I'm a mess and he should leave me while he still can? Or maybe you'll tell him I'm such an emotional wreck there's no need to marry me. He might as well just steal me away like he did with Hestia."

I knew I'd said too much, but I failed to care with all the betrayal and anger I'd been bottling up inside since I found out everyone I knew and loved—everyone I considered to be family—had been lying to me my entire life, only using me to fulfill their own needs or protect their own backs. I was done hiding. If they wanted to kill me, fine. If they wanted to steal me, fine. But whatever they chose, I was going to make it abundantly clear I wouldn't go down without a fight.

"How much do you know?" Epimetheus asked, his face now free of emotion.

"Everything I need to know, I suppose. You created mankind. Your brother stole your creation, remaking them in his own name with Zeus's help, before he kidnapped Hestia, and you had to make a deal to save him." I stared at him, gauging his reaction before adding, "And now you're here for the last piece of the puzzle. Me."

"Pandora, it's not what you think—"

"Oh, really? So you're not here to enslave me to mankind the same way the Titans enslaved your Homo sapiens," I snapped, glaring daggers at him.

He stared back at me, his face going slack. "No, I'm not," he said, lifting his eyes to mine as the shock of my words faded and

he cleared his throat. "I'm here for my brother, as I always am. I hated what the Titans did to my creations and wished to set them free, back into Aether, far away from the Titans' reach, but my brother had other ideas. By the time I'd heard of him making a deal with Zeus, I couldn't stop the plans from being set in motion. I was forced to choose between my twin and my creations. I chose him. And when Zeus punished him for stealing Hestia, I chose him again."

"So what you're saying is, you will always choose Prometheus no matter the cost."

"Yes. That is, until I met you," he said, reaching forward to grab my hand and holding it in his tenderly. I started to pull away, but he stopped me. "From the moment I laid eyes on you, everything I thought I knew about the universe was thrown to the wind. At first, I thought you were a goddess, maybe even one of Aphrodite's daughters."

I snorted at the thought, and he smiled.

"But then you were announced as mortal, and it was like a fire had been lit somewhere within my heart . . . within my soul."

"You didn't even know me."

"I didn't need to. I'd seen you before the celebration, on your way to Zeus's, and thought you were the most beautiful being in all the realms—"

I cut him off. "Wait—you were here that long before the celebration?" I remembered something—glowing eyes watching me from the courtyard outside Zeus's palace. "That was you hiding in the trees?"

Epimetheus smiled sheepishly, looking down at our intertwined hands as if he were embarrassed. "Yes, that was me. I wasn't supposed to be here yet, so I remained hidden. Even then, I knew there was something special about you."

"So, why let him court me? Why not claim me for yourself?" I asked.

"Unlike my brother, I find no joy in things bought or stolen. I find the greatest things in life are earned." He said this as if he resented his brother. "I swear on everything I am, I would never force you into something you did not want."

"But you're willing to stand by and watch as others do exactly that?"

"I cannot stop what is happening, Pandora. Much as I wish I could step in and fix the mess my brother has made, I can't. I don't have the power to take on all of Olympus by myself." He was pleading with me to listen to him, but I was already pulling away.

"Then we have nothing left to say. We both know where we stand, and that nothing can change," I said, walking to the front door and opening it back up. "I think it's time you leave now."

"Pandora, please just let me—"

"No. I'm done listening. I want you to leave."

"I'm sorry," he said, giving in as he walked to the door, his head hanging low like a wounded animal.

"Apologies only go so far, Epimetheus." I slammed the door shut behind him.

CHAPTER 45

I WAS grateful for a few days' peace before Athena finally came to my cottage. It gave me plenty of time to calm down and get my mind together after everything that went down with Epimetheus. Athena and I hadn't discussed where training would take place, and I figured she'd send a message of some sort to let me know our training schedule, but instead, she showed up on my doorstep in the early evening, right as the sun dipped below the horizon.

"Hmm," Athena said, looking around the space.

"What? Not up to your standards?" I snapped, feeling oddly defensive at having her in my home. Sure, it was more average than any of the other places she visited, but it wasn't like I had the luxury of living like the gods and goddesses in Olympus, especially those who were granted a palace on the summit.

"No, it's not that. It just feels . . ." Athena paused, trying to find the right word to explain my tiny home. "Intimate."

I laughed, trying not to feel offended. "I guess that's one way to put it."

She was still looking around when she blurted out, "Guess there aren't a lot of hiding places for intruders."

"Who would want to intrude? Not many Olympians come down this far, probably because they don't want to piss off Demeter by being in her orchards," I said, grabbing a glass of water from the kitchen and taking a big gulp as I leaned against the wood counter.

"As I told you, Zeus is not fond of me training you in combat and battle strategy. My servants informed me they noticed some of his eagles hovering around the property, likely keeping tabs on us. Therefore, it's no longer safe to train on the summit."

"So you came here . . . to train me?" I stared at her curiously.

"Yes." She looked around as if she wanted to sit but wasn't sure if she should. "It's imperative you be prepared for everything to come, but I cannot risk Zeus finding out, so we shall continue your training here."

"When do we start?"

"Tonight. It's best to do this in the cover of darkness. I mentioned at our last session you would need to train for unseen *and* seen attacks. You triumphed in our last battle of the seen threat, so now we'll focus on the unseen," Athena stated, as if it made any sense that I'd be expected to fight such a formidable opponent when I couldn't even see the hand in front of my face.

"Guess I'd better go get my training clothes on," I grumbled before downing the last of my water.

"Wait," Athena said. "I brought you something." She pulled a rectangular package wrapped in twine out of her bag and handed it to me.

Taking the gift, I remained silent, staring at it in confusion. What was happening to her? I'd never known Athena to be a protector, let alone a gift-giver, and recently, she seemed like a totally different being than the one I grew up with.

I unwrapped the gift slowly, carefully untangling the twine. My breath caught.

A full suit of armor.

The black armor glinted in the dim candlelight, embellished with bronze. Holding it up, I realized I'd never seen a fabric like this. It was so soft it felt slippery between my fingertips, and it reminded me of the silk I'd seen in Aphrodite's fabric collection—yet at the same time, it had more resilience than any of those fabrics.

"It's beautiful, Athena," I said, admiring the beautiful craftsmanship. "What is it made from?"

"Spider silk. I made a bargain with Arachne," Athena said, trying to hide her smile, but I caught it.

"Arachne? Must have been some bargain after you stole her beauty and turned her into a spider." I laughed lightly even though I'd always cringed at the story of Athena's spiteful curse. It reminded me all too well of something Hera would have done.

"Yes. Well, I did make it very clear that it was for you, not me, which softened her hate a little." Athena smiled, showing no remorse for the horrendous creature she'd turned poor Arachne into. "She assured me there is no stronger material in Aether than spider silk. When weaved correctly, it is lightweight, flexible, highly durable, adaptable to temperatures, water resistant, and it can help to prevent infection and stop bleeding if anything were ever able to pierce its structure."

"I don't know what's more shocking—that she helped or that you went to her in the first place."

Athena shrugged. "There is one thing the material is susceptible to, which you must use extreme caution around."

"What?"

"Fire."

"Lucky for me, I don't plan on getting lit on fire anytime soon." I laughed, only to have a serious glare pointed my way.

"You may not, but if someone else finds your armor's weakness, they may use it to their advantage."

Fair point. I cringed at the thought of being burned to a crisp.

Athena glanced out the window as a small owl flew by, hooting as it passed. Definitely one of her servants. They were probably making sure the area was clear and safe for us to practice unseen.

Whatever the owl servant had hooted must have pleased Athena, because she turned back to me, and a small smile cracked across her stone-cold face. "Time to train. Go put your armor on."

"Not going easy on me tonight, huh?" I asked, quirking an eyebrow at her with a nervous smile.

"Not at all." Her face lit up in a grin before she walked out to the field across the road, sending a burst of wind to pull the door shut behind her.

CHAPTER 46

THE armor fit my body like a second skin, allowing me to move freely while covering every bit of visible skin, from my ankles to my wrists and all the way up to my neck. I strapped a dagger to my leg and a sword onto my back before turning to look at my reflection.

I looked *powerful* in this suit of armor. Not only that, but I *felt* powerful in it, as if the fabric had woven a sense of bravery and strength into my body.

Lifting my chin in the air, I took my long, dark curls out of the clip they were falling from and quickly braided them, then I twisted the braid over my head like one of the High Olympians' crowns. Satisfied with the female warrior reflected in front of me, I walked over to the field to train with Athena.

I hadn't even closed the front door before Athena's voice rang out to me from the oak tree in the distance.

"Come on, girl. I don't have all night."

Smiling at her in the dark, I pulled the door closed and jogged over to her side, being careful of the dips in the ground as I ran. I didn't want to make a fool of myself by stumbling or falling on my face in front of her.

I made it over to her with only one barely noticeable stumble, and she looked me up and down, her eyes flashing with something that looked a lot like pride. Her lips curled into a grin.

"I hate to admit to Arachne's skill, but she's weaved her spider silk to perfection. It fits your form as if she sewed it directly onto your body, and the braid crown was a bold choice, but I must say, it does look wonderful with your new armor."

My eyes widened at her compliments. I couldn't help but smile.

"We'd better get start—"

I pounced before she could finish, although I should have known she'd be ready for it, since I could hardly ever catch the goddess off-guard. Athena stepped to the side and stuck her foot out, tripping me as I tried to stop the momentum from running through my body at the attack.

I rolled to the side mid-fall so I wouldn't hit my face, and luckily, I managed to land on my back in the grass, which cushioned most of the blow.

"You grunt before you attack," Athena said, with a hand on her hip. "It alerts me to your move before you've even made it."

I grunted in response to that, pushing off the ground into a fighting position and circling her as I tried to watch her own movements.

Athena circled me too and smirked right before she ran at me. I swung my sword at her, and she dropped to the ground, sliding past me and pulling my feet out from under me. My body hadn't even hit the ground before she was on top of me, holding her sword to my throat and pinning her dagger to my side.

"You smirk before you attack." I smiled at her, proud of my observation.

"Good job. You still lost."

"Not for long." I smirked and rolled out from under her, pushing her body off to the side of mine with all my strength.

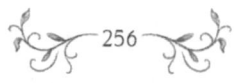

Athena let out a small laugh. "We're just warming up." She stood and picked up my sword, which had fallen to the side during her tackle, and handed it to me. "I said we'd be practicing the unseen tonight, and you can still see me."

I sighed at that, knowing the training was necessary to prepare me for any type of attack that might come my way, but also dreading the soreness I'd surely feel tomorrow morning, after I'd landed on my butt a hundred more times.

Getting back to my feet, I readied myself for the next attack.

Athena won once again, and we did that over and over, until I *almost* had her in a trap—before she evaded it and pinned me with her dagger again.

"You're getting faster. Now, we remove your sight." She pulled a long piece of black gauze from her pocket and walked over to me, grabbing my shoulders to turn me and covering my eyes with the inky gauze. She secured it behind my head, tying it tight, so it wouldn't slip off during the fight.

"How is it that I'm supposed to do this without any powers, again?" I asked as I tried to imagine the incredible task ahead of me. Competing with Athena while not having my sight seemed like nothing short of impossible. So far, the only way I'd had any type of advantage was to watch for visual cues, such as her smirks and the moments when passion flashed in her eyes as her powers longed for the fight.

"Your senses are your powers."

"Yeah, but you're taking the one I depend on most," I argued.

"Exactly. Once you master *all* your senses, not only will you be able to go up against the unseen, but you'll become a greater opponent than you may have thought possible." Athena tapped me on the shoulder, and I listened to her footsteps walking away.

I stood there lost and starting to panic as I struggled to figure out what I was supposed to do.

"Focus on your hearing and your sense of touch to fight me," Athena said from somewhere nearby, but I was too distracted by my loss of sight to focus on the direction her voice came from.

"My sense of touch?" I asked, bewildered. "What, should I start crawling around on the ground until I run into your feet?" I laughed at the idea.

"No," Athena deadpanned, not finding the humor in my question. "You use the sense of touch to focus on the vibration of the ground or the tickle of the breeze when your opponent moves. If you master this, then you'll track them faster than with sight, because many times, the body shifts in preparation of enacting the mind's demands." I heard her footsteps approaching again as she came to stand in front of me. "I'll start by helping you to awaken these senses. I'll move, and you'll track my motions, telling me when I stop and where I'm standing in relation to you."

Athena moved slowly at first, and the air swept over my right arm as she moved behind me, causing tiny strands of hair to tickle my neck. The hair on the back of my head moved slightly as she moved behind me, and suddenly, I felt a tiny shift in the air on the front left side of my body.

The air went still around me.

"You stopped, and you're . . ." I paused, listening as hard as I could strain my ears, feeling like they were stretching from my intense effort as I thought of the movements I'd felt her make. I reached out to my front left side and was about to take a step forward, but I felt a tiny tremor a little more toward the right, dead center of where I was standing. I swiveled at the last second, and my hand connected with a lean, rock-solid arm.

"There!" I accidentally screeched with excitement at my victory.

"Good," Athena said and started to move away from me. "Again."

We did this hide-and-seek game a dozen more times before she decided it was enough for the night, and that I was making

better progress than she expected. This made me grin like a proud lunatic.

"We'll practice every night, four hours past dusk. For now, be on alert at all times. I have a feeling the Keres and the Maniae are only the beginning of the Aloadae twins' attack, and whatever their next move is, it will likely be even more catastrophic than the previous. Do not let your guard down around anyone or anything at any time."

Athena unwrapped the blindfold, and I immediately pulled her into a big, sweaty hug. For the first time in my life, I felt powerful. I felt like the Goddess of Mortal Women.

"Thank you, Athena. For everything."

She patted me on the back awkwardly before pulling out of my grip. "Wear your armor anytime you leave the cottage," she said before turning away and walking down the road to the bridge that crossed into Lower Olympus.

CHAPTER 47

I TRAINED relentlessly.

Even in the daylight hours, when Athena wasn't there hounding me to train harder and faster, I was out there doing it on my own every chance I got.

I may have been born without powers or stamina handed to me, but Primes be my witness, I was going to earn them. I would not stop until I was able to not only defend myself against any attack, but to fight offensively as well.

Besides, Athena hadn't bothered to show up the past couple of nights, and similar to Prometheus, she didn't seem to feel the need to tell me why, so I was left to train on my own.

Fine by me.

I threw my dagger into the tree, nailing the center of the target—a wooden circle I'd imprinted with a beet stain. I'd been out here for hours and decided it was finally time to head in and get started on cooking something for dinner.

Outside the front door, I kicked off my muddy boots, promising to return later to clean them, because I didn't have the energy to do it now. I was about to open the door when someone spoke from behind me.

"Pandora," Athena said breathlessly, making me swivel on my heel toward her.

"It's about time you showed up." I lifted a brow as I took in her appearance.

She pushed past me and walked straight into my cottage, not waiting for an invitation like normal. She wore her usual Ionic chiton, which was fancier than most and showed off her status, but it was covered by a thick, heavy robe, with a hood that covered almost her entire face.

"Come on in," I said, following her into my cottage.

"I'm in no mood for your attitude, Pandora," she snapped.

I stopped in my tracks at her tone and took a moment to look her over, trying to figure out what was going on. I thought she'd moved past her cold demeanor toward me, but it seemed whatever was going on had made her digress back into her normal blunt attitude. The patience and kindness she'd shown me recently were nowhere to be found.

"Why are you dressed like you're trying to hide?"

"Because I am hiding," she snapped again. "The sphinx saw me enter into Lower Olympus, headed toward Demeter's fields, and has reported my whereabouts to Hera. It will not be long before Hera tells Zeus of how I've been spending my time."

"How did you not realize you were being followed?" I asked, incredulous that the Goddess of Wisdom had been caught.

"I noticed the same moment the sphinx did. We looked at each other for a couple of seconds before it flew off. I hoped it would mistake me, not able to believe I'd been caught sneaking around Lower Olympus, but when that didn't work, I hid until there was a clear path to get to you."

"So what now?" I asked.

"I can no longer risk training you. Although, by the looks of the tree out front, it seems you have taken over in my absence." Her tone softened ever so slightly.

"Like you said, I need to be prepared for anything." I walked past her to lean against the kitchen counter. "Are you staying, or did you just come to tell me you quit?" I asked, snarkier than I meant to. I felt a flare of abandonment at the news she was giving up on me out of fear of Zeus's wrath—not that I could blame her. I couldn't imagine going against his command.

"Don't be immature, Pandora," Athena said, walking over to stand in front of me, demanding my attention with her powerful presence as she pinned me with her relentless glare.

"I didn't mean it that way. Everything's coming at me from every angle, and I don't know how to handle it," I said, shaking my head at my rudeness. "It's just . . . I have all this pressure on me to win Prometheus's heart, but knowing what I know now, I don't know how to move forward with that. It was easier to pretend when I didn't know his dark past."

"Understandably. That, however, gives you no right to speak to me with such disrespect." She held my gaze. "I have put not only myself in jeopardy by helping you, but also my entire staff."

I hadn't thought about that. If Zeus found out about Athena, he'd strike everyone loyal to her down. Especially if the sphinx saw Athena's spies in the sky.

"I'm sorry." I sighed, feeling my shoulders drop with regret. She'd done nothing but risk herself to help me when she didn't have to. My paranoia and anger were getting the better of me.

Athena didn't answer at first, but eventually, she nodded, which I assumed meant she accepted my apology and a nod was the best I would get from her.

"Continue training on your own. We have gone through all the basic combat and battle maneuvers. As long as you practice what you've been taught, you should come out of this victorious—or, at the very least, alive."

"That is the goal," I replied.

Athena walked past me, opening the door before she paused and looked at me over her shoulder. "Do what you need to do

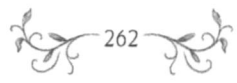

to win the Titan's heart. With him on your side, you could be unstoppable."

I couldn't understand what she saw in Prometheus to think that, but I trusted her more than anyone else in Olympus right now, so I swore to myself I'd make an effort to make things work with him in the times I wasn't training. It may help me to have him on my side, but I would no longer stand by helpless, waiting for others to save me.

Even if having mortality in this divine world was a curse that could come crashing down on me with one wrong move, I vowed from this moment on, I would never stop fighting to survive.

CHAPTER 48

M y body was slick with sweat from a long day of training. I'd decided to come down to the beach to practice my footwork with a sword. I'd practiced it on the dirt and the grass enough that I no longer found it challenging, so I'd decided to get a change of scenery and use the sand to my advantage, going from one end of the beach to the other before laying my sword down and running into the waves.

The cool water felt glorious against my skin, which was red from prolonged exposure to the sun. I'd meant to wear my armor, but the day was warm, and I couldn't bring myself to put it on, so I'd opted for a loose tunic instead. Unfortunately, that hadn't covered as much skin, and I was beginning to regret leaving the spider-silk armor at home.

I dunked my head underwater, wishing I could stay in the sea forever.

A splashing nearby made me emerge, alert as I scanned my surroundings for any threats. I was down the beach from Siren's Cove, and I knew the sirens never hunted this far from their territory, but my body seized up as a form appeared below the waves, swimming in my direction, getting closer at an alarming speed.

I was turning to swim back to shore when a familiar voice called my name.

"Pandora. I thought that was you." Epimetheus swam toward me.

"Epimetheus." I was unsure of what to say after our last encounter.

"I'm glad I saw you out here. I've been meaning to stop by, but I didn't want to make you feel like I was intruding on your space again."

"And swimming up on me isn't intruding on my space?" I asked jokingly, trying to break the awkward tension I could feel between us.

He didn't catch the joke. His slight smile slackened into a frown.

"I'm only joking. I shouldn't have been so harsh with you."

"You weren't wrong in the things you said. I probably deserved it for not reading the situation better." Epimetheus shook his head.

"You didn't deserve it. I was just going through a hard time when you arrived, and you took the brunt of my anger."

"That's all right. All is forgiven." He smiled, closing the last bit of distance between us.

"Good. I'm glad." I smiled back.

"How long have you been out here?" he asked. "Your skin looks like it's getting pink." He leaned in to touch my shoulder, making me wince slightly as he pressed his finger to it, leaving a white imprint on my tender, pinkened skin.

"I was on the beach for a while, but I haven't been in the water too long." I shrugged.

"Were you training with a sword?"

His question made me freeze up. "Why would you ask that?" I asked cautiously, dreading his answer.

"I noticed a female training with a sword earlier, when I started my swim, but I never thought it would be you." He smirked.

"Why not?" I asked, raising my eyebrows at him.

His own brows shot up in kind. "I guess it makes sense, considering the only females I've known to fight with swords are goddesses and Amazons. Figures you would as well," he said nonchalantly, tilting his head as he spoke, deep in thought.

"It makes more sense considering who helped raise me. Athena has been training me since I was a child," I said, brushing off his comment as if his comparison hadn't just made my heart swell.

Epimetheus's eyes lit up. "I never thought of that."

"It's not like I get to practice often, or like I've ever had a need for it until recently, but now, it seems like invaluable knowledge." I only wished Zeus viewed it as a more important skill for me to learn.

"I bet you're glorious in a fight. Much as I wish no harm upon you, I do wish I could see you in battle for myself one day." He grinned down at me, wading closer with each incoming wave.

I stared up at him in disbelief. "Really? You'd support me fighting?"

"How else would one be expected to survive?" he asked, tilting his head and seeming to consider something. "But I wouldn't share your fighting skills with my brother. He wouldn't be as accepting as I am. He's more . . . *traditional*."

My heart dropped a little. This news shouldn't have shocked me, since Zeus had raised me to be exactly what he believed Prometheus wanted—everything I'd never been. Traditional.

"Yet you don't agree with him?" I asked, not understanding.

"My loyalty to my brother does not mean I agree with everything he says or does. There is a lot we disagree on." Epimetheus locked eyes with me, and my heart fluttered. "Including you."

"What about me?" My interest sparked.

"Who would be best for you," he said, holding my gaze with an intensity that burned brighter than Helios.

"Who is?" I asked, breathless.

He reached up and cupped my cheek with his hand. His was rough and rugged, the opposite of his twin in yet another way. "As I said, we disagreed."

His lips were full and inviting as the corners turned up in a sad smirk. I longed to turn it into a smile. I knew better, but something about Epimetheus and the way he seemed to see me with a clarity

no one ever had drew me in like the sea to the shore. Like we were destined to meet.

I leaned in. The water made us much closer in height, leaving only a couple of inches' difference between us.

"Pandora," he said, his voice coming out huskier than before, sending tingles down my spine.

I opened my mouth to speak, but suddenly, his arms were wrapped around me, pulling me so close our noses almost touched, and I could feel his breath whispering across my lips.

I didn't know if the racing in my heart was telling me to stop him or to lean in, but I didn't care in this moment. I wanted nothing more than to feel his lips on mine.

I leaned in.

"I can't," he said, pulling away.

I stared at him for a moment, shaking my head, embarrassed by the thought of what had just almost happened, trying to clear whatever lust-filled daze I'd fallen into. "I know," I replied, turning to the beach to get out of the water.

Epimetheus followed me silently onto the shore. That awkward tension was back between us, worse than it was before.

"I didn't mean to--"

"I understand, Epimetheus," I said, turning to him with a soft smile. "Really, I do. Let's just leave what happened here . . . here. I need to get going anyway."

"Pandora, please let me explai—"

"No need. I've really got to be going." I turned away from him and headed off toward the end of the beach where I'd left my stuff.

"Pandora, please."

I kept walking, not looking back, much as my heart was screaming at me to. He was right. We couldn't do what we'd almost done, but I'd wanted to, more desperately than I could have imagined.

Quickly gathering my things, I was thankful to see Epimetheus hadn't followed me. I headed back up to my cottage, taking a moment to run my hands through the wheat and barley once I was out of sight, admiring the way the golden grains danced in the breeze from the sea, a rippling blanket of gold.

I was so lost in my thoughts, staring out at the grain fields, that it took me a moment to notice there was someone standing in front of my cottage, looking down at me.

Prometheus.

I took a deep breath, pushing my wet hair off my face as I approached him.

"Have I caught you at a bad time?" he asked.

"No. I was just taking a swim," I said, casually wrapping the cotton blanket I'd brought with me around my sword, thankful it was smaller than some of the others I often used. I remembered what Epimetheus had said about Prometheus's traditional views, and I didn't wish to see how he'd react to the knowledge I'd been practicing with a sword all afternoon.

"That must have been a long swim," he said, looking me over. "I've only ever seen men who've been out for hours in the sun get as burned as you."

I looked down at my arm, where Epimetheus had poked me earlier. It was much redder than the last time I checked, having gone from a deep pink to a rosy red. It must have gotten worse in the water.

"I guess so," I said sheepishly, turning on my charm. "I must have lost track of time, but I have some salve inside that will help calm it down."

"Would you like some help?" Prometheus asked, falling into step beside me as I walked toward the door.

Not really.

"Sure. That would be great." I smiled over at him, pretending to be thankful for his help, when all I wanted was to disappear inside and process everything.

He followed me in and sat on the couch while I went upstairs to my bathroom to grab the salve.

"I can get the front of my arms if you can get my back, my shoulders, and my neck," I said, holding the jar out to him when I

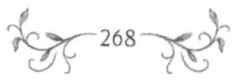

returned. I watched as he took a small scoop in his big hands and rubbed them together.

"Does Apollo make this for you?" he asked, working the balmy salve into my skin.

I couldn't deny, it felt much better having someone else apply the salve to my back than to do it myself, even if I was imagining his soft hands as more rough and rugged.

"Not this one. I made it myself," I said, rubbing some more salve into my forearms.

"Really?" He sounded impressed. "What do you use?"

I turned around and smirked at him. "Trying to steal my secret recipe?"

"Maybe," he said, leaning in as he rubbed small circles into the tense muscles above my collarbone. "I promise I won't go sharing your secrets. I'm just curious what you came up with."

"Well, it's not much. Just a few things," I said, putting the lid back on the jar once I felt like all the burned areas had been adequately covered. "I just mix olive oil, honey, and some fresh lupine and jasmine flowers together until it gets to this consistency. Most of the time, that's it, but occasionally, I add other things."

"Remarkable," Prometheus said. "How did you learn what would work?"

"You do remember I was raised by Demeter . . .? Not to mention, I've grown up in a kingdom where I'm the only one who needs to worry about being burned by the light of day, so it didn't take me long to figure out what worked and what didn't," I reminded him.

"Man has done something similar, but I must say, your salve seems much more effective. The burn has already begun to fade."

"It normally takes a day or two, and then it will be completely gone, other than the tan, which takes much longer to fade."

"It should be healed before our wedding day then. I'm sure you'll be an even more beautiful bride after being kissed by the sun." He beamed down at me.

"It will be healed well before then. I might not even be *sun-kissed* anymore," I said, repeating his phrase for my burned skin, which I'd normally find cute—except now, it only made me think about not getting to kiss Epimetheus in the sun. Something I definitely needed to remove from my mind as soon as possible.

"Actually, that's what I came to tell you." Prometheus turned toward me and held my hand.

I couldn't help but flash back to the similar moment I'd shared with Epimetheus, and how harsh I'd been with him.

"I talked with Zeus yesterday, and we decided, with everything going on with the Aloadae twins and the recent attacks on Olympus, it would be best if you and I married sooner rather than later."

"How much sooner?" I asked hesitantly, knowing I probably wasn't going to like the answer.

"Our wedding is to be held one week from today," he announced excitedly.

"One week?" I asked, stunned at how little time I had left. I'd figured maybe a month, but I could never have guessed it would be as soon as one week.

"Yes. Isn't it wonderful?" He grinned down at me as if I were a trophy he'd won, not someone he cared for. As if he saw me as a possession, not a person.

"Yes, wonderful," I repeated, trying to force happiness into my voice, but instead, it came out quietly, as if I didn't want to hear the words.

"And even better, Zeus has sent out announcements to everyone in Olympus, inviting them to our proaulia the day before. To honor our marriage, he's decided to throw the Olympic Games early and has ensured all Olympians of every status are invited to join."

I'd never witnessed a wedding happen in Olympus before, nor had I seen an Olympic Games, but I'd heard enough about both to know the basics.

"Zeus wants everyone to play games for us?" I asked, not understanding why he'd want to risk another attack on Olympus. Both

previous attacks had happened when all of Olympus was united in one area, and I could see an event as big as the Olympic Games easily drawing the attention of the Aloadae twins. "After everything that's happened, is that really the best idea?"

"Actually, it was my idea to hold the games, but Zeus agreed," Prometheus said, his smile faltering as something like anger flashed across his features. It was there for a split second, and then it was replaced by a look of cold indifference.

It was then I realized I'd never actually seen Prometheus angry. Only Epimetheus had shown his anger in front of me, and even when he'd looked like he was about to rip the world apart, I'd never felt fear toward him, even if I knew I should have done at times. The same couldn't be said of Prometheus in this moment. Seeing him angry was as unsettling as the glass floors of the Olympian Court. As if he could break at any moment and end my life.

"I'm sorry. I didn't mean any disrespect. I was just nervous, what with everything that's happened," I said, avoiding his eye and staring down at my hands instead.

"I do not appreciate you questioning my decisions. If you truly wish to be married to me, you would do well to remember your place."

I stared at him, stunned by his change of attitude. At first, I couldn't understand how the kind, levelheaded man I'd been trying to love could be the same one from Athena's stories, but maybe Prometheus was playing me as much as I'd been playing him.

"I didn't mean to undermine you. I think the games sound like a wonderful idea," I said, forcing a smile onto my lips as I looked up at him.

He eyed me cautiously before his face softened. "Great. I expect you to be ready the morning of, at dawn. I will come by to pick you up so we may arrive together."

"That sounds great." I stood. "I don't mean to rush you, but I need to go to the plateia before the stores close."

"Why the urgency? Couldn't you go tomorrow, when they open?" he asked, quirking a brow.

"I wish." I smiled. "But it seems I need to get a wedding dress made in the next week."

Prometheus lit up. "Indeed. I'm glad to see you so excited." He stood up from the couch, smoothing his tunic. "Very well. I will leave you to it."

I didn't have a chance to answer before he walked over to me, putting his arm around my back and pulling me into him as he leaned down to kiss me. Hard.

My lips stung as he pulled away, but Prometheus was smiling down at me. Looking up at his lips, I noticed they seemed to be tinged with blood. I reached my hand up to touch my own and winced when my bottom lip stung from the contact. Pulling my hand back, I realized my lip was bleeding. That was my blood on his lip.

He noticed but didn't say a word, licking his lips and turning to leave before calling out over his shoulder, "Oh, and Pandora? No more colors for your dresses. I want you wearing white."

I had to bite my tongue not to scoff at that, tasting more blood as it filled my mouth.

White was the color of purity, of innocence, and little did he know, I was anything but innocent. I may not know the man I was marrying, but the more I learned about him, the more I realized he didn't know me either. He wanted to think I was innocent, helpless, only able to survive with him by my side, but screw what Athena said about keeping him close. I would make sure I never needed to depend on anyone but myself.

CHAPTER 49

ENDED up waiting until the next day to go down into the plateia to order my dress, since I was too angry to function after Prometheus left. I'd taken my swords and my daggers out to the clearing to expel some of that anger. I didn't think it would be fair to take my pent-up rage with me. I had to be able to put on a happy face and act as if the most exciting day of my life was only one week away.

The plateia was bustling today, and as I passed by a couple of wagon vendors, I heard my name called from somewhere in the distance.

"Pandora!" a feminine voice hollered. I followed the sound of the next scream all the way to a strawberry-blonde head barely sticking out over the crowd.

Persephone.

Not wanting to get into it with her right now, I ducked down, winding through the bodies that filled the square all the way to the front door of the Weaving Web, where I cracked the door open slightly and slipped in, closing it quickly behind me.

Leaning my forehead against the cool wooden door, I released a sigh of relief.

"Hello! How may I help you today?" Closter—Arachne's only known son, and the owner of the Weaving Web—asked, making me swivel on my heel to face him where he sat behind the wooden counter at the back of the showroom.

"I'm in need of a dress," I said, walking over to him.

"Very well. What type of dress are you looking for?" he asked, stepping out from behind the counter and heading over to the rack of premade dresses.

"Actually, a wedding dress," I said. "I'm pretty short on time, but I was hoping I could pay to have it expedited."

"Oh, how exciting!" Closter said, lifting his body—legs and all—off the ground, as his four extra limbs, which were the legs of a spider, emerged from his tunic. "What is your time frame?"

"Six days." I smiled sheepishly at him.

"Oh! Are you the happy couple the Olympic Games are being held in honor of?" he asked excitedly.

"Yes. That would be us," I said, going along with him. "So, do you think it can be done?"

"Most definitely, my darling. Shall we look over some fabrics in the back? I have some special pieces I think would look beautiful on you." He pointed to the door that led to the back room, where they kept the spools of fabric.

"That would be wonderful." I smiled, relieved.

"Follow me then," he said, holding back the silk curtain separating the fabric room from the showroom with one of his spider legs, while his arm, which was as dark in color as his charcoal spider legs, extended outward, gesturing for me to enter first.

It always took my breath away how many fabrics the Weaving Web had. I hadn't been back here since I bought one of their white premade dresses for the engagement party.

"What color were you thinking? Most of our fabrics are organized by color and texture, so we can start with the color and then move on to the different material options."

I opened my mouth to say white, but then I remembered what Prometheus had said about color and smiled as an idea occurred to me.

"Actually, I'd like to see them all, if you don't mind."

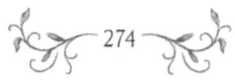

Closter smiled so wide I saw his fangs, normally hidden from view, emerging as he clapped his hands together. "Not at all."

I lost track of time in the back room, Closter going through every single roll of fabric with me before we finally decided on the design for the dress.

"I'll have your gown ready for you by the night before the games. I plan on taking that day off and joining you for the festivities on the summit."

"Really?" I asked, both shocked at the speed he could finish the dress and that he planned on going to the Olympic Games.

"Absolutely. My storefront will be closed, but I'll have a booth up there, run by some of my seamstresses. I figure they can handle the sales while I wander around, close enough that I can assist them if they need it." He paused, writing down prices for the fabric as he figured out the total drachmas I owed. "Besides, the last Olympic Games was so long ago I hadn't even sprouted hair on my legs yet. I figure the next one might come around when I'm too withered and old to enjoy it."

"Well, I look forward to seeing a friendly face there. How much do I owe you?" I asked, looking over to try to see the number he'd written down.

"Oh no. This one's on me. I was just writing everything down so I could account for it in my inventory."

"What? I can't let you do that," I said, setting my pouch of drachmas on the counter in front of him. "Here. Please, take whatever I owe you."

"Nonsense. It isn't every day I get such a special client coming in here for her wedding dress." He reached out and patted my hand. "Just be here the evening before the games to pick it up, and let me worry about the rest."

"Are you sure?" I asked, hesitant to accept his offer but feeling like he wouldn't take the money no matter how hard I pushed.

"Not a doubt in my mind. Now, run off. I have a wedding dress to make." He smiled, clapping his hands excitedly before walking me to the front door.

Walking out into the plateia, I turned to head home, but my eye caught on the metal sign swinging from the marble wall near the entrance to Forging Glory.

Couldn't hurt to get another dagger . . .

I walked over to the large iron door and pulled it open. The smell of metal and smoke immediately filled my nostrils as one of Hephaestus's golden women walked up to me.

"What are you in search of?" she asked, looking me over. Unlike the warm welcome Closter had given me, hers was icy-cold.

"Nothing in particular. Just browsing," I said, walking by her and finding my own way to the daggers.

She didn't say a word, just watched me as I looked over them, her eyes locked onto me as if she expected me to steal or something.

The daggers on display were all beautiful, but there was one in particular my eyes kept returning to. The hilt was made from a polished silver that shimmered even under the dull store lighting, and it had small flowers carved into it, twisting around the hilt and spreading all the way down to the blade. But my favorite part was the tiny cluster of assorted gemstones placed at the top of the hilt, one of which I made out to be an amethyst.

It would be handy to have amethyst in the form of a weapon, not just jewelry.

"How much is this one?" I asked, pointing to the silver dagger.

"Too much for you," the woman said, picking up a minute dagger I'd have better luck sewing with than using in a fight.

"Very funny," I said, refusing to move away from the dagger I wanted. I pointed to it once again and repeated, "How much?"

"Eight hundred drachmas."

"I'll take it," I said, pulling out the pouch full of drachmas I'd brought for my dress. I counted out eight hundred and placed them in front of her.

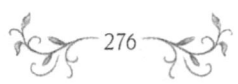

The golden woman collected the money and pulled the dagger out, setting it in front of me and grabbing something else from underneath it. "It comes with a thigh holster, if you want it," she said, holding it out to me.

"I do." I grabbed the thigh holster and tucked the dagger into it before reaching down to lift my tunic. I strapped it onto the top of my thigh, where it couldn't be seen. "Thank you for all your help," I said sarcastically, waving at her over my shoulder as I walked out the door.

CHAPTER 50

NEWS came the next morning of Hades' immediate release, stating his innocence had been proven. What he was guilty of in the first place, other than being close to Hecate, was a mystery. I was just thankful he was free. From the whispers I'd heard around Olympus, Zeus hadn't treated his brother with the necessary respect as one of the big three, locking him in a cage that dampened his powers and hiding him from Hecate until she turned herself over to Zeus—which she'd done in her spirit form, if the rumors were true.

I'd been hoping to hear more about what was going on, since I'd been avoiding most of the Olympians in my life whom I'd normally go to for information. The only one I'd decided I could trust was Athena, and she was coming nowhere near me since the sphinx saw her.

I headed over to Hestia's Hearth to grab a lavender honey cake and a chamomile tea and then walked over to the benches near the river to eat. As always, I found peace in the sound of running water cascading over the river rocks.

I nibbled my cake and watched as a group of young naiads swam upriver toward me. One of them whispered something to the others when she saw me, breaking off from the group to come up to the river's edge and stop in front of me.

She had long, olive-green hair that resembled the river weed flowing like grass in the wind, dancing in the current. Her eyes were a vibrant blue that faded to hazel at the center. Her skin was the same bluish gray as the rocks that had dried along the edge of the river, with fins lining the lengths of her arms and her legs, all the way to her webbed fingers and feet. Gills on her rib cage opened and closed with each breath.

"Hello," I said, smiling down at her.

She tilted her head, studying me, her eyes settling on the cake I was holding in my hand.

"Would you like some?" I asked, ripping off a piece and extending it to her.

She blinked at me before ripping the cake out of my hand and shoving it into her mouth, swallowing the entire thing before smiling up at me as if I'd just become her best friend.

I wondered how old she was. She seemed younger than any naiad I'd ever seen, and perhaps she hadn't learned to speak yet. Most naiads didn't learn to speak above water until they were at least ten years of age. It was the same for most water-dwelling creatures. They had no need to speak the language of the land when they could simply send sound waves through the water, communicating in their own language. I'd always found the water-dwellers' language to be beautiful and swore one day I would learn it, but when Poseidon heard of my interest, he killed any hope I had, saying I didn't have the vocal capacity to reach the same frequency.

"Would you like the rest?" I asked, offering the other half of the cake.

The naiad nodded eagerly, crawling even further up out of the water to grab it and swallowing it just like the last piece. I smiled at her as one of the other naiads in her group swam over, hissing something at her before turning toward me to hiss too, quickly jumping back into the current and joining the group who whispered and glared from a distance. The younger naiad waved goodbye and jumped back into the water, continuing to swim upstream toward the group.

I watched them, thinking of how much I'd miss sights like this even though they weren't always perfect. I didn't know what to expect when I got to the Realm of Man, but something told me it would lack the magic and beauty I'd always found throughout Olympus.

Drinking the last sip of tea, I took my cup back to Hestia's Hearth. It was as I was turning to leave that I ran right into someone.

"I'm so sorry! I didn't see you there . . ." I looked up to make sure I hadn't hurt the other person in my haste, only to find Persephone standing before me.

"Are you avoiding me?" she asked. "I tried calling out to you when you crossed the plateia, but you kept walking."

"Oh . . . I didn't see you," I said, avoiding her questioning gaze.

"Well, did you receive my letter at least? I tried stopping by your cottage a few times, but you were never home."

I had received her letter, but I hadn't opened it—at first, because I was too busy and forgot, and later, because I wasn't sure how I'd feel talking to Persephone again after what I'd learned about her involvement in Zeus's plan. Which was also why I'd avoided answering the door the couple of times I'd seen her stop by.

"I did, but I've been too busy to read it. Sorry," I said, moving to pass by her as I added, "I'm actually pretty busy right now and need to be going. I have more errands to run before I head home."

"Wait—Pandy," she said, turning to follow me. "If it's engagement stuff, I'd love to help. Have you got your dress yet?"

"Yep. It's being made as we speak," I replied, picking up my pace, hoping she'd get the hint and leave.

She didn't.

"Oh, I'm so excited for you, Pandy! I can't believe my little sister is getting married." She was gleeful, blissfully unaware of the way I was feeling toward her. "Oh, and did you hear the wonderful news? Father released Hades!"

"I heard," I replied, refusing to look at her as she kept up with my fast pace.

"Pandy, slow down," Persephone said, pulling on my arm and forcing me to stop walking. "What is going on with you? First, you ignore me—and don't deny it, I know you were—then you go off and move up your wedding date without even bothering to tell me. The engagement was one thing, but I can't believe you wouldn't tell me about this."

"Not everything is about you, Persephone. Believe it or not, I have more important things to do than to tell you everything that goes on in my life," I snapped, pulling my arm from her grip as I finally met her eye.

She looked shocked and maybe even a little scared at my outburst, but all I saw when I looked at my *sister* now was betrayal.

"What? Where is this coming from?" she asked, her eyes pleading with me.

"You really want to know?" I took a step toward her.

"Yes. Please, just talk to me."

"Fine. I know everything. I know you lied to me my whole life, helping me build enough confidence to pursue Prometheus and get him to fall in love with me. But love never mattered, did it? It was just a means to an end, a way to make the horrendous act of selling me off to a life of servitude in a world I didn't know seem sweeter than it really was." I spoke low enough that only she could hear, my anger seeping into every word, making her flinch.

"Pandy, I . . . I don't know . . . what to say." She seemed barely able to speak as tears welled in her eyes. "I just want to fix this. I want us to go back to how things were. We're sisters, remember?"

As she reached for my arm, I took a step back, out of her grasp, shaking my head.

"There is nothing you could say right now to fix this. If this is what sisterhood is, then I want no part of it." I finally pushed past her, leaving her to cry alone, just like I'd had to, more times in my life than I could count.

CHAPTER 51

WITH my bag of weapons slung over my shoulder, I walked the edge of Olympus, following the wall from the lowest point on the west side, where it met the Sea of Poseidon, up to the forests in the north. I stopped by the vegetable gardens below Demeter's palace on the way to grab some snacks to go with the apples I'd snagged from my kitchen. I needed options, since I planned to train in the forests north of Mount Olympus until I had to pick up my dress from Closter this evening, before the Weaving Web closed.

The guard towers on the west wall had double the amount of guards as normal, and another group of four Amazons stood at the gateway. Zeus had definitely upped his security in preparation for the Olympic Games.

Good. He wasn't so egotistical as to think Olympus wouldn't be attacked again.

One of the guards nodded to me as I passed alongside the tower, and I smiled as I continued on into the myrtle woods.

It had been a long time since I'd come this far north, but now I knew my time in Olympus was limited, I was making it a point to see everything I could at least one more time before I left, committing every detail to memory.

The myrtle woods was home to smaller groups of naiads who lived in the streams and small lakes that ran throughout it. The myrtles were just beginning to bloom. Pink, purple, and white flowers were sprinkled across the lush green leaves of the short, rounded trees.

As the myrtle trees grew farther and farther apart, oak trees grew in their place, signaling the beginning of the oak forest, home to the dryads.

I walked through the enormous trees, admiring the way the sun shined through their branches and listening to the leaves as they rustled in the light breeze. I smiled to myself, inhaling their woody scent.

A little further into the forest, I saw a small clearing by a stream. Setting my bag against a tree, I spread my cotton blanket on the ground, grabbing an apple and some snap peas from my bag.

Looking out over the stream, I couldn't help but to pull my parchment and my charcoals out, wanting to capture this moment as a reminder I could take with me. I didn't know what Earth would be like. For all I knew, it could be a world full of sand, with no trees or bodies of water in sight. Primes, I hoped that wasn't the case.

I sketched the stream first, and then a few of the unique-shaped oak trees I found, before pulling my sword out to practice a little bit of footwork. I'd mastered the strength and accuracy of my swings, and I was close to mastering the steps of swordplay, but I still didn't feel confident and wanted to practice in every environment possible. The slick rocks along the river made the perfect training ground.

Brandishing the sword, I practiced the first set of movements.

Swing, step, slide right, slide left, cross, spin, swing.

I did this a few more times, along with a few other practice sets, walking back and forth across the stone, careful to keep my balance steady.

"I haven't seen a mortal in these woods for a long time."

I swiveled around so fast I slipped on the rock, catching myself just before I hit my head. I looked around frantically for where the voice had come from but found no one.

"Over here." The voice sounded again.

I turned in the direction it had come from but still couldn't see anyone—until, suddenly, one of the tree trunks transformed right in front of my eyes. The top layer of bark peeled away, and a woman stepped out. No—not a woman. A dryad.

"Primes, you scared me," I said as I carefully lifted myself off the rock, walking back over to my blanket to gather my things. "I'm sorry if I disturbed you. I'll go."

"You are not like the mortals I've seen before," she said, walking toward me.

"No, I'm not. I'm just going to gather my things, and I'll leave," I said, stuffing everything I'd laid out on the blanket back into the bag.

"Stay," she said, walking closer to me and sitting on one of the large rocks at the river's edge. "I haven't seen a mortal in centuries."

Her skin was made of the same bark as the oak trees, with eyes as deep as the green moss on the ground, and branches grew out of her head like hair, with tiny greens leaves at their ends. It was a long time since I'd seen a dryad, and I couldn't help my desire to stay in her presence, if only for a little longer.

"Are you sure?" I asked, feeling like an intruder in her home.

She nodded. "My name is Trizeena."

"I'm Pandora. It's nice to meet you."

"What brings you to our grove?" she asked

"I was hoping for some privacy away from the hustle in Lower Olympus."

Trizeena smiled. "You are never alone in the forest. Even if you can't see us, we always see you."

"Oh," I said, looking around, wondering if there were more dryads nearby that I hadn't noticed. "Good to know."

"You'd be surprised how many do not realize," she said, running her branch-like fingers through the stream. "Sharing secrets they

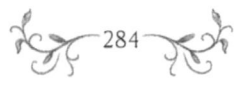

think no one will hear . . . But we hear all and see all who move through our forest."

"What kinds of secrets?" I asked, my curiosity rising.

"All kinds," Trizeena said. "Lies, affairs, rebellion, jealousy, schemes—everything you could imagine has been whispered under our oaks."

"Rebellion? Was that recent?" I asked, eager to know if she'd heard talk of the rebellion that I seemed to constantly hear whispers of but had seen no evidence of for months now.

"Somewhat. It is hard to know exact times when you've lived as long as I have, rooted to the land as surely as the trees we protect. It was within the past season though. The trees had not yet shed their leaves, and we did not smell the sweet scent of myrtles when we last heard the whispers."

"What did they say?" I asked eagerly.

"I will tell you if you tell me of Olympus. I have not seen it since I was young, before I set my roots in this grove."

"All right. What exactly do you want to know?" I asked, smiling at her.

"Everything." She smiled too, scooting to the edge of the rock with excitement.

CHAPTER 52

I TOLD Trizeena everything I could think of about Olympus, from Siren's Cove all the way up to the summit, only pausing when she had questions.

Trizeena was kind, and I couldn't help but relate to her curiosity since we shared a similar story, her stuck living her life in the oak forest, while I'd been contained within Olympus, never leaving its walls. At one time, I would have been just as eager to hear about the world beyond my reach, but now, I wasn't sure if knowing what was out there was worth it. I guessed I'd see soon enough.

"Is there anything else you'd like to know?" I asked.

"Just one more thing," she said from beside me on the blanket, where she'd moved to about halfway through our conversation.

"Well, go on. What is it?" I asked, laughing. I'd never met someone as curious as I was, and I swore to myself I'd make it a point to visit Trizeena more often.

At least, until I was forced to leave.

"Have you ever been in love?" she asked, staring up at the clouds passing by through the canopy of the trees.

"I have loved, but I can't say it's ever been fully returned," I said, thinking of my family and how they'd only ever loved me for what I could offer them, whether that was power, control, or protection from Zeus's wrath.

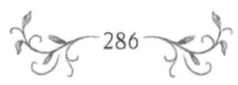

"But you have never been in love?" she said quietly, almost to herself, as if she knew the feeling.

"Have you?" I asked.

"Once." She smiled sadly.

"Will you tell me about it?" I didn't want to pry if it was a sensitive subject for her.

"His name was Vansus, and he was the most majestic drus I had ever seen. Even his oak was twice the size as the others' around him. I'd watched him for years, admiring him from a distance, until one day, a great storm came, shaking our mighty oaks down to their roots. We lost many, including one of our mutual friends, Ronan. Everyone in the forest came together to honor his memory as we burned his tree, returning it to the soil it had once come from and planting a young acorn in the ashes left behind."

"That is a beautiful custom," I said, realizing for the first time the gods held no such celebration of life when one passed—although, granted, most of the time, those who passed were enemies of Zeus.

"It helps us to remember that even when someone is gone from us physically, their spirit lives on in the Underworld, and their memory will live on here, with those they left behind. Through our grief, Vansus and I became very close, until, eventually, we could no longer deny our love for each other." She paused, looking like she was lost in a memory.

"What happened between you two?" I asked.

"Wild ones made it through the wall. Before the guards could track them down, they started a fire in our forest. I didn't smell the smoke until it was too late. By the time I'd made it over to his side of the woods, all that was left was ash, and stumps with jagged tops that looked like daggers sticking out of the charred soil. What was once a place full of beauty and life had been left as bare as the surface of the sea and as black as the night." Tears filled her eyes.

I pulled her into a hug, ignoring the way her barky flesh rubbed against mine, threatening to give me a splinter if I held on too tight.

"I am so sorry, Trizeena. I can't imagine going through a loss like that," I said, shaking my head and feeling a touch of relief that

I'd never had a love like hers, for fear of being broken-hearted when it was taken away.

"I am grateful for the time I had with him." She smiled, less sad than before as she added, "Even one day spent sharing our love would be worth a lifetime of sorrow."

"I'm sure he would have felt the same way about you," I said, knowing nothing of the drus she'd loved but feeling like she needed to hear those words.

"Thank you." She smiled up at me, pushing herself up to sit beside me. "I still visit his oak every morning. Maybe one day, you can come with me."

"I would love that."

We spent a while longer comparing different stories about our lives, and before I knew it, a blanket of darkness had begun to spread across the floor of the oak forest.

"I need to get going. I have to go pick up my wedding dress," I said in a rush, making Trizeena giggle, since I'd told her all about my struggles with the Titan brothers. She'd found this utterly amusing and insisted I shouldn't worry about it, that the universe would make its plans known when I was ready to face them.

"Don't let your worries get in the way of your fun tomorrow. Enjoy everything the Olympics has to offer, so that you can come back and tell me everything I missed."

I pulled her into a hug again. "I'm so happy we met. I promise I'll come back as soon as I can."

"I'll be looking forward to it, my friend." Trizeena smiled, walking back toward her oak tree. Touching her hand to the trunk, she turned to smile at me once more and then stepped forward, into the side of the tree, and became one with it again.

Even having grown up around magic, seeing the magic of nature and those who protected it had always been the most beautiful thing to me. To give oneself over to the land instead of those wanting to control it was something to be admired, and I wished more people had the decency to realize it.

CHAPTER 53

THE lanterns hanging throughout the plateia cast a warm glow across the marble shops, making them look peachy compared to the normal Olympic white, as I made it across the square to the Weaving Web just as Closter was getting ready to lock up.

"Closter!" I yelled out as I jogged over to him.

"Ah, Pandora. I thought you'd forgotten about me." He smiled, opening the door back up into his shop and going around lighting the small sconces in the showroom.

"Never. I just lost track of time," I said, trying to catch my breath.

"Well, better late than never. Just let me go grab your dress." He walked into the back.

I looked around for a few minutes, admiring the mastery in all his designs, until he returned.

"Here it is," he said, revealing a dress even more beautiful than I could have imagined.

"Closter, this is . . ." I stared at the masterpiece in awe, unable to find a word that felt right to describe it.

"I must say, this is one of the best designs I've ever made. You'll make a beautiful bride."

The dress was made of a silky white fabric with strips of golden lace sewn into it, creating an intricate pattern. The shoulders were pinned with golden branches, and the skirt had strips of the same

white-and-gold fabric as the bust. The skirt was pleated, the white and gold separated by subtle strips of color in between. The colored strips started with white at the waist and bled into yellow, then orange and red, and so on, until every color in Iris's rainbow had appeared, getting darker the closer it got to the bottom.

At first, this would look like a white wedding dress, but as I walked and the layers separated, the colors would show through. It felt fitting for the marriage: perfect and pristine, covering the vibrance and uniqueness that most would find unsuitable.

I'd always felt like I needed to keep the most human parts of me hidden, even if I didn't realize it at first, but I'd started to accept the one thing I'd always been trying to change.

Myself.

"It's perfect," I said, running my fingers through the silky tulle that only Closter could have woven so masterfully. Even Athena, although she'd never admit it, admired his skill with fabric.

After Closter refused to allow me to pay once again, I wished him a good night and headed over the bridge toward home.

I may not have been excited for the wedding, but I couldn't wait to wear this dress down the aisle. Seeing Zeus and Prometheus's faces might just be worth the forced marriage—or, at the very least, it would be a nice wedding gift to myself.

THE MORNING OF the Olympic Games had arrived, and I found myself genuinely excited to go. After speaking with Trizeena yesterday, I figured I'd take her advice and enjoy as much of the day as I could, if only to have a good story to tell her the next time I visited. Seeing my wedding dress hanging on the armoire in the morning sun helped to boost my mood as well—so much so, I found myself humming as I got dressed for the day, and all throughout my morning chores.

It seemed as if time had flown by. Prometheus was already standing at my door.

"Are you ready?" he asked, grinning as he looked over the off-white peplos I was wearing.

It was a little cool this morning, and I knew it would be freezing on the summit, so I'd chosen one of the thickest in my closet, wearing it over the top of my spider-silk armor. Its sleeves and its length were long enough to cover the armor, and it had tiny violets embroidered throughout it that reminded me of Persephone. I wished we were on better terms. I hadn't thought of marriage much before the Titans arrived, but if I'd imagined what my wedding would be like, I knew I would have envisioned Persephone with me every step of the way.

"Absolutely," I said, grabbing the hand he extended toward me and pulling my cottage door shut behind me.

It may have been the day before our wedding, but inside, it felt like today was the day my life would change.

"Unfortunately, we'll need to walk. I don't possess the powers of flight like my brother, but we're early enough in the day that we can take our time getting to the summit."

"That would be nice," I said, grateful he'd considered that. Maybe he'd had a rough day the last time I saw him, when he snapped at me for daring to question him. I could only hope this was the version of Prometheus I was marrying, not the other one.

"I'm glad to see you so excited for the games," Prometheus said as if reading my mind.

"I am. I apologize for the other night. I didn't mean to upset you," I said cautiously, looking up at him from under my lashes. I kept my chin level, nervous of how he'd reply.

"I accept your apology," he said, bringing the back of my hand up to his lips to kiss it. "We shall forget it ever happened."

"All right." I waited for an apology from him, but it never came, not even as we walked further through Lower Olympus.

As we headed up to the summit, I felt the drop in temperature as the winds whipped against the loose-fitting peplos, making me shiver.

"Here—allow me," Prometheus said, releasing my hand and pulling me into his side. He wrapped his arm around my shoulder, sharing the warmth of his body with me. "Better?" he asked

"M-m-m-much," I stuttered through chattering teeth, leaning into him to absorb as much warmth as possible.

He chuckled, and I felt it rumbling through his body.

"Good. We're almost there."

I was excited to see the Olympic Games for myself. I still had my worries about whether this was the right time to be holding such a large gathering, but at the end of the day, I had no say in what decisions were made in Olympus. If they thought it was safe, then I probably should too.

The Olympic Games were normally held in Zeus's honor and had been established for a millennium. They were normally bicentennial, and the next one wasn't supposed to be for another decade, but according to Prometheus, Zeus had agreed to move the games up to celebrate our nuptials. The games, normally thrown as a way to thank Zeus for the peace and prosperity in Olympus, aimed to bring everyone closer together. They lasted for a day or two, and alongside the games, a variety of booths sold and traded items, food, and wine from around Olympus.

The Olympic Games were designed to test the players' minds, bodies, and powers. The games were divided into groups, with each group identified by a specific metal.

The High Olympians were gold; lower-level gods and goddesses were silver; and cretes were bronze. Each group competed in rings that were spread throughout the festival, decorated with a variety of courses and challenges, and marked by the gilded metal on the rings' gateways.

As we crossed through the summit gates, Prometheus smiled down at me.

"Sounds like a good amount of Olympus has made it to the games already." Releasing me from where I'd been tucked into his side, he slid his hand across my back and down to my hand, squeezing it as he led me toward the sounds of laughter and conversation.

CHAPTER 54

W E followed the cobblestone road around the side of the Olympian Court. It was still icy this early in the morning. The road surrounded the base of the court, leading to an oak-filled courtyard, within which were dozens of booths. Olympians walked around laughing and smiling as they enjoyed the festivities with an ease I hadn't seen in years.

Maybe I was wrong. Maybe this is exactly what Olympus needed.

My smile grew as a few young cretes skipped by us, heading toward a game ring to our right, with silver gates that told me it was the lower gods and goddesses they were going to watch compete.

I looked over at Prometheus, finding him observing everything with an intensity that seemed out of place in such a joyful scene. "What do you want to do first?" I pulled excitedly on his arm.

Prometheus looked back at the festival and shrugged. "How about you choose?"

"Hmm . . ." I looked at the row of booths, tapping my chin as my heart fluttered with excitement. "How about the booths?"

Prometheus nodded and walked over to the booths I'd pointed at, pulling me along on the arm I'd linked through his own. He walked quickly—too quickly for my taste, because I couldn't look at

the people and the scenes around us, worried I might trip and fall at this speed if I were to take my eyes off the road.

"Is there somewhere we need to be?" I asked, looking around to see if I'd missed something.

Prometheus immediately stopped and looked down at me in alarm before shaking his head. "My apologies. I didn't realize my pace had quickened." He continued walking, this time at a normal rate, only to slow when we reached the first booth.

A tall, slender woman appeared, with ridged horns curling out from the top of her curly blonde hair, and blue eyes that had the same rectangular pupils all fauns had. "Hello. May I interest you in some silk-woven chitons?" she asked, speaking with a slight vibration in her voice.

I looked at the beautiful faun, noticing the texture of the fur covering her face and the small ears peeking out from underneath her warm brown, gray-streaked hair.

"These are exquisite," I said, running my fingers through the silk layers, relishing in the smooth, slippery texture. "Did you weave all these yourself?"

"Most of them. My daughter helps from time to time, but she likes to work with linen, whereas I've always loved to work with silks." The faun smiled at me and walked over to a stack of linens in the corner of the booth. "These are some of hers. They're mostly male, but there are a few female chitons and peplos available if you're interested in linen."

"No, no. I definitely want some silk. A friend of mine recently gifted me something made of silk, and it has quickly become one of my favorite fabrics. Besides, I have many linen chitons, but not yet one made of silk," I said, earning a smile that was so big and pure the corners of the faun's eyes crinkled in delight.

"Well, in that case, I have a few that would fit you beautifully." She started to turn away, headed for a pile of silks behind her, but I spoke before she could move.

"My name is Pandora, by the way."

"Lovely to meet you, Pandora. I'm Filenta."

"Nice to meet you as well, Filenta."

As I looked at the silks in front of me, I couldn't help but reach under the sleeve of my peplos and feel the slippery material of the spider-silk armor. I wished I could show Filenta the beautiful silk Arachne had woven, but I decided it would probably be best not to reveal it now, especially with Prometheus nearby. He didn't like me wearing color, so I didn't want to imagine what he'd say if he saw me wearing a suit of armor to our pre-wedding celebration.

I let her go to work finding the silks she had in mind and turned around to find Prometheus standing there, his back to me. I tapped on his shoulder, and he swiveled around, looking like I'd woken him up from a daze.

"Are you all right?" I asked, worried what could be affecting him like this when he'd been so excited on our walk up here.

"Yes. I just . . ." He paused, shaking his head and rubbing the back of his neck, which I'd come to realize he did when he was unsure about something or was nervous. "Never mind."

"Are you sure? We can go, if you want," I offered, not wanting to, but willing to if he wasn't feeling good or was regretting having the games now he was here. Nothing else seemed to explain why he'd have such a sudden change in demeanor.

"Yes. Finish with the faun, and we will continue," he said, turning his back to me, smiling as if nothing was wrong. But I knew better. There was something he wasn't telling me.

I turned back to Filenta and found four different silk chitons laid out in front of me, each of them beautifully unique. The first was a deep navy with copper pins; another had a mix of violets, pastel blues, and silver pins; and the last two were a deep burgundy with gold pins, and a rich, blue-green emerald with bronze pins. I stared at each of them in awe, unable to decide which of them called to me the most.

"Wow. These are all so beautiful. How could anyone ever pick?" I smiled, running my hands over each of the fabrics, savoring their beauty and softness.

"If you don't mind, I could surprise you and pick the one I believe to be most suitable for you," Filenta suggested.

"I would love that. If you didn't, I'd likely be here all day, and my betrothed would not be happy with me if I were to do that." I smiled, motioning to Prometheus, who stood with his back to us. I hoped Filenta didn't find him rude.

"My pleasure, dear. Let me just get this wrapped up for you, and I'll have you two on your way."

"Thank you, Filenta." I smiled at her sweetly as she went to work wrapping a chiton up, being extra cautious not to let me see which one she'd chosen for me out of the four.

"Here you go, Pandora. I hope it brings you as much joy as making it brought me," she said, passing over a papyrus-wrapped package.

"Thank you so much. How much do I owe you?" I asked, grabbing my satchel to retrieve my coin pouch so I could pay her.

"Oh no, dear. No need to pay for this one. Your company has been worth enough, and I am sure your beauty will have people flocking from all around Olympus to buy whatever it is you're wearing. Just be sure to tell them Filenta made them, and that is payment enough." She smiled and put her hand over mine, giving it a small squeeze.

"You are too kind. If you insist, then I thank you, and you can be sure I'll tell everyone I pass and will wear it all the time. Thank you for all your help. I will definitely be seeing you in the future and buying another chiton from you." I squeezed her hand, smiling too before turning back to Prometheus and tapping him on his shoulder. "Ready?" I asked.

"Yes."

"Well, now that I've done some shopping, do you want to go see a game?"

"If you would like to, then sure. Let's go see a game," he said, smiling and returning to his happy self.

"Let's go see who's playing up in the High Olympians' ring," I said, pulling him toward the gilded gaming ring, which I could already see glistening farther up the road.

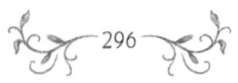

CHAPTER 55

PROMETHEUS and I found some elevated seating on the higher level of the stacked rectangular boulders that acted as both steps and seating. They'd been set up right in front of the ring, wrapping around one side in a semicircle.

"Our first game will be between two of the greatest warriors known to Olympus," one of Zeus's servants announced, extending an arm out to the left side so quickly he sent a gust of wind toward the entry gate, pushing it open. "Our first competitor is none other than Ares, God of War."

Ares came running out wearing a suit of golden armor over a white chiton, with a matching gold helmet, a gold-and-silver shield, his notorious spear, and a sword strapped onto his back.

"And competing against him is the wisest warrior known to the realm . . . Athena."

Athena didn't bother running into the arena making a spectacle like Ares. She walked in, calm and collected, sporting her twin swords at her back, a full suit of gold-and-silver armor, a matching helmet, and her shield.

"A fight between wrath and wisdom. How fitting," Prometheus said so quietly I almost didn't hear him. He never looked away from the arena, which made me think he hadn't meant to say the words aloud.

I wanted to ask him what he meant, but then the fight started.

Ares and Athena circled each other around the arena, neither of them speaking a word, but the looks they gave one another from under their helmets seemed to say enough.

Ares launched into attack first, running hard and fast at Athena, attempting to hit her with his shield, but she was fast and rolled out of his way before it made contact.

Athena dove, dropping to her knees as she pulled one of her swords from its sheath on her back, sliding behind him and slicing Ares across the backs of his knees in one fluid motion.

Ares yelled in fury, spinning at her and piercing his spear into the ground seconds after she was gone. His spear landed in a pool of his own blood instead of in her.

I couldn't help but smile as I watched Athena perform that move. Even if she had left me to train alone out of fear of Zeus catching her, I was still grateful she'd taken the risk and taught me everything she had.

Athena was up and standing, ready to go on the defense, as Ares pulled his own sword and swung at her with all his might. She ducked just in time to avoid a hit to the head and launched herself at him, hitting him right in his stomach with her shoulder and pushing him off-balance.

Ares used the hilt of his sword, slamming it down onto her back while she held on, until Athena stopped, the loss of motion throwing Ares off just long enough for her to slice him across his stomach before jumping out of his reach.

Ares ripped off his helmet, threw it off to the side, and glared, his full wrath on display as he stared Athena down.

"Your wrath clouds your judgement. I've tried to warn you of that before," Athena said calmly, which only ignited Ares' fury.

Releasing a battle cry, he ran at her, slamming his spear into the ground before he reached her and using it to boost himself into the air. He landed behind her, slicing through her side with his sword.

Athena jumped, rolling to the side at the same second as he went for the wining blow, attempting to shove his sword through her back.

"Wisdom fools you into believing you're better than everyone else," he spat at her, not letting her get away for long. He ran after her, spear in hand as he readied himself to throw it.

Athena ran faster, putting distance between them. She turned back in time for Ares to throw the spear and lifted her shield just as it hit. The spear bounced off, landing at her feet.

Picking up the spear, Athena had the upper hand.

Before Ares could react, Athena launched his own spear at him. He blocked it with his shield, but when he lowered himself to pick it up, Athena was ready with four daggers, two in each hand. She threw them so quickly Ares didn't even realize what had hit him until it was too late. He looked down at the four daggers sticking out of his chest and lifted a hand to pull them out, but Athena was there, standing behind him, with another dagger to his side and a sword at his throat.

"I'm not better than everyone, but I am better than you," she said, shoving him to the ground.

"We have our winner!" the owl announced, holding Athena's fist in the air. "Would anyone else care to challenge our champion?"

No one came forward, which made me smile, proud of Athena, even though I'd already known Ares stood no chance against her.

"All right then. Athena is the champion!" the owl announced, placing a gold medal around her neck. "The next set of opponents will be out shortly."

"Do you want to explore some more of the festival, or watch another match?" I asked.

"I don't think anything other than Zeus fighting could beat that," Prometheus said, making me laugh.

"Very true. Should we go get something to eat? I'm pretty hungry after that hike up here." I said this sheepishly, feeling my stomach gurgle.

"Lead the way."

Prometheus helped me up and off the steep boulders before nodding toward the booths for me to lead the way. I followed my nose over to them, finding one booth with both sweet and savory

baked goods. Unable to make up my mind, I ordered a honey cake and a flaky pastry stuffed with a tangy cheese and green veggies.

"Pandora?" a voice called from my left.

Lemenia was walking toward me from the booth beside ours, carrying an apple on a stick dipped in golden honey and crushed pistachios.

"Hi, Lemenia!" I said excitedly, shocked she'd bothered to say hello after all I'd found out about her past with mankind. "How have you been?"

"Wonderful! I got offered a position working in Atlantis, so I've been working on getting everything moved. However, when I heard of the Olympic Games being held in yours and Prometheus's honor . . ." She motioned to him, acknowledging his presence for the first time. It seemed she had accepted me, but not him quite yet. "I just hoped I would be able to see you before we both left."

"That is amazing, Lemenia." I said, unable to resist and pulling her into a hug, at which she froze as if I'd turned the gaze of Medusa on her.

"Thank you. And you? I assume all is going well with the two of you," she said, eyeing the distance between me and Prometheus, which he immediately caught and rectified, grabbing me at the hip and pulling me in close.

"Very. We plan to travel to Earth immediately after the marriage to begin our lives." Prometheus looked down at me, smiling as he leaned in to kiss my forehead—something so tender and surprising it caught me off-guard, making me freeze as much as Lemenia had when I hugged her. "As a friend of Pandora's, you are more than welcome to visit us on Earth anytime."

Lemenia's smile fell, her eyes drifting off, looking like she was lost in a memory for a moment. Before she had a chance to answer, I spoke up.

"Prometheus, would you mind giving me and Lemenia a moment?"

He looked between us, confused at her reaction, and nodded. "Of course." Then he leaned down, kissing me softly before turning to Lemenia. "It was lovely meeting you, Lemenia."

"You as well," she said, forcing a smile, although her eyes were full of despair and sorrow.

As soon as Prometheus was out of earshot, I finally spoke. "I am so sorry about that. He doesn't know of your history with mankind during your time on Earth. Of course you don't have to go there to see me. I'm sure Prometheus will allow me to come back and visit once in a while," I said, wishing I believed it and knowing deep in my heart I didn't. "After all, my friends and family are all here in Olympus."

"You have no reason to apologize. As you said, he does not know my past." She smiled, reaching out and grabbing my hand in her own, the smooth ripple of her scaled skin feeling cool to the touch. "I just wanted to come here to say I'm sorry for how I treated you that first time we met, and I hope whatever future awaits you in Gaia's realm is nothing short of miraculous. Not everything there is as horrendous as mankind. In fact, many parts of Gaia's realm are breathtaking. Prometheus seems like he'll be good to you, but never let your guard down. If there is one thing I've learned about mankind, it's that they will stop at nothing to get what they want, and I have to assume the Titans that watched over them are more similar than we may think."

"What are you saying?" I asked. Was she trying to tell me Prometheus was using me? That mankind would fight for what they wanted? I already knew all this and couldn't understand the point in her telling me any of it, other than to remind me to be careful.

"I am saying keep your eyes open. The realm of Aether may be known as the wild lands, but the realm of man is far more savage."

Lemenia and I visited a little more, but ultimately, I couldn't stop taking my eyes off Prometheus and where he sat in the distance on a gray stone bench, watching everything around him with utter fascination.

"I need to get back, but it really was nice seeing you. I was shocked you called my name, but I'm glad you did."

"I'm glad I gave you another chance on the trail, rather than pushing you off the side of the mountain," Lemenia said, laughing, and I couldn't help but laugh along with her. I couldn't believe she'd gone from looking at me with such hatred and fear to seeking me out as if she considered me a friend.

I walked over to the bench Prometheus was sitting on and filled him in on Lemenia and why her reaction to his invite had made her upset. I was worried he might get defensive of the humans, but instead, he was extremely understanding.

"Blending of species is not always easy. I cannot fault either side for their actions," he said in response, passing me the pastry I'd ordered and a napkin.

I groaned as I bit into the savory pastry, and Prometheus smiled as he asked, "Good?"

"Want some?" I offered, holding it out for him.

"If you don't mind." He leaned in and took a bite from it. He didn't say anything as he chewed, but his face said it all. He liked it as much as I did.

"Not bad for being Olympian-made, huh?" I joked, which made him laugh.

"Not bad at all." He took another bite out of the pastry.

After I'd finished eating and had given him one final bite, I stuffed the wrapper into my satchel until I could find somewhere to dispose of it.

"Is there anything you'd like to do?" I asked.

He shrugged. "I guess we can walk around and see if there are any more good games starting."

"Let's go then," I said, following him across to where a bronze gaming ring had been set up. A crowd was forming around it, and unlike the High Olympians' ring, this one didn't have any seating, which forced everyone to stand around, hoping they could see over the Olympians in front of them.

CHAPTER 56

Just before we'd made it to the group of cretes surrounding the ring, Prometheus froze, stopping so fast I nearly fell, as he was holding my hand.

"Are you all right?" I asked, finding him staring off into the crowd in front of us.

Something that looked a lot like fear flashed across his face. He opened his mouth to speak before shutting it again.

"Prometheus? What's going on?" I asked, looking around to see what had the Titan so startled and finding nothing but Olympians enjoying their day.

"I think we should go," he said.

"Go? Go where? What's going on?" Starting to get worried, I pulled on his arm, forcing him to look down at me as I asked again, "What is going on?"

"Nothing." He shook his head and pulled me away from the cretes' ring. "Come on—let's go back to the booths on the other side."

"But why?" I asked, pulling against him, trying to make him stop and explain what was happening. Prometheus was too strong, however, and every pull I made against him only resulted in him pulling me harder behind him. I got the feeling he wouldn't even

stop if I fell, and so I tried my hardest to keep my footing and to keep up with his pace.

Walking as fast as I could, I opened my mouth to ask what his rush was, but then my legs began to shake, making me stumble.

"Are you okay?" Prometheus asked, turning around hesitantly as I steadied myself.

"Yeah. Did you feel that?" I looked around to see if anyone else had felt the shaking and found dozens of other Olympians looking around too, just as confused as I was.

I started to walk forward to ask if they knew what was happening, but after two steps, the ground trembled. Not a shake like the first time, but a vibration that felt like it was coming from deep within the center of Mount Olympus.

"We need to go, right n—"

The shaking began again, cutting Prometheus off as screams filled the festival. I stumbled again, this time falling to the ground.

I looked up from the quaking cobblestone road to find a dozen or so other Olympians around us had fallen, same as me.

"What is happening?" I asked as the summit stilled and festival-goers started standing up, many moving to help gather goods that had fallen from the booths all around us.

"How could it be happening here? It's not supposed to be here," Prometheus whispered almost to himself, shaking his head and digging his palms into his eyes as he started to spiral into the mental warfare in his mind.

"What do you mean, 'not here'?" I grabbed his wrists, trying to pull them away from his eyes before he dug them out with the heels of his hands, to no avail. He was starting to lose it, and I wasn't sure how to bring him back.

But then I remembered something Epimetheus had once told me.

Releasing him, I looked at Prometheus and sucked in a deep breath to prepare myself. Then, drawing back my fist, I sent it sailing at him with as much force as physically possible, until it made contact with the target I was imagining on his bare cheek with a loud crack.

His eyes went wide, and his hands dropped to his sides as if they'd gone limp. He looked at me in utter shock, but to my relief, it worked.

"I'm sorry. I didn't know what else to do." My cheeks flushed as embarrassment took hold, and I worried I'd made a mistake in punching him, especially when he grabbed my shoulders hard enough I knew I'd bruise.

"Pandora, we need to go. Now," he said, looking around as if something would attack him any minute.

"Why? What's happening?" I asked, still not able to see anything in the places he seemed to be staring off into.

"I can't. We need to—"

Suddenly, Mount Olympus began to shake again, even harder than it had before, making it nearly impossible to stand in place. Screams rang throughout the festival, but the loudest screams were coming from the festival entrance, where Olympians were running in every direction, screaming in absolute panic.

"It must be them. It must be the Aloadae—"

I was cut off when Prometheus was knocked to the side by an enormous piece of rubble that had fallen from the top of the court. It rolled into him as the mountain continued to quake.

"Prometheus!" I screamed, running toward him to help, but he was already rolling the piece of stone off him and getting to his feet, rushing forward to meet me halfway.

"We need to get you to cover," he said, pulling me along with him.

My feet were practically dragged along the cobblestone as I struggled to stay upright with the constant movement of the mountain.

"What do you think is happening?" I asked Prometheus again, yelling over the chaos as we ran, dipping and diving, through Olympians running around frantically, trying to find safety, same as us.

"I think maybe . . ." Prometheus paused, looking up at something above me before yanking on my arm so hard I was sure my shoulder would dislocate from its socket. "Pandora, run!"

Not having time to see what I was running from, I followed Prometheus as fast as physically possible. I could see shelter in the distance, where the back door to the court stood, and I almost smiled in relief—but suddenly, my foot slipped, sending my body tumbling to the ground. I didn't stop until my face slammed against the stone street, hard enough that I could taste blood pooling in my mouth.

As if the ground shaking wasn't bad enough, now my whole world was spinning from the impact. I struggled to focus my eyes on Prometheus, whom I could barely make out in the distance running toward me.

Grabbing me under my shoulders, Prometheus hauled me to my feet, shaking me roughly to stir me into a semi-conscious state before yelling, "Come on. We. Need. To. Go!"

He practically dragged me behind him as I struggled to stay conscious, but then a tumbling, rolling noise sounded from behind us. I swiveled around just in time to jump out of the way of an enormous piece of rubble rolling down the road, straight into us.

I thought I'd made it when I launched my body to the side, but as I tried to stand, I screamed in agony as a flaring pain coursed through my body. It took me a moment to focus on where the pain was originating from, and I found it was worse in my right leg.

I looked down, having trouble focusing at first, until my vision slowly cleared, revealing my leg pinned under an enormous piece of marble, more than ten times my size. I couldn't see the extent of my injuries, but if the searing pain told me anything, it was that it wasn't good, and my mortal clock had just started counting down.

So much for the armor under my peplos.

I stared at my leg for a minute in shock as tears started streaming down my face. Or maybe that was blood. At this point, I really couldn't be too sure. I looked around me, trying to find Prometheus.

"Prometheus!" I cried out repeatedly, for what felt like hours, between sobs, until finally, I caught sight of him.

"Pandora!" he yelled, running over to me, skidding to a stop at my side and looking up at the enormous stone crushing the life out of me.

"Help me, Prometheus," I said, panicked, through my tears. "I need you to get this thing off me. My leg—it's got my leg pinned."

"I-I-I can't," he stuttered, his eyes full of regret.

"What!" I cried out. "What do you mean, you can't? Please! You have to help me!"

He just lowered his head, shaking it as he backed away from me slowly. "I can't," he said, continuing to back away. A crete brushed past him, knocking him off-balance.

"Please." I reached for him. If he left me, I'd die here. "Please don't leave me here."

"I'm sorry," he said, his form fading from my sight as the smoke engulfed him.

Abandoned, with nothing but my tears, screams of terror flooded in from all around me as the sounds of battle began somewhere in the distance.

I looked around one last time, hoping to see Prometheus returning to help me now the smoke was clearing, but I found nothing. The screaming had all moved north of me, toward Zeus's palace, but the shaking never stopped, only intensifying, until it was so strong I could make out the rhythm. It was as if there were a heartbeat in the mountain itself. No—not a heartbeat. Footsteps. Lots and lots of footsteps.

Movement caught my eye at the bottom of the road, and I squinted, hoping it would help me to see the mystery figure better.

"Help! Please, help me!" I yelled to them, praying to the Primes someone, anyone, would find me and get me out of this mess.

The figure turned in my direction, lifting its head into the air and sniffing before releasing a bloodcurdling howl.

More figures appeared behind it, and almost simultaneously, each of them dropped from two legs down to four, contorting into monstrous beasts with the body of a bear, spikes along their spine, and an enormous rack of antlers that were sharp enough to spear anyone who had the misfortune of getting in their path.

The creatures sniffed the air, walking around before grouping in the spot where I'd fallen. They licked at something on the ground. I touched my head, feeling the wet warmth of blood, and as I pulled it back, looking at the glittering red on my fingertips, a sickening understanding settled within me. I'd broken skin, and they were scenting my blood.

As if they could sense my thoughts, the group of creatures whipped toward me as one before charging in my direction.

I watched as they ran, claws scratching the cobblestone road, so sharp sparks flew off the ground with every lunge they took, and closed my eyes, tears streaming down my face as I accepted my fate.

This was it. This was the day I would die.

CHAPTER 57

JUST before the creatures made it to me, a massive animal dropped from the sky.

At first, I thought it was the sphinx, but then I realized it was missing her wings and her human face, leaving only the body of a male lion, its enormous paws ripping one of the creatures down with it as it landed.

The creatures barely had time before it was shredding into them, ripping off limbs and tossing them in every direction, until there was nothing left.

At first, I was relieved, but then the thing turned, looked straight at me, and ran.

I screamed as loud as I could, hoping still that someone was close enough to hear me through all the chaos. But then, as suddenly as it had arrived, the lion's form changed, shifting into a man. No—not a man. A Titan.

Epimetheus.

"Pandora, it's all right. I'm here," Epimetheus said, dropping to his knees on the cracked, dirt-covered cobblestone . He cupped my cheek with his hand. "Pandora, it's all right. Everything is going to be all right. I'm going to get you to Apollo, but we need to move. I'm

going to help," he said in a rush, looking back and forth between me and the massive stone on top of my leg.

"You came," I said breathlessly, finding it hard to speak as my words slurred.

"Yes, my goddess, I'm here. I'm going to get you out of here, okay?" He smiled down at me as if I were the most beautiful being in the world to him, even though I knew I was covered in blood, sweat, and tears—but that never seemed to matter to Epimetheus.

He examined my leg before finding a large piece of metal that had likely come from one of the game rings. He wedged it under the rock next to my uninjured leg, which he carefully moved to the side so he could step in between the metal wedge and the rock. Pushing the metal rod down as hard as possible, he lifted the boulder off my leg and shoved it hard near the top with his shoulder, sending the deadly rock toppling over.

I almost smiled with pride, but it never reached my face as I looked down, taking in the full extent of my injuries.

My leg was completely crushed. In some places it was flattened, where the bone must have just shattered, such as around my thigh and my calf, but at the joints on my knee and my ankle, the bone had simply pierced through the skin. Now the heavy stone had been removed, blood began to rush back to my injuries. At this rate, it wouldn't be long before I bled out, and the look on Epimetheus's face told me he was thinking the same thing.

"I am so sorry, but this is going to hurt," he said, not waiting for me to respond to—or worse, process—what he'd said before he picked me up as carefully as possible under my legs and my back, cradled me to his chest, and carried me to the court.

I screamed in agony as he carried me. My vision was blurring, and I tried my hardest to fight off the darkness threatening to consume me.

Epimetheus hastened his pace, nearly running, with me in his arms.

The court was packed full of Olympians, but somehow, Epimetheus was able to find Apollo quickly among the ever-growing crowd.

"Move!" he yelled at the people separating us from him, making them all rush out of his way, likely fearing the murderous edge in his voice.

"Epimetheus? Is that—?" Apollo's face was covered in worry. He was in the middle of setting the broken arm of a lower-level god when his eyes landed on me, and the rest of his words fell short as he swept his arm across the space beside him, clearing it before pointing Epimetheus to it. "Set her there. She's losing a lot of blood—I need to work fast."

Apollo rushed around grabbing a few things: gauze, water, and some metal tool that looked like it had pincers.

"Where is Prometheus? I thought she arrived with him, not you," Apollo said, looking around as if he would appear from the same direction as us.

"I don't know. Prometheus was gone when I found her like this."

"Hhhh . . . ft . . . me," I stuttered, struggling to speak as blood filled my mouth.

"What?" Epimetheus asked gently, sitting beside me and holding my small hand within his large, rough one. He rubbed his thumb in circles on the back of my hand as he leaned in closer, so I wouldn't have to make as much of an effort to speak.

"Left . . . me," I managed say before falling into another fit of bloody coughs.

Epimetheus held my hand tighter and watched as Apollo leaned over my demolished leg, wrapping it in warm rays of healing energy that encompassed my leg like a blanket. The flares of power licked at my shredded skin, sank into the deepest wounds, and patched the mangled muscle, torn ligaments, and shattered bone piece by piece. It was euphoric, every flare of power washing away more pain.

"He left you?" Epimetheus asked, looking like I'd struck him.

Not trusting my voice yet, I nodded.

Apollo put a hand on his shoulder in a comforting gesture as he said, "For what it's worth, I'm sorry. There are few things worse than the betrayal of a loved one. Believe me, I am well-versed in a brother's betrayal. I see it day after day with the three brothers of Olympus."

"How could he have done that?" Epimetheus whispered almost to himself.

"Where is he now?" Apollo asked.

"What?"

"Where is your brother now, Epimetheus?"

"I don't know," he replied, the shock fading from his face as he said, "I need to find him. There was an army coming up from the east, led by Otus. It won't be long until they reach the summit. Is she safe with you?" He nodded in my direction.

I opened my mouth to speak, to tell him not to go, but Apollo must have nodded, because before I got the chance, Epimetheus was running. Away from me, and into the chaos.

I let Apollo's magic finish its work, and when I felt healed enough, I sat up, testing the leg that had been crushed and finding I could swing it with little to no pain.

"Careful," Apollo said, rushing to my side from where he'd been helping a young crete with some minor injuries. "You are nearly healed, but don't push it."

"I have to go after him," I said, pushing myself to the edge of the stone slab and standing up.

"Who? Prometheus?" Apollo asked, adding, "Don't worry. Epimetheus went to find him."

"No—you don't understand. Something is wrong with Prometheus. I need to find Epimetheus." I unhooked my peplos from my shoulders, letting the heavy fabric drop to the ground, before stepping out.

Apollo stared at my armor, looking like he wanted to ask a bunch of questions, but he didn't get the chance. I was already on my way to the opening in the side of the court.

I had my armor and the dagger I'd bought in Forging Glory, but I needed something else. Looking around, my eye caught on a silver sword that must have been lost in battle, lying about twenty feet away, on the other side of the exit. Not seeing any enemies, I ran out, grabbing the sword in one swift movement, and set off to find Epimetheus.

CHAPTER 58

THE festival grounds had become an all-out battlefield. Olympians of all power levels and species were fighting alongside one another as hordes of bloodthirsty creatures flooded in from every side, using the roads connecting the palaces around the Olympian Court.

There was too much going on, and I had no idea which direction Epimetheus had headed.

Looking around, I noticed a large Corinthian column that had toppled over. It was still mostly intact and leaning against the second story of the west palace.

I ran over to the column and climbed up it as fast as I could, thankful for my healed leg and the damage done to the once smooth surface, because it gave me more traction, helping me to climb faster. I made it to the balcony on the second floor and looked out over the destruction covering the summit of Olympus.

A loud bang from my right shook the palace. I ran over to that side to see what had just happened.

My gaze shot down to a group of creatures holding bows with barbed arrows that had been dipped into the bright green slime of the Loxican, a monster that roamed the darkest parts of Aether and contained a poison known to affect even the most powerful of gods. It paralyzed their bodies—and with it, their powers—and glowed bright green in ominous warning. The creatures were aiming at something flying above them through the sky, tracking it with their bows before releasing a string of arrows in its direction.

Whatever they were shooting at survived, because all their attention was in the sky as they grabbed another arrow at the same moment as Athena arrived. She rode a Chimera into the battle, charging directly for the group and yelling something at the Chimera right before it opened its jaws. It released an enormous roar that rained fire down across the entire area, burning the group shooting arrows, along with another group of incoming enemies that had just entered the grounds, in one fell swoop.

Movement overhead caught my eye, making me look up just in time to see a falcon soar across the sky, heading to an area where smoke billowed, in the direction of the oak forests.

I sucked in a breath, praying to the Primes that Trizeena was safe.

I looked back to where the falcon flew and saw the moment it dropped to the ground, turning into a man. *Epimetheus.* Sliding down the column, I ran toward the area where I'd seen him land.

I was nearly there, taking the sharp turn around a pile of rubble blocking the road, when I saw them and skidded to a stop.

A group of creatures stood between me and my path to Epimetheus, their attention on me. The menacing look in their eyes made me take a couple of steps back, wishing I'd thought this through.

Then they charged.

Remembering what Athena had taught me, I ran at the two closest to me, dropping right before their swords ran through me. I slid on my knees past them, with my sword in one hand and my dagger in the other, using them simultaneously to cut the tendons at the backs of their knees, rendering their legs useless.

A battle scream caught my attention as another creature came flying at me, sword raised and ready to strike. Rolling out of the way, I twisted around onto my belly, then I jumped up and launched myself onto his spiny back, running my sword across his throat. Jumping off his body, I let him slump down and turned to the remaining two.

Crouching down, I waited, ready for their attack.

"You Primes-forsaken Olympian whore. I'm going to kill you for that," the creature holding the axe said. He had green scales, slanted, glowing yellow eyes, and a long tail that was wide at its base, tapering at the end.

"Not if I kill you first," I said.

His smile revealed a row of dagger-sharp teeth that reminded me of the sirens. He nodded to the crete standing beside him. The satyr holding the spear nodded, moving to circle around me.

They were going to try coming at me from both sides, but I wasn't going to let that happen. I stared straight ahead at the green-scaled crete, watching the satyr move around to my side.

"Do you really think this will work out for you?"

They both laughed.

"I am a goddess after all." I launched at the satyr, my sword impaling him through his torso and holding him there as I brought my dagger up to his throat. I sliced across it in the same motion as I pulled the sword out of his stomach.

One left.

I turned toward the last crete just in time to miss his blow. He swung his axe over his head as I rolled out of the way.

"You're dead!" he roared as I jumped to my feet, sword at the ready, seconds before he ran at me.

I threw up my sword in a defensive stance, and he swung the axe down into it with such power the impact rattled me all the way to my bones, almost making me drop it. I couldn't let him get many more hits on me like that. I feared the weapons would be able to take more hits than my body could withstand. I was strong, but he was nearly twice my size, with enhanced abilities. I needed to end this. Fast.

I dodged a few more of his attacks, and finally, I saw my opening.

Running straight into him, I waited for the moment the axe came over his head. I noticed that once it began to swing, the weight of the axe threw him off, making it hard for him to adjust mid-swing. That was when I would strike.

When the axe was over his head, holding my sword in my right hand and my dagger in my left, I threw the dagger, aiming for his chest, and jumped out of the path of the axe.

The dagger hit home, making him falter, but he didn't go down. Not missing my opportunity, I took advantage of his shock, running up from behind him and piercing him straight through the heart.

With no time to waste, I pulled my sword from his back, flipped his lifeless body over, and ripped my dagger from his chest. Then I followed the cobblestone road toward Epimetheus, hoping he was all right and I wasn't too late.

Littered with rubble, the road was difficult to maneuver, but I saw a clear path near one of the collapsed Olympian Court entries that could get me to Epimetheus. Passing by dozens of dead and injured that I wished I could help, I swore I'd come back for them once I found Epimetheus.

Movement ahead caught my eye.

A large shadow figure walked leisurely along the road toward Zeus's palace. Creatures parted like water around the figure as it passed. It was the same shadow figure I'd seen the afternoon following the siren attack, the day I met Epimetheus. A couple of creatures joined the group, following behind the figure as he passed. One of them I recognized immediately as her copper-red hair flashed in the sun.

She noticed me the same time I noticed her. Realizing I was severely outnumbered, I ran behind a pile of rubble and waited, hoping she would seek me out and even the odds.

I peeked through one of the large cracks to the group of creatures and couldn't help but smile as I watched her break off from the group, heading my way.

Backing up a little further from the group, I bolted between a couple more rubble piles, making myself able to be seen for her to follow, until I ended up in a small area cleared of rubble, tucked behind one of the boulders in wait.

"I know you're here little mortal," she taunted, her voice growing closer and closer with every word. "I was wondering when we'd get to meet again."

I stayed quiet, watching her closely until it was time to strike, but then the unthinkable happened.

Filenta appeared. She was covered in dirt, but other than that, she looked relatively unharmed. But she was walking straight toward the redhead, and it would only be seconds before she noticed her.

Not wasting any more time, I jumped out from my spot, launching myself at the copper-haired goddess, pulling my dagger out and holding it to her throat. She stilled instantly, and even though I was standing behind her, I could almost feel her smile as she said, "Ah, Pandora. I didn't realize I would get two prizes if I followed you into this trap."

So much for the element of surprise, I thought, as Filenta looked between the two of us, her brows scrunched together and her eyes wide as I held the dagger to the woman's throat.

"Filenta, I don't know what you are doing here, but you need to go—now. Go find your daughter and get far away from here."

"What is happeni—?" Filenta started.

"Yes, what a wonderful idea. Go get your daughter. Might want to hurry while you're still alive."

"But what about you?" Filenta asked, her fingers playing with the loose thread of her peplos as she looked between me and the opening to leave.

"I will be fine. Now go."

Filenta nodded hesitantly, moving over to my side to pass. I was opening my mouth to thank her for listening when a sharp elbow hit me in the gut, knocking the air from my lungs and forcing me to lose my grip on the goddess in front of me.

I barely had time to blink, let alone catch my breath, when a shriek snapped my attention to the space Filenta had just been occupying. She was gone. Scanning the area, I found her across the open space, pinned up against the mystery goddess in a similar way to how I'd held her previously—except, instead of a dagger, she held her clawlike nails at her throat, tight enough that I knew with a little more pressure she would draw blood.

"Let her go," I seethed.

"Now why would I do something stupid like that?" She picked up one of Filenta's blonde curls, twirling it around her finger, her eyes not leaving mine as she added, "This little faun is exactly what I've been craving since I arrived. Couldn't risk leaving a trail of bodies, though, my master wouldn't let me, but now everyone is fair game."

"She is not who you want—it's me. So let her go and just take me," I offered, crouching down and dropping my dagger to the ground, lifting my hands slowly to show my surrender.

"That's a pretty tempting offer." She smiled, looking between Filenta and me as if she were making the biggest decision of her life. Tilting Filenta's head to the side, she inhaled the air deeply, her smile growing wide enough that I could see how sharp her teeth were. Her two canines were significantly longer and seemed to be extended as she breathed in.

She looked over at me, meeting my eyes. Filenta's neck was still stretched to the right, and the goddess smiled right before sinking her fangs into the side of her neck.

Filenta and I screamed at the same moment. I dropped to the ground, grabbing my dagger, and ran at Filenta, knocking her limp body away from the redhead's with all the force I had. Then I crawled atop the goddess and wasted no time in stabbing my dagger deep into her heart.

"You . . . can't . . . stop . . ." she struggled to say as she coughed up blood, gurgling out each word, "us."

"Maybe not, but I stopped you," I said, climbing off her and pulling my dagger out from her chest with a sickening crunch.

Filenta was a few feet away, lying on the broken cobblestone, blood flowing freely from her neck as the color washed from her face.

"Filenta? Filenta, it's Pandora. You're all right. It's over. I'm going to get you out of here," I said, moving her carefully so I could pick her up.

She opened her mouth to speak, but no words formed. Her mouth simply opened and closed like a fish gasping for water.

"It's okay. You're going to be okay," I said, trying to reassure her as much as myself.

Her body convulsed as I held her in my arms, blood bubbling up from her mouth as she struggled to catch her breath. I held onto her, helpless in her last moments, watching as the life faded from her bright blue eyes.

Tears streamed down my face as I looked at the sweet faun I'd only just met, but who'd shown such kindness and warmth that I'd immediately loved her. Wishing I could stay with her, and knowing I couldn't, I wiped the tears from my cheeks and gently laid her down, silently promising myself I'd come back for her and not leave her in this cold, hard rubble a moment longer than necessary.

Making my way back to where I'd seen the shadow figure and a group of creatures heading, I dipped in and out from behind piles of debris, careful not to be seen, as I followed their path down to the courtyard behind Zeus's palace.

The shadow-cloaked figure stood in the center of the courtyard, along with dozens of creatures frothing at the mouth. All of them were deadly still, watching as the King of the Gods fought Otus and Ephialtes high in the sky above his palace. The Aloadae twins pushed Zeus closer to the ground with every blow.

I looked between the fight in the sky and the group below, and it didn't take me long to realize what they were planning. The Aloadae twins were pushing Zeus right into the enemies' hands.

The figure raised his hands in the air, sending tendrils of inky shadows that looked like smoke from his fingertips to form a cloud above him. He brought his hands to his sides, along with the cloud of darkness, until the shadows were lying atop them like a blanket, making them invisible from above.

Zeus continued to descend toward the trap, glancing down every now and then, not able to see anything but a dark cloud awaiting him below.

Unable to ignore what I was witnessing any longer, I decided wherever Epimetheus had gone, he'd need to hold out for a few minutes longer so I could help save the god I'd grown to despise with every fiber of my being.

I wondered what he'd say if he could see me now, risking my mortal life to save the almighty Zeus.

I took a step forward at the same moment as Epimetheus appeared out of the corner of my eye, emerging from behind another building. He turned into a falcon once again as he flew out, circling up the side of the mountain before turning, tucking his wings into his sides, and diving as fast as I'd ever seen a winged creature dive, swerving between creatures as he made his way underneath the dark cloud. Finding an opening behind the figure, he quickly transformed back into his god form before making his presence known.

I waited for a moment, not sure how I'd make it to him without alarming the figure standing in front of him. But then Epimetheus spoke, ruining any chance I had of surprising the mystery figure.

I stepped closer, making sure each step was slow and deliberate, as I watched the creatures surrounding the two of them, ready for their attack. But none of the creatures moved. None of them even looked in my direction. It was as if they were the puppets and the figure in front of Epimetheus was holding their strings.

"Whatever you're doing, I suggest you stop before things get really ugly for you. Those monsters are going to do nothing but piss him off. Even if you catch him off-guard and shoot some smoke from your fingers at him, he'll still have the upper hand," Epimetheus said, trying to pull the mystery figure's attention away.

It seemed to work, because their body froze, going completely rigid at the sound of his voice.

"Well, are you going to introduce yourself, or should I help get Zeus down here first? I'm sure he'd love to meet his would-be assassin," Epimetheus taunted.

"Is that before or after he kills me?" an all-too-familiar voice asked. Shadows poured away from the figure in waves, and then he turned around to face Epimetheus, revealing the tanned skin, dark, wavy hair, and deep brown eyes I would never forget.

Standing before Epimetheus was his brother, my betrothed.

Prometheus.

CHAPTER 59

"**B**ROTHER?**"** Epimetheus asked, staring at his brother as if he were a stranger.

I ran over to Epimetheus's side, ignoring the creatures, who still seemed to be in a trance waiting for Prometheus to give his command.

"Ah, my love. I'm glad you're here to see what I've been working so hard to accomplish before we leave," Prometheus said, his voice so tender and sweet it made me sick.

"I'm not going anywhere with you," I spat at him, gripping the sword in my palm tighter, my other hand dangling near my dagger.

"Don't you see? I did this all for you. For your kind. You will never be free unless all the Olympians are dead." Prometheus was pleading with me as if I'd trust anything he said. He'd helped the Aloadae twins to invade Olympus and in turn had been the cause of hundreds, if not thousands, of Olympian deaths, including Filenta's. I'd never trust him again.

"You're a fool if you believe killing innocents will bring peace on Earth," Epimetheus said to his brother. "Pandora will never love you—not after what you've done."

Prometheus laughed. Not his usual laugh, but one that was deeper, darker. "Now who's the fool?" he said, his softness fading

back into calm rage. "She will never love me, but it's not the killing of innocents that stops her . . . it's you."

I froze.

Does he know about Epimetheus and me? Did he see us that day at the beach?

"What is that supposed to mean?" Epimetheus asked.

"I've seen nearly every moment you've spent with her, trying to steal her away from me," Prometheus seethed. "I've seen you save her time after time, visiting her cottage, flirting with her, nearly kissing her." He looked me over, confirming my fear, before turning back to his brother. "I even saw the first time you came across her, while you hid in the oaks in front of this very palace, spying on Zeus for me."

"You weren't even here then," Epimetheus said, staring at his brother as if he didn't recognize the person standing in front of him. I wasn't sure I did either.

"I was. Pandora saw me, though she didn't realize it at the time." He looked at me. "Didn't you, love?"

"Who was the woman? Your partner in forming the rebellion in Olympus," I asked, ignoring the confusion on Epimetheus's face, my blood boiling as I thought of the life fading from Filenta's innocent eyes.

"Oh, darling. I didn't form the rebellion. What the Aloadae twins said about Zeus at the celebration was true. He has made a lot of enemies, many of whom were already within his walls. The rebellion has spread far and wide—not just through Olympus, but the entire realm—and that woman you saw me speaking to was one of many who lead within its ranks."

Epimetheus and I locked eyes, sensing the truth in his words. Fear washed over me, momentarily clouding my anger.

"How long?" Epimetheus asked.

Prometheus looked at him, raising a brow.

"How long have you been involved with the rebellion?" Epimetheus asked again.

Prometheus shrugged. "Since the Aloadae twins approached me with it two decades ago."

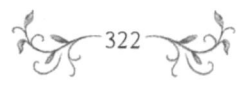

"You've kept this from me all this time?"

"Of course I have. You never had the stomach to go against Zeus with Hestia, and I knew you wouldn't with *her* either." Prometheus glanced pointedly at me.

"Her? We didn't even know about her until we arrived in Olympus," Epimetheus said, not understanding what he meant.

But I did.

"I was created twenty years ago."

Epimetheus turned toward me, and understanding flashed across his features. "What did they offer you, other than Pandora?" he asked, eyeing his brother cautiously.

"Earth and unrestrained access to Aether and the magic it has to offer." Prometheus smiled sinisterly.

"You must have known you'd never succeed," Epimetheus said, taking a step toward his brother, making Prometheus's grin intensify.

"I can glimpse the future. And the future says otherwise."

"Your visions are only partially true, and even then, the future is constantly changing. You can't rely on them for something like this." Epimetheus was pleading with his brother now.

"They've been correct so far," he said, looking between me and Epimetheus, a smug, knowing grin on his face.

Epimetheus looked over at me with the same intensity as always, and for once, I couldn't deny my feelings. I may not have known if it was love I felt for him, but there was something undeniable in our connection.

"Who she loves is not the problem right now. *You are*," Epimetheus said, throwing Prometheus's words back at him. "Stop this now and help us defeat the Aloadae twins, and maybe, just maybe, Zeus will spare your life and not send you to Tartarus."

Prometheus smiled, his eyes darkening—not in the way Epimetheus's had, but filling all the way to the edges of his eyes, like black ink spilled on a page. "The only person being defeated today is Zeus. Now, stand back before I do something I'll regret," he threatened, raising his hands and making the creatures around us twitch in warning.

Epimetheus looked over at me. "Are you ready?" he asked, and I knew exactly what he meant without him even needing to explain.

I nodded, looking back at Prometheus, who looked between the two of us and shrugged.

"So be it."

He dropped his hand, and the creatures launched into attack. Epimetheus and I turned, putting our backs together to face the threat in front of us. I swung my sword, slicing the first of the creatures right in the stomach before dropping to my knees, bringing my sword with me and plunging it into the creature's heart.

The next one was on me in an instant, fighting to pull me away from Epimetheus. I was too close to swing my sword and instead pulled my dagger from its sheath on my thigh, stabbing it with one hand into the eye of the creature coming at me. I ripped it out and sheathed it again as two more approached, one from each side. Stepping forward just as they were about to hit, I swiveled on my heel. As the creatures collided with each other, I swung my sword as hard as I could without spinning out, aiming for their necks. I felt it as the sword sliced through skin and bone, beheading them. Then I turned back around, expecting to find a couple more, but none were left.

I spun back to Epimetheus, finding he'd shifted into a combination of animals, all of which I wasn't sure of, and was holding the last remaining creature above his head. I thought he was going to rip it in two, but instead, he turned to his brother and chucked the creature at him, sending it flying right into Prometheus. It knocked him off-balance long enough that Epimetheus could make his move.

I moved to run, but it was as if I were glued in place. My eyes grew as I took in the tendrils of shadow wrapped around my legs like a python.

I looked up just in time to see Prometheus launching a stream of shadow at Epimetheus, capturing him in a similar way to me.

"Where did you get these powers?" Epimetheus grunted, fighting against the shadow's hold, unable to break free.

"You haven't pieced it together yet?" Prometheus looked at me. "What about you, Pandora? Have you figured it out?"

I glared at him, wishing I could reach my dagger to throw it at him. It wouldn't kill him, but I'd make sure wherever it landed hurt.

"No?" he asked, surprised, as he glanced between the two of us. "I thought it was obvious."

Thunder cracked above us, but no lightning struck. Epimetheus and I looked up just as Ephialtes took aim with Zeus's bolt, striking the King of the Gods down with his own power.

"Impossible," I whispered to myself, unable to believe the sight before me.

Zeus's unconscious body fell from the sky, disappearing from view.

"Prometheus, don't you dare . . ." Epimetheus warned, catching on to something I must have missed.

"Sorry, brother. You chose your side, and I've chosen mine. I guess our family was always doomed to fight against one another." Guilt flashed across Prometheus's face for a moment, and then it was gone, replaced by an unsettling happiness as a scream sounded from nearby, drawing mine and Epimetheus's attention.

Otus was riding off on what I could tell was a hydra from the six heads—which should have been impossible, since they'd gone extinct along with the dragons, thousands of years ago. Squinting at its legs, which looked to be dangling low from its body, I made out the shapes of two figures, one grasped in each of its talons.

"No!" Epimetheus screamed, finally breaking out of the shadows and hurling himself at Prometheus—but Prometheus was faster. He threw up a shadow wall, which acted as a shield between him and the wild animal trying to claw its way through to the other side.

I'd never seen Epimetheus lose control like this, but I couldn't blame him. I felt a rage like I never knew existed as Prometheus disappeared in a cloud of shadows.

"Was that who I think it was?" I asked, staring in the direction they'd flown off in.

Epimetheus nodded, confirming my fears. "Artemis and Hera."

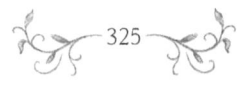

CHAPTER 60

"WHERE do you think he landed?" I asked as Epimetheus lifted another broken column out of the way on our search for Zeus in the rubble surrounding his palace.

"I think he's somewhere over there," he said, pointing to the opposite side of the palace. "We just need to clear our way over to it."

"This is taking too long. It would be faster from the air," I said, glancing from him to the sky.

"You're right." A small smile formed on Epimetheus's lips. "Stay here. I'll find him and return to get you."

"All right."

I wanted to tell him I was fine and that I could meet him at Apollo's, but I didn't want him walking in alone—not with Zeus injured and very possibly still unconscious. It wasn't that I thought Epimetheus would do anything, but the same couldn't be said of the others in Olympus.

Epimetheus flew off in search of Zeus, returning a few minutes later with his body draped unconscious over his shoulder.

"Right where I thought he'd be," he said. "Ready to go?" He stuck his hip out for me to jump on, so we could fly over to Apollo's healing center in the Olympian Court, where Epimetheus had taken me earlier.

I nodded, climbing on, and Epimetheus flew us as quickly and carefully as possible, landing us in one of the few remaining entryways into the court. Apollo was across the room, bouncing back and forth between the wounded, wrapping them in golden light as his healing powers flowed over them. It was mesmerizing.

"Is that Zeus?" someone whispered nearby, and then another, and another, until the whispers had spread throughout the room, making their way to Apollo before Epimetheus had even reached him.

"What happened?" Apollo asked, examining his father, his brows creased in worry as he pointed to the empty table one of his assistants had cleared. "There."

Epimetheus set Zeus down on the stone table, similar to the one I'd lain on earlier, and unstrapped the fibula holding the peplos at his shoulder, pulling the material down to expose his chest. Black streaks decorated Zeus's bronze skin, pulsing as if they were alive, like a current was moving through them.

"Ephialtes struck him down with his bolt," Epimetheus said, low enough for only me and Apollo to hear.

Apollo shook his head. "No. This is not just the work of lightning. Dark magic is at work here. They must have done something else when they struck him down."

Knowing what little I did about the workings of dark magic, I knew that couldn't be good. I'd once heard dark magic referred to as a parasite: once you used it, or once it was used on you, it latched on, feeding on the light in your soul and leaving behind only the darkest parts of yourself, until there was no light left at all. I could only hope Apollo figured something out before it was too late, because if I knew anything about Zeus, it was that he wasn't lacking in dark desires.

"Can you help him?" I asked.

"Yes, but it will take time." Apollo looked around at the chaos filling the room. "I can't do it here. I'll take him to my palace and get him situated. Can you get things settled here while I'm gone? I've healed those who came in with life-threatening injuries, but there are many who still need bandaging, splints . . . Well, you know all about that, Pandora." He motioned to me.

"We've got it covered," Epimetheus said, stepping back to land by my side. "Just save him."

"I will," Apollo said, informing a few of the cretes who'd stepped in to help heal at his side—a few of which I could see where Meliae—before carefully collecting his father and shooting off through the entrance we'd arrived through.

"What now?" I asked Epimetheus, looking around at all the blood, sweat, and tears covering every Olympian in the room.

"We help," he said, leaning down to assist a young centaur who'd broken his hoof.

The care Epimetheus took with the young boy warmed my heart as I helped an elderly nymph wrap her wrist nearby. I'd lost track of how long we'd been helping when a familiar female voice called my name.

"Pandora!" Persephone ran over to me and pulled me into her embrace, hugging me as if she hadn't expected to find me alive. "Primes, I was so worried about you. I was at the Olympics and saw you sitting with Prometheus in the High Olympians' ring watching Ares and Athena's fight, but then I lost track of you in the crowd, and when everything happened and I couldn't find you, I feared I'd lost you," Persephone said, rambling a little but still holding me in a hug. "I don't know what I'd do without you. I'm so sorry. For everything. I'll spend the rest of eternity making it up to you. I swear on the Primes."

"It's all right, Seph. I forgive you," I said, hugging her back and relishing in her embrace. I hadn't been willing to admit to myself before this moment how much I'd missed her.

"Thank the Primes. I've been a wreck without you," she said, finally releasing me to wipe her tear-soaked eyes.

"I have too," I said, smiling at her and trying to hold back my own tears, worried that if I let them fall, they'd never stop.

"I heard you were the one who saved my father." She looked over at Epimetheus, who just nodded in reply. "I know how you feel about him, but thank you. I hate to admit it, with all the cruel things he's done, but he is still my father, and I can't help but love him."

"I understand," Epimetheus replied.

"I will have your back when my father wakes up," Persephone said to him. "He's not going to be happy when he hears of everything they've stolen from him."

"No, he is not," Epimetheus and I said at the same time. We smiled at each other as we spoke, which made me laugh at our synchronicity.

"At least it's over for now," Persephone said.

I looked at her sadly, shaking my head. "If only things were so simple."

The battle may have been over, but the war had just begun.

⚛ACKNOWLEDGEMENTS ⚛

FIRST AND FOREMOST, I want to thank all the readers who took a chance on *Pawning Pandora.* I do not have the words to explain how grateful I am for all of you and how much your support means to me. I hope you enjoyed the world and the characters as much as I do, and I can't wait for you to see where the rest of Pandora's story take us.

Kourtney, my phenomenal developmental editor, you gave me all the confidence and courage to keep writing. Even when I rewrote half the book and dropped it down from a double POV to a single POV. Your advice throughout the entire process gave me the clarification I needed to let Pandora's character and story soar to new heights. I can never thank you enough for caring about this story as much as I do, and I cannot wait for you to read book two!

As for the beautiful map in the front of the book, that is all thanks to the mystical and magical map illustrator, Virginia Allyn. You took my scribbles and made them into a masterpiece. Seeing my world come to life in the map was the first moment I felt like I had truly created something to be proud of, and I can't thank you enough for giving it so much love and attention throughout the entire process.

Another person who brought my book to life is my cover artist and formatter, Rena. You have so much talent, and the amount of creativity and patience you have in every project blows my mind. I can't believe you created a cover so beautiful even my dreams looked lackluster in comparison. I adored working with you and getting to know you over the past year, and I am so excited to work with you again and somehow get you some sourdough bagels to try!

Bryony, I don't think I have the words to explain how much I appreciate and love you as a person and an editor! You have been an absolute dream to work with during the copy/line edit and proofreading process, and I honestly can't imagine going through everything with anyone else. You are so kind and knowledgeable in everything you do, and I feel so lucky to have found you, gotten to know you, and to have the chance to work with you. Thank you for not only always being there when I need questions answered or a quick read-through on extra content, but for being there for me when I struggled with all the health and family problems that fell upon me this past year.

Lani, a.k.a. Lanerd, you are the best friend and chosen sister a girl could ask for! You were there for me through every step of the writing and publishing process. Whenever I was stuck or had too many opinions flying around, you were always my constant and the one I could count on to help me make decisions. I truly don't know how I would have made half these decisions without your input as an experienced and diverse reader, but also as a trustworthy and dependable friend. Thank you for always being there, ever since we were kiddos running up and down Cow Creek Dr. together, when we weren't sneaking through neighbors' back yards to follow the creek to get from one house to another. I can't wait for us to be old and gray, eating sourdough bread and gossiping about books like we do now!

Most importantly, thank you to my family for always being there for anything and everything I could ever need. Mom, you were there for me 24/7 whenever I had mental breakdowns or panic attacks, was jumping with joy, crying with pride, and everything in between. I would not have been able to accomplish this with most of my sanity still intact without you. Thank you for always being there when I needed a shoulder to cry on or a hug to keep me going. You are and always will be the best mom in the world to me.

Dad, in some ways, you listened to this book as much as I wrote it. You were there for me every time I had a crazy new idea, and even though most of them went over your head, you were always so supportive and willing to be open-minded and learn about the subject I was writing. You are the greatest father I could have ever asked for and the most supportive, hardworking person I know. I only hope one day I can be as successful in my writing career as you were in your career, and I know if I work as hard as you do that my dreams will come true. Without you instilling the confidence in me to chase them no matter how far away they seem, I would never be on the journey I am today, and I am beyond grateful to have a father who cares about me as much as he cares about my dreams and supports them no matter what.

Aunt Kathleen, even though you weren't able to be as involved throughout the process, every single time I caught you up on my book and where I was in the process, the pride and joy I saw reflected in your eyes gave me the biggest and best confidence boost I never knew I needed. Your excitement propelled my own and gave me the energy to power through even when I struggled to find my way. Your kind heart, excited energy, and constant unwavering support will never be taken for granted. To me, you're not an aunt but another mother, and I will always be so thankful to have such a wonderful human being in my life.

And finally, my sweet little Lulu. Your cute little furry face and snuggles got me through the highest and lowest of times, and you are not only my emotional support animal, but you are beyond doubt my soul animal. I can't imagine life without you next to me. We are going to get you all the pup cups in the café when we start writing book two!

Thank you everyone for reading *Pawning Pandora*. I hope you enjoy all the adventures, trials, and tribulations as our characters journey into the unknown lands of Aether.

ABOUT THE AUTHOR

WILLOW B. DAWES was born and raised in Northern California. When she's not lost between the pages of a book or a new story, she can be found writing, spending time in the garden, cooking, or traveling with her family and her fur babies. With an iced coffee in one hand and a blank sheet of paper in the other, she wields her words, forging the path toward new worlds.